INCURSION

THE DAKOTARAPTOR RIDERS
BOOK ONE

STANT LITORE

Westmarch Publishing | 2021

MORE FROM STANT LITORE

COLOSSEUMS FOR DINOSAURS

The Running of the Tyrannosaurs
Nyota's Tyrannosaur
The Screaming of the Tyrannosaur

THE ZOMBIE BIBLE

Death Has Come up into Our Windows
What Our Eyes Have Witnessed
Strangers in the Land
No Lasting Burial
I Will Hold My Death Close
By a Slender Thread (forthcoming)

OTHER TITLES

Ansible: A Thousand Faces
Dante's Heart
Dante's Rose

The Dark Need (The Dead Man #20)
with Lee Goldberg, William Rabkin

&

Lives of Unforgetting
Lives of Unstoppable Hope
On the Other Side of the Night
Write Characters Your Readers Won't Forget
Write Worlds Your Readers Won't Forget

REVIEWS FOR *INCURSION*

"Straight for the heart and delightfully weird." – Joseph Brassey, author of *Skyfarer* and *Dragon Road*

"Stant Litore's work blends an array of singular characters, prehistoric creatures, and an imaginative landscape into a dazzling vision, *The Wild Wild West* meets *Jurassic Park* meets *Sucker Punch*—but beautifully weirder, exploring a frontier that is at once alien and yet familiarly human. His writing is deft and delivers, drawing a perfect balance between the real and the fantastic, whisking you away on a fast-paced journey with characters you will feel deeply for. Mythical and marvelous, this is storytelling at its very best." – Samuel Peralta, *The Future Chronicles*

"Stant Litore's *Incursion* brings a new and fantastic universe alive, packed with vivid characters and colossal beasts—yet amidst the story's intense action and swirling dilemmas, he never loses sight of his *raison d'être*: the power of human connection." – Richard Ellis Preston, Jr., author of *Romulus Buckle and the City of the Founders*

"A story that charges as hard at the heart as the fierce, raptor-riding heroines whose passion and mission make *Incursion* a deeply satisfying read. I can't wait for the next book in what promises to be a much larger tale." – James van Pelt, author of *Pandora's Gun*

"Masterful worldbuilding, immersive prose, and authentic characters create a tale of adventure and love you won't want to put down." – L. J. Hachmeister, author of *Triorion*

"An exuberant romp filled with dinosaurs and colorful characters, brimming with Litore's trademark big heart. It also carries shades of Anne McCaffrey's Pern, and is sure to please any lover of interplanetary adventure." – Travis Heermann, author of *The Ronin Trilogy* and *The Shinjuku Shadows Trilogy*

"Stant Litore has created a story about a fascinating world with brilliant characters, superb action, and a mystery I want to read more about. Also dinosaurs. Lots of dinosaurs." – Steve McHugh, author of *The Hellequin Chronicles*

"In these dark days, we need reminders of what makes us human: community and song, collaboration, story and hope. *The Dakotaraptor Riders* gives us those reminders. Woven onto the warp and weft of a rich folklore that feels completely authentic, and yet contains threads that will make contemporary folklorists grin, this tale of clashing philosophies, racing dakotaraptors, and abiding love is a salve for a wounded soul. It reminds us not only that the fight can be won, but that the fight is worth waging against the forces of destruction, of cruelty and colonialism. This book is *The Dark Is Rising* for science fiction. Read it, and let it braid your frayed threads whole again." – O.E. Tearmann, author of *The Hands We're Given*

INCURSION

STANT LITORE

WESTMARCH PUBLISHING

2021

The characters and events portrayed in this book are fictitious. Any similarity to real persons, living or dead, is coincidental and not intended by the author.

Stant Litore is a pen name for Daniel Fusch.

ISBN 978-1-7362127-1-4

You can reach Stant Litore at:
www.stantlitore.com
www.patreon.com/stantlitore
zombiebible@gmail.com

for everyone who survived this past year
and really would appreciate riding a raptor
over the wild prairie today

1

I AM STILL SWEATY FROM TAKING DOWN THAT PRIDE of hyaenadons, and my wife thinks she can outrace me, thinks her dakotaraptor can slice through the prairie grass faster than mine. But my raptor Ihira and I once took a gallimimus in full stampede; we once leapt from a cliff, my raptor catching the wingtip of a swooping quetzalcoatl in her jaws. We skidded wildly down the rockface with the great reptile crashing and flapping about us, its zebra-striped pycnofiber plumage cutting Ihira's face like shards of ice, the entire world a fever of feathers and screeching and tumbling rock, and we *survived*—and if my wife thinks she can reach the trees first, *I am Sasha Nightwatcher*, and my dearest Katya is *very* mistaken.

A command to my raptor, two quick chirps and a warbling trill, and we close with Katya's raptor, Daphne; she veers left toward the trees, with the prairie rolling endlessly on our right. My blood screams for pursuit. I chirp at Ihira and she responds, veering after my wife as smooth as a trell over the waves. Already we've left the other dakotaraptor riders and the heap of slain hyaenadons far behind. We dash along the line of Catha trees, crisscrossing each other's paths as if braiding our way over the prairie. The Catha trees have multiple intertwined stems and they grow horizontally as often as vertically, braiding together like lovers, branches bursting in every direction, aswarm with pink and roseate leaves. Laughing, Katya ducks her head to avoid branches. I chirp a command to Ihira and we swerve out into the prairie grass, violet and tall as my thigh. We round a bend in the forest's edge, and Daphne swerves out too, nearly crashing into us. Katya points across the grasses. Ahead, across the prairie is a tall white rock and a small stand of Catha trees all by itself, sprung up maybe where rainwater has collected in the rock's shadow. So we have a destination now. It's a long way out. It'll wind our raptors, but Ihira and I *will* get there first.

Still laughing and bent low over her raptor's shoulders, Katya taps swift commands on Daphne's neck with her fingers, and they burst into a sprint that shocks me with its speed.

"Going to let her get away with that, girl?" I chirp and trill to Ihira, gripping her neck feathers to keep my balance. Her body surges beneath me and we flash through the grass, fast and faster, striving to overtake my wife and her younger, sleeker raptor. Katya's braid bounces on her shoulder and her drum bounces on her back as she rides, and the wind carries her glee to me. Screeching, three-legged haia explode from the grasses in front of her, scattering in all directions, wings flapping frantically in search of flight. Her raptor falters a moment, and I laugh as we draw abreast. Timing it just right, I lean from the saddle, cup my wife's cheek in my hand, and startle her with a kiss. Her mouth opens softly and *oh, that's going to be a good kiss*, but then our lips part. My Ihira is pulling ahead, pulling me away. I tighten my grip on Ihira's neck feathers while I gaze back over my shoulder, grinning like a fool. Yekaterina's eyes are hot with excitement and there is a flush in her cheeks. There's heat between my thighs, too. This whole day is hot. Hot from the pitched battle with long-jawed and lethal hyaenadons. Hot from my blood demanding victory. Hot from the sun on fire, low in one half of our sky, and the mighty rings ablaze with light, filling the other half. As I turn my face forward, sweat is trickling down between my breasts and from my cropped hair into my eyes, but I blink it back. That white rock—I'm going to get there first. I snap my wind goggles down over my eyes, the tint in the lenses changing the world to gold. I lean low over my raptor, desiring no resistance against the wind. I chirp and I sing my commands to her, and Ihira's body is powerful and swift, and the tall grass lashes at my leggings. That grin has not left my face and the warmth of my wife's mouth has not left my lips, and right now this wild crazy world is *so right.*

We are both nightwatchers, and so are the two dozen women on raptorback we've left kilometers behind us. Seers on their coatls patrol the prairie from the sky; we patrol from the grass. If hyaenadons or wild medveds threaten the herds or the domiks, the lodges of our people, or if a raiding or slaving party comes at us from the mountains, we stop it dead and leave them bleeding on the prairie. This year, we have to handle incursions from the stars, too; the sky over our planet Peace only *looks* peaceful. Hooked to my saddle braids are a kopye—a fighting rod for visiting lightning and flame upon any threat, the same kopye my mother wielded, the one she pressed into my hands when she taught me—and two knives, coils of rope, an awl and strips of leather, a canteen and a raptor bowl and a cookpot, the last two wrapped in thin hide to keep them quiet. There's a bedroll and a collapsible shovel behind me, a heavy pouch of rocket flares, a light pouch with a brush and war paints, and a tinderbox. At my belt is a shorter coil of rope and a ring clasping sixty pages of thin metal, my mother's book of the Founder. Mine now, I guess. There's a spyglass in my jacket pocket. My clothes are supple lambeosaur skin, soft on my body but durable. Kneehigh boots keep my feet and calves safe from the woolly agonda, though mostly I stay on Ihira's back; walking is for farmers. Yekaterina is attired much as I am but also carries a small drum slung behind her shoulders. My hair is dark and short, hers is Founder's gold, long and braided, and she is beautiful. No one would have trouble telling us apart. Nor our raptors. Her Daphne is slight and quick with the most vivid feathers I've ever seen; my Ihira is almost midnight-dark, and that stray coatl we caught a year back raked a deep scar through the right side of her face, just missing the eye. Katya and I have plenty of scars too, only ours are on the inside.

The wind in my face is so fast, I believe I could ride with my wife all the way back, two hundred fifty kilometers, to the banya in our settlement, pull off her jacket, toss her into the hot water, and follow her in. The thought of it makes me wild and I laugh. Ihira cuts through the grass more swiftly yet. It is those trees we must reach and not a banya. I lean forward even more, offering little resistance to the air. Without parting my lips,

I hum the raptorsong that each of us sings the first night we mount the saddle, and again on the second night of testing when we ride without saddle:

We ride not with reins but with will
Not with whip but with heart;
Your raptor is not your slave,
Your raptor is not your steed,
She is your breath and sinew,
She is your war cry and battle screech
You are her will and her compassion—
Her claws, your cunning;
Her violence, your vigilance;
Her swiftness, your daring;
Trust each other,
Help each other,
Feed each other,
For braided together, you are one being,
One story,
One song.

My wife is falling farther behind. Suddenly Ihira's jaws open and she *screeches*, a rending cry of defiance and glory. Not a hunting-scream—dakotaraptors hunt more silently than anything living—but a war-screech, the competitive challenge of a raptor whose blood is up. I feel the screech in my own blood and I scream with her. Behind us, Daphne screeches too, but my Katya is silent. Were I to glance over my shoulder, I would see her hair like a braid of golden corn in the wind; I would not see her eyes beneath her goggles, but I know they would blaze with fire.

But I don't glance back. The trees are just ahead, looming pink and tangled out of the grasses, and I bend *low* over Ihira's neck, trilling, urging her faster, *faster*, because we are going to dart under those trees at perilous velocity and I will reach up and pluck a blossom from those branches, and later I'll weave that blossom into my wife's hair—after Ihira and I win! Another hundred meters—fifty—twenty—*ten*—Ihira screeches again, and I too, my voice ringing out over the prairie—this race is *ours*!

Something drops over my shoulders and snaps tight around my arms and torso. Quicker than thought, I am yanked backwards out of the saddle. Ihira races on without me; I twist like a harra and somehow I land on my feet. Daphne flashes past to my left; I have a quick glimpse of Katya paying out rope on her lasso. I'm jerked into sudden motion. For a wild moment, I'm pulled after her, grass blades whipping my shoulders and cheeks. But I can't run at raptor speed. I fall, sinking into the grasses as if into water. The ground smacks me hard.

I'm dragged through the grass a moment, then I stop. I roll onto my hip, my arms roped to my sides. I can't breathe. I can't see what's happening above the grasses, but I hear Daphne's scream of triumph and my wife's laughter and I know she's reached the trees; Ihira must have veered to the side, startled, when I fell. I shake my head, furious and admiring and completely winded. I hear Ihira's war-screech, and that quenches my anger, gets me focused. A dakotaraptor is not a steed but a fellow nightwatcher, one of your pack, one who wears her war-paint every night in her wild plumage, one whose respect you *earn*, one who will bite you or gut you if you take her for granted, like a lover, one without hands but with talons and teeth, with battle in her heart. With her blood hot, Ihira is likelier to attack her sister Daphne than submit to the race's outcome; I need to calm her.

I fight for air and get just enough to whistle a series of quick chirps, commands to settle, to keep her claws on the planet's soil, to heed me. I hear her answering trill, and though she is silent in the grass, I can tell she is moving again, circling, watching, but not attacking. I want to laugh with relief, but before I can get enough breath for *that,* Katya has reached me. She stands over me with the sunset on her face and a coil of rope over one shoulder, and she presses her boot gently between my breasts, holding me to the earth. I can't rise. I'm missing a boot, and my cheeks and chin burn from the lashing of the stiff grass. I squirm against the lasso. Feeling the braided rope tighten, I lie back, listening to my heart's quick thunder. I gulp air, oxygen rushing back into my lungs, and every part of my body is *alive.* My wife pushes her goggles back and her eyes, shining with victory, take me captive. She signs, *I win.*

Wrath flashes like fire in my veins. Other nightwatchers—Sveta and Veroshka—think me weak. Without any kin to back me, I am just an unbraided strand. If *Katya* were to think me not good enough, I'd break.

"I was…faster," I pant.

My raptor's at the trees. Yours isn't. She grins. *I win!*

"You *lassoed* me!"

She wrinkles her nose. I should be too angry to find that adorable, but—

You know you let me, she signs. Her eyes shine. *You like seeing what I can do.*

Something in her eyes takes away what little breath I have, and oh, breathing hurts. Can't stay angry when my lungs are all squeezed like this.

"I do like seeing what you can do," I whisper.

She touches my cheek, and I make a soft, soft little noise, and her face above mine flushes.

My wild golden girl. Now she's got me smiling too. Nearby, Daphne lets out a long trilling cry, as proud of her victory as my wife.

2

"WELL." I AM PANTING. "YOU HAVE ME TIED UP, dear one. Again. This is the start either of something bad or something…*good.*"

Reading my lips, Katya laughs. Her laughter is loud and pure and lovely. Many women stifle their laughter, keep it quiet. Show too much feeling, and other women will judge you. But Katya doesn't realize how *loud* her laughter is. She never holds it back. It makes me love her.

She straddles my chest, a knee to either side, her hands gentle on my wind-weathered cheeks. Nearby, all the Catha trees whistle their music—not human music but lovely nonetheless. Katya's eyes are just above mine, green as the sea, and I can't breathe. My anger at her trickery is forgotten. *Everything* is forgotten. She kisses me, and there's nothing left in the whole world but her.

She keeps me very busy for a while, and afterward, we're both panting. Nearby in the grass, their earlier tension forgotten, our dakotaraptors nestle together, as if they're lovers, too. They *do* react to our moods, so who knows? Rather than lift her hands from me to sign, Katya speaks with her lips instead, a flurry of small kisses for my cheeks, my neck, the tender place behind my ear, my eyelids. I don't mind.

After a while, I wriggle. "How long are you going to leave me tied up?"

Then she does take her hands from me, so that I regret having said anything.

But she signs, *All night.*

So I feel better.

* * *

The Catha boughs whistle, melodic and quiet. Out in the prairie, the glows—the slow dreamers that stay burrowed by day—have lifted their eyestalks out of the soil. Above the grasses they sway. Their eyes shine faint and lovely, silver and drinking in starlight. Our planet's rings are big in the sky as if radiant with love, and the night air is cool on my flushed skin. My thighs quiver, and I can't seem to catch my breath. When my wife pulls away at last, I am still bound, so I try to wrap my legs around her. "Don't leave me," I whisper.

Katya's eyes fill with tenderness, but with amusement, too. *I would never*, she signs. Then she kisses me. I give myself in that kiss, my heart pounding, everything in me a song of love. When Katya lifts her face, I make the smallest whimper in my throat. I can't help it.

She shakes her head gently. *But sometimes, Sasha, you have to let go, just a little.*

My throat tightens. *I know*, I sign back. *But—not tonight.*

She smiles. *Anyway we'll need a canteen and a drink*, she signs, and nods her head toward where the raptors are snuggled together, half-asleep, beneath the Catha boughs.

But my love is still humming in my blood, in every vein of my body. As is *right*, for we are the humming people, who sing at every birth and sing at every death, and whose bodies hum with joy at a lover's touch. The people for whom a new song and a story bring the highest price at an autumn barter. The people the Founder taught to fill their bodies and their land with melody. Holding Katya's gaze, I open my legs and say, soft as the night, "You can drink me."

That sets her giggling. Giggling almost too much to drink.

Almost.

***

The trouble with having spent the evening racing across the world at raptor-speed and then necking among the roots of trees is that we really have no idea where the rest of our pack is. But we know where they're *supposed* to be, fifteen days from now, and we have more than enough time to get there, so at dawn's light we decide to do a little more scouting on the way. That's because it helps salve the guilt of cuddling at our ease while the others work, not because it's necessary. It's been eighty-three days since the last incursion. Maybe the invaders have given up. Maybe they're bored. Maybe the last time they saw two dozen women with painted faces charging down on them on the backs of a dakotaraptor pack, it was too much for them. Maybe they've gone in search of a planet that doesn't have women like us.

Eighty-three days is a long time.

Katya and I strike out into the prairie. The grass is violet and up to our knees, and our raptors vanish into it; we only know Daphne and Ihira are here because we're riding them. But even after the line of Catha trees disappears into the grass behind us, we have no fear of losing our way. We're in the southern hemisphere, and we always know where north is—it's where the rings shine in the sky, ablaze with burning white sunlight by day, lighting the prairie softly for love by night.

Sometimes at night after love, Yekaterina asks me for a story. I never refuse her. I tell her of the time the first seer fled Grandma Yaga's domik, leaping from her door onto the back of a quetzalcoatl; he left Grandmother grasping a fistful of plumage, with a wild madness in her eyes. I share the tale of the two sisters, one kind, one cruel, and which one left Grandmother's walking hut in a beautiful cloak of therizinosaur feathers, and which left in pieces, as Yaga scattered her bones over the frozen prairie. And I tell her of the time the Founder's daughter slaved for a year and a day in Grandmother's domik, then stole a song from her lips as she slept. She used it to charm the dakotaraptors, so that today our raptors respond to a whistle or a chirp or a brief melody. "Or to the drumbeat of your fingers," I tell Katya, and she smiles.

There are few things Grandma Yaga respects, but she loves a good tale and she admires feats of cunning. In memory of the time the Founder's daughter outwitted her, today when a woman of our people becomes a nightwatcher, she must perform some such act herself. The other dakotaraptor riders, who she wishes to join, give her a seemingly impossible task after dark, requiring all her speed and cleverness and daring. If she can complete it, she joins the pack. If she can't, she must tan hides or grow corn or do something else; only the quickminded can ride the prairie and dare the threats of killwind and wildfire and the wickedness of slaving men. Katya says for her test she had to get a sekaya nut with wisps of white on its shell, the kind that only grows on vines near the top of a yacca—but that she and her raptor had to achieve this without climbing one of those high fungal spires. My bold Yekaterina knew, as her testers did, that there was a caravan of the coastal people nearby on their way to barter, and these people find sekaya nuts a great delicacy. She undertook to flit into their camp and steal away a sekaya by night. While the travelers danced by their fires or slept in their wagons, she slipped into the wains where their food was kept. The sekaya when she found it was round and large as her hand. A boy nearly caught her on the way out, but she surprised him with such a kiss that he could only stare after her, stammering, as she sprinted from the tent and sprang to Daphne's back.

My own test was to steal a long hair from a medved's mane while it slept, then race back before daybreak. The medved was being hunted by Ticktock slavers—the hated Ticktocks who mine beneath rock and soil, who snatch people from caravans and from domiks in the cropland, setting them to dig in the dirt or toil in bed—and there was the danger they might capture me. I knew Veroshka and Sveta and others doubted I could do it. I didn't know if they were right, but I knew I had to try. My mother had been the quickest, the most cunning and clever of the nightwatchers; before her death, she had taught me to wield her kopye and to ride Ihira. How could I fail her?

Unbraided, others called me. Kinless, weak, unbraided from other lives. A strand that would fray and snap under tension. My mother and one surviving sister had been the last, and before I mounted Ihira to ride out and snatch a medved's hair, they were gone. I rode out alone, as one who is unbraided must, but though I didn't ask for help, Katya gave it.

She and four others led the raiders on a wild hunt through the Catha trees while I searched for bear spoor. The beast had carved out a hole beneath gnarled tree roots. I left Ihira elsewhere in the wood, fearing her scent would wake the bear; I rubbed Catha leaves and resin into my skin and hair to disguise my own. Then I crept to the burrow where the medved slept like a living mountain of hide and muscle, the sound of its breath filling the den. Its fur was luminous, eerily phosphorescent in the dark. I wriggled in beside it, got the hair, and wriggled out—right into the grasp of a Ticktock, a slaver! I remember my terror but I remember my fury too. I writhed and kicked and got his back to the den and hollered a battle song. The medved woke at my chanting and came out of the den like roaring death and seized the slaver from behind. Any man grabs me without my sayso deserves to get ripped open by a bear. He let my arms go with a cry of pain, and I snatched his watch from his belt and fled, panting. I whistled for Ihira. She came silent through the trees and I leapt to her back.

Nearby, seven slavers had cornered Katya and Daphne against a thicket. One had dropped a rope over the raptor's neck; another lay on the ground with his belly sliced open. Several were advancing on my wife with ropes and metal hooks. The thought of losing her made my blood burn and made me sick enough with fear to retch. And it was near dawn and I was at risk of failing the test, but I'd rather spend my life tanning lambeosaur hides than see my wife made a slave. Ihira and I tore into them from the shadows and it was a red night.

At sunrise, I presented the medved hair to the other riders and completed the rite that made me a nightwatcher. I lifted the kopye my mother left me, that elegant rod of silver metal that spews lightning and fire. Forged in the oldtech smithies of the arcology cities on the edge of the sea, the kopyes are traded to the mothers of our settlements at the harvest barter by long-bearded merchants who accept our woven blankets and medved pelts in wrinkled hands, before returning with them to those gleaming towers that touch the western sky. The mothers say that tens of thousands of people live in each arcology, as leeches might swarm in a pool. Yet how can such a thing be? I wrinkle my nose, imagining the smell of sweat and the reek of urine in a place where there is no prairie wind in your face.

Veroshka scowled and Sveta's eyes assessed me, but each of the nightwatchers, one after the other, set a hand on my shoulder and gave me a slender strap of leather, pressing it into my palm. Each one dyed a different color. Midnight for Veroshka and violet for Violetta, the orange of flame for Sveta, green for Nadya. To each of them I gave in return a leather strap I had prepared, a red the hue of the last moment of sunset, almost as dark as night. Katya was last, pressing into my hand a strap as yellow as her hair, and when I gave her my red, she kissed me. Barely daring to breathe, I braided the others' straps around my kopye, the way the other nightwatchers' lives would now be braided about my own. Each of them braided mine with theirs—though Veroshka hesitated. The leather straps braided around the kopye's smooth metal provide you with a firm grip. It is the presence of your pack that keeps your hand from slipping, keeps your grip strong and your breath steady as you spin the rod and stab or slash with fire. With your kopye braided, your pack is always with you as you ride out, as you watch the night for threats, as you fight for our survival.

I have braided the kopye every day since. The weaving of the humming people—beautiful carpets of agonda wool in the domiks and saddle blankets for our raptors—is meant to last, but braiding is something you do anew each day. We who watch the night, protecting the people, the fields of corn, and the herds, we live unsettled and always moving; we work with leather and awl, and we do it in the saddle. Out here, we know that memory is something you have to *do*. Each day, as you braid your kopye, you're telling the story of your nightwatcher pack. Even if one strap is gone, even if one nightwatcher has perished between one sunrise and the next, the pack persists. The people are protected. There is hope.

That first morning, I braided the long strand of medved hair in with the leather straps—a small gesture of defiance after seeing the glances Veroshka and Sveta gave me. *I can do this. I belong here, braided with you, running our raptors on the prairie. I do. Though my kin are dead, I am not kinless! I am the daughter of Annika Nightwatcher, and I stole the medved's hair.*

Later, when Katya and I were alone again, we rode out into the tall grass and made love under the blaze of rings in the open sky. Afterward we sat with our backs to our raptors and opened the Ticktock's watch. We watched its weird hands tick in a circle, its sound melodic but monotonous, as if it were trying to hold the day inside of a song but didn't know how to vary its rhythm. It unsettled me, but Katya gazed at it with delight, feeling it tick in her hand, and I let her have it as a gift. I unbraided Katya's hair and she laughed with me, then braided it again before it was time to go back.

Why don't you just cut it short, like the rest of us? I signed.

I like it long. Her eyes flashed with pleasure. Her hair is sun-gold and she is vain about it, and deserves to be. I love to run my fingers through it. That morning, she stopped me, took my fingers and kissed them, and teased, *Anyway it means I am still stronger than you; I have* two *braids, one on my kopye, one on my head. You only have one, Sasha my love.* And she laughed, and I found myself smiling.

The sekaya nut, the medved hair: those were our tests, Yekaterina's and mine. But Mila the Founder's daughter who began it all, the first dakotaraptor rider—she had the most difficult test of all: to steal a song from Grandma Yaga's own mouth in the ghost country. I'd rather dare the slavers and the medved's teeth. But I like telling the story of her deed, and it makes Katya smile. These tales of Grandma Yaga, of the times she bested our ancestors or the times our ancestors bested her, these are all stories that my mother gave me during the cold winters when I was a girl. My mother had a story for every occasion. I like to think that when she died, she entertained Grandmother with them, and that the two swapped songs and tales like old friends while Grandma Yaga's walking domik strode on its raptor legs over the death-cold, brittle prairie. For all I know, my wily Mom challenged Grandma Yaga to a storytelling contest and they're at it still, and one day she'll win and Grandmother's hut will carry her back to us across death's frozen prairie, and Mom will walk right into our settlement and give me a hug. My eyes sting, so I bury that bit of dreaming deep.

Katya has a living mother and a whole thicket of family. Sisters and aunts and cousins. Even a brother or two. So many that I think she sometimes feels as alone as I, silent among many, her tale unheard—except on the prairie among the nightwatchers, where there is only one Katya, adored and known. Though I wonder if any of the others really *know* her. Sometimes, when I look in her eyes, there's such gratitude there at being *seen.* Her kin braids hang from the edge of her saddle, vibrant and colorful, tying up her gear and telling a dozen tales of who she is—yet none of them tell the whole story, the one I see when her hands move in the air, signing what's in her heart. My own saddle braids are a dull earth color, no tales of living kin. My story is more a tangle than a braid, anyway: I can't find the start or the end of it.

While I have no kin braids, I do wear our wife braid around my thigh, under my leggings, its leather soft against my skin. Katya wears hers, too; when she is naked and our bodies are intertwined, I see it there or touch it in the dark, and my heart gets so full it hurts. The night of our wiving, we each braided the leather around the other's thigh for the first time. *That* was a night.

I carry our public braid, too, around the sleeve of my jacket, our colors twining together, gold and sunset. There is only the one public wife braid, and Katya lets me carry it. Well, not *lets* me. I begged her. It's the one story I have that isn't just one of my mother's winter tales.

Katya has many kin, many lives braided around her own; mine were taken at rainfall.

* * *

Yet Katya's love is a comfort at night, and beneath the stars, beneath her kisses and her hands, I forget to grieve for a while. We are both young—we're nightwatchers—so our lovemaking, whether swift or sensual, is frequent and repeated. How much sleep does a woman really need, anyway? By day, one of us can sleep on raptorback while the other stays alert. We can take shifts. By night, we're well rested and ready. Like our raptors, we've chosen to be nocturnal.

Not that I want to miss *everything* the day has to offer. There's a lot to look at. Sometimes distant yacca gleam on the horizon—slender green spires hundreds of meters high, in stands of seven or eight. Flocks of haia leap from the grasses in their thousands sometimes, veering and banking in scintillant hues, dancing in the sky. The loveliness of the rings never really gets old. Sometimes there are thunderstorms. Sometimes there are *bad* thunderstorms, and we have to dig a shelter in haste. If the killwind lashes the prairie, it is nice to have Katya holding me tightly, but we're almost too terrified for love. But sometimes the sun is high and there is little wind and the whole world is still and hot, as if time has slipped away for a tryst with *her* lover, and won't be back to trouble us for a while. Then the drowsiness on the prairie is peaceful and my whole body feels heavy. Even my heartbeat seems to slow, a drumbeat like the pulse of a planet. If we go long enough without speaking, it's easy to lose our humanness for a while, to just *sink* into the prairie, becoming part of the silent grass and the warm air and the slow surge and roll of loping dakotaraptors. Sometimes I just watch Katya for a while. She is more at home in her body than I am, and graceful, though she would laugh hard if I told her so. I like the way a strand of her hair strays against her neck as we ride. I like the curve of her ear. I like the confident way her hands move, her fingers tapping a quick rhythm on the soft down of her raptor's throat, to guide the beast to the left or the right, swift or slow. Katya can chirp and trill at her raptor if she must, but somehow she has found it easier to train her using hand signals, varied series of taps for different commands. I watch Daphne respond to her without protest, as though her fingers are tapping spells, as though it's magic. My own dakotaraptor sasses *me* terribly, chirping and squawking back. I raised the girl from an egg, so she knows *I* am the older sister. Still—sass! I'd hate to ever have to catch and tame a wild one, the way we're taught to do if we're ever stranded in the deep prairie without a ride.

No chance of that, though. Katya would never let anything happen to me out here. Anyway, it's so quiet. I don't think things *do* happen this far out. Drunk on the sunlight and the peace, I share that thought with Katya. She gives me a look and shakes her head. *Don't tempt it!* she signs.

Though she relaxes in my arms at night, on raptorback Katya never stops watching. From time to time, she plucks her spyglass from inside her jacket and scans the horizon. I don't bother to reach for mine. The mother herds are out there on the prairie, just out of sight, defended by whistlers on saddled triceratops; we watch the perimeter for perils. *What are you looking for?* I ask Katya.

I don't know, she signs after putting the spyglass away, *but the last incursion burned a domik. It made a lot of fire. I think I'd see it.*

Sometimes she glances at the sky. I wish she wouldn't. *There's nothing up there,* I tell her.

Her eyes are deep. *That's what worries me. Hyaenas are only quiet right before they attack.*

I gaze up at that sky that is as empty as it is beautiful. "But there hasn't been an incursion in eighty-three days," I say.

3

"BUT THERE HASN'T BEEN AN INCURSION IN EIGHTY-three days!" I cry.

I think Grandma Yaga has been listening every time you said that, Yekaterina signs. Her face is pale.

I close my mouth quickly, regretting the words. Too late to call them back.

Between us and the cool, shaded water we've sought, the whistler lies crumpled. She has a bullet in her cheek. Seven more in her breast. Bullets in the soil, the grasses torn up, bark chipped off the side of Catha trees by the nearby pond. That means an alien weapon, from a world orbiting another sun.

Neither Katya nor I dismount; we just sit our raptors under the whistling boughs. Nearby there's a bit of a watering hole, shallow and muddy, with one dimetrodon half sunk in the slime, watching us warily. That's what's watering the stand of trees here. There are footprints—triceratops, I think—where the whistler must have gone down to the water to refill her canteen and maybe her partner's, too. Only she went; there's only one set of tracks. She was fired on when she got back to the edge of the tall grass, and that's where she toppled from her saddle. There's blood on her and blood on the violet plants. My heart sinks into a deep, cold place. We just gaze at her body a while, uneasy. Sometimes chirping or tapping a command to stop our raptors from bending their heads to feed on the whistler's flesh. The raptors ate lightly last night, and Ihira chirps a protest. Her eyes gleam with keen intelligence but with a dakotaraptor's ravenous voracity, too.

The whistler has been stripped of her jacket and leggings, leaving her in her undergarments and a blouse dark with blood. A terrible thought makes my belly queasy, but there is no sign that her attacker did *that* to her. Her assailant clearly wasn't a Ticktock. In past incursions, such invaders have come through our grass one at a time, and mostly men, but I don't see any tracks for this one.

The whistler hasn't been dead more than a day. No time yet for maggots to crawl under her skin or prowling hyaenadons to find her corpse and feed. Even so, she doesn't look human anymore. She's shrunken. Empty. There are dull stones set above her cheeks—barely recognizable as eyes. They're hard to look at. Too much like my mother's. I blink quickly. I wish the woman's eyelids were closed. There is a reek in the air.

We came to this mudpond for the same reason the whistler must have—to fill our canteens. Water is scarce out here but you always know where it is—it's wherever you see a stand of tangled Catha, pink against the grasses and the sky. We haven't filled the canteens yet; they hang at our saddlestraps, forgotten. Anyway, it's no good filling them now. A woman died by this water too recently; her ghost might have walked in it.

That's a messy death, Katya signs. *If I die young, I don't want to die with holes in me. I show up like that at Grandma Yaga's domik, she'll take one look and laugh herself silly.*

She died fast, at least, I sign back. The whistler's face isn't twisted in fear.

But with holes in her.

There are worse ways.

Katya watches my face a moment. *You all right?*

I will be.

Katya nudges her raptor closer. *Hey. I'm here.*

She reaches across and grips my fingers. I grip back.

I hate corpses, I tell her.

We've seen a few.

Hate them still.

She lifts my fingers to her lips and kisses them, and there's a flutter of warmth deep in my body but it's not enough to thaw the chill at the nearness of death.

She takes her hand back and signs, *Going to look around the other side the pond. Maybe there are tracks there.*

I peer across the brown stillness of the water at the far trees. "Be watchful."

She gives me a look. Watching is what nightwatchers *do.* Her hands move quick. *Sasha. Nothing's going to kill me; I'd kill it first. Let's do our work.*

My throat tightens, but I nod. She's right, but I don't have to like it. I know what that reek is I'm smelling. It's the reek of loss. It's the smell of my mother's body the morning I had to bury her. But I look in Katya's warm eyes and remember that she lifted my mother's body with me, that her hands beside mine patted the soil over her. That she drummed while I sang over her dirt, so that my mother would not be without a song to barter with Grandma Yaga on the ghost prairie. I force a faint smile. Seeing it, Katya nods. She taps the lasso at her belt, bringing a blush of memory to my cheeks and reminding me she is more than ready for any contest. Deftly, she unhooks her kopye from the side of her saddle and snaps it to full length, a metal rod springing from a forearm's length to a meter and a half. She ignites it with a crackle and hum of heat. Both ends blaze in slender blades of blue fire, and her eyes reflect the flame. She holds her kopye near the middle not just with ease but with *grace*, for the kopye is not just a weapon but a song and story, a tale of the pack's strength that we place between our bodies and death, that we wield in arcs of spinning flame. The grip beneath Katya's fingers is wound about with our pack's leather straps: Nadya's wild green and Violetta's prairie violet, and the dying-of-day red that is mine. When my wife rides, she rides with the strength and bravery of all of us.

I leave my own kopye clipped to my saddle. Though I'd feel better if it were in my hand, Ihira and I stand a way out from the trees and we'd see in plenty of time if anything was coming at us.

Anything other than a bullet from an alien weapon, that is. I swallow.

Daphne springs into motion, a muscled and lovely animal. Katya rides her slowly through the Catha trees, giving the dimetrodon in the mud a wide berth. Those can be hot-tempered and vicious. Soon the riot of pink foliage conceals my wife and her raptor, and my heart beats faster. "Let's do our work," I whisper to Ihira. She bobs her head as I walk her, exploring the grass in a wide circle around the body, looking for sign. I am calmest when there are things to *do*. Facing death is easiest when Yekaterina and I are both riding against some threat under the night sky, painted and screaming, charging down hyaenas on raptorback, where we can defend each other. Maybe Sveta and some of the others doubt I can be relied on to back another woman in battle, but Katya and I know different, *yes* we do. We've battled together plenty, been splattered with blood from the same beast.

This is different. It's when we're parted that I get anxious—when we're out of each other's line of sight. Death takes you when you're alone, and I know how quickly someone can be torn from you.

But my wife is right to check around the pond. Bullets can scream through the air a long way. Whatever invader fired his alien weapon at this woman might have done it from the other side of the water, and Katya might see the tracks of whatever beast he was riding. As I search, I hum the nightwatcher's promise, a comfort to my raptor and myself:

I have run my raptor on the prairie,
seen settlements burn,
watched red rain fall,
heard slavers in the corn,
smelled wildfire on the wind.

I do not smell wildfire now, but I *do* smell decay. I catch sight of broken blades of grass and urge Ihira deeper into the violet surge of it, singing softly under my breath:

We will be compassionate and never cruel,
vigilant and not vicious,
bold as Vilya who broke the medved's back,
brave as Nadya who faced the Screaming Ship,
cunning as Mila who brought the song.

If our people are sick, we will find healers.
If our people are starving, we will find the herds.
If our people are captive, we will cut the ropes from their wrists.
If our people are fleeing, we will guard their passage
through cropland and prairie and wild forest.
If our people are silent, we will sing their tales.

And when Grandma Yaga comes for us at last
we will greet her with a story and song
and say, "Welcome, Grandmother.
We are ready for the last ride."

And I do find something in the grass, twenty meters from the body. Saddlebags, cut open, cans of food and sheaves of dried jerky spilled into the grass. That is strange, because who would leave *food* behind? Also the whistler's clothes are here, rifled, then discarded. Jacket and leggings. A wind rises in the grass, tugging at my short hair and my shirt. Ihira's uneasy; she smells something. I wish she could tell me *what.* I stroke her neck feathers to calm her, chirp softly to her, then slip down from her saddle to take a closer look.

The whistler's garments are better made than ours. Probably got them at a barter off merchants from the far coast. The pockets have been emptied, and from what I can tell the devices of her trade have been thieved from her: her bone whistle, her blade, her tools for prying stones loose from a ceratopsian's foot or for cutting parasites from its hide. I glance back in the direction of the body, remembering. Even her wrist bracelet of beads patterned in the colors of her herd is gone. So is her mount, though I doubt the invader took the animal. Riderless, the ceratopsian probably just lumbered away and rejoined the herd.

Now that I'm out of the saddle, I can feel the trembling of the soil under my feet, the passage of that herd. When I strain my ears, I can just hear the distant murmur that is their lowing. When I stand on my boot toes and peer over the grass, I can see the edges of the herd a few kilometers away. The mingled triceratops, styracosaurs, and pachyrhinosaurs form a horizon line of green and golden and russet hide, a place where the violet prairie appears to *stop* and become something else. There is no cloud of dust; the vegetation underfoot is too thick—and right now they're grazing rather than migrating. If we sprinted our raptors near, we would see them, their rolling backs, their heads bobbing, the shields of bone behind their heads lifting and falling like waves, their lethal horns stabbing at the sky. And yet this is only an outlying band. In the deep prairie where the mother herds roam, tens of millions of horned giants flow over the grass. The mother herds can drink a river dry or take a week to cross it. If they pass too near a settlement, the shaking of the ground beneath their feet can collapse shelters and cave in wells. That's one reason we have whistlers, to ride along the edges of the herd and guide it with their bone whistles pitched too high for human ears, or to trail the smaller bands that break away.

The wind quickens. Even at this distance, it brings me the heavy musk of the dinosaurs and, not quite hidden beneath it, the more pungent reek of the oleni, the long-legged skitterdeer that hide among the herds, peeking over the ceratopsians' backs with their long eyestalks. I turn, take the pommel of Ihira's saddle in my hand, and hoist myself onto her back again. She shies a few meters, chirping. "Easy, girl." My voice is soft. "I'm spooked, too." I turn her and ride back toward the trees and the water and the whistler's body.

That body isn't *right.* Whistlers aren't like nightwatchers, taught and trained for velocity and violence and nights of facing death and outwitting it. Whistlers are made for slow life, for life amid teeming masses whose musk settles over the land like an unwashed blanket. If hyaenas or worse come, the whistlers send up flares to alert the seers who can then alert us, then slip back into the safety of the herd until we arrive. Even slavers won't trouble a whistler. Too much at stake. No one wants the mother herds untended and unwatched. Ticktock raiders will wait like venomous agonda in the grass until a whistler passes, then try to cut a few young styracosaurs out of the herd. But if a whistler sees them, they'll flee. *No one* attacks whistlers; no one risks the herd. So there shouldn't be one dead out here. How do we untangle this mess and braid a tale from it that makes sense?

Katya rides her raptor up from the trees, to my relief, and pulls up alongside me. She puts her hand on mine, over the pommel of my saddle. I turn my hand palm up and twine my fingers with hers. Then Daphne destroys the moment, nipping lightly at Ihira's neck. My raptor squawks. I chirp twice and nudge her over a bit.

Behave, Katya scolds, and taps a few quick signals on her raptor's neck. Then she signs to me, *See? I'm back safe. Breathe, Sasha.*

I'm trying. What did you find?

Her face falls. *Nothing.*

I glance out at the wide prairie. Maybe the woman's attacker wasn't lying in wait at the water. Didn't care about the water, had enough already. Maybe he came from *out there*, from the wild grass, riding in while the whistler filled her canteen. Briefly I tell Katya what I found.

"It doesn't lessen the mystery," I conclude. "What do we do now?"

Katya reads my lips. Her eyes get this familiar glint like she's about to cheer me up, though I never know whether to expect a kiss, a lasso, or a song. Instead, she simply signs, *We're nightwatchers.*

She's right.

We are nightwatchers, each of us wild mothers to our people. We ride out. We put ourselves between our people and death. That's what the Founder did long ago. That's what generations of nightwatchers have done. That's what my mother did. That is how we survive and sing. The seers patrol the skies, we patrol the prairie; the mothers of each settlement gather the harvest and get our people traveling to safety before the red rainfall and keep them fed, while we fend off threats on the journey. We nightwatchers have the most difficult part in our people's tale, the part with the fastest tempo. We have to outthink and outrace and outfight hyaenas and slavers and invaders from the sky.

We live by our speed and our cunning, beating back fear with a song, with the beat of our heart or the beat of a drum, outwitting death as long as we can. That's what we do.

We didn't do it quick enough to save this whistler. But now that we know there's death on the prairie, we can stop her attacker from taking anyone else.

I think the invader went north, I say, pointing to where I found the discarded clothing and the ripped-open saddlebags.

Yekaterina glances that way, then back. *Whistlers travel in twos,* she signs. *Where's the other?*

Good point. I pluck my spyglass from my jacket pocket, snap it open, lift it to my eye. Yekaterina does the same. I scan the north and east, she scans the west and south. Above us, the rings blaze in an arc of blue and silver fire. When I lower the glass, she points, and I lift it again to check. Not a dead trike or another dead whistler, but something both useful and hopeful: way out there in the prairie, a tiny flash of red.

"Let's go," I say, and trill to Ihira. My raptor protests; there is still an uneaten body here, and she doesn't want to depart. "Come, girl," I whisper, repeating the command. Beside me, Katya's eyes shine, her love of adventure awakening, stronger than any dread—that boldness and hunger for thrill that makes all the other nightwatchers, and me, adore her.

We lope forward through the grass, swaying in our saddles. Approaching, we can see it clearly: two meters of red ribbon snapping in the air each time a gust catches it, one end tied securely to the top of a tall grass stalk. When

I reach it, I lean from the saddle and catch it in my fingers. I don't know the material—it's nothing the humming people make—but it's soft and strong.

Katya already has her glass to her eye again. She points.

Out there where the wind sends ripples through the grass like waves in a sea, there's another flash of red.

"A trail," I whisper.

Invaders don't leave markers for the vengeful to follow. This is a whistler's work.

Katya and I confer. Clearly, there *were* two whistlers, and one is alive.

And she's left her herd.

Where is she going? I sign. *Why would she do that?*

Don't know. But she's not running away. Katya wrinkles her nose in thought. *She tied ribbons.*

She wants someone to follow. So she needs help. I caress Ihira's neck feathers absently, and she makes a low purr in her throat. *Is she pursuing whoever killed the other one? Hunting, like we would?*

On a triceratops. Amusement dances in her eyes. *Pretty slow hunt.*

I'm thinking fast. *Maybe she thinks her quarry doesn't expect to be hunted and won't be in a hurry. Or she just doesn't care, and has to pursue however she can.* Yet—she left her *herd*, the one thing a whistler never does. I gaze at that distant ribbon, trying to understand. *Maybe the two whistlers were close.* Isolated together for months on the prairie, surrounded by their vast rumbling herd of ceratopsians, they had to be.

Ihira warbles and shifts her weight. I grip the pommel of my saddle quick and chirp to her, instructing her to stand still. She cranes her neck around to hiss indignantly at me, and I chirp the *halt* command again. This is no time for Ihira to decide she's restless and bolt across the violet sea with me on her back. Daphne trills softly and Katya bends and rubs her cheek against her raptor's neck feathers, her hand resting on the animal's neck.

The prairie looks as timeless as ever, out here, yet I *feel* time rushing past. We have hard choices to make. An incursion, and it's not a full pack that's found it but just the two of us. No way now to find the other dakotaraptor riders in this wide land. Not til rendezvous. And however peaceful this prairie and the distant rumbling herd and the wide blue sky looks, sometime recently an invader's ship broke across it, descending from above in hot fire. Maybe at night, while Katya was kissing me and neither of us were watching closely to see one speck of light darting across the stars. There's a flash of cold rage in my blood. These invaders shouldn't be tumbling out of the sky at us; they should stay on their own planets where they belong. We have terrors enough that rain on us without them. And it shouldn't be just my wife and I, just the two of us to face the invader's brutal weapons; we should have our pack. Maybe some of them—*Sveta*—would be reluctant to ride to my aid. But they would ride anywhere for Yekaterina. We should rush out of the grass, two dozen of us in war paint and screaming at the man who has set unwelcome feet on our prairie. Graceful, bald Neveah with her thirteen throwing knives in beaded sheaths on a belt running from shoulder to hip, knives shaped like feathers; giant Nadya with her sea-green hair and bladed gloves on her fists, gauntlets that stab, and her battle cry that shakes the prairie; wild Veroshka with her midnight tresses and bolas at her saddle braids, ready to spin through the air at a touch; Violet with their javelins and their deadly aim, and their trophies braided, grisly, to their saddle; my wife with her kopye and lasso; I with my mother's kopye. One day I'll add a second weapon. For now, mastering my kopye is trouble enough. But we should be here right now, all of us. We should all be riding down this killer.

Hard choices.

Follow the ribbons? Katya signs.

Or ride for the nearest settlement? I ask. *Warn them a whistler is dead, maybe two; that their herd is untended and trampling along its way.*

We could split up. She frowns.

No. My fingers press together so hard they hurt. *We're stronger together.*

Katya gazes at me with sudden intensity, and I blush. But there is no doubt in her eyes, none at all. Try as I might, I can't prove myself to the other nightwatchers, but I have *never* felt like I have to prove myself to Yekaterina. We faced the red rain together in a creekbed the night we first kissed. She has seen me at my most vulnerable, my most shattered. And if *she* doesn't doubt me…

We *are* stronger together.

Her eyes flash. *Then let's find the hyaena who did this to her.*

Pride in my heart. So *what* if it's just my wife and me? We can do this.

Let's ride back first, I suggest. *Bury the dead.*

She shakes her head. *We've lost time. Near midday now, and that other whistler could be riding naked into a killwind if she's facing an invader's bullets alone.*

We have to. We can't leave her there.

No choice, Sasha. Even her own left her. We have to find that invader, fast. No one else can.

I am stricken. *We need to sing over her!*

Yet how *can* we, really? We don't know this whistler's story. How can we bury her when we don't know her story? And how can we bury her before the battle is even done, when her killer is still out there, slaying the innocent and leaving their bodies in the grass? I hesitate, something inside me trembling. But there's no time for hesitation. "You're right," I say, against the pang in my heart, and I snap my wind goggles down over my eyes, the golden tint of them changing the hue of the world.

Katya nods and wheels Daphne about, tapping signals on her neck, swift and rhythmic, directing her toward the second ribbon. I follow on Ihira. We'll ride hard. We have a whistler to save and a killer to find.

As we ride, I rip open the satchel of coatl flares where it hangs braided to my saddle. I lift one high and slingshot it into the sky. It ignites above our heads in a flash of white, but as Katya and I crane our necks back, I soon lose sight of it. Those flares soar high, and the light at the end is not easily seen by human eyes. But long ago, the Founder's whitejackets *changed* the seers' eyes; if one of them is up there, they'll see it. His quetzalcoatl will bring him clinging to its back to this place to see more. Surely the whistler's partner sent up a coatl flare, too? Yet no coatl has dropped yet from the wide blue expanse to examine the body as we did or to care for it and then carry word to our pack and others. That kindles unease in me. Maybe it was just that the other whistler had only one flare left, and it failed. Such things happen.

As we speed through the grass, wind in our faces, old grief lassoes itself tightly around my heart. What is wrong with me? Why do my eyes sting with tears I don't want to shed? That body behind me is none of my kin; I have buried my kin. Grandma Yaga requires a burial and a payment in song, a story of your life sung by those who remember you, in exchange for passage in her walking domik across the frozen prairie. If none remember you, if none sing of your life's deeds after you are gone, then you are left to wander in the endless frost, in an empty land where blades of brittle, frost-rimed grass break at a touch. Empty but for other ghosts who wander there like you, silent and without stories. Sometimes you hear Grandmother's cackling laughter in the stillness, her hut sprinting by on its raptor legs too quick to catch, no matter how fast you and the other ghosts run.

At my mother's grave, I sang for hours.

I sang til my voice gave out.

There was no one else left to.

Now all I have of her is her stories and her copy of the Founder's book in its ring of metal discs at my belt. I drop my hand to it, feeling with my fingertips the tiny symbols burned into the cool metal by our ancestors before they left their emptied vessels on a green cliff by the sea, to grow wild with moss and lichen.

Suddenly Katya cries out and points to our left. There is something red in the vegetation as we pass—not a ribbon this time, and all but hidden behind the tall violet blades. The wind tugs at the grass, revealing glimpses of it, and I catch my breath. My heart suddenly pounding.

It's a rainmaker.

It resembles a cactus from old Earth, a saguaro, but with a dozen stalks no more than a meter tall, each a vibrant and lethal red.

It is not water they're fat with.

I call to my wife, "How long until rainfall, do you think?"

Katya's face is set, all her laughter gone—for the moment. *Fourteen weeks? Sixteen? Who can say?*

Later in the year, near harvest, when the red cacti grow taller than the grass and are easier to find, dozens of masked diggers will ride out from our domiks on their long-clawed therizinosaurs to scour cropland and prairie alike and rip the cacti out of the soil. The red rain is terrible and claims many of us; without the diggers, it would be cataclysmic, as it was for the Founder and our ancestors. Even with them, it is terrible enough.

But the red rain is tomorrow's problem.

Just ahead in the violet grass is that second marker; once there, we'll stop and find the third through a spyglass. Then the fourth, then the fifth. It's all we can do. No other way yet to braid up the unraveled strands of this day. Ihira squawks as we ride, and I comfort her with quick chirps, not blaming her one bit for being uneasy. I am too. I am bewildered by these signs left by a whistler who *left her herd.* Fearful of this threat that has fallen from the sky, after eighty-three days of peace. Distressed by carnivorous cacti in the grass.

For her part, Katya's shoulders are tensed and alert, her braid tapping against her back as she rides, but I can tell, looking at her, that she is also *thrilled*, too. My wild golden wife loves a threat. Gets bored when things are quiet.

Through my goggles, the light is golden and warm and the grasses nearly black. Blades of grass flick against my boots as we ride, Ihira and Daphne cutting across the land swift and straight. But the sight of those swollen red cacti is beaten onto my mind like a bruise.

The red rain killed my mother and my kin.

4

FIFTY-THREE RIBBONS AND ZERO ANSWERS LATER, we locate the second whistler, who is *not* a woman. Rare to find men tending the herds. And he is definitely not killed and dead—though he rides a triceratops that looks near it, seeming older than the gutted ships at Landing by the Sea. It's an immense, hoary bull with watery eyes, cracks in its hide, battle-scars across its face, and only one horn, sporting several red and gold ribbons flickering in the breeze. The other horn is broken off just above the eye. The man who rides this bull on a long felt saddle, swaying with the trike's rolling gait, is younger than I, and stranger than I by far. I consider him carefully as we ride up. There are worry lines in his face. His hair is pale, not gold like Yekaterina's but almost white. Someone has drained all the color out of his face; maybe his parents made a bad bargain with Grandma Yaga when he was a baby. As if to make up for his pallor, his shirt and trousers are dyed red and gold, though the colors have faded with wear and sunlight. At first I don't get a good look at his eyes, because he wears a hat with a ridiculously wide brim, sticking out well past his shoulders, as if it is designed not only to shield him from the sun but from the red rain itself. The hat shadows his face until he lifts a hand to tilt it back as we ride up. His eyes are youthful but grave. He has tied his whistle to the back of his wrist with leather straps as if afraid to lose it—or afraid to forget his charge, the herd he has left behind. Perhaps the whistle is tied there to urge him to survive whatever encounter lies ahead and then ride back.

The trike shies at the raptors' approach, lowers its horn. The whistler caresses the soft skin behind its frill, murmuring to the aged triceratops bull in a soothing tone.

"Evening, girls," the whistler calls to us. I dislike his accent. Not from any settlement *I* know.

"Peace," I greet him warily. "I'm Sasha Nightwatcher; she's Yekaterina Nightwatcher. We're watching cropland and prairie. We saw your ribbons."

He chews the inside of his cheek for a moment. His eyes assess us. Reaching into his jacket, he pulls out a round device, much like a seashell the size of his hand, but of gleaming metal. There are designs traced on it in silver; they catch the sun and gleam. A watch. I feel a chill, because I know where timepieces like that come from. A bit of Ticktock loot, much like the one I gave Katya. I stare at it, wondering how he got it, wondering who he is, why he's out here far from herd and duty, rather than waiting with the trikes and styracs for a seer to respond to his coatl flare, or ours. The uncanniness of his choice to ride out here trailing ribbons like drops of blood has me on alert; maybe there's something about this incursion I don't know, some threat I don't understand.

The whistler opens the watch's shell and peeks inside. "Appears I spaced them well," he says after a moment.

"My clock told right." Without any smile of greeting, he tucks the watch away in his jacket. "Did you bury Ellie?"

A pang of guilt.

There wasn't time, Katya signs.

He is watching my face rather than Katya's hands, and he sees the answer there. His face twists with grief. "I should have stayed. Ellie's people believe you need a burial."

'Ellie's people.' Who are you? Aloud, I say, "We sent up a flare."

"So did I. No one came."

I swallow, my mouth suddenly dry. All the way here, Katya and I watched the sky. No sign of a coatl. No sign of help. Where *are* they? The seers are usually swift to respond.

We are all silent a moment. Wind in the grass.

I am uncertain how to proceed. This whistler hasn't shared his name yet. How can we know his story if we don't know his name? This day is becoming a tangled mess, but we're nightwatchers; it's out task to untangle the tale of the day, find the threat and deal with it, and braid up the story after, keeping our people safe so more of us are alive to tell our stories this winter. Why hasn't he said his name? His words are few and abrupt. Questioning us, when we should be questioning *him.*

He's strange, I sign to Katya.

She looks pensive. But then our eyes meet and she flashes a smile. *Cute, though.*

You think everyone we meet is cute.

Nope. Now her eyes sparkle with real humor. *Only the cute ones.*

The whistler stares at her hands, then at her face. I bristle, but the look he gives her is not one of lust but admiration. I suppose if you ride a lumbering triceratops, crawling across the skin of the planet, you *would* admire women who ride raptors, free and swift.

"Why *are* you out here," I blurt, "away from your herd?"

He meets my stare. "There's a man out here killed Ellie. Wasn't her time of death. There's justice owed." Something cold and lethal flickers in his eyes and though he has no kopye and no weapon, only a bone whistle for herding ceratops, for just a beat of my heart I fear him. Then he glances out over the prairie and the moment passes.

No, not *cute*. There's something hungry in him. Too hungry for a whistler.

"You want that invader," he says, "same as I. Will take you there, if you help me."

I blink. Katya looks startled, too. We're used to riding ahead, fast and far, to help and defend. "Are you suggesting we ride together? That's not a raptor your saddle's strapped to."

"No, but he's sturdy."

You're cute, Katya signs, *but you're slow.*

He watches her hands move, then frowns slightly.

With a shock, I realize *he doesn't understand sign.* Glancing at Katya, I realize she knew at once. But I reel. How does a man over six years of life not understand *sign*? Another tangle in this day that I haven't time for.

"He isn't *fast,*" I tell him.

"Don't need fast."

"Listen. Raptors could cross the entire prairie in six days, take you sixty. We can't wait for a ceratops."

"That's where you're wrong. This killer, he's in no hurry either. Sauntering over *my* prairie like he owns it. Killing who he will, feasting on what he pleases, not a fear in the world. I could probably *walk* and catch the arrogant bastard before he leaves this planet."

I don't think I've ever walked as slow as a triceratops, Katya signs in dismay. She peers ahead, where the grasses wave and sigh in the breeze. Then she signs, *Let's go look.*

I nod. Both our raptors spring forward, away from the nervous trike.

"You won't find the trail," he calls after us.

We're nightwatchers. We'll find the trail.

For a bit, Katya and I ride in long, sweeping circles around the whistler and his trike, searching for signs in the grass.

We don't find the trail.

No broken off blades, no trampled brush or spoor. The lack of it is bewildering.

I bring Ihira to a halt. Katya and Daphne stop beside us.

Katya looks thoughtful again. She pets Daphne's neck a moment, then lifts her hands to sign. *You remember the stories of Koschei, stealing lives, then flitting away as a shadow?*

I shiver. *I hate those stories.*

The puzzlement in my wife's face would be comical if I weren't so distressed. *Sasha, are we following a ghost?*

All around us, the prairie tosses endlessly, violet and vital. *It doesn't look like Grandma Yaga's country.*

Katya brightens. *Maybe* we're *ghosts.* Her eyes sparkle with silent laughter. What has her so cheerful? *Maybe*

Grandma Yaga's country looks sunlit and violet to ghosts, and only appears gray and dead to the living.

That's a strange thought.

It's a strange day. She glances at the whistler and his trike. *Come on. Let's go make it stranger.* She taps quickly at Daphne's neck, and her raptor rushes through the grass toward the whistler in a burst of speed. Startled, I chirp to Ihira and we pursue.

Katya's in a mood; though I don't understand it, it stirs my heart. Maybe it's meeting the whistler that's done it. Katya likes people. She'd be happiest riding with fifty nightwatchers or drumming in a circle with forty kin. Me, I'm happier alone with her out on the prairie or in a banya full of steam. I don't need people. People always let you down in the end, or die. Except Katya. Katya isn't *people.* Katya's my wife.

I hear her wild laughter. Her braid dances on her back. The old triceratops lowers its frill and horn, but as Daphne and her laughing rider bear down on him, the trike turns and bolts. The whistler curses, clinging to the animal's back. He takes a quirt from his belt and starts striking the animal's shoulder; it lifts its head and bellows, its voice deep and resonant, a triceratops bull. I scowl. No nightwatcher would ever treat her raptor so, and I am surprised to find a whistler would treat his trike like that.

Katya brings Daphne flashing past the trike, and the animal digs in its front feet and stops, nearly launching the whistler from its back. His hat spins away through the air. It lands perched on the tops of a tall grass plant like an overfed harra too plump to burrow. Riding in, I lean from the saddle and snatch it up. Just ahead, the trike stands braced, turning its head from side to side, to face first

Katya, then me, then Katya again, lowering that horn at us in warning. Its eyes roll, and breath puffs from its nostrils. I bring Ihira up alongside the bull, leaving five meters of healthy distance between us out of respect for that long, ribboned horn.

Without his hat, the whistler's hair looks even whiter. He stares at me glumly, but then he cracks a grin wide as Katya's, revealing good teeth but a gap where one's gone missing.

"Is that bull going to charge us?" I call to the whistler.

"You keep scaring him like this, he just might."

Katya laughs again. Catching my eye, she taps the lasso on her belt. I blush hotly. I know she means to signal that she's prepared to lasso the trike if it charges, but my heart is hot with the memory of a *different* capture she made with that rope.

"All right, whistler," I say. "What trail are you following?"

He shakes his head. "No trail. I know where he's going." His gaze flicks to my wrist. "I'm partial to that hat."

I lift my hand, twirling his hat on my finger. "You abandoned your companion to take off after what killed her. You must be awfully *confident* of where you're headed."

"Whistlers know their prairie." He nods at the horizon. "This prairie's mine. Only place in this world that is." He looks yearningly at the hat.

I sign to Katya, *We could turn back, get the others.*

Katya shakes her head. *It would take us days to find them, or we never would. Rendezvous's not for two weeks.*

I don't like this. "We should turn back."

"That killer took my partner," the whistler says. "*I* ain't turning back. He needs to bleed for what he's done. You helping me, or you just going to flash your raptors around us in pretty circles and give Old Man a heart attack?"

Katya signs, *We aren't turning back.*

"What can you tell us about the invader?" I ask. I toss him the hat and he snatches it out of the air.

"His garments were worn," he tells us. "He's been out on the prairie a while. It's why I think he's taking his time." He settles the hat firmly on his head and glances across the grasses toward the distant band of ceratopsians. They are too far away now to see, though I imagine Ihira can still feel the rumor of them in the earth under her clawed feet.

"All kinds of damage done," the whistler mutters. "And before it's done, the herd's path will be *all* messed up. Could have made enough on this migration to buy my first slave. Could have had a girl to kiss my thighs on the next ride out, to cook a meal or two and ease the bite of solitude." He chews the inside of his cheek. "Or a man," he adds after a moment. "Not particular, long as they're pretty."

My blood goes cold as he speaks. So *that's* the reason for the strangeness of his voice and manner. I am suddenly certain we've fallen in with an invader of another kind. And I know now where he got that watch in his jacket. It's not *loot*; it's *his*. "You're a *Ticktock*. From the mountains."

Katya's eyes widen.

"Was born so," he says gravely.

"You're no *whistler*!" I hiss, backing Ihira away. Our whistlers don't keep slaves.

He tips his hat. "For a rainfall or two now. Turns out, your people provide for whistlers better than mine provide for clock keepers."

My anger must be hot enough for Ihira to feel, because she hisses. "*Your* people raid our herds. Steal hides."

His eyes are guarded. "Often as not." After a pause, he adds, "You asked my name, Sasha Nightwatcher. It's Dmitri. Dmitri Andreivich."

I bristle. That's a Ticktock name. A Ticktock tells you who gave his mothers seed, as if that's worth a tale, as if that's what matters to his story—if he tells you anything at all before chaining you for his mines. But he never names his mother or her wife.

"Not a raider though," Dmitri says quietly, watching my face. "I'm a whistler. And whistlers are the same all 'cross the prairie, no matter their tribe. Whistlers are their own tribe. Most the year we're out here in the long grass with only each other and the blazing stars for company. And that killer took one of us. One of *ours*. So you can hate me, you can hate my accent, can hate the Ticktocks' slaving ways." His eyes are cold and intent. "But I don't rightly care. I care that you have raptors. You're fast, you're lethal, you look *smart*. You're going to help me get my justice."

Katya signs, *That we are.*

We can't travel with a Ticktock, I sign briskly. *He might get it in his head to slave us.*

He can try. Katya's eyes shine with that wild humor of hers. *On that old trike. If he wants.*

My hands are quick and curt. *That's the other thing. We'll never catch anything trailing behind a trike.*

So let him trail behind us. Katya taps Daphne's neck, and her raptor walks forward through the grass at a quick step. The Ticktock chews the inside of his cheek, watching. If we were going to travel this slow, we could've stopped and buried that girl. I chirp a command to Ihira, and my raptor wheels toward the horizon. I glare over my shoulder at the whistler. Fury burns cold in me, and my voice is ice. "When you buy your slave, Ticktock, if she's one of ours, you let her go. Or him. The humming people are a free people. Have been since Landing. They don't make good slaves."

He meets my gaze. "I'll consider it."

"You do that." Three quick chirps, and my raptor leans forward; I sway with her. "And try to keep up." Then we are running through the tall grass. A flash of violet, and Katya is beside me on her Daphne. I drive Ihira hard, so that we flicker through the grass faster than wind, though I know we'll have to stop soon and let that triceratops catch up, since I have no idea where we're going. But right now, I have anger to burn. Katya glances at me with concern as we sprint, leaving grasses swaying in our wake.

5

AFTER CRAWLING OVER THE PRAIRIE A WHILE AT THE lumbering pace of an old trike, we're near frantic with the need to sprint again, and I'm anxious and craving action enough that I could just about pick a fight with a *tree* for lack of another foe. Even Ihira and Daphne are restless, and Katya keeps braiding and unbraiding a lasso, over and over. But it's getting dark. We camp the night in a narrow gully, a crack in the land just wide enough for Dmitri to squeeze his triceratops into—though that takes some doing. The massive animal balks, and Dmitri gets his whistle and blows tunes we can't hear. His trike does, though. It snorts and lifts its head, its single horn slicing the air, but eventually the scarred old bull complies. I bring Ihira to a halt and exchange a look with Katya. She shrugs. Half a day that Ticktock has ridden beside or behind us, yet he remains a mystery. What unseen passions drive him to ride after a foe he can't hope to kill, leaving herd and duty behind? What louder duty summons him, what bone whistle in the night that he alone can hear? For that matter, what duty has called the seers out of our sky, so that they no longer come to a flare? To my unease, the prairie dusk is full of songs I can't hear and tales I can't braid.

There's just a trickle of water left in the gully, and after unsaddling our raptors, Katya and I are able to fill our canteens by lifting water, a little at a time, in cupped hands and pouring it in while the other holds the canteen. Down here, we're screened by the tall grass and by a few Catha trees with wide, wide branches, their roots dug deep to drink up the scarce water. If that invader is out there scanning the prairie with his spyglass tonight, he won't see us. Doubtless in the morning he'll see the triceratops, if he's attentive.

But he won't see the raptors. With their violet feathers, *they* blend in.

* * *

Katya and I dine on salted triceratops jerky and slices of dried apricot. Dmitri opens a can of cold beans and spoons them into his mouth with a bit of hard biscuit. We don't share. No campfire—the night is warm, and this isn't food you have to cook, and anyway we don't want a pillar of smoke betraying our pursuit. I share my jerky with Ihira, who snatches bites of it from my hand with quick bobs of her head, tickling my palm with her teeth without cutting my skin, but Katya lets her Daphne slip away in the silent dark to hunt. I'm not about to let my own raptor stray too far for a quick summons back. If the Ticktock tries anything, he'll find Ihira's claw shearing through his belly. But instead, he seems occupied with his beans and biscuit. I find myself staring at his hands. He takes the glove off his right hand while eating but leaves his left covered. His hands are long and slender—a Ticktock's hands, for shunning work and scribing numbers and arcane symbols while his slaves prepare his food and heat his bedding—but *this* Ticktock's right hand has grown calloused from work on the prairie, like a whistler's hands. He dresses like a whistler, too, and no Ticktock I ever heard of rode a triceratops like that scarred old bull. This thinking of him as a whistler one moment and a Ticktock the next is no good—if I don't know *what* a threat is, how can I defend against it? He glances up at me and our gazes meet. He seems to read my fear and my hate as easily as Katya reads my lips. His own lip curves upward a little at the corner, but there's no mockery in it, just a wryness and a weariness. A whistler's humor, maybe, from a life lived in slow patience and hard work on the vast prairie. I look away, flushed as if I've been caught at something, and I tear at the jerky with my teeth.

The meal is brief but it's enough. Afterward, Katya unslings the drum from her back. It's a narrow bowl with a bit of tanned corythosaur hide stretched over it, bound in place with a beaded cord. The cord is a gift from her sisters, like the beaded armlet just below her left shoulder, each bead the size of one of my teeth, strung on six strings of pachycephalosaur gut, for the six elements: earth, water, fire, air, space, and song. The beads are many hues, but especially violet for the prairie, blue for the sea, red for the heart. The colors of the humming people. Her sisters made that armlet and the beaded cord on the drum too, several of them working together. I don't have such an armlet or cord; my sisters are in the ground.

Katya clasps the drum between her knees and begins beating a wild cheerful tune with her hands. Her eyes close, and she smiles. I smile, too, untensing just a bit, because my wife is happy. I can hear the sound; she can *feel* it. It's a good tune. Even Dmitri looks at ease as he leans back against his triceratops' pebbled hide. He starts to tap the beat on his thighs, and I realize I am doing that, too. The first drumsong of the night ends in a long roll of sound as Katya's hands move almost too fast to see, and after the last beat of it fades in the air I let out a whoop, and Dmitri lets out a ridiculously loud fart. From the beans, I expect. I make a face, and Katya's eyes fly open. She must have caught a whiff, because she laughs that wild laughter of hers and almost falls over backward, laughing so hard. The triceratops opens one eye and shuts it again. Ihira makes an anxious chirp, and I press my cheek to her neck, holding her and stroking her feathers, torn between irritation at this stranger who upsets my raptor and upsets *me*—and pleasure at my wife's joy. It takes a while for Katya to recover and start rolling the next beat.

She drums for a quarter watch at least while the dusk deepens and the rings start to burn bright in the dark. I marvel that her hands aren't tired. Once the drumming's done and my heartbeat slows, the day's weariness starts setting into my limbs, but I am still tense. There is a stranger in our camp. I guess he feels tense, too; though the sun's long set, he's still wearing that hat.

The worst part about having Dmitri down here, leaning against his resting triceratops—a living, breathing mountain in the quiet dusk—and watching us with those flinty eyes, is that his presence wreaks havoc on any plans I might have with Katya tonight.

The *second* worst part is that he watches me pray.

Katya doesn't pray much, but she doesn't mind me doing it. After she has finished drumming and is spreading her bedroll, I take some of the soft soil near the water, dark and damp in my cupped hands. I close my eyes and hum softly a while. Then bend my face and very slowly, tenderly, kiss the soil. Then I return it to the ground and put my hands over my ears and listen to the water song of my blood, of my own body. I let my breathing grow deep and full. I've needed this. Ever since leaving a body unsung.

When I lower my hands and open my eyes, Dmitri is still watching me, and I feel strangely naked.

"Kissing soil gives you a mouthful of dirt," he says, his tone thoughtful and perplexed.

"What would you know about it?" Rage torches its way into my blood. There goes all my calm from prayer.

Katya glances at one of us, then the other, worried.

"Easy now," Dmitri murmurs. "Meant my words to do no wounding."

"I'm not *wounded*."

"That a true thing?" His eyes seem to peer deep into mine, and I don't like it.

I glare at him. "I am honoring the Founder."

"By kissing dirt?" Now he sounds almost … amused. "You'd have more fun kissing your wife."

"Not while you're watching," I snap.

She can kiss me later, Katya grins.

To my surprise, he dips his hand and gets a palmful of soil in his gloved palm. Lifts it near his chin, smells it. "Saw Ellie do that once," he says. "But only once. I was all shy then, and didn't ask." Gently, he kisses the dirt.

And now my feelings are a tangle. I don't know if he's reverencing the Founder or mocking me or meaning to honor the dead whistler or just trying to understand, and the uncertainty does nothing to cool my anger. Still, I answer the question he's trying to ask. "With earth in my hand, I listen to her song in the earth and her song in my blood. Don't you Ticktocks revere the Founder?"

He tips his palm and lets the earth trickle slowly, gently from his hand. "Different Founder."

"What?"

Katya looks shocked, too.

Dmitri's eyes glint in the starlight. "Ticktocks have a different Founder."

"You came here on the ships, same as us. Long, long ago."

He shakes his head. "Different ships. Ours arrived first. We'd already hatched the first herds when you all dropped out of the sky."

I gasp. "That's a lie."

His face goes dark. "I am no liar, Sasha Nightwatcher."

I regret speaking. He looks … dangerous, somehow, with his eyes dark like that. I have my mother's kopye clipped to my belt tonight and not to my saddle braids, but I've enough discipline not to reach down and grip it for comfort like a girl still preparing for her nightwatcher test. I return the whistler's stare without flinching.

Katya signs, *Tell us about your Founder.*

Dmitri watches her hands, then glances at me. "What's she saying?"

"She says you're not even a *good* liar."

Katya looks almost as furious with me as he does. My cheeks flush. I wonder which of them I am trying to pick a fight with. I wanted to be in her arms tonight, and I suppose I am all kinds of frustrated right now.

Don't do that, Katya signs. *You don't get to speak* for *me, Sasha.*

I flush a little with shame and sign back, *I'm sorry.*

Dmitri watches the exchange and says quietly, "You're the one what's full of lies."

I don't react. "She's asking you about your Founder."

He plucks a blade of grass, pops one end in his mouth, chews on it. He is always chewing on *something.* Like a triceratops.

"Clockmaker," he corrects me. He reaches into his jacket and plucks out the round watch, large as his palm, that we saw him checking earlier on the prairie. He presses a small knob on its side and it pops open like a seashell. There's a rhythmic slow ticking. He lifts it so that the firelight shines on its polished shell, and he looks at me, then at Katya. "He made the clocks we carry with us, wherever the tribe goes. Clocks that tell time on a dozen worlds but ours, so we will never forget the universe is not just the soil and flesh of this one planet but a dozen scattered and set rolling among the stars like a child's baubles. So we will never forget this one hour is only one, there's another before it, another after, and the worst hour of all is only a temporary and passing thing, terrible in its being but soon to be slain, severed by the knifelike finality of the hour hand."

I stare at him as he speaks, aghast. I'd thought he'd go on forever talking only in short phrases, a man who barely gives his name and isn't quick to tell his story. Now he's talking. I glance at Katya. She looks rapt, as if it's one of *my* tales she's listening to.

"But that goes for the more pleasing hours, too," Dmitri adds. "Round and round the hands turn, one twelve after another on Earth, one fourteen after another here, one seven after another on the seas of Escape, one nine after another on the lava plains of Hostility, one twenty after another in the floating cities of New Kenya, and wherever you ride and wherever you stand even if it's on the other side of the stars, nothing is permanent. The clocks remind us."

I glance at the stars that are out now and starting their cold burn. This talk of other planets chills me. Other planets are where our ancestors were slaves and where the invaders drop from. Our time in prairie and cropland is impermanent enough and plenty to worry over.

"That's grim," I mutter.

"It's necessary." His hands holding the timepiece are reverent as mine when I'm holding warm earth; he traces the carvings on the top of his watch with his gloved fingertips. I lean forward slightly, peering, troubled. Those carvings—are those signs, like the ones in the Founder's book I carry at my belt? Maybe his watch is telling a story, but it's a story I don't know how to hear. I can't read the signs; I wonder if he can.

"What planet's time does *your* watch tell?" I ask, bewildered.

"This one's." He gives it a bittersweet look. "The time of my people, the time of the Clockmaker's heirs. At least I hope it does. It's been a long time since I could sync it with the others." I recognize the pain in his eyes—it's grief. He lifts his gaze from the watch. There's—respect—in his eyes. Well, there'd *better* be. But I'd know better how to respond if there was hate there instead. "Can't imagine how you nightwatchers do what you do with no watch to tell your time, to help measure the distances. I need a clear sense of how far I'm traveling, how many days I might be, how many supplies I need; I can't flit over a couple hundred kilometers between sunrise and dusk like you can. Imagine you noticed."

I scowl. I certainly did. We barely *moved* over the prairie today.

But we do have a watch. Katya's eyes spark with mischief. While I translate for her, she reaches for her saddle and the bags tied to it and retrieves her own watch, the one I gave her the morning I became a nightwatcher. I stare at it, startled.

You carry that with you?

It's a gift from you, she says. *It's lucky.*

She reaches across the fire, holding out the watch. The Ticktock's eyes widen and he accepts it with trembling fingers, as if the moment is holy to him. He opens it and peers inside. I can hear it ticking.

"It's loot off a Ticktock I killed." There's an edge to my voice. I suppose I'm warning him that we are not to be messed with, that we have killed Ticktocks at need and can do so again. If he needed any warning other than the dark eyes and sharp talons of our raptors. Sensing my tension, Ihira nuzzles my side and I caress the feathers behind her eyes.

"If you're trying to rile me," Dmitri says without looking up, "you might consider there's no love lost between me and the clan I was born to." He stares moodily at the timepiece. "*This* one belonged to Nikolai's clan. You can tell by the gold tracery. But this clock's telling all *kinds* of wrong." Hushed, he adds, "Could wind it for you."

Katya shakes her head, smiling. She signs, *It looks old.*

I translate.

"It *is* old," he says. "These watches all come from Landing. From the Clockmaker's ship. The Ticktocks been keeping them wound all this time. Some are cracked now beyond all repair. Maybe three hundred ten, three hundred twenty left in the whole world." Gently, he hands it back. I see his fingers tremble again.

Katya takes the watch, tucks it back into her jacket.

"Thought you had slaves make them," I say.

He snorts. "Slaves dig up iron and smelt it, raise rock haia for food, keep the caves warm. Slaves don't touch these." Old sadness settles in his eyes. "Though *I* hardly know. I carry a watch but do not own a slave. I'm the poorest Ticktock you'll ever find, and who knows if my clock tells right?"

A silence settles between us all, heavy and uncomfortable, and suddenly I am aware again of the prairie above and all around us, of the wide and empty night, only not empty *enough.* I think of that body far behind and her ghost stumbling its way through pale ghost grass somewhere in the far distance. A yearning takes hold of me to have Katya pressed to my side, to find solace in her warmth. I lean back against my raptor, and Ihira nuzzles my cheek with the soft end of her snout, offering what solace *she* can. I rub my cheek against her a moment, too, grateful, and she warbles and sets her foreclaw on my arm, the points of her talons sharp but only barely pressing at my skin. Gentle girl. She had to learn that. I remember Mom carrying Ihira to me as a hatchling, placing this young raptor in my arms when she was barely longer than my hand. Her curved shearing claws, one above each rear foot, were tiny, but they cut into my arm, making me wince. Yet her feathers were soft on my skin, as they are now, and her eyes were round and liquid and as deep as forever, and I couldn't breathe, gazing into them. I held Ihira all night and didn't sleep, just felt her heartbeat against my arm. She was so small; I kept her warm. Now, she is larger than me by far, and she keeps me warm.

It has been a weary day and my hips feel the ache from the ride—first swift, then all too slow—but I am not in the least sleepy. Nor is Katya, I expect. She thinks this Ticktock is *cute*. What *is* he, though? He travels slow on trikeback like a whistler and I saw him kiss the earth, but all his talk is of clocks and chained slaves and coldness.

Somewhere out in the dark, a chaka screeches. My heart pounds, as it does whenever I hear one. A chaka is too small to attack a woman, but there is something primal and terrifying in its screech. Small animals freeze in the grass at the sound, and none flee when the chaka makes its dive and snatch. Ihira and Daphne hunt and pounce silently as shadows, their violet feathers concealing them in the tall grass, but the amphibian chaka that glides in the night-dark likes to announce its presence and its kill.

The invaders that come to our world in sleek, gleaming ships, they are as crafty and silent as Ihira and Daphne. It might be better if they were like the chaka, screeching as they descend; then at least we would know when they are about to strike.

The moment passes, and there's just a low rumbling sound from the triceratops. And a slight wind over the prairie, making the grasses toss and sigh and setting the Catha boughs whistling. Their melody is wistful and sad tonight. Like the trees are mourning that death behind us and other deaths ahead. I shiver. This Dmitri has infected me with cold thoughts.

I catch Katya looking at me. She signs, *He told us about his Founder. Tell him about ours.*

He doesn't deserve to hear about ours.

Katya looks angry again.

I flush and turn to the stranger. I know Katya wants a story because she doesn't love the dark—when *two*, not one, of her senses are quiet. Night is a time she likes to fill with touch or talk. I guess I prefer it that way, too. All our people are like that. We want our tales before sleep. Even on the first winter night after rainfall, when the humming people have gathered again in hiding, with our collapsed domiks carried on our backs and on the backs of dinosaurs, each person sings their tale of someone who didn't make it, someone the rain took. And all the stories of those who survived the red rain and those who didn't are braided together in one telling that night.

Katya is right; I didn't think to be braiding tales tonight with a Ticktock, but he gave a story, and Katya and I need to give one also. My voice starts a bit slow because I know how to tell *Katya* tales but I don't know how to tell tales *he* can hear. "Our Founder is Yelena," I say. "The Prophet-Singer, from old Earth. She saw the old world burn and doused the fire in her tears. Like my wife, she could not speak." I falter and glance at Katya, who smiles encouragingly.

"But," I go on, "she sang the music of the gods from her throat. She teaches us to hum. She teaches us to hum not only with our throats but with our bodies, to hum with such joy at all of life." My voice rises with excitement, even though it is an outsider I am sharing this cherished story with. There is joy in the telling itself. "She visits you on your deathbed, where only you can see her, and she hums with you. She visits you in the womb before you are born. She visits you in the pleasure-surge in your body when you are with your wife. She brought us here across the stars, singing, leading us with her melodies to our new home."

Dmitri chews the end of a blade of grass as he listens. Then he says quietly, "Craziest thing I ever heard. Beautiful, though."

I glare. I *knew* better than to share a sacred tale with this Ticktock in whistler's clothes. "Music and love are the only things in the world that *aren't* crazy."

Dmitri grins. "Love's the craziest thing there ever has been or ever will be. But that's all right. If love isn't crazy, what's the point? I like your Founder."

Katya signs, *I like yours too.*

I bristle. *Don't. Don't do that.*

Do what?

Flirt with him like he's one of our pack.

She blushes. *Who's flirting? I just said I like his Founder.*

I know what you said.

Sasha—

He's a feral slaving slowrider and I don't need my wife making eyes at him. I'm tired.

You're in a mood. After a moment, she signs, slowly, *I love you.*

I glance down, ashamed at my outburst. *I love you, too.*

Ask him how his trike lost its horn.

I blink.

Go on. Ask him.

I stare at her.

I'm changing the subject. She gives me an impish grin, and I shake my head, my lips curving in a smile despite myself. I can't—I can't *stay* angry when she grins at me like that. How does she *do* that?—just flow so easily from one mood to the next? She rides her moods in a raft, bouncing along on the rapids with her eyes full of laughter, while I flail and drown in mine.

I try to bury my unease. Yekaterina flirts. Always. I know that. She flirts like a raptor in spring, but I've never seen her kiss another girl. But I know that look in Katya's eyes. That same look she gave a baby haia she found stranded once in the grass, lifting it in her cupped hands. That same nurturing and tender look she gives *me* sometimes. She doesn't need to be giving *him* that look; Dmitri has lost someone, as I have, and I suppose he's alone out here, but he is no baby bird.

My gaze bores into him now, while he sits there lanky and young under that ridiculous hat: *Don't be charming my wife.* He doesn't appear to notice my discomfort. While we've talked, he's taken out a small bladed tool, only a few inches long, with a hilt wrapped in what looks like microraptor hide. He's working with slow patience to pry a rock loose from the treads of his boot. He has probably been watching our silent talk, but he gives no sign of it. Behind him, his triceratops settles his head on his front paws and closes his eyes. His one horn lifts and falls softly as the animal breathes.

"How did your triceratops lose a horn?" I ask.

"Is that your question?" He works the stone loose, holds it up between two gloved fingers to get a look at it, then tosses it aside. "Or hers?"

"Hers. She likes you, for some reason I can't fathom."

Those dimples. "I'm a likeable fellow, as it happens."

Sasha, my wife signs. *You know whose braid is on my thigh, ridiculous wife.*

Well don't you go forgetting it.

She smiles. *I would never.*

Dmitri watches our hands and this time I catch the bewilderment in his eyes.

"How do you not know sign?" I ask suddenly.

"Sign?"

"This." I sign at him, rudely, *Your mother fucked a medved the night she made you.*

Katya giggles.

"There are a lot of people who can't speak the way you do," I tell him pointedly. "How do you talk with them if you don't know sign? What do you do at a barter?"

He shrugs. "Not a lot of people like that among the Ticktocks."

Puzzling. "Why?"

He is silent a while. Katya and I both watch him. The ringlight is bright on his face. His triceratops starts to snore, a thunderous noise that makes me jump.

He glances warmly at his trike. "Old Man's missing a horn. Your wife's missing a voice. I'm missing a thing, too." He takes his left glove in his teeth, pulls it off, holds up his naked hand. I let my breath out slowly, realizing what he meant. His left hand has no fourth finger—just a thumb and three.

"Ticktocks don't learn sign." His eyes catch the ringlight, bright and intense. "And they don't ask, *How did your trike lose a horn? How did you lose a finger?* None but my mother—and you—and my partner dead—have ever seen this hand."

"Why?"

He looks at me evenly, then gestures at my saddlebags. "Ever been hungry? *Real* hungry?"

I glance at the bags of jerky hung from the saddle, where I've lain it on a white rock by that trickle of a creek.

Dmitri nods, as though I've just confirmed something. "Down here on the prairie, you've got a world of plenty. Herds. Winged flocks. Further toward the sea, croplands, right? Catch yourself a meal or grow it. Harvest in a hurry before rainfall. Backbreaking, but food enough that they can send you girls out on raptorback looking for trouble. Right now you're not planting, you're not hunting, but your people don't feel the lack of your labor. No one back in your settlement is crying because her baby starves while you carry all that food across the grass. Up in the mountains, is different. There's less. Always less. Winters are bad. Ticktocks don't raid you because they're mean, they raid you because they're *hungry*. And Ticktocks don't feed sickly children."

I gasp. Katya goes pale.

I stare at his hand, feeling sick, thinking I understand now why a Ticktock is down here on the prairie, guiding herds alongside other tribes' whistlers. "They'd have killed you? As a child?"

"Mother hid it." With quick, practiced movements, he tugs the glove back on, restoring the illusion of a five-fingered hand. "Mothers all 'cross the world love their babies. That's a true thing." He motions at Katya with his chin. "Mean no disrespect to your wife. But I don't know sign."

The pain in his eyes shames me. "I'll translate for Katya," I tell him quietly. "But you can talk to her directly. As long as you look at her and she's looking back, she can read the movement of your lips. She'll know what you're saying."

"That right?" He looks at her, and she nods. She is smiling, but there's such sorrow and empathy in her eyes, he actually blushes at it, then coughs to clear his throat. "Seen you ride, Yekaterina. It's nothing sickly. Three of us instead of one to hunt down what killed Ellie. That's a firm number. Am grateful. Am glad you weren't born a Ticktock. Now pardon me, both. Going to be needing sleep."

And with that, he settles back against Old Man's leg and tugs his hat down over his eyes, shutting out the ringlight, the conversation, and us. Alone in the dark with his memories. Old Man opens one eye and as I watch, he shifts position, placing a thick leg against his rider's side, as if to cuddle him and keep him warm in the prairie night. My breath catches at the sight. It's like something Ihira would do. That's a whistler's bond with his animal, akin to ours though different. How did a Ticktock—from a people to whom all others are merely things to use—form such a bond as that?

Katya's face is pensive, too. Remembering suddenly how I've acted, I flush with shame. I catch her gaze and sign, *I'm sorry about earlier.*

About that. You don't get to speak for me, Sasha. You don't get to decide when I ride into peril or when I don't, nor what words I want said to one who isn't reading my hands.

I know. I … I'm sorry. I am, my love. I'm tense. Eighty-three days without an incursion, and now…

You're not tense, Sasha. You're angry. Her eyes are deep. Concerned. She signs, *You need to take a breath sometimes, for me.*

Hard to breathe when enemies are falling from the sky at us, or sleeping in the gully beside us.

He's not an enemy. He's a whistler.

He's a Ticktock.

Sasha, listen to me.

My temper flares. *You listen.*

Her eyes flash with anger, and I lose the trail of my thoughts and finish weakly, *He's a Ticktock.*

If he tries a thing, there's four of us and one of him.

Four of us: Yekaterina, Daphne, me, Ihira. I glance moodily at the creek. She's right. Doesn't mean I have to like it.

She reaches for my hand, squeezes it. Then signs, *Look, there's danger out here on the prairie tonight that scares me, too, frightens me until I'm half a ghost, but we're quick and we're smart. We can do this.*

You can. You're not unbraided, I sign back, my throat tight. *Not the one who'll break if you lean on her.*

Katya goes very still.

Then her hands move slowly, very slowly, her eyes shining in the firelight. *You overheard that?*

I can hardly breathe, but I manage a nod.

Sveta didn't mean that, Sasha.

Oh yes, she did.

Out here on the open prairie with Yekaterina, I haven't had to think about what I heard. Haven't had to look the others in their faces. But some reason, now it's all rushing back like a flash flood after sunthaw.

It was a few nights back, right before our nightwatcher pack took down that pride of hyaenadons. Near a stand of Catha and a creek, we'd camped around four, no, five fires. Ihira was out hunting. I'd lain down early, tired, and drowsed a bit, but woke to hear murmured talk by the next fire over. Cracked my eyes open a slit but otherwise didn't let on I was awake. Don't know why. The rings were lovely and unexpectedly bright in the night sky. The Catha boughs were whistling a little in the breeze but quietly, and I could hear the other women. Veroshka and Sveta were there, and Katya had walked over to join them and was crouching with her kopye across her knees and her braid over her shoulder. They were signing, of course, but Sveta had started speaking, too.

"Why, Katya?" she asked.

Katya's back was toward me and I couldn't see her reply.

Sveta went on, "You're the best of us, and you don't even have to brag about it, we all know."

Veroshka started to say something, and Sveta sighed, "Shut up, Veroshka."

But Veroshka spoke anyway. "I don't know about *best.* It's pretty ropework—"

Sveta blushed. "Very pretty ropework," she said quietly.

"—but it'd take more than pretty ropework to tie up a wild *spinosaur.*"

Sveta bit her lip, and I could just about *hear* her thoughts: *It wouldn't take more than your pretty ropework to tie me up.* That's what she was thinking, plain as morning sunlight. My blood burned.

Katya signed something, and Veroshka flushed darkly. Sveta grinned.

"All I'm saying—" Veroshka began.

Sveta held up her palm. "We know, sister. We know. Took down a wild spinosaur. You and your Zima, all by yourselves. With just your kopye and a bolas. And once it was down, you tore its throat out with your bare teeth, or something. We've all heard it."

Veroshka's eyes blazed. She stood. "I need to see to my raptor. You two flirt all you want."

She slipped away from the fire. Sveta giggled, but Katya didn't laugh. I could see the tension in my wife's shoulders, and the sight of it calmed me a bit. Sveta could *flirt*, but my Katya didn't want her.

Still, I didn't understand why Katya's shoulders were all tensed like that until Sveta spoke again, running back up her trail to her original question, the one she'd been asking when I first woke. And when I heard it, it was all I could do not to gasp, not to let them hear I was awake.

Sveta lifted delicate fingers, pushed her crimson hair back behind her ear. "All right, maybe Veroshka thinks she's good as you, but I know I'm not. The others know it, too. There's never *been* a nightwatcher can do what you do with that lasso, or run down a trail like you can. So why you with *her*, Yekaterina? Why'd you wive with *her*?" There was a sudden intensity, maybe a sadness now in Sveta's voice.

Again, I couldn't see my wife's response. Almost I couldn't even see Sveta's face lit up by the firelight, because my eyes were playing watery tricks on me. But I could hear Sveta's voice clearly enough, louder than the murmurs from the more distant fires. "Ever since you were a little girl, Katya, you've taken care of anything that's broken. A haia with a shattered wing, a weakened corythosaur calf. You even chose the *smallest* dakotaraptor. Though you were right about Daphne, I admit. She's fast. And gorgeous as the dawn. But Sasha…" She sighed. "She's *unbraided*, Katya. Kinless. You can't *depend* on her. Can she be trusted to do what it takes to protect the people, when she has fewer people to protect?" She paused a moment, probably watching my wife's hands. "No, listen. We love you and dammit, you need to hear this, Yekaterina. Your lasso flies true because there are so many lives braided to you; their strength flows into your arms and into the rope and makes you strong and swift. But what does she have? Not a one. Less braided even than *I*. She's a single strap, a weak strap. You lean on her, she'll break. And then where will you be?"

I closed my eyes and cried then, hating myself for the silent tears because crying is what I did when I held my mother dying in my arms at fifteen, when I couldn't save her and all I knew to do was cry like a child. But try as I might, I couldn't stop these tears. Even Sveta thought me useless. Even *Sveta*, the one woman in our pack who might have understood my grief. Flame-haired Sveta, daughter of two peoples, with only half her kin on this side of the mountains, unbraided forever from the forest tribes. Even *Sveta*. Betrayal bit at my heart. I wondered if at each dawn,

Sveta, Veroshka, or any of the others truly braided my strap of red leather around their kopyes, or if they left my strap in their saddlebags, fearing its inclusion would make their braiding weak. I could check by daylight but I already knew I wouldn't dare. I didn't want to know. My secret and unspoken hope—to be one among sisters at last—was dashed. I had no sisters. I had no family. I had no mother, no kin. All I had was my raptor and Katya, and the other women wanted her. Who wouldn't? That was the undercurrent beneath the river of Sveta's words. She was saying it clear without saying it aloud: *You could have any woman here; you could have me. And you picked her. You're a fool, Katya, a beautiful fool; you picked the weakest girl, the one who will fail you.*

* * *

Ihira nudges my cheek with her snout, and her breath washes warm across my neck. I put my arms around her but resist the temptation to hide my face in her feathers. Katya's eyes shimmer. *Oh Sasha*, she signs, and touches my cheek. A shiver runs through me but I will *not* cry. A little desperately, a little defiantly, I turn my face and brush my lips across her fingers.

They're wrong, my love, she signs. *They're so wrong. You're the strong one, the strongest woman I've ever met. You held your own mother while she died and you did not break.*

"Didn't I?" I whisper. Then, louder: "You take care of broken, kinless things. Isn't that what the others say?"

Katya's nostrils flare and her eyes go hot. *I'm drawn to what's beautiful, broken or not!*

So you do *think I'm broken!* I sign.

That's not what I meant, and you know it, Sasha.

Even if I am *a single strap, I can survive and fight just fine! Ihira and I took down a feral coatl! I snatched a medved's hair! I am a nightwatcher, the same as Sveta or big-as-a-mountain Nadya, and I can handle mysel—*

She shuts me up with a kiss. A furious, deep, long, loving kiss. Her kiss is sweet, and I taste sweat and prairie wind and her. For one wild moment, her love floods away my pain. I melt. After the kiss, her eyes are fire.

Yaga's teeth, Sasha, if you could just see what I see. —I could slap Sveta right now.

My smile is like a raptor's; it shows my teeth. *I'd like to see that.*

Bet you would. Her signing is gentle. *I need you to breathe, Sasha. I need you to just breathe. I don't want to see the woman I love living in pain.*

My eyes sting, and I blink furiously. How is it she always sees inside me, like that?

Come on, she signs. *Let's look for Daphne.*

I nod and trill a command for Ihira to stay, then glance at the Ticktock. He is still lying against his snoring trike, with his hat over his eyes. No sign of whether he heard my outburst or watched us kissing. My wife takes my hand.

We climb out of the gully together, grasping roots to pull ourselves up. She slips once, and I catch her, pulling her into me.

Her eyes shine. *See? Strong Sasha.*

I am caught by her eyes. She probably slipped on

purpose. I almost kiss her, but instead I heave her up toward the top of the gully.

That scramble leaves us dusty and hot, but then we reach the top and stand in the cool shade of a Catha tree, gazing out together across a prairie turned silver and black by the fall of night. Up here, we can feel the wind; it tugs at our hair. I am still holding Yekaterina's hand.

No sign of Daphne yet. I tilt my head back and look at the sky. The rings are behind us and the stars before us. Nowhere do I glimpse a swooping coatl. That problem is a welcome distraction from the turmoil in my heart, but it worries me, too.

I let go of Katya's hand, to sign. *Where are they? We've sent up two flares.*

Katya's hands flash. *I worry.*

I have eight more. We could send up one now.

In the dark? The seers only fly by day.

Two unanswered flares. I watch the dark grasses ripple in the wind. *What will we find out there tomorrow, Yekaterina?*

Same thing as today, same as the next day after. Peril.

You like *the peril,* I accuse.

I like a thrill. She grins. *Each of our hearts beats a different drumbeat. Yours is strong and loud and loyal. Mine is fast.* She glances back toward the gully. *That whistler's heart beats steady...and quiet.*

Like a clock.

Katya searches me with her gaze.

They tried to slave you once, I remind her.

She lifts her wrists, showing them to me, before signing, *No bonds on my wrists yet.* Then her face gets serious. *You listen to me, Sasha, because we're on a hard trail, a trail we can't even see, with death and Yaga's cackling at its end, and maybe more thrill than even I'm ready for, and to catch our quarry, we're going to need each other. Even that whistler and his triceratops, slow-crawling over the ground as he is. You're hating on him, but remember he is only a boy. And more alone than you or anyone I know.*

And you think he's cute. I regret my words immediately. Too late to call them back.

Katya looks at me sharply. *That's what's gnawing your toes, Sasha Nightwatcher? If I didn't kiss Sveta, what makes you think I'd get all wet for the first lanky whistler we meet?*

I flush. *Just promise me when you're thinking about inviting a man to the domik for a few nights to plant children, we'll have a long talk.*

Well, not too *long. When that night comes, I might be in a hurry,* she teases.

I take a breath. Then another. *How do things get so tense so fast, out here? We need a night or two in the banya, don't we?*

Yes.

We're getting entangled in that whistler's story, and I don't know how to braid a tale from this mess.

The way we always do. She considers me, her face full of thoughts. In the gully behind and below us, the fire is dying to embers. Ihira chirps once. Old Man still snores. Then Katya walks out into the shoulder-high grass. I follow. When the grass sighs all around us, Katya turns to me. The light of one of the nocturnal glows, its tall eyestalk waving nearby, lights up my wife's face and hands. She signs,

When winter cracks the crops with ice
when white fever knocks your beast from the sky
when the killwind has torn your domik to splinters

when you haven't a thread of garment to wear
and only two drops in the cup
when your bones quiver with illness
when the red rain is falling and there's screaming in the grass
when you've buried your daughters with your own hands
when even Grandma Yaga's hut on raptor legs has left you alone behind
when you are outcast
when the prairie before you is wide empty as forever
when the frost eats your fingers
when your feet crack and bleed
when you have nothing left

there is still kindness
there is still seeing each other, eye to eye,
there is still holding one another for warmth
there is still sharing your last morsel
there is still kindness
there is still loving
there is still love

Before she is done, I am singing the words softly while she signs. The song calms me, reminds me of who we are. It's the Founder's song.

Katya holds my gaze as she signs. *Sasha, that boy is a stranger, and he is strange. But he has lost everything. His people. His one friend. Even one of his fingers.* Her eyes are serious, pleading. *We have to help him, since we couldn't help the other.*

I feel a chill. My mind fills with the image of that dead whistler with the bullet in her face. We should have buried her. I glance over my shoulder at the gully. I can't see

Dmitri's Old Man, but I can certainly hear him. That Ticktock has known grief, as I have; when he speaks of his dead Ellie, there are coals that burn behind his eyes.

We could leave, I suggest. *We could ride through the dark, maybe catch the invader by dawn. Even if we don't know where he is or where he is going, the direction we've been riding is clear. No need really to delay for this Ticktock and his trike. Why should we?*

Because his heart drums as true a beat as ours. He breathes the same air. If he dies in this pursuit, Sasha, or alone on the empty prairie, he will be buried in the same earth. But who knows him? Who will touch the soil and sing of his life?

We've only known him for a day.

That's enough to make a song.

Her eyes shine with conviction, and her words twine through my heart's soil like roots seeking deep water. I am troubled. Katya and I wived less than two years ago, and I am still learning her. There is always more to her. Because she is lovely and silent (until she laughs) and speechless (until she signs), strangers at first look at her face the way they might look at a lake surface, barely glimpsing all the life in her, the thoughts that flash like schools of fish through her depths.

She is as deep as I or anyone else. She has suffered as much. Even though her family lives and breathes, unlike my own, she has suffered too. There is such music, compassion, and wisdom in her heart.

Maybe the Ticktock—Dmitri—is deep, too. Maybe I have been gazing at his face as at the surface of a lake. A troubling thought.

Thought you'd chafe more at this slow journey than I, I tell her, *that you'd be eager to rush on ahead, seek a new thrill.*

I catch movement out the corner of my eye. Daphne is flitting toward us through the grass, quiet as the wind. Katya sees, too, and her face fills with joy. *Oh, I'll seek a few thrills tonight,* she signs.

Something has me feeling tenacious, like a dimetrodon with its jaws in its prey. Unable to let go. *Boy or no,* I sign, *lonely exile or no, we have only his word for what he is, and he might be telling us a tale. We better alternate watches until daybreak. I don't want to wake tied across his saddle on my way to the Ticktocks' slave caverns.*

Katya smiles as her raptor comes up; halting by her, Daphne nudges her shoulder and coos. Katya pulls herself into the saddle and there she is, silhouetted against the stars and lovely as midnight. She grins down at me, reaches and clasps my arm, and pulls me up with her. I settle in behind her, my heart drumming a quicker beat now, realizing she means to ride with me across the grass, away from the gully, to some place private and quiet beneath the sheen of those rings in the sky. Half turned in the saddle with her eyes gone all half-lidded and sultry, she signs to me, *Stop worrying about how you'll wake. What makes you think I'm going to let you sleep tonight at all, wife?*

6

WE SEND UP A THIRD FLARE at the first glimpse of dawn. Though it is soon invisible to my eyes, I gaze after it into the sky, wondering where the coatl riders are. *Where* are our seers? It's their job to *see* us; it's what they're *for*.

Our breakfast is hasty: dried apricot, a few strips of ceratops jerky, and a wafer each of dry prairie bread. Afterward I crouch by the creek and lift water in my hands to wash out my mouth, then wash my face. It feels good to wash away the grime of travel, even just for a moment, though what I *really* need is that banya. I close my eyes as I scrub at my cheeks. Then gentle hands take mine; when I open my eyes, there are Katya's, green as the sea. She kisses me, long and long, and when our lips part she flashes me *such* a smile before rising and stepping away. My blood thunders in my ears. *That* is the way to start a long day's ride.

Dmitri is adjusting the bridle on his triceratops—a barbarous contraption that no dakotaraptor would ever permit, nor would any nightwatcher ask one to. He glances up as I lift my saddle and winks at me. I flush hot as summer. He knows Katya and I stole out into the grasses last night, and—

Well, *I* could keep quiet, but Katya…

My face burns. Our loving isn't for *his* ears. I keep my back to the Ticktock as I saddle dear Ihira, checking the straps, talking to her in quiet chirps and trills. Her eye is very dark and wet, and I give her a kiss on the little ridge of skin above it. Then I hide my face in her feathers, my arms around her neck, until the blush fades. After a moment, I feel her foreclaws behind my shoulder, and my heart is warm as a hearth. Her breath soft by my ear. My raptor.

Dawn opens the sky in glory as we mount up. Impossible to describe dawn on the prairie. The stars vanish, a few at a time, like small creatures ducking into their burrows beneath the grass when raptors rush by. Then the last stars are gone. The rings are touched with fire, and the horizon turns the color of love, then the hue of flame, and the sun breaks the horizon to our right and the prairie grasses turn a dozen shades of violet at last, tossing and waving and rippling with color and life. It shocks and stuns the eyes, every morning.

Dmitri departs first, his triceratops lumbering down the gully to find a gentler ascent. Katya and I have no such need; our raptors can *leap*. And anyway it's time to feel the wind of a hard ride in our faces again. But as we wheel about, Ihira letting out a screech to greet the dawn, I see it.

On the other side of the drying creek, half-concealed behind a broken Catha tree, *right there*, where we missed it in the twilight: a paw print, large, three-toed, pressed deep into the softer dirt by the water.

Katya sees me staring and she looks, too. We both stare. Then our gaze follows along the line of the creek. More prints, terribly far apart. Maybe a day old.

We glance at each other.

"Shit," I say.

Katya nods, her eyes wide.

And this morning had been so *beautiful.*

"*Hai!*" I cry, and I chirp a series of swift commands to Ihira. Katya taps Daphne's neck rhythmically with her hand. We surge up out of the gully, our raptors scrambling up the scree, then leaping the last bit to land hard on the prairie above. Then they lower their heads, straighten their backs, and *run* alongside the gully. The speed is exhilarating. So is the anger pumping in my blood.

Soon, I pull Ihira up; she squawks a protest, then lopes lightly near the edge of the ravine. I have one hand grasping her neck feathers, the other on my hip, within a quick grab of my kopye. Below us in the gully, I can see Dmitri's Old Man lumbering along, leaving his own heavy prints by the water.

"Ticktock!" I cry.

He glances up. His eyes glint under the shadow of his hat.

"You didn't tell us we were trailing a *tyrannosaur*!"

"You didn't ask," he drawls.

I am so furious I can't get words out. Picking up on my stress, Ihira hisses. Katya slows her raptor alongside mine. Her eyes shine with excitement. Katya *would* find hunting a tyrannosaur exciting.

"Besides, if I'da told you," Dmitri calls up to me, "you might have run back where you came from, and that'd be the end of my justice, near about. Didn't know yet if I could depend on you."

I jerk in the saddle as though slapped.

You can't depend on her.

Sveta's voice.

"I am a *nightwatcher*!" I press my hand over my heart, shaking. "My mother was a nightwatcher. My grandmother was a nightwatcher. My great-grandmother! We are bold."

"I believe it. But I didn't know you at first. And last night when I might have said something, I was right distracted. Thinking about this." He lifts his gloved left hand. "The tyrannosaur slipped my mind."

"How does a seven-thousand-kilogram tyrannosaur just *slip* your mind?!"

"This one's smaller, I think." He ducks his head lower, holding tight to Old Man as the terrain down there gets less even. "If I read the prints right."

Katya catches my eye. Signs, *If it's a smaller species, maybe…?*

It's a tyrannosaur, Katya.

She bites her lip.

"So," the Ticktock concludes, "now you know."

Now we know. I seethe. "You ever dealt with one of the invaders' tyrannosaurs, Dmitri?"

"Can't say that I have."

"Neither have we," I shout back.

Katya signs to me, *He doesn't let it show, but he's desperate.*

I bite back the things I *want* to say. Have to stay focused. "Anything else we should know about, Ticktock?" I gesture to the horizon. "Any more surprises I might not like?"

"Well. He's got a deathclock."

"A what?"

"A *deathclock*."

I hold back a growl. "I don't care if he has a *clock*. Do I look like a Ticktock to you?"

Dmitri grunts. "Well, I heard it from afar. Time I rode up, Ellie was dead and he was gone. Flash of color in the far grass."

My heart is at my feet for you, Katya signs. *I know what it is to be alone.* She taps one of her ears with her fingers.

That stabs at *my* heart. I edge Ihira near enough to reach for Katya's hand. Last night, I was moaning about being thought unbraided and kinless, and I forgot the one way in which my Katya is far more solitary than I, riding forever on a silent prairie without sound or speech. Though not without a good beat on the drum.

She squeezes my fingers.

Then I translate for Dmitri, the way I've promised her I would. Dmitri gives my wife a respectful nod, and Katya gives me a grateful look, and a new thought is braided into my heart: that despite all her kin, I have made my wife less *alone*, even as she has made me. Our gazes meet, and the realization near takes my breath away.

"One day," Dmitri calls up to us, "the clock stops for each of us. Even for a tyrannosaur rider. And it's good that we're three for the hunt. That's a firm number."

"A what?"

"A number you can trust." With his teeth, he pulls the glove off his maimed hand, showing me his thumb and three. "Four's an *infirm* number. Sickly and weak."

"How can a *number* be sickly?" I demand, taken aback.

He shrugs. "Just is." He ungloves his other hand, lifts his fingers to show me. "Three, five. Also seven, eleven, thirteen, seventeen, nineteen. Those are *firm* numbers. Two *should* be, but hardly ever is. Ellie and I traveled as whistlers do, in twos." There's pain in his voice, and guilt. "Now she's dead."

"That's ridiculous," I snap. "Your friend didn't die because there were two of you. She died because the invader had a tyrannosaur and a gun and didn't care if herds are left untended."

"Maybe," Dmitri says. "Still glad we're three."

Katya has been gazing out at the distance. Now she turns to me and signs, *Now a tyrannosaur's a thrill!*

Katya love, some thrills are too big.

She laughs. *There is no such thing. That's what 'thrill' means.*

Dmitri lifts his whistle to his lips, blows silent notes, then holds on tight as his triceratops lurches toward the wall of the gully, lumbering up onto a natural stair of large slabs of white rock. That stair doesn't look like it could hold the beast's weight, yet up he comes. Old Man clambers up, surprisingly agile, then surges out of the gully just behind us, that single horn first, then his head, snorting and blowing breath and digging in hard with his forefeet as he pulls his enormous mass up. The edge of the gully gives way, but the triceratops throws his weight forward and is up and half tumbling, half running into the grass before he can slide back. Dmitri takes off his hat and lets out a whoop. "Not dead yet, Old Man!" he yells, grinning.

That Ticktock's going to get us killed, I sign. I gaze out over the grasses. Somewhere out there is a powerful, carnivorous predator that masses thousands of kilograms and can snap a dinosaur's back in its jaws. I can't see it, but it's out there. I wonder how the invader got it down here out of the sky. The invaders have oldtech, like what used to be in the ships that are now overgrown with moss at

Landing by the Sea, or maybe like what we're told can be found in the arcology towers on the coast, where wonder workers forge the kopyes and other useful tools the merchants bring us at barter. Maybe the invader's own metal lander is *big.* Or maybe he rapid-grew the animal from a vat, the way the Founder's whitejackets did in my mother's stories. Except the Founder didn't grow a *tyrannosaur* or creatures meant for killing people. She grew what would be useful to us. Tyrannosaurs belong in old stories of the worlds we fled, not here leaving prints in our own soil. I shudder.

Katya's eyes are intense. *Right, let's plan. Sasha my love, we should split up. You've got to get to the others at rendezvous, tell them. I'll trail this thing.* Her grin bares her teeth. *I can find it.*

What?! No. My hands are vehement. *A tyrannosaur isn't a sekaya nut for you to just ride in and snatch.* There's a cold knot in my belly. Already, I am kinless. A snap of a tyrannosaur's jaws, and I might be wifeless too. *We stay together. We'll fight it together.*

Her eyes are deep as the sea. *Sasha, we might both die.*

Then we'll have quite a story to tell Grandma Yaga. Anger and old pride surges in me. *We'll spin a tale that will keep Grandmother up listening for three nights.* I hold her gaze. *But we aren't dying today. Never been anything living or dead that could take both Daphne* and *Ihira out. We took the hyaenadons.*

Her lip quirks. *We had help.*

Eight or nine. But we did all the work.

Something feral flickers in her eyes at that. *You're right. We did.* She taps the coil of rope attached to her saddle and grins. *And I can lasso it. I lassoed you running full tilt, and that tyrannosaur will be too big to miss. Come on then, you've convinced me, Sasha. Let's go find it. Together.*

Eighty-three days. We went eighty-three days without an incursion. And now…

This might just be the most damn foolish thing I've ever done, and there aren't even any other nightwatchers here but Katya to prove myself to, but I'm still burning with adrenaline, and I nod. *Let's.*

That triceratops has already lumbered on across the prairie, rolling as it barrels through the tall grass, leaving a wake behind it, while my wife and I have dallied a moment to decide whether to go ride to our likely deaths. Now Katya taps lightly behind Daphne's eye, and her raptor sprints after Old Man. Katya's braid bounces against her back as she rides. I hear Dmitri call back, "Glad to find you bold as you say," and I would scowl, except I'm distracted gazing after Katya, heart-struck with my wife's beauty in the dawn, with the sheer strength of her.

"That Ticktock's going to get us killed," I whisper to Ihira. She trills softly as if agreeing. And I signal her to pursue.

7

WE FIRE A FOURTH FLARE at the sky near midmorning. Still no quetzalcoatl. But Katya sees something else, and points it out to me, and I gaze up at the sky in wonder and dismay. High to the west, far away, I can glimpse a swift, gleaming surface, moving fast and leaving a white trail behind it across the blue. It is lovely and terrible, that mark across our sky.

Our quarry escaping? I sign.

Katya shakes her head, her eyes wide with wonder too. *Been watching it for a bit. It's getting a little closer to us, not drawing further away.*

Another incursion? Doesn't that give me the chills.

I don't know.

I say nothing aloud. If Dmitri's going to hide a tyrannosaur from us, we can hide a lander from him.

The lander—if that's what it is—passes above us and flashes to the east, and then it's gone over the horizon. After a while, the white mark across the sky fades too, though that takes longer. Still, it gives me a small thrill of hope. I don't know why that invader tried to mark our sky like that, but its mark was temporary. So are the tyrannosaur prints back by the creek, it occurs to me;

eventually a bit of rain will swell the creek and wash those prints away. Katya and I exchange a determined look; it's our task to make sure the invaders themselves prove temporary, too.

Perhaps to take my mind off that evil in the sky as we ride over the prairie, Yekaterina asks me for one of my mother's stories. I cast a glance at the whistler, and that resolves me, because there is a thing I want this Ticktock to hear. I do my best to tell the story in both sign and speech, because it is also Katya I am telling the story for, hoping it will make her smile. This is the tale:

There once was a girl whose mothers tended a field of maize. She sheltered with them in a domik of Catha wood on the edge of the cropland. They had a good stone well, and they cared for a tamed, plodding ankylosaur, a behemoth of muscle and bone that pulled their plow in the spring. Each year before rainfall, they piled its shell high with sacks of corn and rode the ankylosaur forty kilometers to the harvest barter, to trade the maize, still in its husk, for salted meat and grain and agonda wool for making clothes. And for glass beads from the arcologies on the coast, for making armlets and prayer nets and braids for the ankylosaur's saddle and harness. And one year, when the girl's body was ready—and her heart—she met a stranger at the market, a young man with a pointed black beard and eyes the color of ice. He had come down from the high mountains, and brought that much of the cold with him; he was an icewalker. He was not kinless, but his kin were far away; unbraided from his tribe, he yearned for connection with a hot and terrible longing. He could speak barely any of her words—she was of the humming people, like you and me, Yekaterina. But he sang love songs to her in his own language, and she sang him one of hers, and they were soon kissing behind a heap of corn sacks. He was hungry, his hands rough, and he lit quite a fire in her.

On her way home, he followed her through the tall grass, with a cloak of violet wool that made him difficult to see, but she knew he was there. She kept glancing over her shoulder and smiling to let him know it was all right. "What are you looking at?" one of her mothers asked.

"The haia leaping in the grass," she said. "They are strong and happy."

"They should be," her other mother said. "They don't have to plant, or harvest, or weave, or cook, or trade, and they can flit naked through the grass from sunrise to sunset."

"I might like to flit naked through the grass—from sunrise to sunset!" She said this loudly so her lover would hear her.

Her mothers shook their heads and prodded the ankylosaur to sway more swiftly homeward. "You'll be naked in the grass after dark," her mothers told her, and the icewalker following her didn't know what they meant, only that it made the girl laugh.

They were home soon enough, with the sun low and the harvested cornfield with its broken stalks mournful in the perishing light. The mothers glanced anxiously at the sky; with harvest done, they didn't know how many nights were left before they must hide from the red rain. As they busied themselves unloading the goods from the ankylosaur's back, the girl told them she was feeling ill.

They checked her for sunstroke and fever, then made her drink water with drops of hajaka in it and sent her to bed, concerned. No sooner was she in her bedding than her bearded icewalker slipped in and joined her there. There was much undressing and kissing and touching, though they spoke only in whispers.

"I don't want my mothers to hear," she told him softly. "Cover my mouth with your hand, and I'll cover yours." And they did that. And the dancing they did in her bedding was very good.

But even as she shuddered and shook with pleasure, and at the very moment before he would have had to pull himself out of her and spill, the sun set. Her eyes changed first. Then her throat and breasts and arms grew a soft down of feathers, all in the time it takes for a single beat of a lover's heart. The icewalker gasped and squirmed under her, trying to remove himself from her body. In the next moment she was growing until she filled the domik; he slipped out of her and rolled aside before he could be crushed. While loving, she had forgotten, you see, that she needed to be outside before the sun could dip below the horizon.

She broke her mothers' domik into kindling and lifted her long neck from the shattered roof and trumpeted at the stars, so loud the icewalker's ears nearly bled. Then she stepped clear, dragging half the domik's frame of wood and hide behind her, with her bedding caught on one foot; she shook it off, then rose on her hind legs. Her tail swept through the air just above her lover's head; the wind of it knocked him to his back. And she bellowed again at the sky. She was a woman, but she was also a brachiosaur.

Grandma Yaga had braided a spell around her when she was a baby, and on every seventh night, she would walk the prairie in a brachiosaur's hide rather than a young woman's. While she was a toddler, she was still a little brachiosaur, and her mothers would prepare a bed of straw by the fire and tuck a wool blanket around her. Later, they'd lay three blankets over her by the well. Now that she was a grown woman, they had quite given up, and would just let her slip out the door and over the grasses before dusk, to change beneath the open sky, out where she wouldn't trample the corn.

Now her mothers came running from the pen where they'd been settling the ankylosaur for the night. Reaching the edge of the cornfield under the stars, they gawked at the ruin of their domik and the rolling bulk of their magnificent and immense daughter. *And* they caught sight of the icewalker getting shakily to his feet with his pride dangling between his thighs, quite undone by the sight of his lover adorned with feathers and ten meters tall.

The icewalker's blood burned with fury. "What trick is this?" he cried. "I have a woman whose body and heart I desire and who also desires mine, but I cannot hold her in my arms at night?" When the mothers explained, he said, "I will go to Grandma Yaga and get her to unbraid this spell."

"You will need something to trade her," one of the mothers said.

The other mother removed from her throat a necklace of silver disks. "Take this," she told him. "These are books from the world where the Founder was born. These are many stories; our family has remembered and told them since Landing. Trade them with Grandmother."

Now I don't know whether the mothers sent him to Grandma Yaga to change the spell on their daughter or whether they hoped Grandma Yaga might eat him and scatter his bones from the window of her domik. They had not liked finding the icewalker with their daughter, and they had not liked losing their shelter. But the icewalker was a young man, thinking only of the girl's soft thighs and her moans at dusk, and he did not notice how the mothers' eyes were hot with cunning. He let them place the silver disks about his neck. Then he put his clothes back on and his boots, and he left while the night was still dark and the girl still trampling in the distance. He walked through the corn and through croplands on the far side and then out toward the deep prairie, because he was an icewalker and walking is what icewalkers do, even over the most frozen terrain across mountains that touch the sky, and because you cannot *ride* into Grandma Yaga's country; the dead arrive on their own feet, and the living who seek her must do so too. The only thing you are permitted to ride in her country is her walking domik, and then only if you pay a price.

The noon sun rose and the rings blazed in the sky, but then their light dimmed and the sky went gray and everywhere was fog. The grasses grew brittle with ice, snapping against his thighs as he walked. Ghosts in the fog moaned at him as he passed, but he walked too quickly for them to grab hold of him. Then he heard the creaking and rattling of Grandma Yaga's hut, and her domik of triceratops bone and hide loomed out of the mist, rushing toward him on its tall raptor legs. Lanterns flickering with blue fire swayed and clattered against its frame. He stood in its path, and the domik stopped just before it could crush him. Yaga opened the hide flap over a window and peered out at him, her cold eyes glinting in the blue lanternlight, a dozen braids in her silver hair. She lifted a hand; her fingers ended in long claws. "Who are you? You're not one of the dead."

"I breathe," he confirmed. "My heart beats. There is still song in my blood."

"Then what are you doing here? Why are you in my way?"

"I wish to make a trade."

She snorted, then ducked inside, went to her door, and tossed down a rope ladder for him to climb up. Inside, her domik was small and cramped. There was a lute made of white bone with strings of human gut rather than lambeosaur. There were cups made from skulls, and the buttons on Grandmother's coat were shiny and made of pale bone, too. Quilts of vivid purples and reds were piled on her bed of rib bones. A giant mortar and pestle were shoved in one corner, a microraptor with indigo feathers curled up purring beside it. A fire burned in a pot. The icewalker glanced at the smokehole in the roof, but there were no stars there. No stars are visible on death's prairie.

Grandma Yaga tapped his chest with a heavy ladle. "What do you bring me, boy? A liver? Your beating heart? Might be tasty. Ribs to repair my bedframe with? You have strong ribs, I can tell. Or perhaps…" She licked her lips. "Perhaps a story? Do you have a story for me?"

"I have a thousand stories and one," he said. "Yours, if you braid a spell for me, if you give me a way to keep my lover bound in a woman's body." Boldly, he lifted the necklace in his hands, showing her the silver disks.

A wild light shone in Grandma Yaga's eyes. "I like your trade. I like it much. Better than a heart. Better than hot blood. There are *many* hearts in those stories, and I will feast on them until the stars burn out and the ground in your world is as cold as the ground in mine. But you are not one of the recent dead. What gives you the right to trade with *me?* You must earn that right. Complete three tasks for me, you who are not dead, and then I will trade with you."

He chafed at the delay, but he agreed. When you are in Grandma Yaga's country, it is unwise to anger her. Yet you must be cunning and relentless, resourceful and persistent as the roots of Catha trees, if you wish to get out of her country again.

For the first task, Grandma Yaga took him to a canyon filled with mist, and in the deep cold under the fog were nightraptor eggs. Grandmother would gather a few each year and hatch them, and after the hatchlings grew to their full length, they would provide fresh legs for her walking domik. There were as many eggs in that canyon as there are blades of grass on the prairie, and the eggs were black. She told him, "One white egg, a raptor's egg from the world of the living, has been lost in here by mistake. Find it."

He climbed into the pit and searched. There was no day and no night in the fog, no spring and no summer, no rainfall and no harvest. Only winter. Frost bit his hands, his beard rimed, his eyelids froze open. Still he searched, *still* he searched. At last, he brought Grandma Yaga the egg, held cupped in hands like blocks of ice. He carried it to a fire she'd lit by her raptor hut, and she cackled and cracked open the egg over a pan and fried it. She had him sit and she whispered a spell over her fire, and the flames' heat thawed his hands, and his fingers were whole and no longer black with death. She offered him the egg to eat, but the icewalkers know about Grandma Yaga too, even as we do, and he knew that if he ate anything while in her country, he would never leave it. So he refused her. She cackled again and ate it herself. Starvation bit at the icewalker's belly the whole time he was in her country.

She set him two more tasks, and he completed each, at great peril. He had to make her a quilt out of the clothing of the dead, and for a long time he hunted ghosts on the frozen prairie, to steal their garments. He brought more than she needed and she offered to make him a cloak to keep him warm in the fog, but he knew better than to wear anything made in her country. He lay shivering on her floor, wrapped in the tatters that were left of his own garb, while all night Grandma Yaga snored beneath her heavy quilt of dead men's clothes. If he drowsed at all, Grandmother's microraptor stirred from its place by her mortar, darted toward his feet, and nibbled at his toes and his arches. He did not sleep the whole time that he stayed in Grandma Yaga's country. And he forgot how to dream.

In the morning, Grandma Yaga hopped out of bed refreshed, her eyes shining, and set him his third task. He had to catch a spinosaur under the ice of the river that waters the forest of forgotten songs, and bring her two of its teeth so she could carve them into drinking horns. He hurried to his task. Under the dark ice, the creature tore off his leg and ate it, but he pulled two teeth from its mouth and then crawled back across the prairie. He trailed dark blood through the frozen grass; all the ghosts gathered to drink it. Reaching Grandma Yaga's domik, he held up the two teeth, then blacked out from blood loss. When he woke, she had lit a fire again and had sung spells over him and given him a leg made of wood that worked almost as well as the old leg had. She had carved the drinking horns and she offered him one filled with golden nectar, but though in her country he thirsted until his throat dried and cracked, he knew better than to take the drink.

"Three tasks have I completed," he said, taking the necklace of books from his neck and offering it to her again. She squinted at him, then reached out one withered hand, and he dropped the necklace into her palm. Then she cackled.

"You should not have made this trade, man whose blood is hot," she said. "You would not accept your girl as she is. That makes you a fool, and little pleasure will you have of her, mortal. Better had you learned to ride her high above the plain by ringlight, and hold her after to keep her warm against the dew when she becomes a woman again, nude and shivering in the grass. You desire to contain her and all the wildness of her heart, and a woman cannot *be* contained."

In trade she gave him a necklace of braided rope decorated with brachiosaur feathers black as midnight, for the girl to wear to prevent her body from changing. He took it in his hand and departed from Grandma Yaga's walking domik. Following her directions precisely, he left her country, walking until the frozen blades of grass thawed and the sky became sunlit instead of gray, until he saw the field of maize and the ruin of the domik where his lover and her mothers awaited him.

The girl came running to him through the corn. When she reached him, she was frightened. But she knew who he was; she stepped near and touched his face. That's when he realized he had changed. He had white hair and a white beard. His eyes hid among wrinkles the way wanini hide in their burrows. His hands were crooked, and they hurt. He had one wooden leg. He was old. He had slaved for Grandma Yaga for years on death's prairie, but for the brachiosaur girl only a single night and a single day had passed. She took him in her arms and kissed him, ignoring her fear and the warning it gave her, and then he put the rope with black feathers about her neck. It tightened, snug against her throat, and she could not remove it as long as the icewalker lived.

His years away and his aging had made him bitter, and he was unkind to her. He watched her after dusk each night. He watched her at the barter, fearing she would find the arms of a younger man and kiss his thighs. Sometimes he beat her, which is a thing that is not done among our people, though it might be among foolish icewalkers and slaving Ticktocks. "You would not do this to me if I didn't wear this," she cried, tugging at the feathered necklace, which remained tight about her neck; she couldn't break it. "If I were a brachiosaur, you wouldn't dare beat me, for I would crush you at night!" But he did not hear her, and each day he became more cruel. The flames of her cookfire flickered without warmth, and she drank tears with her evening stew. Her mothers, in fury, considered whether to kill the icewalker and bury him in secret under the corn, perhaps telling their daughter that he had gone away and abandoned them, or that he had been snatched by a hyaenadon or fallen into a ravine. But before they could, the lovers had a baby, a little girl. The whispers at night about killing him ceased.

Then one night, with the rings bright in the sky, a slaving party came to the cropland. The slavers seized the two mothers and chained them. The icewalker tried to fight them with a shovel, but his hands hurt and his back had grown crooked with age, and his arms were weak, and his wooden leg cracked as he fought. A slaver stabbed him in the gut, and he died in the dirt outside his lover's hut, clutching at his belly. The last sounds in his ears were the creaking of Grandma Yaga's domik, and the moaning of the ghosts on death's prairie welcoming home the thief who had stolen their clothes, and Grandma Yaga's cackling in the wind.

The brachiosaur girl stood at the entrance to her hut, the wind tugging at her hair, with her baby weeping in her swaddle-net inside the shelter behind her. The slavers approached with cruel laughter, to chain the girl, but as the icewalker's last blood sank into the soil and his heart beat its last pulse, she tore away her gown and ripped off the chain of feathers from her neck, and became a brachiosaur. In thunder of sinew and muscle, she crushed the slavers, smashing flesh and bone. People living in domiks far away across the cropland heard her bellowing and her trumpeting cries and the trample of her feet, loud over the fields of corn.

In the morning, the mothers managed to pick the locks on each other's chains. They brought out the baby safe from the domik, and they found the girl a long way out in the field, sleeping in the corn, in the middle of a crushed and flattened circle the size of a brachiosaur. But she was a woman again. Her heart had desired love but had desired freedom more. After she had fed her baby, she buried the icewalker, and the corn grew ears that were ice blue above his grave. Every seventh night, she would walk out naked far over the grass away from the corn, and then roam over the land with the wind in her feathers. And she was happy. Her daughter did not change at night but grew a mane of midnight feathers down her back.

* * *

I finish the story, and Katya claps her hands twice, grinning. She hasn't heard this one before. I grin back. I guess I've told my mother's tale well. I sign to her, *You are lovely and wild as a brachiosaur, my Katya.* She gives me a look that changes my blood to fire.

Dmitri starts laughing. I haven't heard him *laugh* before, and it startles me. He actually has a good laugh.

"What amuses you?" I ask, unsettled.

"The girl!" he says. "If *I* changed into a brach at dusk, I wouldn't be looking for some human lover to ride on my back or collar my neck with feathers. I'd go find myself a brachiosaur bitch large as a mountain and fill her with eggs. Think of that! Two brachiosaurs loving at night. We would shake the earth." He laughs hard, and leans over to whisper something in Old Man's ear. The trike doesn't laugh.

"The story isn't really about fucking," I protest. "It's about freedom."

"What's freer than brachiosaurs fucking?"

Honestly, all our stories are about fucking, Katya signs. Her eyes flash with mischief.

You're not helping.

I give the Ticktock a pointed look. "This one's about how you can't make a person your slave. Braided rope around another's wrists or her throat tells a tale about her she didn't consent to, a tale where she is captive and a thing to be used, rather than a person with a story you need to hear."

Dmitri chews the inside of his cheek. We ride quietly for a few moments, matching the rolling gait of his triceratops.

"It's a good story," he says at last.

Do you have a story to tell? Katya signs.

I translate.

Dmitri tips his hat low to hide his eyes a bit. "I don't."

"What will you tell Grandma Yaga when you die, if you have no story?" I ask.

"Yaga only eats humming people. In the mines, we have our own ghosts."

"But you're riding *her* prairie."

He grunts. Then tips his hat back and looks at us both. His trike bellows, and he reaches down to stroke the soft skin behind the animal's frill. "The stories I have are not like yours. They are hours on my own life's clock, and they hurt too much to tell."

As if to make the point, he takes his watch out, opens it, and reads whatever story it has to tell. Then shuts it and puts it away. "Getting close," he says.

Katya has been watching me with a thoughtful expression. *You like that story because it's like us*, she signs.

Is it?

Well, I am *wild as the brachiosaur girl,* she reminds me.

A pang of hurt as it occurs to me what she's hinting at. *You think* I'm *like the icewalker?*

I'd thought Dmitri was like him. Not me.

She gives me a serious look. *'A hot and terrible longing.' That's you. You don't know how to let go, either to one you've lost or to one who is with you. My Sasha, you're so afraid that if you let go and just breathe, I'll be gone.*

My eyes sting.

But I won't ever, Sasha, she signs.

But I don't treat you as a slave!

She's quiet for a moment. Then the look she gives me is a gentler one that lights fire between my thighs. *I am, though. When our blood is hot, I tie* you *up, but my heart is in bondage to you forever, Sasha my wife.*

I am relieved by the shift in topic, leaving the story behind for now like one of Grandma Yaga's ghosts, wailing after we've stolen its clothes. My wife has a way of *looking* at me, and she is doing it now. *Maybe I should lasso* you *tonight,* I sign.

She glances quickly at Dmitri, her cheeks flushed. He glances back. His eyes widen slightly. He lifts his bone whistle and blows a silent note, and Old Man begins to run ahead in that rolling ceratopsian manner. Katya drops back to walk her raptor beside mine. With her so near, my heart races.

He can't overhear us. He doesn't know sign, I remind her.

Oh, that boy's perceptive enough. But I don't care. Her eyes burn with heat. *I want you like fire wants a forest.*

And, like a forest, I burn for her.

She touches my cheek, and I hers. Leaning from our saddles, we kiss.

Then, her eyes hot, Katya tells me, in quite some detail, exactly what she means to do with me the next time she has me alone and captive in her lasso. Until I'm squirming in my saddle, biting my lip to hold in a moan.

* * *

A few times this afternoon, I take out my spyglass to get a good look at the horizon. Just endless prairie and sometimes a distant blur of trees marking water. Nowhere a gleaming ship or a charging tyrannosaur. It depresses me. Katya signs to me, *This is taking forever. Maybe he has already left our world.*

I don't like that thought. I don't want the invader to leave our world; I want him to die on it. I want to send him to Grandma Yaga so he can find out if Grandmother finds his bones as worth cracking for marrow as she finds ours. I want those people up there among the stars to know they can't keep doing this. But Dmitri and his trike are a hobble, and we limp through the grass, hot and sleepy and bored. Maybe I should tell another story.

But it's nearly sunset. I hear hyaenadons in the distance. Their eerie laughter, rising and falling out there on the prairie—it chills me. I remember the flash of their teeth when we fought them beside the other nightwatchers, several nights back, and the blue flame of my kopye as it took a hyaena right in the snout. Of the creatures our Founder brought to this planet, I like hyaenas the least.

When the Founder lived, other planets than ours were *terra*formed—given air or heated or cooled. Peace didn't need that. Our seasons are temperate and our air is rich with oxygen. But there were and still are lots of creatures here that want to kill us. So the Founder and her whitejackets *fauna*formed the planet, introducing new life to render the world more welcoming to her children—to us. That's how the mother herds arrived, their genomes chosen by the Founder because ceratopsians produce far more meat and hide than the cattle and bison of old Earth. That's how the hyaenadons got here, too. Among the most voracious predators in the Founder's book of life, they were unleashed to exterminate several organisms on this world that were harmful either to us or to our herds. But the massive hyaenas themselves filled the niche our ancestors wanted vacant, and we have never been able to get rid of all their prides in the centuries since. They breed fast, they are versatile in finding new things to eat, and they possess a ferocity and cunning that is terrifying in the dark.

I hope they aren't in a hunting mood, I sign to Katya.

Maybe they're hunting invaders. A flash of a smile. *Like we are.*

Maybe. The thought of whoever killed that whistler waking to the sight of hyaenadon jaws closing over his face brightens my mood. So does the sunlight on Katya's hair. She *is* wild and glorious as the brachiosaur girl. But then my mood falls, because her words to me about the icewalker still rankle—how can *I* be the icewalker? how can she see me like that?—and I need to work out some of my stress before it makes Ihira anxious and skittery. I unstrap the kopye from my saddle braids and, making sure Ihira is far enough from the others for safety, I snap the rod to its full length and begin spinning it, moving through the fighting forms for combat from raptorback, forms which my mother taught me before her death. The nightwatchers say *no one* ever fought as Annika Nightwatcher did, and I believe it; in her hands, the kopye was more than just a rod of metal and heat. It was a part of her, as much so as her raptor or her own arms. She moved with wild grace when she taught me. She *danced* as she spun her kopye, a circle of blue fire about her body, as if she ignited the air itself. I suck in a breath. I push back my frustration that I can't wield the kopye as well as she, and my doubt over whether it is truly *mine*, whether I truly have a place among the hues of my pack woven around the grip. Doubt is not a part of the song the kopye makes in the air, the high-pitched hum of defense and death. My *Mom* gave me this kopye. She hoped and she believed in me. I have to believe too, because she did. And one day, I will dance as she did.

And at that thought, for a moment—just a moment—I feel like Mom is *here with me*, guiding my hands and my breathing. I *feel* her, as I spin the kopye on one side of my saddle, then the other, then behind my back and over my head. As if I might turn at just the right angle, at just the right instant, and *see* her, her eyes shining with pride in her daughter. My throat tightens. *Mom.*

Dmitri's voice breaks the spell. "I am much amazed." There's wonder in his tone, and amusement too. "Your rod is bigger than mine, I'll admit."

Katya nearly falls from her saddle laughing. She must have read his lips.

I glare at Dmitri, wanting that brief sense of Mom's presence back, thirsting for it the way a girl lost with no canteen thirsts for water. "It's a kopye, not a cock, you barbarian."

He grins under the shadow of his hat. "I know what it is, Sasha. Ticktocks buy them too, from merchants come to barter. Our enforcers use them."

That incenses me. The kopye I hold is not for keeping slaves in line or whatever else Ticktocks want to use it for. And it's not for dark caves inside of mountains. It's for the flash of sunlight and the fire of the rings. It is my mother's tool of choice, and it is *mine,* and braided about its sleek metal are the lives and leather straps of the other nightwatchers, whether they accept me or not. "Men by the sea might make these," I tell him curtly, "and Ticktock men may *use* them, but the nightwatchers *wield* the kopye. We understand the kopye. We put it between our bodies and death. We dance the dance. We survive."

"As we all hope to," Dmitri says. But then he's quiet for a while, which pleases me.

I caress the feathers at the back of Ihira's head to calm her, because she tensed up when I did. Then I go back to my practice, but I am distracted now. Arrogant Ticktock.

Katya is still giggling, hunched over Daphne's neck and out of breath.

After a bit, I snap my kopye shut and return it to the side of my saddle and look about me with more alertness, because of what I've spotted in the grass. We are passing entire clumps of rainmakers. So many. The diggers will be after them later in the year, but the roots twist through the ground for kilometers; it is impossible to completely eradicate them. I wonder if the invader rode past these, too, on his tyrannosaur. I wonder if he understood what they were. If he realized these were not *plants* he was looking at.

The Ticktock knows. He gives the rainmakers a long look. "I don't much miss the other Ticktocks wanting me dead," he confides from Old Man's swaying back, "but I do miss the Rain Clock."

"What's that?" I ask.

"It's a rain clock." Seeing our bewilderment, he adds, "A clock what tells when it'll rain. When it'll rain red."

Katya and I stare at each other, in shock.

She signs quickly, *Is he joking with us?*

I chirp to Ihira, and we swing alongside his trike. Katya flanks him on the other side. Old Man shies and warbles a moment, and his eyes dilate, but I think he's getting used to our raptors.

"Do you mean to tell me the Ticktocks have a way to know when the rain will start?"

"Don't you?"

Katya and I exchange a look. *This is a thing we need to tell our people.* If we could trade for this knowledge, barter for word of when the red rain will fall—Yet, the thought of trading with *Ticktocks* is an uneasy one. Still, this 'Rain Clock' could save lives. Knowing when the rain would fall, that would have saved my *mother's* life. How could the Ticktocks have such a thing and not share that knowledge? I give Dmitri a horrified look.

Katya signs, *You are full of surprises, Dmitri Andreivich.*

I translate for her.

Dmitri's lips curve in that wry smile of his. "Not a person born isn't full of surprises. Every clock telling a slightly different time, every drum with its own beat."

I catch my breath, because his words are so much like Katya's to me last night: *Each of our hearts beats a different drumbeat. Mine is fast.*

With a sweeping gesture, Dmitri indicates the violet grasses. "From here, each blade of grass looks the same…"

Intrigued even in the midst of my turmoil, I finish that thought. "…but up close, each is different. Unique."

He nods, and points at a stand of Catha trees some distance ahead of us. "And from here, those trees look the same, don't they?"

"…but up close, each is different."

"Grass, trees, people. Anything that dreams and breathes is like that." The smile he's using now warms his eyes.

"You don't really talk like a Ticktock," I say.

"No, I talk like me."

I just stare at him.

Well. This Rain Clock, whatever it is, is something to think about later. Today has problems enough. I glance ahead at that distant wood. There will be water there, cool in the throat and sweet on the body, to wash away the dust. A creek or a stream or even a small river, dark and quiet between the trees. Catha trees trouble me by day, because they block my view of the open prairie. But they comfort me by night; their wood and their sap is toxic to the red rain. Our people make our domiks from triceratops hide stretched over a round frame of Catha wood, and we coat the hide in Catha sap for good measure. And the whistlers house their herds during rainfall, until winter, in wild canyons and ravines that can be roofed over with a wide thatch of Catha branches. So at night, when the world is dark, Catha trees comfort me. If I wake from dreams of rainfall or my mother's screams, I wake to the tossing and the wind melody of the tree boughs, and I am comforted. And when Katya is there, she can hold me until my trembling passes. A Catha wood after dark is a lovely thing. I glance at the sky. Good thing it's near sunset.

I look to Dmitri. "That's a good place to halt. We can camp, eat, send up another coatl flare before dusk."

"Imagine we could."

And, I think to myself, we might find prints by the water, to tell us how far behind we are.

I share a glance with Katya, my hands flashing quickly: *Let's ride ahead. Take a look.*

She grins and taps Daphne's neck. In an instant, both our raptors are sprinting through the grass, leaving Dmitri behind. His Old Man bellows at us, low and deep. We ignore him. After slouching along all day at triceratops speed, it feels good just to run with our faces to the wind. I drop my goggles over my eyes, bend low over Ihira's neck, and urge her to greater speed. Daphne paces us and Katya signs, *Race you!*

Ha! I remember how the last race ended.

This might end the same way. Her eyes blaze. Then she drops her goggles, hiding them. But there is no hiding her grin or her excitement.

I blush. *The Ticktock isn't* that *slow. His trike will catch up.*

I better enjoy my wife quickly, then! With a laugh, she unhooks a coil of rope from her belt and lashes my raptor's flank with the end of the rope. Ihira squeals in surprise and bursts into that wild velocity that under the wide sky only raptors can get. Katya is laughing wild as a hyaena behind me. My heart pounds. Maybe she really *does* intend to lasso me again. Holding tight to Ihira's neck feathers, I whisper near her earhole, "She'll have to catch us first, Ihira!"

We cut through the grass, swift as sunlight. The ringlight doubles our shadows, which run beside us on our right. Katya's laughter follows me, and I am laughing too, and the world I see through my goggles is touched with gold. A rainmaker cactus rises just a bit above the grass ahead of us, and rather than swerve to miss it, I urge Ihira faster—we can flash by it or leap over it.

But just as we reach it, the rainmaker bursts in an explosion of red and purple fluid, spattering the grass and Ihira's side and my boot, and I cry out at the shock, but my cry is drowned in an abrupt, cracking thunder of sound. *Now* we swerve, Daphne and Ihira both; as we do, I see movement by the Catha trees ahead.

A tyrannosaur rises from the violet grass before the line of trees, surging to its feet like a cresting wave, two and a half meters tall at the hips, its plumage gold and flame, as if the sunset has been given flesh and sinew and a fury to devour all life. All along its snout are ridges of white bone, almost as if the roots of its teeth are exposed above the jaw; it is one of the smaller, fiercer species, the one called *reaper of death.*

Swaying on the beast's back in a saddle of leather and bone is a man in a blood-red coat and veil and hood, and a cloak billows crimson behind him. As the tyrannosaur charges toward us like living fire, the man swivels a gleaming gun, mounted at the front of his saddle. Its barrel is longer than a kopye, and I have barely time to scream before it spews thunder and smoke again, rattling like a storm as the deathreaper bears down on us.

8

NO ROAR, NO SCREAM LIKE RENDING METAL, the way the stories describe the cries of tyrannosaurs bred for the arenas in Sol system, centuries behind us. Instead it *coos*, its ancient and birdlike voice reverberating in its wide nasal passages. But not like a furred harra a child might hold cupped in her hands, whose cooing is gentle and sweet. The tyrannosaur is hundreds of times a harra's mass. I feel it more than I hear it, the animal's presence so massive and vital and overpowering that when it calls, all reality quivers in response. The soil beneath us, the Catha trees, the air, the very bones in my body *vibrate* with the force of it.

Katya and I divide, Daphne flashing to the left and my Ihira to the right, making two targets. The deathreaper charges toward my wife, but the gun follows me, and I hear the *thwick thwick thwick* of bullets ripping up the grass behind me. My heart pounds. I bend low over my raptor, hoping the tall grass will make us difficult to see. Leaning half to the side from my saddle, I pluck my kopye from my belt and snap it open, extending it into a meter and a half of gleaming metal. I thumb the button that ignites it. The ends crackle with blue fire. I chirp quick commands to Ihira, and we arc toward the tyrannosaur until I see the beast ahead of us—we rush at its right flank. The gun swivels, following us, *sweet Founder* how many bullets can that thing fire, and as my heart stops and my blood is ocean in my ears and the world slows around us like the last instant in a dream, as we rush near enough that I can see the invader's eyes above his red veil, I realize we aren't going to make it—that gun is almost *pointing at my face*, the bullets are ripping the ground *right at Ihira's feet*, it's going to carve through my raptor's side and my leg like dozens of sharp teeth, like the jaw of the universe slamming shut on its prey, and I can hear the rattling of Grandma Yaga's raptor hut creaking across the prairie at me, or is that the rattle of the gun—I open my mouth to scream—

—rope wraps arounds the barrel of the gun, and the gun is ripped from its swivel. Yekaterina's lasso yanks it out over the grass. Daphne carries my wife around the tyrannosaur from the other side, my wife with her eyes blazing like the sun, battle fury in her face, her mouth open in a war-scream she can't hear but I can. She flicks the lasso loose, sending the gun crashing into the prairie, vanishing in the grass, invading metal swallowed up and gone from sight.

We pass each other, our raptors slicing through the grass along opposite circles. The deathreaper has stopped its charge; it turns, opening its striped jaws and *cooing* again.

I veer close and Ihira leaps, seeking to slash the deathreaper with her shearing claw—the red assassin's gaze meets mine—but the deathreaper's head slams into us from the side, knocking Ihira and me into the grass. Falling from her back, I roll so she won't crush me. She tumbles, crashing through the vegetation, squawking and bleating with the shock of it. I leap to my feet, adrenaline drowning my body's bruises, the kopye blazing in my hands. The deathreaper looms over me, teeth like knives. I thrust the rod at its descending maw. But again a rope saves me; Katya's lasso wraps around the tyrannosaur's snout, tightening and snapping it shut; my kopye takes the beast in the underside of its jaw. Blue lightning crackles along its skin and now it *does* scream, a high-pitched squeal through its nostrils, and I smell the reek of burned flesh. The deathreaper stumbles backward through the grass, dragging Katya and Daphne after it on the rope, as an adult might tow a toddler. That beast is *immense.*

The invader draws a sidearm from where it's holstered at his shin. He lifts it and fires in one swift, skilled motion; I hear Daphne's shriek of pain. An explosion of red from the dinosaur's hip, and the raptor's leg collapses under her. My wife leaps free of the saddle, still holding the rope, still screaming wordlessly. The tyrannosaur shakes its head rapidly back and forth, sending my wife whipping through the air on the end of the rope. Katya won't let go.

Ihira regains her feet, shaking her head twice. Then she hisses and sprints at the tyrannosaur. I grasp her neck feathers and swing myself to the saddle as she flashes past. She leaps, nearly losing me from her back, this time digging her claws into the deathreaper's hip and clinging there. The invader flinches to the side as Ihira's jaws snap shut where his arm was an instant before, but he does not evade my kopye. The end of it slams into his side and again there is blue fire and cooked meat and the invader tumbles from the saddle. I hold onto Ihira's neck feathers with my other hand, desperate, as the tyrannosaur rolls and thrashes beneath us, furiously trying to shake both us and Katya. As the deathreaper staggers to the side, I catch a fever glimpse of the invader, a red blur in the grass behind. A glimpse of Katya in the air, still clinging to the end of her lasso with gloved hands. A glimpse of a green hide and the lifted horn and the stampede of Old Man toward us from the distance. Quick decision. Heart racing, I leap from Ihira's saddle onto the feathered shoulder of the tyrannosaur, grabbing a fistful of plumage to stop myself from sliding down its side. I drive my kopye into the back of its neck. A crackle, and the tyrannosaur rears with a scream. I lose my grip, tumbling. The edge of the invader's saddle slams into my hip, flipping me; I land on its rump near the beast's tail, the breath knocked out of my lungs, but I catch a grip of short feathers just above its hind leg. Gasping for air. Ihira is on the ground again, hissing at the beast, circling, watching for a chance to strike. The deathreaper drops its head and rushes forward through the grass. I snap the kopye to my belt and climb hand over hand to the saddle. Katya is being dragged behind us through the grass but somehow is keeping her feet, running and skidding at a terrifying pace that might break her legs if she falls or hits a rock. One hand on the rope, the other swinging a *second* lasso in the air, even as she is dragged. If I had a hand free I'd pump a fist in the air and scream her name because she is magnificent and she is my *wife* and not even a reaper of death can stop her!

I gain the saddle, groaning as my body realizes how bruised it is. The Catha trees are tall and pink before us, and we're about to slam into them. Ihira comes at us from the right, slashing with her claw at the tyrannosaur's leg to hamstring it, but again the deathreaper rams its head into my raptor, battering her aside and off her feet. But the dinosaur has turned aside from its charge at the trees; this behemoth of flame and death surges under me, muscled and furious, as it turns in a circle. Snapping a coil of rope loose from my belt, I knot one end swiftly about the pommel of the creature's saddle. My turn. With the other end, I make a lasso and hurl it swiftly at a knot of thick tree branches. It catches. A tether. Katya's second lasso falls over the deathreaper's neck, and then she is at the trees, too, on the other side of the dinosaur from my tether, knotting the end of one rope around a stout Catha trunk. Then she runs for another tree with the end of her second rope in hand. The deathreaper makes to charge her, but I snap open my kopye and slam it into the side of the creature's bound jaw. It flinches and tries to turn toward me, and I slide off its back. Ihira runs up and I catch her saddle and vault up; then we're away through the grass. I'm already snatching a second coil of rope from the saddle for another lasso.

The tyrannosaur strains and thrashes and coos through its bound snout. Katya and I work fast, looping multiple lassos around its neck, each tethered to a different tree, some to the deathreaper's left, some to its right, the ropes tightened until it can't move, only thrash and tear at the ground with its hind claws. That animal is mighty but *we* are nightwatchers! Two final lassos capture its legs, bringing it crashing to the earth at last, and Katya and I leap onto its hip, knotting the ropes tight, as it bucks beneath us. Our eyes meet and I take her by the hair and kiss her hard, my teeth cutting her lip, her surprised cry muffled against my mouth. I taste blood and Katya.

Something like a fist hits my hip and I crumple, falling out of my wife's arms, tumbling off the tyrannosaur into the grass. I twist, striking the ground with my elbow, hard. I squirm away from the tyrannosaur's bulk before it can crush me. I catch a brief glimpse of Katya standing on the downed beast, silhouetted against a red sky, snapping her kopye free, her braid swaying at her back, her eyes blazing. *My Katya*, lovely and lethal in the sunset. Facing her, the invader strides toward us through the tall grass, crimson cloak billowing behind him, his sidearm lifted, smoke trailing from the barrel. I stare at him dizzily. I've been shot. Sweet Founder, I've been shot. My eyes sting. They were right. I really *was* the weak strap, the girl without mother or kin, the girl who fails.

My hip is a roar of pain. I can hardly breathe for it. For just a moment my eyes close. Time goes sluggish. I can feel the long blades of grass against my body, one of them tapping my cheek like the ticking of a Ticktock's watch. Here on the ground, the alien scents of this day—the tyrannosaur musk and the strange new smell of gunfire—are fainter; the scent of crushed grass overwhelms everything. I can hear my heartbeat … and something else. I am *certain* I can hear my mother's soft breathing, as if she stands over me in the grass, as she did that day long ago when I first saddled Ihira, when Mom first taught me to ride my raptor.

Mom.

I don't dare open my eyes, for if I do, she will be gone. I'll just lie here listening. As Katya has asked me so often to do, I'll just … breathe.

In my memory, I have just fallen from Ihira's back at high speed, and I am winded. Ihira stands nearby in the grass, waiting for me. Mom reaches her hand down, but I don't take it. *I can't, Mother. I can't.*

Her voice is deep and melodic, a voice for braiding up the night with stories. *Yes, you can.*

I keep falling. It's too hard.

Get up, daughter.

Just let me lie in the grass a moment, Mom.

She crouches beside me, hands between her knees. She looks at me. Her hair is black as night, her eyes gray as steam rising from the flanks of a ceratopsian herd. Her face and hands are wrinkled and strong and kind. She moves them, signing as she talks, as our people often do. *You keep falling, do you?*

Yes, Mom. Tears of shame burn against my eyelids.

You know what you have, Sasha?

I shake my head.

She takes my hand in hers, presses the smooth metal surface of the Founder's book into my palm, closes my fingers over its pages. The book is still warm from her hand. *You have a bruised hip, two bruised ribs, a cut lip, dirt on your cheek. And you have the Founder's book and your mother's stories and the blood of a nightwatcher in your body, and you have a whole lot of hope in your heart. You have hope, Sasha. That's what you have. Hope. It's the best thing that ever was or ever will be. Spun from stories, stronger than medicine, older than this world. Hope is what braids our lives together. Hope carried our people between planets and hope carries us through the red rain and hope will carry you. So will Ihira. Now get on your feet, daughter, and get in her saddle and ride.*

Yes, Mom.

My eyes shoot open.

I've only had them closed a few moments. Katya stands on the bound tyrannosaur's back, tall and strong as Mom might have. Her kopye flares with blue light. She leaps, and the next bullet passes her in the air. The invader tracks her to fire again, but his hand sprouts a blade of shining metal and a blossom of blood, and his gun falls into the grass. There is a knife through his hand. If the invader screams, I can't hear it above the roar of my own blood in my ears. But he plucks the blade out of his right hand with his left. He wields the blade, making it his own, raining blood into the grass. But then *another* knife sprouts from his hip. Then the triceratops bears down on him; Dmitri is already holding a third knife ready for the toss, but Old Man strikes first, driving his horn through the invader's side. The trike lifts his head, carrying the invader through the air, speared, and yet the invader still fights, slashing at the horn with his knife, to no effect. The triceratops tosses his horn and the man slides off it, rolling into the grass, leaving Old Man's horn slick with blood.

Fighting for breath, I get to my knees. Katya is running toward me now. I glance down but don't see blood. I glance at the horizon. No sign of a domik on raptor legs. No death coming for me yet.

Hope. Now get on your feet, daughter.

With a groan, I stand. Near me, the deathreaper thrashes in its ropes, its eyes rolling, torn blades of violet grass tangled among its red feathers. Its legs are bound but its feet kick together, claws gouging ravines in the soil. No death's harvest for it today.

I am dazed. But not dying. Katya reaches me, throws her arm around me, and then my head is in her lap, her face above mine. Above her head is a sky lit with flame and the delicate silver of our planet's rings. I feel a tug at my belt, then she lifts her hand, shows me the metal circle of the Founder's book, which I have carried on my belt since my mother's death. It was her book. And her mother's before her. And *her* mother's. Back all the way to Landing. Now its thin, tightly-packed metal pages are warped and bent; it will never be read again. A bullet is captured in the twisted metal. I gaze at it in wonder. My hip is screaming and will probably be as purple as my raptor, but the bullet never tore through the leggings into my skin. The Founder was always placing her life between her people and peril. My mother, too. She placed her own body between me and grisly death, at rainfall. Now she has saved her daughter again; that disc of metal is all I have left of her besides the kopye and her stories in my memory, and it kept the bullet from my flesh and bones. My throat tightens. "Thanks, Mom," I whisper.

Katya touches my cheek and I realize my face is wet.

She presses the Founder's book into my hand—it's hot, but not enough to burn—and she dips her head and kisses me then, quickly. Then signs, *Daphne.* Terror in her eyes. She helps me sit up, then runs into the grass, sprinting back the way we came, toward where her raptor fell.

9

IHIRA REACHES ME, NUZZLES ME WITH HER SNOUT, hard enough to make me wince. I wrap an arm around her neck and hold on, letting my brave raptor pull me to my feet. "Good girl," I groan, "good girl." With a whimper of pain, I climb to her back, holding tightly to her neck feathers. I clip the metal ruin of the Founder's book to my belt and chirp my commands to Ihira. She walks, snout low, nostrils flaring. We're looking for that man in red. To one side I see Katya as she runs through the grass. Dmitri slides from Old Man's back and approaches the deathreaper with a fresh coil of rope. The tyrannosaur kicks, captive and enraged, powerful muscles rippling beneath its feathered skin. I cast it a resentful look; my wife's lassos that bind it were supposed to be for *me* tonight. Instead—a cold knot in my belly—tonight we might be burying a raptor.

The sky is still full of light, the sun just kissing the horizon, as if the planet hasn't rotated even a meter while we fought for our lives. I am sweaty and out of breath and faint with pain; I would have thought the battle a day in length, but maybe it only lasted the length of time it would take to sing the Founder's song three times through.

With a shout, the invader rises from the grass before me, startling a squawk from Ihira and nearly a squawk from me too. The man's red robes are torn and darker where he's bled, where a triceratops horn impaled him, yet he *stands*. He pulls another gun, a slender-barreled thing he can hold in his left hand. But we're on him before he can use it, and my kopye knocks him into the grass with a crackle of burning flesh and the scent of meat.

Yet, as we ride past him and turn, he stands *right back up*.

I cry out, jerking to the side as he fires. The bullet shrieks past my ear. Then Ihira is on him, her shearing claw tearing robes and skin and belly. The man sways on his feet, drops the gun into the grass to clutch at his belly. A mass of entrails slithers out into his hands, steaming with his body's heat. He drops to his knees, then to his back. I restrain Ihira from dipping her snout to feed, and I hold my kopye lifted.

I stare in horror. The invader's movements as he lies on the bloodied ground are not those of a dying man but of a determined one. His hands shake as he presses the coils back into his belly. Behind him, the deathreaper thrashes and lets out another thunderous coo. The man stares up at me, dark eyes above his veil, cold with hate. His blood-soaked fingers press the last of his intestines back into his gut, and his skin starts to seal itself, like two lips closing; then the gash in his belly simply *isn't there*. As if a healer has stitched him up and overseen months of recovery in just a few heartbeats. And more. There isn't even a *scar*. Just smooth skin red with spilled blood. I gasp. My hands tremble. I cast a glance over my shoulder. The others haven't seen; Katya is out in the grasses with her raptor and Dmitri is looping more rope around the tyrannosaur's legs.

The invader forces himself up on one elbow.

"Oh no, you don't." I slide from Ihira's back, chirping at her to stay put. I snatch a leather cord from the saddlebags and lunge. Seizing the man's wrist, I rip his arm out from under him. He lands on his belly, squalls in pain. I wrench his arms behind him. He is *strong*, but I knot the leather swiftly about his blood-slickened wrists, breathing hard.

Out of the corner of my eye, I see Dmitri coming toward me. "No, I've got this," I call to him. "Help Katya." Grasping one of the invader's bound arms just below his shoulder, I start dragging him toward the trees. The tyrannosaur lunges at me, still fighting its ropes, but half those ropes were tied by my wife and those are nightwatcher knots, and that animal is *not* getting loose. Strain as it might, it can't reach me.

I slam the invader's back against a tree. Above his veil, his eyes flash with hate. But he is shaking, tremors taking his body as though the sunset hour is cold to him. Maybe the shock of battle and the shock of his wounds is catching up to him. He writhes and I almost can't hold him; I rope him tightly to the tree. Stepping close, Ihira thrusts her head at him and screeches. The invader looks cooly into my raptor's jaws. No wince, just a narrowing of the eyes like he's angry. There's something strange about those eyes. They're shadowed under his hood and he isn't facing the sunset, yet there are flecks of fire reflected in them, like embers.

"Back," I snap at Ihira.

Her jaws close. She cocks her head to the side and stares at our captive with hungry, silent intensity. The branches whistle faintly above us. The invader kicks at me, and I press my boot down on his thigh to hold him. Breathing hard, I cinch the knots and check them. Then, with cold wrath, I lean close and hiss in his ear, "*You came to the wrong planet.*"

Then I straighten, breathing through my teeth as my body reminds me of its bruises. Ihira gazes at me with one unblinking eye. "Watch him," I tell her, "but don't eat him. We need answers." She chirps. To a dakotaraptor, *don't eat him* is more of a suggestion than a command; I imagine the invader, who rides a feathered carnivore as we do, understands that. I hope it makes him sweat under his hood.

With his gaze on my back, I stagger through the grasses toward where the looming triceratops marks the position of my wife, her raptor, and our strange traveling companion. Ihira remains behind. Soon the grasses hide me from raptor and captive alike. The violet blades are as high as my cheeks, and I swim through them more than I walk. A wind has swept up and those blades of grass flow about me like a song in the sunset. Clouds in the northwest are turning orange and red, all the hues of wildfire. This is our prairie and it is beautiful, but there has been blood spilled in it today.

The others aren't far away. Old Man's ponderous body forms a wind shelter; in his lee Dmitri is crouched beside Daphne, who is on her side, grasses crushed beneath her. Blood runs down the dakotaraptor's leg. Katya is pulling items from the trike's saddlebags, laying them out within the whistler's reach. Holding a wide-bladed knife, Dmitri carves away the feathers from Daphne's hip, clearing an open space around the sucking bullet wound. Seeing that Ticktock, an invader himself, bending over my wife's raptor like a hyaena over carrion, with that knife in hand, I shout and run the last steps toward them.

"What are you *doing*?" I snap.

"Fixin to help this bird." He glances over his shoulder at me and his eyes are grave.

"You get your hands off her."

Katya touches my arm, but battle fury is burning in my blood.

"I can help her," the Ticktock says.

"I don't trust your hands on her, slaver."

"Don't *have* to trust me," he says, a flicker of anger in his eyes. "Just have to let me help her."

Katya squeezes my arm.

Just then, Daphne lunges at Dmitri. I'm just quick enough to grab her head. I wrap my arms around her jaws, holding them shut, and the raptor hisses. Her head thrashes from side to side, dragging me off my feet. I hit the ground hard on my bruised hip and yelp in pain, but I don't let go. She struggles to get up, to get where she can shear and rip with her hooked claw, but one leg won't hold her weight. Dmitri throws himself onto the raptor beside me, lending his mass to the struggle. Daphne is smaller than Ihira but she is *strong*. And as long as that Ticktock is messing with her hip, she's going to want to bite and tear. Katya knows it, too, and approaches Daphne with rope. It takes both of us fighting her while Dmitri holds her down, cursing, but then Katya gets several loops of rope around her raptor's snout and ties her jaws shut. The raptor whines. Weeping quietly, Katya throws her arms around her dinosaur's neck and presses her cheek against her neck feathers. I touch Katya's hair, my heart hurting.

"Right, we won't get bit," Dmitri says hoarsely. "Sasha, hold her down while I cut out this bullet."

No time for distrust now; I need to keep this raptor off him. Shakily, I let go of Daphne's head, step around my wife, and straddle the raptor. I can feel her body surging under me as she keeps fighting to stand. If it weren't for her injury, I couldn't hold her down. I don't have a lot of weight on me. I find myself saying softly over and over, "Shh, shhh, I've got you, I've got you," and I don't know if I'm talking to Daphne or Katya or both.

Dmitri works fast. He picks up a long, sharp bone with a seeking point, very narrow and from no animal I recognize. With it, he pokes at the wound, then starts digging in the dinosaur's flesh. Daphne's whines get frantic, and she bucks me off her but I climb on again. Dmitri uses one hand to spread the wound open and keeps probing.

"Yaga's ribs, what are you doing?" I ask him.

"Digging," he grumbles.

"I can see that."

"Then let me *work*." Without taking that bone pick from the wound, he snatches up another tool, this one made of white orra wood and shaped like a long-handled spoon with a deep curve to it. There are tiny symbols burned into the orra, sigils like those on his watch. Ticktock magic, maybe. The end of the spoon is small, and he gets it in the wound and begins working both tools while blood flows out over his hands. At last I understand. He means to scoop out that bullet like a mouthful of borscht if he can get at it.

Katya has her face turned from me, pressed to Daphne's feathers while her raptor screams through its nose, and Katya's shoulders are shaking. "She'll live," I tell my wife; though she can't see my lips, I have to say it. "She'll live."

"Not if I don't get this bullet out," Dmitri mutters.

I round on him. "Shut *up*."

He lifts his gaze from the wound, and his eyes are haunted. "*You* shut up. There's enough noise coming from the raptor, *and* I have to worry about getting dirt in the wound or getting her claw ripping through my belly if you don't hold her down tight. So *you* shut up and let me work, because I've got enough under the sun to distract me."

I keep quiet, because he's right. I hold Daphne down as best as I can and I watch him work his Ticktock magic. He bites one lip and worries at the inside of the dinosaur's leg with his tools. Sun's fading and it'll be getting dark soon, another reason to hurry. I could make a fire and lift a torch for him to see by, but I can't do that *and* hold down three hundred kilograms of panicked dinosaur. Back by the trees I can hear the tyrannosaur thrashing, and out across the prairie I hear the laughter of hyaenas, chilling my blood. What do they have to laugh about? This is not an evening for laughter.

It takes a while, and I have sweat through my clothes and I've got sweat running down my back and between my nates from fighting Daphne, but at last Dmitri gives a low cry of triumph and pulls something small and gory out of the wound. He drops the bone pick and takes the item in his fingers, dries it on the trampled grass, then lifts it to the red light of sunset. That slug of metal is the length of my fingertip to the first joint. So small, to inflict so much pain. Dmitri shakes his head in awe. "Never seen anything like it," he murmurs. "The timekeep and his clockmen would pay prettily to see this, wouldn't they?" Shaking his head, he pockets it.

"Will she be all right?" I ask raggedly.

"Hope so. Sometimes wounds go bad. Better chance now, though, with that metal out of her. Hold her, I'm going to sew her shut."

I nod. My body is a haze of pain from bruises and from Daphne's bucking beneath me. Dmitri gets a tiny needle and thread from the assortment of supplies by his knee, and he gets to work. It's a wonder to see it. His hands are deft and quick and skilled. He's done this kind of healing work before. His eyes looked haunted before he found the bullet. Maybe when he has tried this before, it hasn't ended well. Now that he isn't digging in the wound, Daphne's struggling less, too. Or maybe she's just tired. Her chest lifts and falls like a feathered ocean under me. I risk letting go with one hand and placing it on my wife's shoulder. Yekaterina is trembling like the invader was, but the pain is in her heart, not her body. For a nightmare moment, I imagine losing Ihira and having to raise a new raptor from the egg or first, to get safe out of the prairie, having to undertake the lethal peril of capturing one wild in the grass. I think of seeing *Ihira* labor for breath, seeing her eyes go dull, seeing her *die*, and I feel sick. *Oh, Katya.* "I love you," I whisper, though I know she isn't looking at me to read my lips or see me sign.

But then Dmitri finishes. He returns his tools to the saddlebags and pats Old Man on his frill; the triceratops is chewing his cud, watching us with one wary eye. I climb off the raptor and hold Katya. "I'm sorry," I whisper, my cheek to her back, my arms around her. She is still trembling. She reaches down to her boot and plucks her long knife from its sheath there, and saws the rope off Daphne's snout. When the dinosaur is free, her warbles of pain and fear are heartbreaking. Katya turns her face to mine and she is a mess of tears, her face pale and her eyes ablaze with fury and death. I can't breathe; I've never seen her like this. She removes my arms gently but firmly and rises to her feet.

"Katya?" I ask softly.

She doesn't take time to sign. She just strides out into the grass with that knife in her hand. I get to my feet, and as she disappears into the tall grass I realize she's heading for the Catha trees. I have to force my body to move; the bruising is bad. First I stumble, then I walk, then I break into a run. She is moving fast, and even as I come out of the tall grass, I see her bearing down on our captive, her knife reflecting the sun's last embers. And my heart burns as hers does to see him dead, but I remember his body sealing up a wound, like no invader we've seen before, and in a flash, I realize we *can't.*

"No!" I cry to her.

But she can't hear me.

Ihira cocks her head to the side, puzzled, and steps back. The deathreaper lifts its snout and coos without opening its mouth, that deep coo that makes my body resonate like a drum. The captive lifts his head, casting a defiant glare at my wife. I run toward her.

Her knife flashes.

Then my arms are around her. Her knife plunges into the invader's shoulder, missing his heart. Katya turns on me, her eyes wild, and we fall, fighting, punching and kicking in the dirt. One of the tree roots slams into my back and I cry out. Katya twists around to grab at the knife, still sheathed in our captive's shoulder. Gasping, I grab her hair, pull her back. Then we're wrestling. The tyrannosaur's coo makes even the ground beneath us quiver.

I get my foot in Katya's belly and I flip her, rolling onto her and grabbing unsuccessfully for her wrists. Her nails rake my cheek. "Damn it, Katya, *stop*!" I scream. I grab her hair again and hold her head to the ground. I try to muscle her into yielding. She kicks, so I straddle her. Her nails dig at my arm, but my jacket prevents her from doing any damage. We fight, panting, for a few moments. Then she collapses under me. There are tears on her cheeks.

"I'm sorry," I whisper. "I am so sorry, my love." I fight for breath. "I know he hurt your Daphne, I know he did. But we need him captive. We need to question him."

She won't look at me. I let her go and I fall to my side in the dirt, groaning. She doesn't make any move to get up, so after a moment I crawl over to our captive, whose eyes are dull with pain, and I wrench the blade from his shoulder. He hisses in agony. Blood flows from his shoulder at the removal of the knife, but already I can see it slowing. He says something in a language I don't recognize, the words biting and furious.

"Shut up," I tell him.

Fatigued, sweaty, covered in dirt, covered in bruises, I stagger back to my wife. I toss the bloodied knife to the side, and I sit by her; I draw her into my arms. She pushes me away, her hands abrupt against my shoulders, and I feel the wound of it like it's me her knife's been sheathed in. "Katya," I whisper.

She rises, silhouetted against the last of the sunset, and walks into the grass. To see Daphne, I know. I stare after her, needing to get up but at this moment too exhausted, too bruised, too heartsick to do so. I lie back against the mossy soil, a gnarled Catha root under my back, feeling at each breath like the next might break me apart.

***

Moments later, the Ticktock staggers out of the grass with his hat in his hand, his face even paler than usual, hair sweaty across his brow. "That crazy damned raptor is napping," he mutters as he slumps to the ground beside me. "Old Man's with her. I cleaned the wound best I could, rubbed hajaka on it. If I got it clean enough, she'll be fine. Might even have the full use of that leg after a while, but I wouldn't push her hard." He settles the hat on his head.

A flash of grief and fury. *Pushing hard* is what nightwatchers and their raptors *do*. How will Katya catch me, racing for Catha trees, if her raptor's limping? She'll need more than a lasso to make up for that. And seeing Daphne's pride wounded will break her heart. *My Katya.*

But also I look at Dmitri with new eyes. He is still strange under that hat, but he helped us against the invader. He took care of Daphne, though he nearly risked her slicing him open. He didn't have to do any of that, not for us, but he did. He treated us today like we were kin.

"Thank you," I tell him.

He turns his head and tips his hat up, gets a good look at me. "What did you say?"

"I said thank you."

He blinks. "Might be so exhausted I'm hearing ghosts talking in the grass. Say that louder, Sasha Nightwatcher. I want to be sure what I'm hearing." His lip curves.

I bite back a retort and instead I say, clearly, "Thank you, Ticktock."

He grins. Then lies back and settles his hat over his eyes. "Damn," he says.

But now I am thinking of Daphne's wound, and the bullets that tore at the grass, and the wild swivel of that gun almost as long as a person is tall, and my blood starts to heat. "Why didn't you tell us he had a long gun like that?" I say, quiet and cold. "On a saddle? I've never seen a gun like *that*."

"Did tell you." Dmitri speaks without looking up.

"You certainly didn't."

"Told you he had a deathclock."

"You said a *clock*! How is that a *clock*?"

"Not my doing you don't recognize a clock when you see one." He stifles a yawn. "It's a timepiece that keeps the time of death, a sharp crack of sound dividing the hours of life from an eternity of silence."

I stew, not having words for everything that's boiling in me.

Freaking Ticktock.

The sky is still too light for stars, and the rings are splendor. Ihira walks over, violet and regal, her head high. I wonder suddenly if she's worried for Daphne, too. I chirp to her, and I get to my feet, groaning. She nuzzles me; I hug her briefly and kiss the top of her head, just above her left eye. "Thanks for keeping me alive," I whisper. I give her neck a good petting, then stoop to retrieve the knife from the ground. It is still bloody, so I wipe it on a patch of moss before tucking it carefully into my belt.

All right. Let's see just what we've caught.

Putting an arm around Ihira's neck and leaning on her but trying not to *look* like I am, I walk with my raptor toward the invader from another planet. We leave Dmitri lying behind us. He might be falling asleep for all I know. *Deathclock*. Why did I *thank* him? I burn with irritation.

As we approach, the deathreaper tries to roar with its mouth tied shut as we approach. Ihira hisses at it, and I caress her neck feathers and chirp quietly near her earhole. Then I slip my arm from around her neck. Suppressing a shiver of instinct, I crouch in front of the tyrannosaur, near enough I could reach out and touch its snout with my fingertips if I wanted to. It strains to get at me. The ropes creak and the Catha wood groans. The tyrannosaur's breath washes across my face like a hot summer wind, but fetid. Holding my breath, I marvel at the wildfire of its feathers, flame in the sunset. I gaze into the deathreaper's dark, dark eye. That small-mammal-in-the-grass fear that my body and blood have inherited from distant grandmothers millions of years dead makes my heart pound and my palms sweat. Yet pride swells in my heart—I am a *nightwatcher,* and whether or not I am the weak strap wound around the kopye, *I* took down this tyrannosaur, I and Katya. Pride is louder than my fear. Pity, too. Hesitating, I *do* reach out and touch its snout, soft as Ihira's. It struggles to open its jaws but can't. Its eye rolls, and I realize it is afraid.

"I am sorry you're bound," I tell it softly. "You are a beautiful animal, but you don't get to eat me."

I stand and give the deathreaper a steady look, daring it to thrash all it wants. Then I turn to approach the captive toward whom I have less pity and more fear. Ihira follows me, a few steps behind.

While the tyrannosaur kicks and bucks against its bonds, the invader tied to another tree is quieter, alert, watching us from beneath his red hood. He glances once at Ihira, who eyes him as she might a juicy, summer-plump haia. The invader's robes are ripped where the triceratops gored him, and his belly is exposed where Ihira's claw cut open his robes and his flesh, but his skin has *healed.* Not even the white line of a scar to show where she spilled his innards. His breathing doesn't even sound labored. I reach him, but I don't crouch; I stand over him. Gently, fearful of what I will find, I pull back the torn cloth from his shoulder where Katya stabbed him. There *is* a wound there, but even as I stare, the blood flowing from it slows to a trickle and the edges of the cut start to close like a kiss.

"Sweet Founder," I whisper.

What *is* this magic? Here is a thing beyond Dmitri's Ticktock medicine. Can Grandma Yaga reach somehow between the stars to touch and curse the flesh of another world? A strange impulse takes hold of me, to touch his skin, to know if his flesh is *real.* Instead, I draw my hand back with a shudder.

"You've done a lot of hurt for just one person," I tell him, "yet you don't seem hurt at all." I sign it, too. "Are there more of you?"

He is silent. He might almost be asleep like Dmitri for all he reacts, except that beneath his crimson hood, his eyes catch the sheen of the dying light like a brachiosaur's after dark. Something isn't *right* about his eyes.

"What is your name?" I ask.

He says nothing. Just watches me.

I reach beneath his hood, catching his veil and pulling it away from his face. This time he does flinch, just a little. I force his hood back onto his shoulders. It's the first time I've been able to get a good look at him, and I gasp. He is *young*, younger than Dmitri, I think. How many winters has he seen? Fifteen? Fewer? Maybe too young to have kissed or been kissed, though evidently not too young to have killed.

His head is completely shaven. He doesn't even have eyebrows. His skin is pale as though the sun never touches it, ever. I stare at the strangeness of him, taken aback. He stares up at me not with a captive's fear but with contempt burning in his eyes. His eyes—they *change* as I watch them. The irises shine like metal and they rotate, a little bit one way, a little bit the other, and his pupils shrink and dilate as they do. As if these are not eyes but Ticktock clocks embedded in his face. I have never seen eyes like these.

"What is *happening* to your eyes?" I whisper.

Still, his silence. Nearby, his tyrannosaur thunder-coos with its jaws closed. Its talons tear at the dirt but with its legs bound in place, it can't find any balance.

Unready to stare too long into our captive's metallic eyes, I glance at the veil in my hand. I have no idea what material it's made from. It's soft but strong. It doesn't appear to be woven or sewn. I drop it to the ground. "What is your name?" I ask again.

When he doesn't answer, I add, "All things that breathe, and many that don't, have a name and a story. Only in Grandma Yaga's country do ghosts wander without names. What's yours?"

Slowly, deliberately, he jerks his head forward and spits on my shin. I suck in breath through my teeth. His spittle trickles down the side of my boot.

We stare at each other.

"You want me angry?" My voice goes quiet and cold. "I'm already angry. You've killed people. People that didn't need to die. Like that whistler. Ellie. You shot her. And you shot my wife's raptor. I am all the angry you'll need, invader. Save your spittle."

Those clockwork eyes seem to count heartbeats of time, more alien than the timepiece Katya carries with her in her saddlebags or the Ticktock in his jacket. The tyrannosaur snorts desperately through its nostrils. Out in the prairie behind us, hyaenas whoop and laugh.

I bite out the words: "*Your name.*"

"Took veil from face," he says in cold fury. His accent is thick, but I can make out the words—they're words I know. He *does* understand our language. I *thought* so. His people have been watching us, listening to us. "You want see my face. Want hear my name?"

"I do."

He sneers. "Have no right my name, no right my face, no right my blood. You, me, different hatching. You, wombgrown. Born slimy, spattered with blood, misshapen. No millions in blood, no strength in skin to heal scratch, no loyalty, no love for Mother in heart." His lip curls. "Not human. Born ungenomed *animal.* I not give my name to *animals.*"

Well.

I struggle to understand. He speaks of hatching. Of *hatching*, as from eggs. As if these invaders dropping from our sky are like the deathreapers they ride. How can that be?

I take a breath and start again. "Who is 'Mother'?"

"Mother." His face—it changes. His contempt fades. The sheen in his eyes burns very bright. He is facing me, but he is looking inside himself. Maybe at his memories. It's a rapturous look. Is that how I looked, when I told Dmitri about our Founder? "Mother," he repeats, more softly. "Mother's eggs birth us. Mother's blood defeats death. Mother's dark fluids bring sleep in long plummet between stars. Mother's millions heal wounds, make sinew and bone strong."

"I don't understand."

"Mother is *here*, in blood. She listens, sees. Mother gives strength. Gives steed for ride, thunder and teeth. Gives gun for fight, gives planet for conquer." He lifts his chin, and his eyes blaze with fresh defiance. "Am *good* son. I make planet safe for Mother's eggs."

"This is *our* planet," I snap. "For *our* children."

He works his jaw.

In fury, I tell him, "You spit at me again, and so help me, I will *let* Yekaterina cut out your tongue."

Laughter in his eyes now. A hyaena's cold, violent laughter. No tremor of fear in him, and that … I shiver at that. He is our *captive*, tied to a tree, his veil torn from his face; surely he must be afraid.

"I grow new one," he says.

"What *are* you?" I cry. "The previous invaders couldn't … do that. What you do!"

"What I do?" he sneers.

"That." I point at his shoulder, his belly. "Washing away wounds like silt in a creek."

"Others only scouts."

Again that contempt in his tone, but directed this time at his own people, not at mine. Maybe I can push for answers that way. "Maybe *you're* only a scout," I taunt him.

His eyes go cold. "Am deathless."

The hairs rise on the back of my neck with a whisper of the coldest stories my mother ever told. "Koschei," I gasp, shaken. In my heart, I can hear my mother's low voice telling me a winter tale: *Koschei cannot be hurt or killed because his life is not inside his body where it can bleed out but is hidden inside a bone whistle, which is hidden inside a doll's belly, which is hidden inside a dark kedr tree, deep within a vast forest in Grandma Yaga's country where there are thousands of dark kedr trees. His eyes are not human eyes; they gleam like reflections of ringlight in a pool, lovely but cold. He comes in the night out of the air, snatches children from their mothers, snatches wives from each other's arms. He is hungry, not for meat but for a kiss. At the touch of his lips, your ghost is sucked out and your body is deathless as he, but there is no girl left inside it. He cannot die and he cannot be killed.*

My hands tremble. "Koschei!" I cry.

No recognition of the word in his alien eyes. But he runs the tip of his tongue along his lower lip and lifts his face. "Bring for eat. I starve."

I step back so fast I almost trip over a root. Trembling, I lift my fingers to my lips. But the young invader is tied; he cannot lunge at me, cannot reach my mouth to kiss me.

"What do you *want* here?" My voice quavers, then goes knife sharp.

His nostrils flare, as though he can *smell* my fear. "Want meat." He bares his teeth. "Maybe want *your* meat."

My hands are shaking; I force them to stop. I take a deep breath, another. Whispering in my heart,

bold as Vilya who broke the medved's back,
brave as Nadya who faced the Screaming Ship,

—I am a *nightwatcher*. And this man—this koschei—is not some ghost stealer from my mother's tales. Surely he is not. Surely. He is flesh and blood. I have *seen* him bleed. Though I haven't seen him die ... I choke back a whimper. That story used to give me such nightmares when I was a child, such that my mother stopped telling it. She would pull me into her arms and kiss my hair and say, "Sasha, my little love, you have to be bold. The prairie night is full of scary things. You have to be brave." And if I was still shivering, she'd say, "Brave as Nadya," and she'd tell me the story of the Screaming Ship and Nadya with her vast net of feathers, red and violet and gold and black. Standing on the edge of the ghost prairie to keep the ship from reaching her people.

Bold as Vilya who broke the medved's back,
brave as Nadya who faced the Screaming Ship.

My breathing is slower now. The koschei is only taunting me so because he saw me afraid. My face flushes with shame that he saw me weak, and the shame kills my fear. Anyway this invader is not trying to steal my ghost. It's physical meat he craves, with a belly empty after battle.

Feigning disinterest, I gesture toward his tyrannosaur, which no longer strains against the ropes. It just watches me with its eyes dark as secrets at the bottom of a well. "That one wants one of us to eat. I don't believe you do. And you can stop trying to scare me, koschei. I have you tied to a tree. I could give Grandma Yaga your bones."

"Have tied?" A tiny snort of a sound.

"I do. You've likely noticed the ropes."

He stares at me, his irises rotating. I clench my teeth. No ropes could hold Koschei in my mother's tales.

The koschei settles back, closes his eyes, shuts away their gleaming clockwork. "If not give meat, give sleep. Mother's millions burned like suns, can smell their smoke. Want rest and forget. Sight of you, stink of you offends."

"Thought I smelled tasty."

"Smell wombgrown *animal*," he sneers. "Like unwashed cow."

A … cow? A cow triceratops? "Where is your lander?"

He opens his eyes, jerks his chin suddenly toward the captive tyrannosaur. "Untie *her*, more talk."

"I might. When it's safe. I have no quarrel with her."

"Starve tied." The clockwork in his eyes rotates. "Not her belly. Her heart."

I let out my breath. This pushes back my fear: the way he is looking at his tyrannosaur. Here, at last, is something I understand, something to make him less strange, less full of terror. This young man, he is another tribe's nightwatcher, *that's* what he is. Bound to his dinosaur, heart to heart, maybe as surely as I am to mine and Katya to hers. I, too, dislike the sight of the deathreaper bound, though I dislike the thought of being its meal tonight more. This koschei heals, but maybe he's capable of feeling pain. Maybe he feels pain for his deathreaper.

I drop to a crouch before him, eye to eye, one nightwatcher to another. My voice is gentler than it was. "Your creature doesn't *belong* here. But I'd never starve her. I'll see she's fed. And by the song in my blood, I swear I'll free her in the morning, when we go. But do you a kindness to me also. Tell me what song is in *your* blood, koschei? Where do you come from? Where is your lander? Your ship? You want to scare me, fine, scare me. Scare me with a tale of invaders that drop out of the sky. Make me shiver. Tell me what peril I have to fear. Tell me about your ship."

His eyes glitter with hate. "Is not *ship*, girl savage. Is not *ocean* up there. Is empty black. No air, no food, no water for drink. Always fire of suns leaking through metal, killing. Is not *ocean*, is only death. *Ship!* You animals think *ships*, waves, sun for sail, wind for face. Is why you stay on planet, crawl like snail, not flit between worlds. Is not *ships*. Is bullets."

"Bullets?" I whisper.

"Mother's bullets. Aimed, all your hearts. Behind bullets, all Mother's children, come for live your domiks, harvest your corn, use your raptors." He nods at Ihira.

A stab of fresh terror. "Don't you *look* at her!" He gazes at Ihira not as you might gaze at a companion but as the mother of a settlement might look at a half-grown lambeosaur, to assess whether it has enough hide yet to be worth the skinning. So much for kinship between dinosaur riders.

He is watching my hand. Startled, I realized I've lifted it, ready to strike him.

"Made *angry*." His lips curve in a slow smirk. "Made scared. Is good."

I struggle to hold in my rage. "Yes, well you enjoy that." I turn my back to him, breathing a little hard, as though I've been running. Maybe it's the bruises in my side that make standing and talking so difficult.

The koschei's voice behind me is mocking. "Want ship? Want see ship? Walk through trees. Maybe find … *ship*. Maybe good eyes, 'koschei' eyes." He laughs.

I stiffen. *Walk through trees*. I glance back at him. The koschei's face is lit eerily by the ringlight and the fading sunset. Can I take him at his word? Was that a taunt and not a lie? I do not know his name. Our names are passed down from our ancestors, generation after generation, gifts from our grandmothers' grandmothers, who gave us this planet, gave us our liberty and our herds and our songs. Names are how we are braided to lives past, not just present. To know the name of another woman is—a powerful thing. Encoded in the name is an entire story of where she comes from.

I know Yekaterina's name.

But this youthful invader hides his name the way he hid his face behind that veil. I do not know his mothers and his grandmothers and their deeds. I do not have any tales of them leaping off a cliff on raptorback to catch a swooping coatl, or guiding triceratops herds with whistles of bamboo or bone. I do not know what his people have done, or what they might be capable of.

"Maybe find ship. Maybe good eyes, or maybe blind savage." He bares his teeth. "Good game? Like children play. Want hide and find?"

"You rot against that tree," I tell him.

I walk past Ihira, answering her query with a chirp of my own and a gentle pat on her flank. By the edge of the tall grass, I find Dmitri on his feet, gazing out speculatively across the prairie, his hat on the ground where he was resting, his watch open in his hand. As I approach, he snaps the timepiece shut. "We followed him forty and one hundred kilometers across open land, and more north than east." His eyes blaze in the dying sun and his voice quivers with anger. "He came forty and one hundred kilometers to kill my partner, and maybe millions of kilometers across airless space before that." He turns to me. "Bold of you to talk with him and not kill him dead."

"Well, that's what I want to talk with you about, Ticktock." I pitch my voice low. "I learned a thing. You might get Old Man and come with me. We need to find that koschei's ship." I gesture at the snarl of Catha trees.

"In there, is it?" He slips his watch inside his jacket. "It's dusk, Sasha."

"Best time to come sneaking up on his lander all stealthy. Best time for an ambush, if there are more like him."

There's a hardness in Dmitri's eyes that I haven't seen there before. "If there are more like him, we're like to die."

"I don't think there will be. They've always landed alone." Yet I swallow, thinking: This one's different than the ones we've encountered before. This one's a koschei. This is unknown prairie we're riding across.

"But you want to be cautious, is that it?"

"That's it." I don't like the idea of a surprise between now and dawn. I want this incursion to be *over.* Granted, the Ticktock and his trike are not who I would have chosen to sneak through a wood in the near-dark with, but I need a second pair of eyes and I sure don't like the thought of leaving a Ticktock man near Katya when she's in this state, even if he *did* patch up her dinosaur. An invader's an invader, and a Ticktock's a Ticktock, and it'd be best if I don't forget that.

Dmitri gives me a serious look. "All right. I asked for your help. Not going to turn it down now. Let's go." He stoops, lifts his hat from the ground, places it back on his head, its ridiculous size silhouetted against the end of day. Then he plucks the bone whistle from his belt and lifts it to his lips.

I nod and return to Ihira, my thoughts flitting fast as haia over the grass. We have to find that ship, have to *know* if he came down alone. And much as my wife and the Ticktock both would like to see him dead, I suppose we'll have to keep the koschei captive a while yet. There's so much we need him to tell us. We'll keep him with us until the rendezvous; then the other nightwatchers can help keep him. Having him with us, under watch, will *not* have a pleasant effect on any plans Katya and I might otherwise have for keeping each other warm in the night chill. The Ticktock we might be rid of at last, but this invader will be with us for the duration.

Reaching Ihira, I stroke her neck feathers gently, and the soft down under her jaw. I take the beautiful wedge of her feathered head in my hands and turn it so that her right eye gazes on our bound koschei. She warbles.

"Yes, I *might* let you eat him," I tell her. My smile is a pale thing. "Later. But *watch* him." My voice goes low and dangerous. "If he moves, kill him. Or cut him open again, at least."

She shifts anxiously and I press my cheek to hers. "I have to leave you here, girl, while I scout this wood. Someone's got to keep my Yekaterina safe. Daphne's hurt. My wife, too, in a different way. Just—protect them for me until I get back, all right?"

She chirps, and I hug her neck, tightly. As I let go and look up, I hear Old Man coming, the great beast huffing as he lumbers out of the grass. He slows and walks over to his rider, a moving mountain of hide and horn. I shake my head and follow his wake back out into the violet grass, trying to still the drumming of my heart as I do.

I find my love sitting by Daphne, her head down. Her drum is between her knees; she caresses it without tapping any beat. Daphne is breathing slow and steady, still asleep.

I step close, my footfalls soft and my movements slow so as not to disturb the dakotaraptor. I sit beside my wife. When she looks up, her face is tight with anguish. There's a hot temper in her eyes, something feral, a naked fury I have seen once or twice turned on others but never on me. I nearly choke. Her hands flash through signs rapidly. *I ever set to kill a man again, don't you step in my path, Sasha Nightwatcher. I'll kill you dead, too.*

That hurts so much, I can't breathe. She turns her shoulder to me, puts her arms around Daphne's neck and presses her cheek to her dinosaur's, crying silently. I lift my hand to touch her shoulder but I stop, for fear she might flinch. Breathing quick, holding back the killwind of my own pain, I remember that a nightwatcher's bond with her raptor is deeper even than her bond with her wife, that my own bond with Ihira is in the marrow of every bone I have.

Your raptor is your breath and sinew,
She is your war cry and battle screech
You are her will and her compassion—
Braided together, you are one being,
One story,
One song.

If it had been Ihira—

But wives are braided together too. That's what wiving *is.* Two stories in one braid, each beautiful, both stronger for being together. A nightwatcher's braid with her raptor and her braid with her pack may be strongest, but the wife braid matters *too.* I touch our braid on my jacket—its leather straps of sunset and gold—and I feel the more delicate braid around my thigh. When I am without kin and I can't trust how tightly I'm braided to my pack, the wife braid with Yekaterina and the raptor braid with Ihira are the only ones I have, all that truly keeps me from being unbraided, kinless, lost.

So I clasp my wife's shoulder, squeezing gently, just to let her know I'm here. She doesn't look up, and I have a thousand words stuck in my throat that I want to say to her, but I can't say them to her back where she can't see. And I don't dare wait; it's getting dark. But she's *my wife*, so I sit by her a little, anyway. Her shoulders shake. I'm angry too, angry and hurt and desperate. After a bit she glances up, tear-streaked, and I start to speak but stop to wait while she lifts her scarf to her face, drying her eyes so she can see. Her eyes are puffy and red. Some strands of her golden braid have come loose, and she's a sight.

I keep my hands slow. *The whistler and I will search through the trees, see about finding his lander. Might be brief or might be long. Need you watchful and safe. I'll leave Ihira. I'm bruised up but I can walk.*

She nods tersely. The rage is fading from her eyes and she looks tired, and I just want to hold her. I pluck the invader's knife from my belt, place the hilt in my wife's palm, and close her fingers around it. I hesitate, then dip my head and kiss her fingers.

She pulls her hand away, and I hurt. She folds up protectively for an instant, bringing her arms in, pressing the hilt to her breasts above her heart.

"Please don't kill him yet, Katya. We need to talk to him. This incursion's different and we need to know why. To keep our people safe."

Safe, she signs—a crossing of the wrists, then an opening of the arms to show vulnerability and trust. Her eyes are numb.

I nod and get to my feet, feeling as weak and as like to tumble over as Sveta and the others think me. I pet the tuft of feathers behind Daphne's head gently. Those stitches in her hip are an ugly sight, but not half as hideous as an open wound.

I love you, I sign to Katya. Then I add, *Stay alive, my love. Alive until sunup.*

Alive until sunup: that's the nightwatchers' cry. We all yelled it—or signed it—several nights ago when the hyaenadons sprang out of the grass at us.

But Katya has already turned back to Daphne and doesn't answer. She shakes her raptor gently awake, and I slip away, more worried than I can remember being in a long season.

***

The koschei has his head bowed and doesn't look up. Resting, maybe. *Yeah, you rest while you can. At least you get to.* But his deathreaper lifts its head as I approach and it coos, so that my bones tremble. The koschei we have to keep captive, but I have no idea what to do with his tyrannosaur, how to turn it loose without getting ourselves eaten. Guess that's a problem for the morning. Got far too many problems tonight already.

I go kiss Ihira on the top of her head and pluck my kopye from her saddle. I stand, running my fingertips over the leather straps around the grip. In the fading light, I can see Katya's golden strap, leather dyed almost as bright as her hair. I blink quickly, then scrub my eyes furiously with my hands. The men here do not need to see me cry. *I* do not need to see me cry. I clip the kopye roughly to my belt, breathing hard. I use my anger at myself, at the koschei, at Daphne's injury, at this whole damn night, to get my feet moving again.

Swaying in the saddle, Dmitri rides Old Man near, though the trike's eyes roll a bit at raptor and tied tyrannosaur. The whistler must see in my face what I'm feeling. "She'll be all right," he says. "Your wife. If that one had shot Old Man…"

"What do you know about the bond between woman and raptor?" I say bitterly. "You're just a Ticktock who's stolen a trike."

His eyes are sad. "I'm a whistler, and Old Man is all I have left in the whole dry world." He holds out his hand. "Mount up. Old Man'll carry you easy enough."

"He will not. I'll run alongside."

Concern in his eyes. "You're all kinds of bruised and battered. You think Old Man is slow, but he's faster than your two feet, and that run will hurt you something."

"I'll run alongside."

He stares at me a moment. "I'm not fixin' to slave you, Sasha."

"That's what a slaver would say to get me relaxed and riding in his saddle."

He sighs. "Well. Had to try." He digs his heels into Old Man's side, and the great bull lumbers forward into the shade under the twisting trees. I cast a glance back over my shoulder, see the invader staring into the grasses with those intense eyes of his. Katya and Daphne are out there, just out of sight, though I know they'll limp over here to the open ground by the trees soon. I shiver. Maybe I shouldn't leave her. But Ihira is standing by the koschei, near enough to slash him open at need, and as *often* as needed, and her eyes and her teeth are sharp.

I hug myself briefly, then take a breath and sprint into the trees, following Old Man and his nine-fingered rider, groaning at my body's protest. We have to find the ship. We have to know if this incursion is a thing we have just defeated or if there is more fighting to be done. And if there is—how do you defeat the deathless? A chill in my heart.

Though we have fought invaders before, ripping them out of our world like weeds out of cropland soil, we still know so little about them. We know little even of the star system these invaders come from. It has been a long time since we sailed its seas and walked its prairies, a long time since we kissed its soil and buried our dead beneath a sky lit by two moons instead of rings. That system where humanity was born had only eight planets, where ours has fourteen, two of which hold life. The eight planets were named Messenger, Love, Earth, War, Father, Eater of Children, Skies, and Wet; their names are in the Founder's book. When we left, Earth was scorched and poisoned, and most humans lived on the red sands beneath the moons of War. We came here and named our planet Peace.

10

UNDER THE WHISTLING TREES, WE RACE THE DUSK. My sides burn as I run alongside the triceratops, trying to keep up. Now that I'm not on raptorback, I have a different appreciation for Old Man's power and speed. The scents under these trees are damp and deep. We couldn't hear the water from the edge of the trees, which means it's some way in and this isn't a line of Catha but a stand, or even the start of a small forest. You find those sometimes on the prairie because Catha roots travel long to reach water, and near as we can tell, the whole stand of trees is a single organism, digging its roots into wet soil but sending up new trees everywhere. So we hope to reach the water, cross it, and get out the far end of this forest quickly, but we can't be sure that we will.

My heart burns with worry for Katya. I hope she'll be all right. I hope her raptor will be, too. The Ticktock is strange, but his hands are skilled and he has Ticktock magic in his saddlebags.

He nudges Old Man closer and I eye the trike warily; its feet are large and I am not planning to be stepped on. It hurts too much to run, as it is.

"We're two," the Ticktock frets. "An unsafe number."

Like him and Ellie. But I shake my head and point at each of us in turn. "You. Me. Old Man. We're three."

He brightens at that.

"Why isn't two a 'firm' number?" I ask.

He looks pensive. "Don't know. By all rights, it *should* be. It's not made up of smaller numbers, as infirm numbers always are. Still, two isn't *safe*. It's always been that way. Ticktock homes always have three windows or five, looking out over the mountain slope. One Ticktock and two slaves makes three, and that's firm. You can keep meals cooked, beds warmed, the water clock tended and flowing with three. Just two together, there's too much work and not enough hours to do it in. So even though two is firm, it's unwise. Don't know how you and Katya manage it."

"We're four. Daphne, Ihira, Katya, me."

Dmitri lifts his gloved left hand, the hand that's missing a finger. "*Four*'s an infirm number," he reminds me.

"That doesn't make any sense."

"Doesn't have to make *sense*. Numbers just *are*. Carved right into the skin of the universe like the fine lines in the skin of your fingertips."

"But why?" I ask. "Why do you think that?"

He gazes down at me from his saddle and shakes his head. "Sasha, Ticktocks don't *make* the world the way it is, they just keep the time. If you don't watch the time and keep your numbers firm—the number of windows, number of slaves, number riding over the plain—then time eats things away a little faster, little easier. Eater of Children ate away my finger even while I was still in the womb."

"Eater of *Children?*" I whisper, a bit horrified. That is the name of a planet orbiting the sun our ancestors fled—but that is not the tale *I* would have chosen to carry with me to Peace.

He gives me a wry look. "You nightwatchers have your Grandma Yaga, cracking bones for marrow in her walking hut. We have Eater of Children. Old Time himself. He has a starvation in his belly and bones."

I stare at him, aghast, as I pant alongside his trike. All this talk of firm and infirm numbers and slaves and work. What do the Ticktocks have so much 'work' *for*, anyway, up there inside their mountain fastnesses where the red rain can't get at them? Though I suppose there aren't a lot of cornfields in the mountains—but I always thought they raided for their food. I wonder how many Ticktocks there *are*? Maybe too many for raids to feed. Dmitri's few tales are tales of hunger; even his gods are hungry.

Two seems like a good enough number to *me*. "Anyway," I tell him, "if you're relying on two slaves to do your work and *you're* not working, why not two free people working together, and no slaves at all? You would get the same done or more."

"Don't try to out-rithmetic a Ticktock," Dmitri remarks wryly. "And you're mistaken. Never been a Ticktock born didn't toil until his hands go crooked."

"What do you need slaves for, then?" I demand.

"It's the *kind* of work," he says, then changes the subject. "You think there might be others at the lander?"

My throat is dry. "One man, one ship. That's how they've done it before."

He chews the inside of his cheek. "But, as you said, this one's not like before."

"No. No, he isn't."

"You see his eyes?"

"I was standing right in front of him," I remark.

"That man's clock tells all *kinds* of wrong." Dmitri looks pensive. "You said *koschei*. Wouldn't mind knowing what that is."

"One of my mother's stories. The death of Koschei the deathless."

"Wouldn't mind hearing the story."

"Well, I'd mind telling it."

In my memory, my mother tucks a few strands of my hair behind my ear while our lamp's lambeosaur oil burns low, casting flickering shadows across the hide walls of our domik, and she continues her tale. *Koschei came for the second of the three daughters next. Her mother and her brother and her younger sister had bound the doors shut with lambeosaur hide and rope soaked in yacca sap, and they had put out the fire and closed the smoke hole, so none could enter. But Koschei did. He sent his shadow in first, slinking along the ground under the wall of the domik. And because a shadow needs something to cast it, where the shadow went, he then appeared, too. He came silent and quick and stood over Vera's bedding, without waking her kin. He stooped and touched her cheek with fingers cold as a corpse. Her eyes shot open and she would have screamed, but he kissed her and stole her scream and stole her breath and stole her ghost. She had her eyes open and she cried and tears were hot on her cheeks, but when the kiss ended, the tears dried and there were no more, not ever again. No tears or laughter or cry of love or cry of pain. Just the empty girl. Koschei's eyes burned hot in the dark because he had a belly full of ghost, and their light woke the others…*

I shiver and try not to think about the rest of it. It is dark under the trees, and that is *not* a story to tell in the dark. Anyway, my mother's stories, when I share them, are for Katya. Not for any slaving Ticktock. Not for these trees where a lurking invader might hear. I shove *that* thought back hard too, because the last thing I want on my mind as I trot blindly beside Old Man in the gloom is the thought of another burning-eyed koschei lunging at me, shadow first, then grasping hands and pale lips.

"I hear water," I say suddenly.

Dmitri nods.

The trees before us are twisted and close, but Old Man nudges his way through and I follow. A few long, streaming pink leaves brush my cheek, soft as a kiss, but startling me and making me jump. I have been thinking too much about the koschei's kiss in that story. Ahead, I hear the triceratops splash into water, and then I'm in the open too, on a sandbank, with a wide stretch of river before me, the water slow and strong. The last light of sunset glimmers on its surface. The rings rise from the trees across the water, with a few stars coming out above us, pale and faint and far from the rings. Catha trees sway in the dusk on the far bank, and I can hear their distant whistling, as if the trees on that side and the trees on this side are singing to each other. It takes my breath away.

The water is not deep enough for spinosaurs, but I see two dimetrodons resting some distance down the bank, sailbacked and long-snouted with jaws full of teeth. Brought here by the Founder to hunt and devour the venomous hasks that infest these waters, eels as long as a raptor, the dimetrodons were bred and modified by her whitejackets for a dry climate and high aggression. I watch them out the corner of my eye, but neither slips into the water to swim upriver and come at us.

"Well, here's the river," I say. "So now we know how deep the forest goes." I take off my belt, with its kopye and canteen and mangled Founder's book, and set it beside a large white rock, too big to lose sight of. I start unlacing my boots. "Can Old Man swim?"

"He can."

"Good. So can I." One boot, then the other. I eye the other bank, noting the distance, then the current, judging its speed. Yes, I can swim this one. I take off my jacket, wincing as my muscles remind me again that today a tyrannosaur slammed me across the prairie like a child's ball. I *think* I can swim this. Clenching my teeth, I pull my shirt off over my head.

"Sasha—" Dmitri says.

I feel his gaze on me. Ticktocks slave women sometimes. But my kopye is still at my belt, in easy reach. And I'll want dry clothes in the night chill after this swim. I toss the shirt into the pile by the rock and start on my pants. I try to ignore how much it hurts when I breathe. "You afraid of a woman naked, Ticktock?"

"*Afraid* is not quite the word. You're as purple as Ihira."

I glance at him over my shoulder. His face is flushed, but that is real concern in his eyes. Now *my* face is heating. I look away quickly. "It's a good color," I mutter, tossing my pants down.

"Not on a woman, it isn't."

I toss down my underclothes, too. But I leave the wife braid bound about my thigh; that, I'll take with me as I wade, and dry it later.

"Look across the water, Sasha. At the far bank. What do you see?"

I take a look. The Catha trees are still, no breath of a breeze. If there were another deathreaper there, with plumage like the dying of the sun, it would be *very* visible. "Nothing."

"Whole lot of nothing. Look closer. *At* the water."

The little hairs on the back of my neck rise, as if I'm standing under a lightning storm. I stare at the water, trying to identify what has made me uneasy.

There.

For a moment I can't breathe at all.

Just a little way upriver, the water near the far bank is parting and rushing, white, in small rapids, around something big. Too big to be simply a submerged rock. *Big.*

I wade into the river, the water cold and bracing, biting my skin, waking my whole body. With the water at my thighs, I stand in the shadow beneath twisting branches, my toes in the soft river silt, and I stare at those rapids that don't make a lick of sense.

"What is that?" I breathe. "Why is the river *doing* that?"

Dmitri doesn't answer, so I set out to get answers of my own. Bending at the waist, I plunge my arm into the river up to my shoulder. The water's cold is sharp against my chin and neck, breasts and belly. I scoop up a stone from the riverbed. Straightening, I send it on a long arc through the air. It spins over the river, then bounces off the air above those rapids. And the air *ripples*; it shimmers like summer heat dancing. For the briefest instant, I see a gleaming surface, like steel. Then it's gone, and there is just that heat shimmer, then nothing at all, just trees and water.

"Yaga's teeth," I whisper.

Behind me, Old Man snorts, an explosion of sound that startles me.

"Found his lander," Dmitri remarks.

Right there in the river, like it was set there to cool after falling in flame out of our sky. But hidden from sight, like a spell, like wild magic tucked into a domik with raptor legs.

"It's a veil," I whisper. The koschei has veiled his lander the way he has veiled his face. But it's not a very *good* veil, when we can see the water churning about it like that.

Then something else occurs to me. My body ablaze with fury, I turn and wade back, striding up out of the river at Dmitri. "You. Ticktock." I'm not yelling—sound carries over water—but I *am* livid. "You knew where he'd be. You knew where we were *going*. Why didn't you warn us he was in these trees? You could've gotten us killed, Katya and me!"

Dmitri pales and glances down, hiding his eyes under the brim of his hat. "My clock told wrong." His voice is gruff. "I am grieved and sorry. I know a canyon, forty kilometers that way." He points. "Figured he'd hid his ship in it when I saw his beast run north over the grass. Only he didn't set it in the canyon. Seems he has other ways to hide his ship. My clock told wrong."

He looks so ashamed, my anger goes out like damp coals. I turn and squint again at that disturbance in the river. The koschei didn't hide it *that* well. Why did he put that lander here in the river? Did he need to cool it off after it fell through our sky, like a stone dropped into water in a banya? That would have made a pillar of steam, though—not very subtle. Or did he think the dimetrodons would keep people away? Or did he mean to land it here at all? Well, I have enough questions to fill a night's tales; I better see about getting answers.

Glancing at my belt and kopye, I hesitate, torn. But my kopye won't be any use to me in the water, and it will sure be difficult to keep dry.

I glance warily at Dmitri. "Touch that kopye," I say quietly, "and I hope it burns your hands off."

He shakes his head. "Your cock is safe with me."

I think he's trying to make me laugh—as Katya would—but I am too uneasy. "I'm going to see if there's a way inside that lander," I say. I hear the Ticktock suck in a breath.

I wade out until the silt falls out from under me and I have to swim. My head breaks the surface and I glance down the bank. I don't have to worry about hasks, but I *do* have to worry about dimetrodons. The two are still resting on the bank. Loud splashing behind tells me the Ticktock is riding his trike right into the river. That triceratops is conspicuous and I've half a mind to remonstrate with his rider, but I decide I haven't the time. I strike out hard for the other bank. I'm a strong swimmer, stronger than Katya, I think, though we have few enough opportunities to race each other through water. The Ticktock doesn't try to race; I hear his splashing recede behind me. That's just as well; he got an eyeful enough back there on the bank, and he can just as well wait til I get back before getting another.

The river is strong but it's slow, and the burn of my muscles as I fight its current would be pleasant if the water wasn't so cold and if my bruises didn't make me gasp and splutter and almost drown in pain. It takes longer to cross the river than I expected, but at last I reach the foaming water I saw from shore. I fight against it, and suddenly I feel the smooth, unseen surface of the lander, invisible metal slick beneath my fingertips and against my shoulder. The river slides me along it and I panic a moment, but then my fingers catch some groove in the air; there's a shelf here, and with difficulty I pull myself onto it and stand, with my feet on a hard surface I can't see, raised a third of a meter above the river. The surface of the lander is recessed above this shelf, and when I press my hands to it, it whispers like the wind and the air ripples like water. Then the surface parts before me and there is an opening in the air and darkness inside it, where an invisible door had been. The entrance is circular and two meters across, and I am standing on the lip of it. Panting softly, my hair dripping down my back, I peer inside. I can't see or hear anything within, just the splash of the water against the ship's side below my feet, and a low bellow from Old Man half across the river. So *this* is where the koschei came from. It's like I'm staring down a hole in the world. If I fell down that hole, would I keep falling for all time, like you do in a dream? Fall right through the planet and out the other side and tumble into the endless dark?

I touch the wall just inside the door, and suddenly there is light. I gasp. Not an oil lamp or a firepit, but pale light gleaming from the walls, the floor, the ceiling. Light without heat, as if it's *ringlight.* Not a hole beneath me after all, but a corridor terminating in another round door, with two identical doors to either side. The floor is pitched at an angle, as if the ship is tipped almost on its side like the domik in my mother's story after the brachiosaur girl burst out of it. The light is eerie; I don't like not being able to see where it comes from. Shivering, I take a step into that corridor, passing through the veil around this ship as I might one day pass through the veil of mist into Grandma Yaga's country. I shiver; the air in the ship is cold on my wet skin. I am stepping into a ghost place. Yet I *have* to. The icewalker strode into the ghost prairie to undo a spell; the spell I hope to undo is a spell of incursion and violence, a spell written on a whistler's flesh and in Daphne's hip, a spell of bullets that might be written in other bodies yet, and to unbraid that spell, I will enter the domain of Grandma Yaga herself if I have to.

Bracing myself against either wall with my hands, I step carefully, to keep myself from sliding down its angle and smacking up against the door I see meters below at the far end. I wish I could drop my hand to my hip and touch the Founder's book for comfort—the bullet embedded in its metallic surface proof both of the malice and violence of the koschei and of our ability to withstand it—but I am naked and the book is on the shore with my kopye, canteen, and clothes, and even if I had it on me, I wouldn't dare take my hands from the walls. Sliding or falling down this alien corridor would be *terrifying*.

It's silent in here, not a sound at all. Perhaps there are no other koschei here. In this total quiet, surely I would hear them breathing? I strain my ears, wondering if I will hear Grandmother's cackle through the gleaming walls or if I'll open a door to find her sitting at a table dining on a woman's flesh, licking human grease from her fingers or cracking a fingerbone between her ancient teeth. My hands tremble. This is a ship of the dead.

My skin crawls as I reach the doors—one before me, a second to my left, a third to my right. No matter which I enter, the other rooms will be at my back. If I step through one of these doors, what if some invader *does* slip into the canted hall behind me and puts an alien bullet in my back, where this time no Founder's book, no gift from Annika Nightwatcher, can stop it? I freeze, unable to bear that sudden thought of some quiet koschei in the ship, a deathless man who doesn't even breathe, whose heart doesn't beat as mine does, who exists in a ghost country more silent than the world in my wife's ears.

Again I hear my mother's voice in my heart: *Sasha, my little love, you have to be bold. The prairie night is full of scary things. You have to be brave.*

"Brave as Nadya," I whisper, my heart pounding. I remember Nadya in my mother's story, standing with her feathers streaming in the ghost wind on the edge of the dead prairie between the Screaming Ship and all her people. Even as I stand here, now.

"Brave as Nadya," I whisper, "brave as Nadya. Yes, Mom."

In the pale light, I turn my head and examine the door to my right. I don't see an *edge* that I can lift and pull. The gap between door and wall is nothing more than a thin line like a crack in old leather. Carefully, I brace myself against the wall by the door, then run my fingers across it. There's a soft sound like one of those farts that's more noise than air, that you don't want to admit to making. The door *rolls*, then splits in a dozen places and opens like a flower. Its pieces recede into the wall and are gone, and there's just a hole there. The room inside is dark. My heart pounds.

"Mom," I whisper, "I really wish you were here."

And suddenly anger flares in my heart. Rage at my mother for leaving me when I was only half grown into a woman, when I *needed* her. The fury is irrational because my mother died *saving* me, but the fury is real nonetheless. Shaking with it, I am able to shove back my terror and dart through the door.

Soon as my feet touch the floor inside, the room lights up the same way the corridor did. That's little comfort, because the interior is unnerving. There is an oval table with its single leg fastened to the floor, and I let myself slide in and fetch up against it. When my palms touch its surface, colors ripple across it, then glyphs of some kind, not like those in the Founder's book. I touch one and it vanishes. Swallowing, I risk a further glance around this fearsome place. Nothing in here is familiar. The space is much smaller than the inside of a domik, and there are no cushions or carpets or pouches filled with beads or bones or pretty river rocks, or any of the things a girl of the humming people might collect. All the surfaces are smooth and white. There are *things* in the walls. I don't know what any of them *are*. Some have eyes, dead eyes the size of my hand, and I try not to look at them. Above the table, several orbs the size of my fist float in the air, completely smooth like eggs but black like a tyrannosaur's eye. One is within easy reach but I take care not to touch it.

Beyond the table, set in the wall ahead and below, is another door. Leaning against the door is a thing no larger than a child's doll, half a meter tall. It gleams like bronze. It is naked, and it has a finely sculpted face, the details intricate and carved with great care. Its eyes are closed, its face peaceful. It has both breasts and a cock, the way sometimes one of the humming people is born *two* instead of one. That slows the pounding of my heart, brings a touch of calm—here is something I can understand, something I know. Among the nightwatchers, Violet is like that, and one of Katya's aunts is, also; her aunt is two, and she has a bit of a beard. Unlike her, this little doll has no hair, just a scalp smooth as an egg. No hair between its thighs or even in its armpits—that's *strange.* And it is so small. Yet it is the only thing in this ship that looks at all like one of us, the only thing unthreatening.

Still not trusting my feet or my balance in this *other* place, I make my way along the rim of the circular table, hand over hand, until I'm around it and can slide to that far door. This door doesn't open when I bump it, nor when I run my hands over it, so I slide down and sit with my back to it and look at the doll. Up close, the details are even more remarkable. It looks alive, though its breasts do not lift and fall with any breath. Gently, I touch its hand, then gasp as the bronze eyelids slide open. Its eyes are smooth and all pupil, entirely that same golden bronze as its skin.

The doll's lips open, and it speaks in a voice quiet but melodic. I don't understand its words; they are not in the language of the humming people, nor in the language of the caravans from the coast. I stare into its eyes, my heart captured by wonder. What *is* it? Was it made, or was it born? And how can I even tell, inside this lander that was shot at our planet by a man who says *he* was made and not born? Is this tiny person his doll, his captive, or his child? If his captive or his creation, she is more kinless even than I, less braided to any other lives: for surely nowhere on Peace are there bronze people like her.

"Are you a toy?" I ask her gently. Her fingers where I clasp them are cold. "Or are you a woman?"

She speaks again, and her voice is dulcet and lovely, but I still can't understand the words. There are no chains on her wrists, but surely she is not slumped against this alien door inside this alien vessel by choice. I can't imagine what a horror it must be to live trapped in this ghost place, where you can't see the stars or the rings in the sky, where you are alone and cold as a ghost. "Do you want me to get you out of here?" I ask.

She tilts her head to the side like a raptor. I point to the open door I came through. She shakes her head, sings more words at me, words whose meaning is as veiled as this lander, as veiled as the koschei's face. The strangeness of this encounter overtakes me—two women, one of flesh and one of bronze, leaning naked against the door, neither understanding the other's words. I wish I had something to give her, to clothe her or feed her or let her know that she has landed on Peace and everything will be all right.

Except that everything won't. Not nearly.

Outside, though I can't see it, it will be getting darker, and her silence grips me with sorrow. I have no way to hear her tale, her loss or her grief. When you don't know how to tell your tale or no one knows how to hear it, it becomes concealed inside you, wrapped about your heart, choking you.

I can't stay, I tell the little ghost girl. I sign the words to her. *Can you swim? If you follow me, I'll get you away from here.*

After a moment, she signs back. It is not our sign, but it looks like *I am home.*

But that can't be right. *This is no home,* I sign.

I am home.

Then why is she sad?

I gaze into the doll's eyes, and sorrow tightens about my heart. She believes she is where she needs to be, yet she remains alone. I know what that is like.

She signs more after that, but I can't understand the other signs. I am, for the first time since I was four, as illiterate as Dmitri. If Katya were here, maybe she might understand more of it, or we might unriddle this alien sign together.

I let go of her hand and rise slowly to my feet. "I have to look through the rest of the lander," I tell her, signing and speaking. "Then I'll come back." I try to tell her that promise with my eyes, too.

With effort, I walk back up the sloping floor. As I step through the door, I glance back and our gazes meet. The doll still rests against the far door, completely still, and her face, in the angle of her eyelids and her lips, conveys an expression of such loneliness that my heart breaks. Then the door slides shut between us. I lean braced against the wall beside it, feeling like Karine Nightwatcher in my mother's tale of the woman who rode into the ghost prairie to get her wife back, finding her wife among the ghosts only to discover her wife no longer remembered her name or their life together. *I am home*, the doll signed, listless as a ghost. I shiver, torn.

If our people are captive, we will cut the ropes from their wrists.

That is the nightwatcher's code. But nothing binds her that I can see, unless her bonds are veiled from my eyes the way this ship was. She is so small; I could lift her and carry her with me—but I am no slaving Ticktock, to take a woman from her *home*.

Is she a woman, and one who is two? Maybe she *is* a doll, given a semblance of life by some spell bartered from Yaga. Yet—yet—that loneliness in her face. If Katya were here, she'd sign a joke and startle a laugh from the doll's face, and then I'd know for sure, because only living, breathing things with souls and stories *laugh*. Katya would know what to do.

If she were here.

If she weren't furious with me.

If she were speaking with me.

The pang in my heart gets me moving again. Yekaterina—I have to get back to her. I turn toward the door to my left, the door that was to the center when I first came down this corridor. It opens as the other did, and I reach in and tap the wall so that the interior lights up. Then I peer in without entering.

This room is even smaller, less than four meters across. In the center is a metal container of some kind, filled with liquid. A transparent screen of some alien material covers it, separating the green and brackish fluid from the air. Tubes run into the container at different points, connecting it to the walls. The container is just large enough for a person to lie down in, and with a shock I wonder if the koschei does just that. Perhaps this is his banya, his bath or his bed; surely he does not sleep on the table in the other room with the doll, not during the long night between the stars. But if so, how does he breathe, with his bed full of green water like that? Is it a bath, then? Does he sleep on the floor beside it? Surrounding the nightmarish bed on the walls are buttons, pressed everywhere into the smooth metal like river pebbles into a dirt floor, the way a child might decorate. On the far wall is a thing stranger yet—a great sheet of glass or something like glass. Through it I can see the river; that end of the room is underwater, and the water is already dark. I peer into it, catching glimpses of movement—bottom plants, and once a bright flash like the phosphorescence of a fakl, one of the nighthunter fish that lure and devour the molluscs that graze the riverbed with their slow mouths after dark. How beautiful it must be to stare through that window at sunrise, to see the darting hues of our world's boneless fish. Is that why he landed this metal horror in the river, to see things of beauty under the water without getting wet? I wonder if the koschei landed by dark or by day. If by day, did he rise from that liquid bed and gaze out into the river for a while? Why did its beauty not capture him and hold him here? Why did he have to get up and find a gun and a tyrannosaur and come after us? I bristle with frustration. I still haven't *learned* anything about the koschei or about incursions yet to come. The only thing this lander has shown me so far is that the koschei is alien to our world, to the ways of our planet and the dreams of our hearts—and that, I knew already. At least I have confirmed he came alone. Except for that little bronze woman.

I wonder if she ever comes into this room, to gaze into the river.

I wonder if she is waiting for the koschei to come back.

I am sorry, I whisper to her in my heart. *You will be waiting a long time.*

* * *

The last of the three rooms is the largest. It is shaped like a corridor itself, with a row of canisters about my height running down its middle. The walls to either side are pocked with tiny objects like scraps of flint in a glacier in the icewalkers' mountains. These are thousands of small cases, each the length and shape of a finger, cylindrical and black. I reach out a hand instinctively, as though to pluck one from the wall, but I draw my fingers back at the last moment. Instead, I turn and peer into the tall canisters. They are filled with the same brackish fluid that has drowned the koschei's bed—if bed it was. Most the canisters are empty, but two at the end are not. One contains the corpse of an infant tyrannosaur, withered and featherless, curled up at the bottom of the container with its neck bent backward in a rictus of painful death. I swallow and glance into the other container. This one holds another infant deathreaper, but its body is misshapen. It has three small arms, two left and one right, and only one withered leg. When I press my hand gently to the glass—the first surface inside this ship that feels warm to the touch—the tyrannosaur's eye opens, and it looks *right at me*, startling a cry from my throat. I jerk back, slamming into the wall behind me and wincing. The tyrannosaur kicks its leg feebly, turning in the green liquid, its nostrils flaring—somehow *breathing* the fluid, as a fakl or a hask might.

It's alive!

Alive and—in pain.

Unlike the corpse in the other canister, this one is plumaged with feathers of flame like the beast the koschei rode into battle against us. But the flames here are darker, coals dying out in the night that filled this room before I came here. A tiny metal disc, like a page from the Founder's book, is wired to its foot, and tubes of some black material run from its body to the top of the canister. The tyrannosaur's eyelids are half closed, even as it watches me. Its one leg kicks, turning it, but there's barely room for movement. It's penned, but in a stable full of liquid and one smaller than any animal should ever be put to bed in. Something feral growls in my heart.

We ride not with reins but with will
Not with whip but with heart;
Your raptor is not your slave,
Your raptor is not your steed,
She is your breath and sinew,
She is your war cry and battle screech
Braided together, you are one being,
One story,
One song.

This tiny creature, which I could hold in my arms, is not a raptor. But the koschei rides the tyrannosaurs even as we our raptors; he should know better. What has he *done* to this one?

Desperate, I cast about, my palms aching to grip my kopye, to swing it crackling at the glass, to break the canister and free the infant. My kopye isn't here. Nor is anything else. The creature thrashes weakly in that green soup. I shout and launch a savage kick at the glass. The canister trembles but doesn't break. I throw myself at it, screaming, fists and feet. The canister begins to rock, and a few more kicks sends it crashing to the side. It strikes the floor and shatters. Fluid and glass slide down the angle of the floor. The tyrannosaur kicks feebly and I catch it by the ruff of feathers behind its neck to stop its slide. Its tiny forepaws scratch at the air and its head tilts back. I keep clear of its teeth. "It's all right, little sister," I tell it, my mouth dry. "It's going to be all right."

The dinosaur twists in my grasp, getting that one leg under it, scrabbling for purchase. Its eyes roll with pain. It struggles for a bit while I hold back a sob of rage and helplessness and try to think what to do. Those tubes inserted in its back, three to either side of its spine, should I rip them out? Or leave them? But already the creature is slumped and dying, its last breaths whistling between its teeth, its down of tiny feathers soaked in dark fluid. There is something indescribably delicate and pure about the tiny creature, with the fingernail-sized knives of its teeth, with its eyes small and just born yet ancient, eyes meant for gazing out not at a ship of metal and death but at a richly forested and sweat-damp landscape many light years away across the black and millions of solar years in the past.

Now it lies still.

I still hold it by its neck feathers, my heart beating fast.

At least it's free.

I cannot bury it in this metal place, but I press my hand to its soaked feathers and murmur in the ghost quiet of this alien ship, hoping Yaga can hear me in here: "This tyrannosaur was alone and far from any prairie or forest that would make sense to it, but its feathers were fire and its heart was too, and it fought to get to its feet, just like a nightwatcher would."

I hum for a little while. Then I can't anymore, because I'm crying. Furiously, I rub water from my eyes, though my hands are full of that fluid the dinosaur was in, and it stings a bit. This is no time to be helpless or to cry. It's time to get these koschei, these *torturers*, off our planet.

Shakily, I set the little corpse aside and get to my feet, bracing myself against one of the canisters. I glance about at the vials in the walls. I *know* what these are, now. I know it from my mother's stories, and from caravan traders' tales that tease about the oldtech wonders in the arcologies on the coast, and I know it because I have seen this deathreaper with its three arms and its one leg and its eyes full of pain. Those vials in the walls are genome capsules. This is a place where whitejackets work, or where their work is kept when they've finished. I run my hand along the cases in the walls; they're cold. Maybe each of those capsules could create a herd, a pack, a flock of new creatures. This ship is big but its rooms are small, and there's no stable in here fit to hide a deathreaper in; gazing at these capsules, I realize the koschei *grew* his dinosaur once he landed. Like the Founder herself. Only he isn't a whitejacket; he's a killer, trained for taking life rather than making it, and he must have messed up a few times with these canisters, first. These koschei, these killers, they are people without names, without song. People who know only how to scream in hate. People deathless because they are already dead inside, able to look on suffering like that three-armed infant's or loneliness like that metal doll's, and feel nothing, no need to help, no compassion, no desire to shatter the glass. They are people who cannot love or be loved and cannot be killed. I start to tremble.

What was it he said? *And behind bullets, all Mother's children, come for live your domiks, harvest your corn, use your raptors.* This wall with its capsules blurs before my eyes. The pieces all come together now, each detail, each fact strung like a bead on an armlet. I have to lean against a canister behind me so as not to faint. The koschei and whoever sent them—they're settlers. Not just slavers or raiders from another world but *settlers* from one. Like the Founder, they have come here to find food and shelter—but by *taking* it. From us. They're not just here to shoot whistlers or thieve a few triceratops from our herds. They're here to make homes for themselves, maybe on the ashes of our own. They've got oldtech like the Founder had, like the arcologies still have in part. Maybe *better* tech. Not only to conjure a tyrannosaur when they land, but something else, something in their skin, in their bodies, to heal any burn or cut.

Eighty-three days between incursions but it won't always be so. *All Mother's children, come for live your domiks, harvest your corn.* All? How many is all? Are landers going to fall out of the sky at us like rain? How many rivers will be filled with ghosts, how many whistlers killed, how many nightwatchers left like Katya to weep while their raptors bleed in the grass?

I slide to my knees. My hands grope along the floor but there's no soil in here, no warm earth to lift to my lips for a kiss, no way to give the Founder a prayer. I'm shaking. It's hard to breathe. I need earth under my boots again. I can't get to my feet, fears cycloning through my body like bits of uprooted grass in a killwind tornado on the prairie. I crawl for the door. I have to get out of here. I need out, let me out, *let me out!*

11

ONCE IN THE CORRIDOR OUTSIDE, I LEAN AGAINST the luminescent wall and breathe, just *breathe.* I am a bit dizzy. Almost I feel that this lander is breathing, too, all around me, like it is a vast water beast and I am in its belly, swallowed whole yet still alive, but with my heart just counting time like a Ticktock's watch until my breathing stops and I remain lost here for all the years, a ghost inside a ghost ship. But that is not the ship's breathing I hear—just the thunder of my blood in my ears, loud in the silence.

My body's shivering distracts me, the cold and wet on my skin a more urgent demand on my attention than any terror. I glance down at myself. Dmitri is right; I am all kinds of purple. He is also right that the color looks better on Ihira than it does on me.

Groaning like a dying girl, I get to my feet. Glancing to my right, I can see the ringlight and the lovely dusk through that external door that has a river on its other side. But I can't leave just yet. First I will keep my promise, as a nightwatcher must.

Though I shake with sickness and dread, I return to the other room to speak again with the woman made of bronze, the woman who is *two* like Violetta Nightwatcher, the woman who stands only as tall as my knee. But her room feels colder now, even more alien, and she isn't in it. I lean against the table a bit, looking around with bleared eyes. I bend and peer under the table. No doll beneath it. I slide into the far door, but it does not open to my touch any more than it did before. I beat on it with my palms. "I want to help you!" I cry.

No answer.

I press myself to that alien door, shaking. The bronze woman is gone. Maybe she passed through this door and closed it again behind her. Or maybe she climbed up the corridor, frightened by the sounds of shattering glass and the choked gurgles of the dying deathreaper. Maybe she reached the outer door and dove into the river, swimming away from this ship forever, fleeing into our world, more free than the tyrannosaur I broke out of its canister. I hope so. After a moment, I turn and follow her.

* * *

I stand again in that door in the air. After the pale ghost-glimmer of the ship's interior, even the twilight is so bright it's painful. The rings fill the sky above the river, and the summer night air feels clean and wholesome on my skin. I close my eyes and just breathe it in. All right. Time to return to Katya—and Daphne and Ihira. Nothing more to learn here. But I have new questions for our captive, and new fears, and new resolve, too. Time to leave this nightmare ship behind.

I open my eyes, and I am about to dive into the river when Dmitri's shout stops me. Old Man has waded well into the river and Dmitri has taken off his hat—his hair almost white in the starlight—and he is gesturing wildly with it. I look where he's pointing.

Oh.

That's trouble.

The dimetrodon is swimming right toward me. It cuts the water with an agility and speed you might never imagine if you only see them on land. Five meters of ferocity and hunger. It sees me—or smells me. Its sail slices the water, colored black and white like a coatl's pycnofiber plumage. My blood burns with adrenaline.

Dmitri shouts again and lifts my kopye. He has my kopye *in his hand.* I *told* him not to touch it, I told him. I am going to skin that man.

But then he hurls it, and that rod of metal with its leather straps dyed the hues of my pack flies toward me in a high arc, crossing the water as easily as the pebble I flung earlier. Dmitri is strong. Accurate, too, even in the failing light. I lean out of the door and catch the rod neatly in my palm, gripping it and flicking my wrist to snap it open to its full length, a meter and a half of gleaming steel sheathed in its case of lightning-protectant material. I feel the strength of it, the solidity of it in my hand, and more—my mother's presence, her grace as she fought, dancing on her feet and spinning this kopye like a song. I see the leather straps wrapped about the grip, Katya's gold and Nadya's green and Veroshka's midnight black. Whether my wife is speaking with me or no, whether Nadya or Sveta or others doubt me or no, at *this* moment they are with me, and my mother too, and I will fight with all their strength. I will fight like a woman with a thousand kin. A momentary rush of gratitude for Dmitri takes me—he threw me *my kopye*, as a fellow nightwatcher might—and a battle-scream of defiance fills my throat. Into that scream I pour all my grief at solitude and all my fury at the koschei and all my horror at his ship and at the tortures other living beings have endured inside it. I scream all of that at the onrushing carnivore.

Then the dimetrodon is on me, one forefoot braced against the invisible hull a meter from my feet, claws clicking at the metal. It lifts its scaled head, dripping, from the river, a head the size of my torso, its eyes cold as the dark between the stars, and *close*. Its jaws open, revealing a wild profusion of teeth—knife-like incisors for stabbing, rear teeth curved to shear flesh. There are other teeth I can't see, hidden, ready to pin struggling prey. In an instant it could lunge, fasten those jaws in my leg, and drag me, kicking and bleeding, into the water.

I dial up not lightning but flames at each end of the rod, because while lightning might dissuade that dimetrodon, the river would catch its white fire and throw it right back at me and crisp me dark as psittacosaur bacon. But dimetrodons are sensitive to heat—they have to work hard either to warm or cool their bodies—so a torch will do just fine. I jam one end of the kopye into its maw as it lunges. The creature shrieks and recoils, but lunges again before I can take a single breath. Heart pounding, I fall back through the door into the ship. Then its head fills the door and its eyes glint in the ship's eerie light. I stumble and slide back, holding the kopye at the ready before me.

Outside, faintly, I hear splashing in the river and shouting—Dmitri must be charging his triceratops across the current, coming to rescue. He won't make it in time, though.

Hungry death slithers down the corridor after me. It lunges, and I roll to the wall. Its claws scrape my calf, cutting my skin, but not deep enough to catch hold of me. I've got my kopye up lengthwise like a bar blocking my body, and those massive jaws snap shut around it. I get another glimpse of its eyes in the dark, large and liquid and ablaze with light from the burning ends of my kopye. Then it shakes its head wildly, slamming my body into the wall. I hold onto my kopye as tightly as Grandma Yaga holds onto our dead, and I *don't let go.* The world is sound and sweat, my screams and the growling of this hungry creature. I thumb the dial on the rod and fire blazes out, wild and hot, flames running up the curved wall and spilling back to lick at the creature's flanks. Its jaws release my kopye; it hisses, and I tumble, rolling deeper down into the ship. I get a fever glimpse of the dimetrodon, sailbacked and black against the fire, lashing its tail and screaming like a hundred tortured ghosts. I'm screaming, too, fire still spilling from the rod I hold. Then I smack up against one of the doors; it irises open and I drop through like a haia falling out of a net. Inside, I slam into the side of the alien tank, that liquid-filled bed, knocking away my breath. I whimper in pain. Fire roars about me, lighting up the alien surfaces. There are sparks as things in here catch fire that were never meant to burn. Another scream from above me; I look up and there is the dimetrodon, its neck charred, its jaws reaching down through the open door, its eyes filled with fury and ravenous hunger. By the light of the flames I see rows of buttons on the wall within easy reach, and I slam them with my palm. I flip switches. I crank dials. Then all around me there is light, and voices speaking in a language I don't know, and things coming alive in the walls and flashing. My heart pounds in terror. The dimetrodon loses its hold on the rim of the door and topples through, nearly crushing me as it slams into the tank beside me, spattering me with dark fluid. Tubes come loose from the tank, hissing, wires sparking as if holding conversation with my kopye in the secret language of fire. The dimetrodon lifts its head and hisses at the cacophony of light and flame and human voices. I crawl aside and its jaws slam shut over the tubes attached to the side of the tank where I had crouched a moment before. Then there's a wall at my back and nowhere to go. The dimetrodon comes at me, eyes dark as the beginning of time, jaws opening to show all those teeth. I kick wildly at its snout. My heart cries out for Katya, who always stands between me and death, and for my raptor. For the first time in forever, the first time since my mother died, I am completely *alone.*

In that moment, I am certain that I am going to die.

And like a knife through my heart, the thought: *I won't get to mend things with Katya.*

But I still have the kopye in my hands and the courage my mother taught me and the pride of a nightwatcher, and I jab one end at the creature's jaws and pour flame into its mouth—flame and more flame, uncaring if I empty the kopye of fire forever, just needing to *burn* that roaring creature out of this ship. Its head is lit up by the flames. It thrashes and flails. Its screams are horrible. Mine are, too. It twists away and leaps for the door above it, grabbing hold of the edges and slithering up fast as an eel. A flicker of long tail, and then it's gone, screeching and scrabbling its way back up the corridor. Then I can't hear it at all over the flames and the spit and hiss of things burning. Some of the flames blaze purple and green. My heart beats fast as Katya's drum. I turn off the fire from my kopye but half this alien room is burning; even the liquid in the bed tank is in flames, like a lake on the other side of Grandma Yaga's ghost prairie. A drop of something spatters on my naked arm and I scream because it *hurts.*

Move, I have to *move*!

I get up, shaky, and I force my way up the slant of the floor and then jump like the dimetrodon did, catch the rim of the door, and swing there until I get my feet against the wall, and then I scrabble up. Even as I fight for purchase, dark smoke billows up past me, searing my skin and choking my air. I keep my grip on the door but *I lose my grip on my kopye.* I gasp, grabbing at it, nearly falling back, and my fingertips brush the end of the rod—

—and then

—and *then*

—in a moment that lasts a brutal forever, my kopye, *my mother's kopye*, spins away from me in the air, the leather straps bright with color. It flashes down into the bed tank below, my rod of fire and lightning dropping into the burning fluid with a plop.

Then it's gone.

My eyes watering in the smoke, I stare at that tank and those flames, everything in me frozen with horror. My kopye. For a moment I want to slide back into the room below and plunge my arm into that flaming liquid and *get it*, because it is my strength and the strength of the pack and my wife's strength beside me and the memory of my mother fighting and singing in combat in the dawn, but if I do that, if I go after that kopye, I will *die*. That fire below me is a hungrier thing than the dimetrodon by far. With a scream raw in my throat, I turn and fight to get my torso, then my hips over the edge of the door. A great heave with all my remaining strength, and then I'm up.

I'm in the corridor. Smoke flows above my head like a dark upside-down river. The metal is warm now, not cold, under my hands, and there are a few flames still flickering in here, too. But no dimetrodon ahead of me. Coughing and sobbing for air, I climb up through the smoke and then I reach the outer door, the door in the air, and below me is the river and there is the dimetrodon, too, swimming away. Its spine cuts the water. Its tail makes waves in the ringlight on the river surface. It is a powerful animal. I didn't fully respect how *immense* they are, the dimetrodons, until I was trapped in a narrow space with one and it wanted to eat me.

I get to my knees, gasping for breath. I am alive. I am *alive.* But my hands are … empty. Watching the dimetrodon's eerie grace as it departs to leave the fire in this ship a mere nightmare behind it, a note of sadness seeps into my heart. That dimetrodon probably has a den somewhere along the bank, maybe a clutch of eggs. This river is its home, where it feasts on a red harvest of eels and stretches itself along a fallen log when it wants to, lazy and hot with enjoyment of life. *I* am an incursion here; I have come into its *home*, my kopye as brutal and irrevocable as the koschei's mounted gun, as eerie and inexplicable to the dimetrodon as the inside of that ship is to me.

But unlike the koschei, I am not planning to stay.

I dive into the water below. Its cold slap against my body shocks me out of whatever adrenaline surge I've been in, and bruises and pain wake like fire all over my body. Lifting my face above the surface, I moan and almost sink. Straining, I make for the middle of the river and then glance back. Behind me I can see the door in the air lit with a glow of interior flame. Then an immense shape blocks its light, swimming between me and the ship. I gasp, but it is no dimetrodon returning to devour me. It is Old Man.

In the saddle with water lapping his boots, Dmitri gazes down at me and tips his hat back. "I couldn't make it across the river fast enough. Dimetrodon thought it had you." He adds smugly, "Its clock told wrong."

"I can see why the hasks are scared of them," I say, treading water weakly.

"Think I can, too." His tone is dry.

He leans from the saddle, reaching his hand down, and this time I take it; he pulls me into the saddle behind him, naked and dripping from the river. Naked not primarily because my clothes are dry on the bank but because my kopye—my mother's kopye—is gone. *Gone.* I shiver in the trike's saddle, as miserable as I am cold. Even my mother has abandoned me. I have lost her kopye, I have lost the *braid.* Shaking, I have lost my strength—both my own and the strength and support I always hoped and *hoped* the other nightwatchers might give me. I shut my eyes. A foolish hope. The foolish hope of a kinless girl. *Braid her around the kopye, and the braid will be weak.* I think of the pride with which I spun that kopye, fighting hyaenas on Ihira's back or dancing the forms for raptorback combat while we pursued the koschei across the open prairie; I think of how I yearned to wield it the way *Mom* wielded it. Then I think of my wild flailing in tight quarters on the lander, lighting everything on fire and scarce landing a hit that mattered. My throat tightens. Some nightwatcher I am; I couldn't even keep *hold* of my kopye, let alone wield it right. No wonder Sveta scorned me so. Even Katya will barely speak to me now.

Dmitri lifts the whistle to his lips, blows notes I can't hear. Old Man warbles and lurches into motion, almost spilling me naked off his back into the river. Sweet Founder, this is *not* like riding a dakotaraptor. It's more like riding a boulder tumbling downhill. I grab hold of Dmitri's shoulders and hang on as the trike rolls toward the bank.

"What'd you find in there?" Dmitri asks.

Desolate, I glance back at that door red with fire, hanging impossibly above the water in front of a snarl of night-stricken trees. In the oxygen-rich air of Peace, fire burns *hot.* Fire can eat a Catha forest or kilometers of prairie. It can eat its way across the backs of a triceratops herd, leaping from one animal to the next. It can eat a settlement. Perhaps it can eat a ship, leave only a few blackened bones of metal behind. I wonder if the room with the whitejackets' capsules will burn too. And suddenly there is an answering flame in my heart, a flicker of hope, like coals catching fire when you stir them at night, even embers you thought were dead and cold. The koschei might think himself deathless and the invaders might have weapons of unthinkable rage and power, but they are *people* nonetheless. Even the dimetrodon that could rip me in half with a twist of its jaws can be scorched, can be forced to retreat. There is ferocity in my heart. We will *make* these koschei retreat. They are as fragile as any of us, in the end; they and all their craft can burn.

"A world that isn't ours," I answer Dmitri. "All gleaming, slick surfaces and spells and nightmares. Nothing that should *be* here."

* * *

When we reach the shore, Dmitri helps me down from the saddle; I cry out from the jolt as my feet hit the sand. I am shaking like a yurrup you might rip from the soil, and it hurts even to breathe. My hair smells like smoke. It takes me a while to dry and get dressed. Last, I fasten my belt, with my canteen and the ruin of the Founder's book, and by instinct I reach for my kopye before my hand recalls that it is gone. I clench my fist. I hurt. I hurt everywhere. In my skin, in my muscles, in my bones and my heart. It's a long time to barter, and it may be a good while before I have another kopye in my hand, and even when I do, I will still be *the girl who lost her kopye.*

"What's wrong?" Dmitri asks, sitting Old Man's back.

I swallow. "Sometimes you lose a thing and can't get it back."

"I am aware."

There's a strange note in his voice and I look up. He's gazing across the water at the smoke pouring from the mouth of that invisible ship, and I realize the Ticktock is thinking about the other whistler. Ellie. When he turns to me, his eyes reflect the fire. "You did right by me, you and your wife."

I don't know what to say. It occurs to me that I am unarmed and without my raptor or any means of attack or defense other than my fingernails and my feet and my teeth, and I am alone with a Ticktock—

—a Ticktock who might have just *saved* me from being eaten by a sailbacked lizard in the corridors of an alien ship. I glance up at him uncertainly; he has seen me naked and vulnerable. Though I am clothed now, I am weaponless and more naked than before. I hug myself protectively. "Thank you for tossing me my kopye, out there."

There's a kindness in his eyes that takes me aback. "Grisly thing, watching a woman get eaten. Not how I had wanted to spend the night."

"Nor I," I mutter under my breath.

"You going to walk?"

I shift my weight and wince but manage to bite back a moan of pain. I look at him, really *look* at him. There's weariness in his face. This day has dealt its wounds to him, as well. And I wonder if he slept fitfully the night before, while Yekaterina and I cavorted in the grass beneath the rings in the sky. Maybe he lay awake with his back to Old Man's warm hide, looking at the inside of his hat and wondering about the invader we were chasing. Or wondering if we might turn on him, just as a part of me feared he might turn on us. This hunt has put the deep fatigue in our body and bones, for all of us. Now he's watching me, waiting for an answer, and there isn't even a ghost of malice in his eyes.

"Think I'll ride," I whisper.

Hearing the whisper, he reaches his gloved hand to me again.

* * *

It is full dark, and we roll through the trees at a speed that makes me sway. The way I have to cling to Dmitri to stay in the saddle would enrage or embarrass or frighten me but the truth is, I hurt too much to feel anything but *tired.* One arm around Dmitri's waist—that boy is *slender,* he must only pretend to eat when we camp—with my other hand I reach for my belt and touch the Founder's book, my mother's book, feeling the hole the bullet made in it. I've come close to meeting Grandma Yaga face to face quite a few times on this nightwatch, since Katya and I and the others rode out so many nights ago. When I do meet Grandmother, I'll ask her for my Mom back. Don't know what I have to trade, though. I feel emptied out. Maybe Yaga would settle for a song about a pitched battle with a dimetrodon inside a vessel shot at us from another world. Could tell her quite a tale.

There is hardly any light at all under the whistling boughs, and I ask the Ticktock if he fears getting lost.

"Triceratops don't get lost," Dmitri tells me. "That's a thing they don't do."

Certainly Old Man doesn't seem bothered by the dark. Nor Dmitri. But the corners of *my* mind are filling with dark thoughts, though—Daphne wounded, Katya sobbing, the room with the whitejacket capsules, the koschei's talk of taking our land, the splash of my kopye into that burning tank—but Dmitri's mood seems lighter. For the first time since we've traveled together, the whistler starts *chattering*. "I'm grateful," he says. "Glad you two found me and Old Man. You said you'd help catch the man and you did. Got him tied to a tree, and his tyrannosaur too. And then lit up his ship like a midnight clockdance." He laughs. "Might tell him about *that* when we get back."

"Might," I mutter.

"Hm. You all right?" He has noticed my trembling.

"Just cold."

"You're safe, Sasha."

"No one's safe."

"Hm. Might be a true thing." He changes the subject. "Your wife, she'll be all right?"

I shut my eyes tight, remembering the fury and pain in hers. "The braid of her life is a tougher one than mine."

"I believe it. Way she went after that … 'koschei' … ready to cut him into strips of bacon."

Remembering the horrors on that ship, I whisper, "I should have let her." I press my cheek to Dmitri's back and just hold on. Dmitri is warm, and after the battle with the dimetrodon and the cold of the river and the chill of that ship… I just wish my shakes would stop.

"Whatever broke between you two this evening, you'll patch it up." Dmitri's voice gets unexpectedly soft, so that his words get inside me and start doing things there, without my sayso. "You two know each other too well, can tell each other's time, even when your clocks are telling different. I seen it."

"Thanks." I don't know what else to say.

His voice is wistful. "Thinking if I ever take a heartslave I'd want it to be like that."

There's his talk of slaves again. Irritated, I say, "Don't you Ticktocks ever *wive*? Braiding two lives, two stories together?"

After a moment: "Can't say that we do." He adds, "Two's an infirm number."

"Oh, will you ever shut up about your infirm numbers?" I snap. "Numbers aren't firm or infirm outside of ridiculous Ticktock talk."

He glances over his shoulder at me like I've just said the sky isn't blue.

I take a breath. "Anyway, you should try it. Try seeing other people as companions and not *slaves*."

"You're my companions."

I'm not sure if I should feel insulted or not.

Then he adds quietly, "Ellie was a companion."

"Oh." A pang of guilt. I think of her body unburied and the koschei's clockwork irises spinning, and Grandma Yaga cackling over a feast of dry bones. I should have sung a tale for Ellie, but I didn't even know her story. Still don't. Maybe Dmitri does.

Around us, the trees press dark and close, and we ride in silence now. Part of me regrets it. His talk was distracting me from the pain all over my body.

After a while he remarks, "You're trying to say that because we don't wive, we don't *love.* I don't think that's true."

"You can't love a slave," I tell him, and I search for words he'll understand. "You can tell yourself you do, but it's not the same. You can only love when you're both free to range wide over the prairie, riding faster than wind and laughing at life and always coming back to each other at night. You treat your love like a watch you put in your pocket, Ticktock, and that clock will tell wrong. It'll wind down and die. That's not love."

He chews on that a moment, and as he does I feel a pang of something, some dark feeling. I recall Katya's fury at me when I misspoke for her, or when I struck the knife from her hand, or when I clutch her to me too tight, when I cry "Don't leave me" but she needs to. She's all I have, and so I've forgotten that I don't *have* her; I just ride *with* her, and she rides with me. And if my mother hadn't died gasping in my arms, leaving me kinless, if I hadn't lost so damn much, that would have been all I needed, from the start. My throat tightens. I don't want to look too close at what's in my heart right now. What I see in there might look just a little too much like a Ticktock, and it might scare me. "Is that why you can only think in terms of *heartslaves*?" I whisper, my cheek against his back. "Because you lose so much, *starve* so much, and you're terrified of losing more? So that whatever or whoever you want to have near, you lock them up tight in your mines, thinking that way you won't lose them."

"Can't entirely hear your whispers," Dmitri says.

But I am not inclined to repeat myself. Instead I ask him softly, "What was she like? Your Ellie?"

His voice goes hoarse. "She liked to sing."

"She was one of us, then? One of the humming people?"

"She was."

Such anguish and yet such affection in his tone. This man was born a Ticktock but he yearns for love. I can hear it in his voice. He thinks he wants to own a slave, have the things his people have, the things they tell him to have. Yet what he really wants is what Yekaterina and *I* have, or what we *could* have if I'd let go of her just a little, as she asks. Maybe he was raised under rock and soil in the cramped places where the Ticktocks mine and make things, where there isn't sunlight or breath of prairie air—yet even down there, hiding his hand in a glove and looking in vain maybe for more warmth in his mother's eyes, even down there *love* was what he longed for, because love is what all human beings long for and not even the Ticktocks can change that, no matter how deep they tunnel in their rock, no matter how many slaves they bind.

"She sang at dawn," he says, "and she sang at noon and she sang at dusk. She'd taught her styracosaur to warble with her, nearly in tune."

"She rode a styrac?" I imagine the beast, the high crest of jagged bone, the small eyes, the bit of waddle most styracosaurs have.

"She did. Young thing that liked to prance. He kept trying to mate with Old Man. Met Ellie and her styrac the day I met Old Man, in fact. I'd run from—well, I'd run a long way. Mines were far behind. Figured dying on the prairie beat dying in there. Didn't have water or food at all. Not even this hat; that came later. So I figured out here was where my watch would stop. Was getting acquainted with dying, best I could. Sat myself down in the grass, plucked a bit of it and chewed on it, the way you've seen me do. You should try it. Is mighty calming."

I make a small noise that is almost a laugh.

"Well. There I sit. The rings are the most beautiful I have ever seen. We don't live *in* the mines, you know. We have mountain terraces outside the caverns. In the warmer part of the day, or at night if you're wrapped in enough wool, you can stand out there and smell the snow in the air and the stands of kedr on the slopes. Day like that, you can see the whole world, and the rings are white fire in the sky. Except I had never seen them like *this*. Like I saw them that day when I sat dying on the prairie. I gazed up at them and thought maybe—maybe this wasn't a bad way to breathe my last."

I smile, not at the thought of death but at the realization that the Ticktock is *telling me a story* at last. He had tales in him, after all. Even if his mother never gave him any, he'd found at least *one* he could tell. Something in me relaxes. It's unnatural to be among people who don't have stories, who have only the ticking of a clock and a dream or two about what they might have, who see others as possessions, not as people with stories of their own. But maybe *this* man isn't like that. He has a story or two. And he threw me my kopye—even if I lost it after. I close my eyes and listen to his tale.

"There I sit," he says, "smelling the grass, the sun cooking my skin a bit. Then there's this warbling nearby and a huff of breath. I turn my head and there's Old Man. This hoary old bull, all by himself, no herd anywhere. Slow and tired and left behind, his hide as scarred as my heart, and one horn missing. And I saw that and I knew he was my brother. I took off my glove, showed him my hand with my finger missing. Called to him gentle and walked to him slow as snowflakes melt. He let me touch his frill, and I talked with him awhile. Didn't have a saddle, but I got it in my mind that I might die more comfortably on his back than on the ground. I'd never ridden anything before. It took some doing to climb up here, but he didn't mind. I held on to his frill and yipped at him and I don't know if he somehow heard what was in my heart—because I sure had no whistle—but quick as thought, he started pounding through the grass, and I was crouched on his back just laughing like I'd split. You can't imagine what I felt."

"I think I can," I say, and I wish Ihira were here.

He laughs, and it's a good sound. "Suppose you can. Well, I rode him until he stopped to eat again, which was near sunset. A trike may not be fast, Sasha, but he's got endurance like the planet itself. And he'd been galloping so hard under me that we near caught up with the rest of his band. That's where Ellie found us. She was riding back, checking for stragglers. She whistled and Old Man sprinted right to her. She looked at me clinging to his frill and laughed hard as Yekaterina does. 'What are you doing?' she asked. 'On his back like that without a saddle?'

"Well, I was feeling hot from the day and thirsty too, but my heart was ticking like a clock and I felt I could drink the sun and breathe the sky, so I said, 'Kiss me, and I'll tell you my story.' And she did. And I…"

He trails off.

I smile, my cheek pressed to his back. "What color was Ellie's hair?"

"Flame. Like the last sunset in the whole world."

"Red? I thought you said she was one of ours."

"Yours wive sometimes with the forest people."

I think of Sveta Nightwatcher with her head half-shaven and battle sigils on her scalp and her eyes and hair both crimson. "Sometimes."

We're quiet for a bit. His triceratops keeps rolling under me, but I've gotten used to it. Or maybe I'm just half asleep. The trees are vague shadows against the dark, neither ringlight nor starlight making it through their boughs. A breeze stirs those unseen branches, and their melody is quiet and eerie. Catha trees at night usually comfort me, but tonight they only deepen my sense of desolation. I am alone in a dark world full of ghosts, without my kopye, without my nightwatcher pack braided to me, without Ihira's feathered body under my saddle, without my wife's kisses or her laughter that banishes midnight and puts ghosts to flight. Dmitri's sharing of a story lifted my heart but now my solitude returns and cuts into me sharp and knifelike. Riding behind a Ticktock with fires behind me and who knows what perils and losses ahead, I might as well be a captive trussed up and on my way to the mines, as small and alone as I feel tonight.

Then I hear a sound from Dmitri, and I gasp. "You're crying."

"Imagine I am," he says hoarsely. "Been holding these tears back too long, and no burial to shed them at. Eyes and heart have to catch up all at once. Sasha, my clock has told wrong since the day I was born, and I've no way to set it right."

I lift a hand, as if to touch his shoulder or his hair, to offer some consolation. But what solace can I offer? He is a *Ticktock*. Old anger flares in my heart. I don't need his tears right now. Neither does his Ellie, unburied behind us on the prairie with her eyes gazing up at the night sky. I cried all my tears when I held my mother dying; I have none left.

"Our tears can't help the dead," I tell him sternly.

"Tears aren't for the dead. They're for us."

I close my eyes, feeling Old Man roll beneath us. "Tears cost too much."

* * *

Soon the Catha trees part before us, and out from under the branches there is starlight and ringlight, soft on the grass, and we aren't lost after all. There, a short way to our left, is the deathreaper, bound between two boles at the brink of the wood, nostrils flaring, one eye watching us emerge from the forest shade. Katya's ropes and mine still hold it.

"Those are good ropes," Dmitri mutters.

"They're *our* ropes," I murmur sleepily, "and those are nightwatcher knots."

"*Damn,*" he whispers.

Nearby, with her back to Daphne's sleeping bulk, Yekaterina has started a small fire and stretched strips of triceratops bacon on a rock near the coals to heat them. Ihira sits nestled protectively against Daphne, her head and a clawed hand set on Daphne's feathered shoulder, one eye watching the bacon crisp and sizzle. I feel a rush of relief, seeing my wife and my raptor, inhabitants of my more familiar world. My face must be like the icewalker's in the tale I told, approaching his lover's domik at last. I *have* been walking the ghost prairie tonight. Nearby, our captive rests, unveiled and pallid but without fresh injuries, seated against the tree I tied him to.

I call out to him as we approach, rolling on Old Man's back. My voice is raw with the night's anguish. "Burned your ship. Your *bullet.* Burned it like kindling. It's gone."

He just watches me, his eyelids slitted.

My temperature rises. "Did you hear me, koschei? Your ride home is *ash.*"

"More soon," he says.

Then my weariness hits me like a charging hyaena. Old Man sways to a stop five meters from the fire. Katya is staring into the flames. I don't know if she has even heard us. A good thing I left *Ihira* to watch. My raptor lifts her head and chirps at me, plaintive, maybe confused to see me on another dinosaur's back. I chirp back, telling her to stay where she is. I don't want her rushing toward me and scaring Old Man into a skitter; I'd probably fall right off his back, and I flinch at the thought of what *that* would do to my bruises right now.

"Brought back your wife," the Ticktock calls to Katya.

She looks up at last, pale with grief, and a grim anger is burning in her eyes. I swallow. There's a conversation we need to have, and I am already so fatigued. But I'm a nightwatcher; I don't get to leave homes undefended or a story unfinished just because I'm tired. That's a thing we don't do.

Then my wife rises and walks over, and I all but fall from the saddle into her arms, my bruises flaring to life and a cry escaping my lips.

"She's hurt," Dmitri tells her. "Exhausted. Bit burned. Fights like a medved when trapped."

Katya gets an arm under me and helps me toward the fire. Leaning into her, I limp and whimper. Ihira watches me with a worried trill. Daphne is awake now but looks dazed. *You and me both, girl.* The pressure of Katya's arm on my bruised body makes me wince. My breath is ragged but I will *not* sob, I will not collapse, because my wife needs me and the whole world is at risk and this is no time to cry and be useless. I let Katya settle me beside Ihira, and I lean gratefully into my raptor, her feathers soft against my face. Katya gets salves and yurrup oil from her saddlebags and opens my jacket, and I let her. She's gentle for all her fury, but I wince at her touch on my burns and bruises. Seeing the ferocity in her face as she examines my wounds, everything I felt in that alien lander comes rushing back at me. How I thought I was going to die. How I thought I might not see her or speak to her ever again, might have only Grandma Yaga's wrinkled face to look at for the rest of time.

I'm sorry, I sign.

Hush, I'm trying to tend you.

I don't need tending, I need you to hear me. What I saw out there—it scared me, Katya. I can't face this if we're angry at each other, if we aren't together as wives should be, braided tightly as woman and raptor. I swallow. *Katya, I am sorry. I love you, Yekaterina, and I am so, so sorry.*

Her hands freeze. She lifts her face, searches mine. She signs carefully, *What you sorry for, Sasha? Specifically?*

I meet her gaze. *Your Daphne was hurt and near death and you had the battle-fever and I didn't back you up. I know I wounded your heart. If I had Ticktock magic, I'd find that wound and sew it up. I am sorry, my love.*

She dabs a little more salve carefully on my right breast, and I whimper through closed teeth.

This one's blistering, she signs after a moment.

I noticed. I groan. *Yekaterina, say something.*

The anger in her eyes flickers out. Now she looks almost as tired as I. She touches my cheek and I lean into her hand like it's all the warmth left in the world, closing my eyes and trembling a little from the exertions of the night and the exertions of the heart. I open my eyes when her hand pulls back.

She packs away the salve and I watch silently. Nearby, I can hear Dmitri settling his trike for the night. He's giving us space to talk, and I'm grateful. Then Katya signs, *I know why we need him breathing, Sasha. But look. You don't always get to decide things* for *me, wife.*

I want to say, *You decided for* me *that we'd kill him*, but I bite that back and keep my hands still because my mother didn't raise a fool and we need to be listening to each other right now. We're too tired to be setting our tempers on each other. So I just watch her hands and listen to her heart.

She closes the flap on her saddlebag and her hands tremble, just once. She turns and looks at me through a sheen of tears. *You don't get to decide how I speak, to those who can't read my hands. You don't get to decide whether I ride out or stay. And you don't get to decide who I kill. I wield knife and kopye at need. You don't get to decide for me. I love you, Sasha, and I will love you when I'm gray, but sometimes you hold on to me so tight you choke me.*

"I'm sorry," I whisper. "I had to stop you then. I had to."

I know it.

And now I'm near to breaking, because she's right—she wields knife and kopye where she sees need—and because I'm right, and because I have no kopye to wield.

She sees it in my face. *Sasha, what is it?*

All my decisions have gone wrong. I choke. *I got Daphne hurt. I hurt you. I lost my kopye. I lost it, Katya. The kopye my mother gave me when I was a slip of a girl still falling off Ihira's back. I lost the braid. I am a weak strap, Katya. I'm a—*

She takes my face in her hands and kisses me, fiercely, and she tastes like tears. I lift my hands to hold her face too but she forces them down. There is something angry in her kiss, but something needful also. She bites my lip, and I make a small, soft sound into her mouth.

She ends the kiss and rubs my nose gently with hers, and now I'm a tangle of feelings and tears, for all I told Dmitri that I don't *do* tears. "Some nightwatcher I am," I whisper.

Something has softened in Katya's face. She lets go of me and searches her saddlebags. She pulls out a strap of leather dyed gold as her hair, gold as summer sun. Her fingers are warm as she takes my hand. She doubles the strap up and braids it gently around my wrist. My heart is so full, I can't breathe. When she's done, she kisses my palm, then lets go and signs, *You are not alone, Sasha. My strength rides with you. The others can give you theirs again when we get you another kopye.*

I blink quickly, glad I can sign and not speak because I don't trust my voice right now. *If they do.*

You're a nightwatcher, she signs.

A nightwatcher without weapon or defense.

Her hands are fierce. *You're the nightwatcher* I *ride with. Armed or no.*

The leather strap is cool and soft against my skin. And strong, like my wife. I nod.

Grandma Yaga's done cursed us, it's certain. Katya's eyes flash. *But you didn't get Daphne hurt, Sasha. I did. I could have ridden her faster, or lassoed the invader first instead of his gun.*

I could have said: Let's turn back, let's get the others.

But you didn't, and neither did I. I was wrong to blame you, Sasha. If we'd turned back, we wouldn't have him tied to that tree. We wouldn't have whatever you learned in the wood tonight.

Didn't learn much.

Much or little, you can tell me later.

I peel my heart open and ask softly, "Would you really kill me dead, Yekaterina?"

She shakes her head. The slightest hint of her wry smile. And tenderness in her eyes.

Only if you deserved it, she teases. Then she lowers her eyes. *I know you were right, Sasha. I do know. Nightwatchers don't kill their captives.*

No, we don't, I sign.

We aren't forest people on a raid.

No, we aren't. Slowly, I sign, *Vigilant and not vicious.*

She signs back, *Compassionate and not cruel.*

Clever and not clumsy. Except I am. *So* clumsy. I dropped my kopye and my strength into a burning ship and I can't get it back. But Katya has still braided her own strength about my wrist. I gaze into her face, my eyes shining. I smell the bacon burning but she doesn't appear to care.

Nearby, the koschei murmurs some chant full of words I don't know, and the sound of it riles me. It's an unwelcome incursion into our conversation.

He tries to provoke me, Katya signs. *Been trying all night.*

I am aware. What is he singing?

No song of ours.

I listen to it a moment. It is strange and … cold. Its measures quick like feet walking too fast. And with too little variation. Less a melody than a stomping in the grass: defiant, arrogant, a tyrannosaur rider's tune. I don't like it.

You and I, we'll mend, Katya signs. And she touches the wife braid on my sleeve. *I've put some work into this braid of ours. It's worth more than a chance to knife that man. I'm sorry, too.* She glances at the koschei, and her eyes glint in the firelight. *I burned so hot, Sasha. I've got so much rage and grief and shame like claws in my heart, I don't know what to do with it.* Her eyes fill with tears. *Daphne might never run again, not like she needs to.* She caresses Daphne's neck. The dinosaur twitches in pain, and when Katya's face crumples, it near breaks my heart. My wild golden girl, of the laughter and the lasso, is hurting more than I've ever seen her hurt.

I love you, Katya.

And I you, Sasha. I you. She touches my arm. *Now come here and cry with me.*

They'll see.

Let them see. One's with us and the other's tied to a tree. Let them see what they like. You come here.

She takes me in her arms and I take her in mine, never mind my bruises. I pillow her head against my breasts, and I hold her, I just hold her, grieving for her and so intensely grateful for her, for her strength and her wild courage and her deep heart and her love for me. She makes a fist against my shoulder but then opens it and grips my jacket and just holds on. Caressing her hair, I tell her, "Daphne will be all right, Daphne will be all right, I know she will, I know it." She can't see my lips, but she can feel my voice vibrating as I hold her, can feel my care though not my words. "It's going to be all right, it's going to be all right," I keep saying, while Dmitri approaches and tosses saddlebags by the fire and Old Man lifts his head and bellows once to the stars, and the koschei keeps chanting like he's trying to call ghosts out of Grandma Yaga's country. Let him. He can call a thousand ghosts; they can't pry my Katya from my arms.

* * *

It feels like we have lived twenty nights in one, yet it is still early dark with long watches ahead. Katya's weeping ceases. She shudders in my arms a while, then rubs at her face with her hands. I get her one of her scarves from Daphne's saddlebags. Katya gives me a grateful look. Yes, we'll be all right. If not tonight, then later. I hope it. Right now I ache inside and out, so much I can't tell anymore which pain belongs to my heart and which pain belongs to my flesh. I have been clobbered by a tyrannosaur, ripped at by a dimetrodon, scorched by fire and choked by smoke, and threatened by a koschei, and I feared I might never again see my wife. I need sleep the way I need air. Yet one of us has to watch. And my wife has had the greater shock tonight. "I'll take first watch," I tell her. Then sign, *You take second, then wake me for third.*

That brings her out of her grief. *Give me first watch.*

No, you need rest.

So do you. What are you going to do, Sasha, if the invader gets loose or some threat comes out of the grass? Glare at it?

I stare at her in shocked hurt, but at her next words, I realize she isn't alluding to my lack of a kopye.

You're probably too sore to even stand right now, she signs, *don't pretend you aren't.*

I'll stand if I need to. That whisper in the back of my mind—*weak, you're weak, Sasha*—is getting louder, and it sounds like Sveta's voice. I have to do *one* thing right tonight, and get my Katya some rest.

Stubborn, she signs wearily.

I am.

All right, I'll take second, she signs. *But first I need to show you a thing. Found something in the grass.* Her eyes are grim so I know it's important, but I also know she's trying to distract me from the agony my body's in. *Dragged it here, it was heavy. Daphne's hurt, couldn't make her carry it.* She nods toward my right, and I see where she has laid the koschei's swivel gun down, at the edge of the firelight. I gasp, seeing again how long the barrel of that weapon is. This thing was not made to be held like a kopye but to be mounted on a tyrannosaur saddle. Loud in my memory is the thunder of it and the chopping of the bullets in the grass.

Dmitri comes over, crouches beside us, sets a shallow pan over the fire, and pours in a can of beans. Between that and the scent of charred bacon, my belly growls like a dimetrodon. The whistler gives the wasted meat a look of quiet distress, and I remember his tale of hunger among the Ticktocks. But I keep my own gaze on that metal monstrosity in the grass.

He follows my gaze, and his eyes widen. "Now *that* is a deathclock," he mutters.

A what? Katya signs.

I give her a wry glance.

Dmitri reaches for the weapon, keeping his voice low. "Old ones called these guns and cannon, but the truth is they're another kind of clock, and built like one. For timing the tread of death. I can see how it's put together. Look. You press there—but I wouldn't recommend it—and that will send the bullets screaming. That belt of bullets over there by the grass, that feeds in—here. This…" He hesitates. "I think this might be a lock. Keep it from firing when you don't want it to, or telling a time of death you aren't ready to hear."

I eye it skeptically, but I am oddly comforted to know the thing has a *lock*.

"This long part, that's the barrel," Dmitri continues. "And I think *that* there is where the grit is."

"The *grit*?"

"Grit is fine black powder, like the ash of dead hours, only it doesn't crumble at the touch the way ash and the hours do. In every Ticktock home, at the center, there's a clock that tells time by water. This one tells time by fire. Your kopyes, shaped in the arcologies, they don't use grit like this, but liquids." He crouches closer to the gun, runs his fingertips along its barrel. His voice is soft, almost reverent, weighted with the past. "Peoples that came to this world, Ticktocks and icewalkers and humming people alike, we all learned a long time back: you can't tell time with fire, because fire will burn and destroy everything you want to devote time *to*. So we left almost all of our deathclocks behind on the other side of the stars, almost all. Clockmaker didn't expect anyone would *bring* them here."

Yet you've seen ones like it before, Katya signs.

He reads the question in her eyes. "Hm. There's a few like this on the mountain peaks, half encased in ice. Oldtech. For remembrance, not for use. Bigger than this but much like it in shape and function. Thought they were the only ones on this world."

"This gun doesn't come from our world," I remind him.

There's more, Katya signs.

She reaches for her saddlebags in their heap near the fire, takes from beside them a small bundle wrapped in a saddle blanket. She unrolls it before us. Inside are two guns of gleaming metal with stocks of polished wood, much smaller than the one the Ticktock has been fondling. In length, each is the span from my wrist to my elbow. They are nearly identical, except one has symbols etched into its stock, sigils as alien to my eyes as those on the Ticktock's needle.

Dmitri lifts the other one in his hands, turning it, fascinated. He presses a small lever, and the device *opens* and he peers inside. "Sixteen bullets," he mutters.

Katya points to the other gun, the one with the sigils, but she is careful not to touch it. Her eyes flash with fury. *That one has fewer. It's the one he shot Daphne with.*

I lift that one and set it beside my hip. *Then I'll make sure he doesn't get it back.* I nod at Katya, and her eyes shine with love.

Dmitri shows no sign of returning the other. A wild light flickers in his eyes and I catch my breath, wondering suddenly if the Ticktock might barter such alien tech to have his exile rescinded, to claim some place among his coldhearted people. A vision afflicts my mind of Ticktocks with guns coming at us out of the grass, and our charging, battle-screaming nightwatchers stopped suddenly by the crack and fire of these evil weapons, raptors crumpling beneath us as we ride. I hold out my hand for the gun, but Dmitri gives me a look. After a moment, I withdraw my hand. Loath as I am to concede him that weapon, I have no persuasion I can use. He and Old Man have done their part in the hunting of the koschei. And he stitched up my wife's raptor as deftly as you might stitch an unraveled sleeve. And he has lost more to this incursion than we have. He has as much right to the loot as we.

Still, I shiver.

Maybe we should find a quiet place away from the trees and bury these guns where they'll never be found. Or feed them to fire, like the koschei's ship. And yet—this one by my hip is small enough to carry. If I can get it back to the other dakotaraptor riders, we might learn something from it about the invaders and their way of battle. Maybe find some seer from the skies or scholar from the coast who can decipher the sigils. If there is a spell on that gun for the working of untimely death, I'd like to know what it is and how to unspeak it. I'll never find that out if I cast it aside or bury it.

I go to my saddlebag, grunting at the pain in my limbs, and I take out a bit of leather cord and make a quick loop and catch at my belt to hold that slender gun. It is not a thing I want to leave about loose where it might do as it pleases when we aren't looking. I lift it before my face. Its polished wood and metal reflect the sheen of the fire. Why would anyone need such a "clock," or the other, the big one that maybe can tell the time of death for hundreds of people? There is a strange and alien beauty to these devices, but it is a cold beauty, even in the firelight. They do not burn and crackle and sing in the air the way a kopye does. I recall how the koschei plucked this one from his belt and fired it at Daphne. There was a brutality to his movement, but no grace. This is not a weapon my mother Annika Nightwatcher would ever have wielded, nor chosen to teach me. Yet I take everything Dmitri said of it and store those words in my memory, in case I should need them.

Then I put the gun away on my belt. It is heavier there than my kopye was.

I think of the lander, the koschei's "bullet," the bronze doll who I really hope escaped, the room with its canisters and its tortured creatures and its vials of as-yet uncreated life waiting in the walls. *...come for live your domiks, harvest your corn...* Maybe that is the spell written on the gun: a death curse against an entire people. The koschei is not a Ticktock. He doesn't need slaves. His people don't need us to do their work. They just want to mow us down like corn and *replace* us.

I look to Katya. There is fire in her eyes, the same as mine. Dmitri's eyes, also, are full of strange thoughts. And our raptors' eyes shine like metal, too, in the firelight.

"All right." My throat is tight. "Let's talk to him."

Katya tenses, then nods. She rises and takes my arm, and I let her half-lift me to my feet, clenching my teeth against the pain. I don't have time tonight for pain or sleep or shame over the loss of my kopye. This deathclock at my belt and its metal kindred, and that veiled lander burning on the river, they have told me the time. It's time to get more answers from the koschei. Answers about his kind and how to stop them.

12

AGAIN THE TYRANNOSAUR STRAINS AGAINST THE creaking ropes. Katya's ropes hold, and under the soil, the Catha roots intertwine in a net too strong for any deathreaper to tear loose. No tree will be ripped out of the ground tonight, no matter how the creature struggles. At last, the muzzled tyrannosaur settles and just watches us, its eyes like flakes of night.

Katya, the Ticktock, and I are seated before the koschei's tree in a semicircle, as though we are a Three summoned to hear a crop dispute or consider judgment over a thief or an abuser in the domiks of our people. Behind us, there is fresh bacon sizzling at the fire. It will be ready quick; the scent of it makes my belly growl like a medved, and I am not going to get so distracted that it burns. But for the moment, I do have my gaze fixed on this koschei. I face him without any kopye in my hand, without the strength of the nightwatch braided to me. Yet I do not face *this* horror alone; Katya and the whistler are both here. The koschei's irises rotate and gleam, reminding me that he is alien, though his body is flesh and bone and blood.

"Your eyes see?" the koschei taunts me. "Good eyes? See bullet?"

"I did." The memory of it screams in my mind and I shove it back.

He smirks, like a boy at a barter about to steal a kiss.

"You were growing tyrannosaurs in there," I say. "Maybe you grew that one in there." I jerk my thumb toward the watchful deathreaper. "But faster than a raptor grows."

He lifts his chin. "Fast. Slow. Mother chooses."

His chin fascinates me. There is no night growth of stubble on it. This young man doesn't even have eyelashes. He is hairless as the doll on that ship. *Wombgrown,* he called us. As if he himself is a thing that is *made*, like that tiny woman of metal and sign.

"Did they grow *you* like that?" I ask.

He doesn't answer. Dmitri's eyes glint in the ringlight, and I suppress a shiver, grateful for the fire on the koschei's lander. If the Ticktocks ever captured such oldtech—ever learned to *grow* slaves, both human and tyrannosaur—

Everything in me goes cold at the thought.

And the koschei … what if this strange warrior from the stars *isn't* fifteen, as he appears? What if he is five, or four? What if he was grown inside that bullet, in that tank of dark fluids and tubes? What if this—his incursion on Peace—is the first time his feet have touched soil? *Millions in blood*, he said. What if there is oldtech coursing through every vein in his body, growing sinew and marrow, even now, even tonight? Is that where his defiance comes from, too? He is alone, wounded, and tied to this tree; he should be trembling, but he isn't. There should be droplets of sweat beading his bald scalp; there aren't. People held captive smell like fear, but there is no scent of it on him, faint and unpleasant beneath the cook-scent of bacon sizzling behind us. He *should* fear us, but he doesn't. It's the most unnerving thing about him, more than his clockwork eyes or his deathclock guns or his claim that he was never grown inside a woman's body. My mother's tale scratches at the back of my memory: *And her brother, wanting to protect her, waited awake by her bed, and there he caught Koschei at last, in a net of Catha fiber. He dropped a heavy stone on Koschei's shadow, too, to pin it in place and prevent him from escaping the way he'd come. From his hip he drew the kruschev knife the feathered merchant had traded him, and it flashed in the blazing light of Koschei's eyes. But Koschei neither trembled nor moaned in fear. And when her brother plunged the knife into his heart, Koschei laughed a cold, dry laugh. Because his life was not there in his chest and it was not there in their domik, and he could not die. He had no fear.*

I remember the terror pumping in my blood when the dimetrodon, defending its home, fell through that corridor after me, all jaws and rage. Surely this young koschei felt *something* like that when Katya's lasso ripped his gun from its swivel, when I thrust him from the saddle, when he tumbled into the grass, when Ihira's claw hooked him and tore open his belly, spilling his insides like raw meat?

"You are alone," I tell him, "among people you have hurt. Do you *understand*? In your body and bones, do you *get* that? There is no going back, for you. There is no going home."

"This, home."

"It sure isn't. Not for you."

Behind me I hear the crackle and crisp of the bacon. He is listening to it, too. I can tell. I recall how he demanded food before Dmitri and I went looking for his lander. Tied to this tree after wounds that should have been mortal, perhaps the koschei is hungrier than he has ever been.

The thought apparently has occurred to Dmitri, too. He leans forward. "I imagine you might desire food to eat," he drawls. "Even water to drink. It's just possible. You might think about that."

Her eyes hot with anger, Katya signs, *You better think long and well.*

"Nightwatchers don't starve their captives," I say firmly. "But it *is* customary to share a tale when you sit yourself at another's fire. So give us a tale, koschei, and we will give you meat as you've asked."

"Tale," he grunts, his face full of mockery.

"Tell us how you came here," I clarify.

"And when more are coming," Dmitri adds.

And about these guns you bring to our planet, Katya signs, *and whether others will bring more. These guns I hate. Our planet doesn't need your guns.*

He ignores her hands, and I keep the anger from my face. Why does everyone we've met these past few days not understand sign? When I translate for Katya, the koschei sneers and says nothing. The irises in his eyes spin faster.

I lean a forward a little. "Why are your eyes like that?" I ask. "What do you see with those clockwork eyes?"

He appears to look right *into* me. "See … heat. Heat from body, heat from raptor, from woman. See *heat.* See time. See where small, where weak. Things you not see, Mother eyes see."

How? Katya asks.

I translate.

"Millions in eyes," the koschei replies, "in heart, lungs, groin, in limbs, in hands. Ready for see, ready for hunt, ready for kill. For Mother."

Is this 'Mother' a god of his, and not a woman? Katya signs. *The way he talks about her.*

But I can think of a more important question. "This Mother," I ask, "how many children does she have? How many koschei?"

The koschei bares his teeth. "Ask questions, not want answers."

"Try me."

He only sneers.

I really hate him, Katya signs. Her fingers stray to the knife hilt at her boot, and her eyes flicker with something feral. I touch her fingers lightly with mine. Her shoulders stiffen. Then she gives me a wry look.

"I had a mother," I tell the koschei, fighting to keep grief from my voice. "She rode a dakotaraptor, as I do. Grew me in her womb, as you've said. Her name was Annika, and she was full of stories. Does your Mother have a name, and stories?"

"Is Mother."

Dmitri sighs and takes off his hat, scratches at his wild tufts of near-white blond hair. "I didn't follow him across the prairie to talk about his mother. We should kill him and be done." He reaches with one gloved hand as if to grab the koschei by the chin. The man lunges swift as an eel, teeth snapping. Dmitri curses and snatches his hand back.

Katya's eyes narrow. But her knife stays in its sheath.

"That wasn't clever," I tell our captive. "You realize at least two of us want to stab you and one already has."

He spits.

I let the spittle dribble down my cheek, refusing to show any reaction at all. I hear Katya's breath hiss between her teeth. She hands me her scarf, and slowly, I dab away the spittle.

"We aren't killing him," I say sternly, aware of the koschei's gaze on me. "Not yet. We need to get him to the nightwatch."

"Thought *you* were the nightwatch," Dmitri mutters.

"We're *two.* The others might have more questions for him."

The Ticktock scowls. "I didn't track him to go talking sweet with him like a lover at midnight," he says again.

"You didn't track him at all," I snap. "You *guessed.* Katya and I caught him; her raptor took a bullet for it."

"I helped." His voice is grieved.

My anger flares, but I lower my voice, because this talk is not for the koschei's ears. "If you'd told us where you thought he was going, we could have been here two days back. Maybe crept up on him fast and unseen in the grass. Daphne wouldn't have been *shot.*"

Dmitri looks down, abashed.

"I am sorry about your Ellie." My voice is sharp. "But you realize there is more at stake here than your revenge for a companion lost?" My voice rises, but now I'm past caring. "There's a *herd* roaming loose behind us without whistlers, there may be other bullets dropping from the *sky*, and a lot of people might die, Ticktock. A *lot* of people."

His maimed hand clenches in a fist. "Have never worried about *other people*. Other people have never worried about me. Only had Ellie."

I shiver at that, because I only have Katya. But Katya has brothers and sisters and aunts and grandmothers and they have brothers and sisters and aunts, too, a whole settlement full of them, and kin in other settlements of the humming people up and down the edge of the prairie, tending cornfields and tanning hides and stringing beads and making drums and dancing at barter. "Well, we're nightwatchers. We *have* to worry about other people. It's what we do."

"Well, I sure ain't worried about *him*." Dmitri's eyes flicker with anger. "If you won't kill him outright, let him starve, then."

"No. We'll feed him," I growl.

"I wouldn't."

"The day I start listening to a *Ticktock's* advice on how to care for a captive is not today."

Dmitri tries to stare me down. "Not the justice I had in mind."

"You'll get your justice," I say. "Just not this way."

Dmitri gets to his feet, his eyes flickering with anger. "All right. He's your captive, that's a true thing. Doesn't mean I have to like it. But you're foolish, Sasha. There's a clock inside that koschei's body and that clock tells *wrong*. As long as it's ticking, he's a danger to you. You feed him and keep him strong, no telling what his body might do. Healed up right after my trike gored him. I don't like it."

I don't either.

Dmitri leaves us, walks over to the fire, gets his pan of beans and sits there in a huff. I hear Old Man warble, and then I hear Dmitri talking to the trike in low tones.

Katya is watching me, her eyes shining in the ringlight. *He's dangerous. Even now.*

Hardly. He's just pissed. I am, too.

I mean the koschei.

I glance at her, thinking of Dmitri's words. Then I look at the koschei tied to his tree, sullen, with that hint of mockery in his eyes. My heart sinks. The decisions I've made have gone awry. I've lost my kopye. I know the way of a nightwatcher, but I don't know how to battle *this* threat. This koschei shoved his entrails right back into his belly; that scares me so, I may never sleep again.

You're right, I sign.

So what do *we do with him tomorrow?* she signs back.

I sigh. *Suppose we could tie him to the trike.*

A hint of laughter returns, at last, to Katya's eyes, and I catch my breath at it.

Her lip curves. *Dmitri might ride off with him.*

He can try. Our raptors would circle him so fast we'd make a tornado right there in the grass.

Her face falls, and at the look in her eyes, I could kick myself. *Her* raptor won't be running any cyclone tomorrow. We'll be traveling slower than we ever have. My hand seeks hers, and our fingers twine together.

"Hunger," the koschei says.

"I bet you do," I mutter.

He lifts his chin. His voice is proud, taunting. "Walk on planet, herds with millions, eat grass?"

"The mother herds." I nod.

"Flesh for strength, hide for shelter?"

"Yes, the herds give flesh and hide. For *us*."

He laughs, a dry, dry sound. His tyrannosaur coos, and I feel the reverberation in my bones.

"Am planet," the koschei says. "Herds, millions, in blood. Hunger for meat, not grass."

Am planet, am deathless. Our captive sure thinks highly of himself. I exchange a look with Katya. She nods, rises to her feet and returns to the fire. She caresses Daphne behind her head, then Ihira, too. I hear my raptor trill. Then my wife bends and begins stabbing the bacon with a small eating stick and scooping it onto a thin plate of kedr wood. She carries it back to us. The *scent* of it. I lift a strip of bacon to my mouth. The bacon is hot but not scalding, and *ohhh* the taste of it, the grease and flavor. That goes a good way toward restoring my lost strength. Maybe I don't need a braid around a kopye. I just need bacon and sleep. I lick the grease from my fingers.

"There's bacon for you also," I tell the koschei wearily. "… If you plan to talk without spitting in my face. Bacon and beans and water."

"Not need water." A snarl in his voice. His strange eyes flick to the right. "Need meat. Need veil."

I glance where he's looking. Earlier, I had tossed his veil aside. A breeze must have caught at it while I sought his lander; it has fetched up against one of the trees, forlorn and red.

"Why?" I ask.

He bares his teeth. "Face for Mother. Not for you."

"Then you shouldn't have come here," I snap. "You shouldn't have killed people."

"*People*," he sneers.

"That's what it is, isn't it?" I say. I lift more bacon to my mouth, and I try to feed my anger too, so its flickering heat will burn away my fear. Our captive koschei doesn't think of me and Katya and Dmitri and dead Ellie as *people*, to be respected and battled. At best, maybe we are prey—as women to the koschei in my mother's tale. More likely, he considers us an inconvenience, like weeds to be ripped out of cropland soil. Earlier, I tried to talk with him as one tribe's nightwatcher to another's, as one *dinosaur rider* to another. That was a mistake.

"Here," I say gruffly, taking the kedr plate of bacon and crouching in front of the koschei. I lift a strip of bacon to him and he rips into it with his teeth. He eats quickly, chewing and swallowing fast, then lunging for another bite.

The burn of anger spills out in tone. "You don't want to talk, *I'll* talk. You've made a mistake, koschei, coming here. I hope you know it. *Deathless* doesn't make you infallible; you still hurt and you still hunger. You and your kind don't know how battles are fought here, how homes are made, how people are fed."

He says nothing, just keeps eating. Katya's eyes shine. At this moment, I *do* speak for us both.

"I've been thinking about how you attacked, what you've done," I tell him. "I don't know your name or your tribe but I know you, koschei. You try to survive by sheer strength, by power, by a tyrannosaur and a gun that can rip open the prairie with its spray of bullets. But this is the planet Peace you're on now. Subtlety, cleverness, cunning, compassion, commitment to the survival of the *whole* people—that's what makes life here possible. We live by our wits, not by our muscles. By our speed and cunning."

He chews the bacon, not glancing up. Yet my words must have affected him, because he says, "Mistake, landing wrong night, landing river. *Am* cunning. But need land many koschei. Here, one." His eyes shine with rage, but a rage turned inward. "Mistake."

"Hm." So *that's* why his ship was in the river. I bring another strip of bacon near his teeth, let him take a bite. There's only a little of it left now. "Yes, I'd say that *was* a mistake." A mistake that has cost lives. I think about that while he chews. "You came down too soon? Did you crash? Right into that river? Are you *bad* at riding things, koschei?"

He grunts. "Untie dinosaur. Untie me. Maybe see."

"Yeah, you'd like that. Just be glad I'm feeding you."

The koschei takes the last bite, then licks my fingers. I hiss and jerk my hand away. He laughs.

Katya slaps him, her palm loud across his cheek.

I scrub my fingers furiously on my jacket.

Katya signs something that I can't see. The koschei stares at her, his cheek reddened, revulsion in his face. "Savages," he says.

Katya's shoulders are tense, the lines of her face hard as metal.

"Not hear landers," the koschei says to her. His irises spin and blaze in the ringlight. "Not hear beast in grass. Not hear enemy. Not hear lover moan. Silence in ear, weakness in bone." Now he looks at me. "Mother heals; savages leave woman silent, broken."

"What are you, a *Ticktock*?" I snap. My fury is white hot. "My wife isn't *broken*. You speak with sounds and she speaks with her hands. Maybe *you're* the one that's broken."

Again that smirk, as if he is the one with nothing to fear, as if everything amuses him, as if he isn't captive on a world that's alien to him. "Hands tied, hands not speak."

"I'm *not* untying you."

Katya unclips a one-meter coil of thickly braided rope from her belt and hands it to me, cooly. Our eyes meet.

Then, using the rope, I gag the koschei. Now he can't speak at all.

* * *

Returning to the fire with a bellyful of bacon and a heart full of dismay, I slump down by Ihira, lean back, and look at the stars. Tears well up, but I forbid them. My raptor curls her neck around to place her head against my chest, just above my heart. I put my arms around her. "You're a good girl," I tell Ihira, "you're a good girl." I am overcome by her gentleness, this killer raptor of mine with claws that can rip open a lambeosaur or a man, but whose breath is washing softly now across my wrist. The golden strap Katya bound there is a comfort, too. Nearby, Old Man is snoring, and Dmitri has his hat over his eyes. And suddenly I am ashamed of my thoughts of him, or of tech he might barter to his Ticktock kin. This is the man who threw me my kopye, and it was no fault of *his* that I lost it, and no fault of his that we're here now, with a deathreaper squirming between the trees behind us and our heads full of nightmares.

Katya has settled near me with her back to Daphne, and her raptor's head on her shoulder. Katya's own head is down, chin on her breast. I reach across and take her hand, the softness of Daphne's feathers beneath our fingers. Katya squeezes my fingers once; she isn't asleep. I'm not, either; my fatigue is deep, yet I am so full of thoughts. In my mother's stories, the koschei's life was hid away. It had to be found before he could be killed. Blood had to be bartered for it, an innocent girl's spilled at the roots of a kedr tree. But my mother didn't have any stories about *packs* of koschei. "If *many* bullets fall," I say softly, "if it rains silver this year instead of red, we might be bartering the blood of many girls."

Katya squeezes my fingers again, and I realize she has been reading my lips. I squeeze back, because she's right. This is a problem for tomorrow. Tonight has troubles enough. I gaze up at those stars, desolate, no kopye at my belt, no pack riding behind me, just Katya's hand holding me so I don't fall right off this planet into that cold dark. What kind of people grow babies like cornplants and put guns in the hands of children who have never heard their mother's tales, never known their mother's name or felt her kiss on their hair, then send them across the stars to kill? This koschei, does he ever feel the absence of *his* Mother, who he has probably never seen, as keenly as I feel the loss of *mine*, who held me in her arms at dusk and taught me to ride a raptor at midnight?

With a touch of unexpected pity, I realize the koschei isn't some proud nightwatcher among his people, however skilled he might be at gunfire and slaughter. No. He is a slave. Grown and owned even as his tyrannosaur is. I recall the tiny interior of that ship, smaller than most domiks, for a domik of the humming people might include many rooms divided by folding screens, so that kin can sleep and laugh and eat together. For making love, we go outside into the corn or into the long grass. But that lander had no room for kin, and the cold dark above the sky might be no place to take a lover outside if the koschei had one. That lander was small like a cave for slaves in the mountains. A vision takes my mind of dozens or hundreds of koschei children grown inside canisters and grown badly sometimes, like that infant dinosaur with three arms and not enough leg to walk on. Maybe even grown en route between worlds. All of them kinless, all of them unbraided from their people, all of them enslaved and lost. Lost as ghosts on Yaga's prairie, captive as slaves in the Ticktock mines, living without love, existing only to maim and kill. "Deathless"—they don't know they can die. They don't know they can live.

13

I CAN SILENCE THE KOSCHEI FOR A TIME, BUT NO gag can silence my dreams. As I rest tonight against Ihira's feathers, those dreams come upon me fast and deadly, shearing into my mind the way predator talons might shear into my flesh. I tremble in my sleep.

I am fifteen.

I am sitting in a domik, my mother's. Ihira is outside in the raptor stables. There's screaming outside too, but I don't hear it. I sit on the carpets, holding my mother's body, tears on my cheeks. Annika Nightwatcher gazes up at me with glassy eyes, and horribly, her mouth moves, but the voice is my wife's: *Breathe, Sasha, just breathe.* Then she is silent. The rainmaker larva is half-burrowed in her breast, its back pulsing obscenely. Its limbs are *inside* her, and some of its long claws have pierced through her shoulder, gory and visible. Its slimy body is red, swollen with my mother's blood. It's still drinking, but soon it will stop and it may turn and rend me, as well. Her head rests in my lap, and I can't let her go, I *can't.* My sisters perished in the previous rainfall; Mom was all I had left. Tonight she breathed her last while I held her cheeks between my palms, and I couldn't do *any*thing but weep. I am weeping now. At last, so gently, I lay her head on the carpets and bring my ear to her lips, yearning for some whisper of air, some breath across my cheek.

There's nothing.

Just—nothing.

The only sounds in the whole world are the obscene suckling of the red larva, the creak and rattle of Grandma Yaga's walking domik as it swings by outside, somewhere a nervous dakotaraptor chirp, and me—sobbing, useless, and small.

I throw back my head and *scream*. Then I get to my feet. I stumble to the door of our domik and out into the gray dusk because I can not, I can *not* stay in here with that empty corpse that used to have my Mom inside it. I keep screaming, unbraided and alone and of no use to anyone, while others of my people die outside even as my mother has. Just outside the door someone catches me and shakes me, hard. They keep shaking me, and I fight them, certain this shadowy figure is the koschei, his bonds torn loose, his mouth gaping to kiss and devour. I kick and scratch. It keeps shaking me until my eyes fly open.

* * *

It's Katya, shaking me awake. My heart pounds. In the ringlight above me, her hands move almost too fast to read. *We're in danger.* Adrenaline floods into my blood like fire, and I roll to the side, reaching for my kopye. It's not there. With a bite of panic, I recall the flash of the dimetrodon's jaws before my face in the dark.

Then I'm up.

I am twenty. And my mother is long dead, and a nightmare is only a nightmare. I tell myself that.

Katya tosses her kopye to me. I catch it, its heft reassuring in my hands. A wildfire of gratitude in my heart. My wife is giving me *her* strength, her kopye to wield in the cold night. Our fire is down to embers, but I can see the glint of eyes in the ringlight, at the edge of the tall grass. Hyaenadons.

"Ihira," I call, then utter a series of quick chirps. She pads toward me, her eyes slitted, her breath hissing between her teeth. Daphne favors one leg but she's alert, all torpor gone, and Katya leaps to her back. No time to saddle her or Ihira. We'll ride bareback like Mila and her nieces when Peace was new settled. We know how; every nightwatcher trains both with and without saddle. Dmitri has been sleeping against Old Man with his hat over his face, but the trike's eyes are wide, and at a worried warble in his throat, Dmitri stirs.

That's all the time we have. A shape dark as a hole in the world leaps from the grass, landing on Old Man's back with an eerie whooping cry. A second hyaena pounces, sheathing its claws in the trike's hip. Its massive head lunges in quick as an eel's, saber teeth sinking into the trike's leg, jaws fastening. The trike's bellow is terrible. Others rush at us out of the grass, jaws with far too many teeth. Each hyaena is the height of a dakotaraptor, with twice its mass. Screaming, I catch one on the side of the head with the kopye. It jolts, then springs aside, lithe as a haia. I pull myself to Ihira's back and cling as she leaps, her shearing claw slicing air, then flesh, ripping one of the hyaenas open from gullet to gut. Then everything is sweat, and blood in my mouth where I've bit my cheek, and the eerie laughter of the hyaenadons, each of them five hundred kilograms or more, lunging in at us like dimetrodons with dark fur and a wild mane instead of a sail. Long, curved teeth flashing in the dark. Last time I fought a pride of these, there were two dozen night-watchers with me.

I look for Katya. We need to start circling the hyaenadons, drive them against each other and disorient them. Or else get *out* of here. One of the two. I can't see how many there are—just lunging, toothed shadows all around us; there could be eight in a pride, or forty. The kopye lights up one's jaws as it comes at me, and Ihira slams her head into it and knocks it aside. It turns like it's made of water, claws scoring Ihira's flank. My raptor screams, and I hear Daphne's war-screech to my right. "Katya!" I shout, heart pounding. I jab the kopye into the hyaena's shoulder and spill lightning into its body; it howls and then is gone through the grass.

Fear stabs me like a spear of ice. I wheel Ihira about; she's bleeding, but not bad. Now I think to get my wife and flee into the trees where we'll have some cover—hyaenadons prefer to stalk through the grass, surround, and pounce, and they can't climb—but then I catch sight of Dmitri on Old Man. The trike turns and gores a hyaena right through the side with his horn and lifts the squirming beast high, raining blood. But a roiling mass of hyaenas are clawing their way up the trike's rump. Old Man bellows in pain and fear. Dmitri lifts a deathclock pistol, purloined from our captive koschei, even as one of the hyaenas lunges at him across the trike's back. My own pistol is back in the saddlebags by our dead fire. Dmitri's gun discharges right in the hyaenadon's mouth. A flash of light, a sharp crack of sound. A high-pitched yelp, and the great beast tumbles from the trike's back. But there are others.

No circling to contain the pride, then, and no rapid flight. Not all of us are on raptors.

Yaga's *bones*, this is bad. I spin the kopye in my hand and slam it into a beast on my left. Ihira leaps over the dead fire as I hold on with my knees, hands on the kopye.

Ihira lands on a hyaena, bearing it to the ground, seizing the back of its powerful neck in her jaws. Her hind feet rip at it until the beast lies still. Fighting panic, I glance about for Katya, but I can't see her, just the dizzying sway of Catha branches in a sudden wind and the grasses tossing like the sea. Old Man bellows, and I hear a muffled and thunderous coo from the bound deathreaper.

"Wombgrown!"

I glance back at the shout. There's the koschei, tied to a tree not five meters away. He's worked the gag out of his mouth. Those clockwork eyes are spinning and they glint with flecks of silver in the ringlight, like there's metal in that man. "Am deathless!" he calls. "Fight with you! Or all die."

Ihira rips at the hyaena's throat, then lifts her head and screeches her triumph. I snap the kopye out of its spin, holding it out to one side, a lethal rod of metal and fire.

"Fight with you!" the koschei yells.

I hesitate. Truth is if we don't have help quick, we *are* about to die. But—

Just then, a mass of night-dark fur and slavering fangs lunges at the koschei, still tied to his tree. Faster than thought, the koschei kicks, his red boot connecting with the hyaena's jaw with a sharp crack. The hyaena yips and springs back. Then Ihira is on the monster's back, claws and teeth ripping. I hold on to her neck feathers with one hand and spin the kopye in a fresh arc of blue flame with my other.

Even as the hyaena beneath Ihira bucks and screams, the koschei strains at his bonds. His face goes red. A vein stands out against his brow. Then the ropes binding him fray and snap, and he *rips* his arms free of that tree. As I watch in shock, he rises to his feet. "Ungenomed animal!" the koschei shouts at the slavering hyaena. "One day needed. One more!"

My heart's in my throat; our ropes didn't hold him *at all*; he could have done that *at any time*. He wasn't our *captive*; he was simply observing us, up close, while his body healed. If he'd wanted to, he could have attacked us while we slept, while Katya watched alone. That makes my blood run cold.

Katya and Daphne flash by, my wife spinning her lasso in the air. As they do, the koschei grabs and plucks my wife's blade smoothly from its sheath at her boot, then leaps and flips in the air even as Katya glances, startled, over her shoulder. The koschei lands on his feet and sprints for the tyrannosaur. The deathreaper lifts its tethered head, and the koschei grabs one of the ropes and swings himself up onto its neck. Hanging on by the rope, he leans down to cut the tyrannosaur's tethers in quick movements, parting my wife's ropes as if they're merely strands of thread. I've never seen anyone move so fast. Then a hyaenadon slams into him from the shadows and knocks him off the tyrannosaur to the ground, the knife spinning away. They roll together, saber-toothed carnivore and murderous koschei, tumbling among the roots of the trees while the deathreaper screams through its bound jaws. Another hyaena charges at them, but, flashing back toward us, Katya drops a lasso around its thick neck and wrenches the snarling beast off its feet.

"Help Dmitri!" I call to her.

She nods.

Then I snap the kopye to my belt and drive Ihira toward the tyrannosaur; I lean from her back and snatch up Katya's knife where it lies on the ground. Then we're alongside the deathreaper. Holding the knife between my teeth, I grab one of the ropes at the tyrannosaur's jaw and leap from Ihira's saddle to the wild beast's back. A chirp to Ihira sends her wheeling after Daphne toward the floundering trike, to fall upon the hyaenadons with rending tooth and scything claw. As for me, well, I *did* promise I'd unleash the reaper of death before dawn. Might as well do it now!

Hanging onto the tyrannosaur's jaw rope, with my other hand I saw quick as I can through the ropes tethering the massive predator to the trees. The deathreaper's muscles ripple under my knees; the strength of this animal is *wild.* The last of the tethers comes loose and I cut the ropes free of its jaw; when that toothed maw opens, its roaring coo near breaks my bones, its temper as red as its plumage. It surges to its feet beneath me like fire in the wood. Heart sprinting at a rate somewhere between panic and exhilaration, I grip its neck feathers as I would Ihira's and chirp to it. I don't think the deathreaper understands raptor talk, but it understands that the hyaenadons are its prey. With another bone-shattering coo, it charges. Hyaenas scatter before us like leaves at the sheer mass of this running animal. I can't steer it; I balance at its shoulder, holding to the tuft of crimson feathers behind its head. Like clutching flames in my hand. The scent of the tyrannosaur's feathers is unfamiliar; there is a musk to the beast. It is not Ihira. I cannot trust it.

Daphne runs limping toward us with a hyaena on her tail.

"Wife!" I shout.

She glances up. Her eyes widen to see me on the tyrannosaur's back. I raise the knife; she understands and lifts her hand, and I toss it. It flashes in the ringlight. She catches it deftly out of the air. The hyaena behind her springs, and my wife turns and plunges the knife into its throat. Daphne squawks and nearly tumbles to the side but somehow keeps her footing, and Katya keeps her seat, and then the hyaena crumples to the ground and Katya is holding the red knife high, her eyes shining. I whoop for her.

Charging past her, the tyrannosaur nips at Daphne's flank but misses. "Hey now!" I scold, smacking the dinosaur's cheek. "Hyaenas, not wife!"

Cooing in a way that nearly topples me from its back, the deathreaper veers of its own accord right toward Old Man, and its jaws reach in and pluck a hyaenadon from the trike's back, clamping over the hyaena's spine. The deathreaper shakes its head viciously from side to side, and I *hear* the hyaena's bones snap. It yelps in high-pitched agony.

Dmitri is off the trike's back and on his butt in the grass, hat tilted back, face grim, that alien pistol lifted in both hands, firing off shots. Then the sharp cracking thunder of it stops. Just empty clicking. Dmitri's eyes widen. Two hyaenas leap from the squalling trike and run at him, taking him for easier prey.

"Ticktock!" I yell.

There isn't time to hesitate. I fling Yekaterina's kopye at Dmitri even before he looks up—like I'm returning the toss he gave me on the river. He catches it and snaps it to its full length the way he's seen us do, and spews liquid flame into the faces of the animals bearing down on him. The hyaenas shriek as they ignite like torches. I am astonished that I flung the kopye so easily, giving our strength, my wife's and my own, to Dmitri as we might to one of our own pack. Yet I haven't time to ponder it. Tonight at least, his life and ours are entangled. Battle is a tangle where little makes sense; if you survive it, you braid it up afterward with a story.

The tyrannosaur tosses aside the broken hyaena from its jaws and leaps into the grasses, sending me sliding from its back. I catch hold of its feathers with both hands, with my feet dangling against its side, and I hold on because surely the only thing on this planet more dangerous than being helpless on a tyrannosaur's back is lying helpless at its feet. Sweat stings my eyes. Now I can't see the others, koschei and whistler and wife. Too focused on staying off the ground and alive, on surviving these next moments.

The deathreaper whirls, and I almost lose my grip again. Hyaenas dart all about us, yipping and whooping. A *lot* of hyaenas. They lunge in, snapping at the tyrannosaur's legs, at mine. The deathreaper turns in a sweeping circle, an unstoppable mountain of flesh, its tail slamming into a hyaena, knocking it into the violet grass. I hear the crunch and the yelp as the dinosaur seizes another in its jaws. Guess the deathreaper doesn't like these hyaenas either. *No one* likes hyaenas. One snaps at my boot; I kick wildly at its head—that head far too large for its body, a head that is all teeth and snarl. Then its fangs catch in my leggings and I am *ripped* from the tyrannosaur's back.

I'm on my back in the grass. My hands scrabble and I catch up a fallen branch of Catha wood and bring it in front of my face just as the hyaenadon leaps onto me, crushing my air, it jaws lunging to crush *my face*. I drive the branch between its teeth and shove *up*, hard as I can. Its jaws snap shut around the wood and it snarls, its snout centimeters from my cheek, its breath fetid and choking. The hyaena shoves the stick toward my face and opens its jaws and growls, hot saliva dripping onto my cheek. Urine runs warm down my thigh. Whimpers in my throat. My arms lock and it can't close its jaws around my head with that stick in its way, so instead it clamps its teeth into the wood and thrashes its head from side to side, trying to tear the branch from my hands. I just hang onto that branch in panic, not daring to let go as it drags me through the grass and dirt. If another hyaenadon comes up, I'm dead and gone to meet Yaga.

A kopye slams into the beast's face in a burst of blue sparks. The hyaena scrambles off of me, wriggling aside, snarling. Katya grabs my arm and pulls me to my knees. From there, I scramble to my feet. Through the tossing grass, I glimpse one of the raptors—Ihira—leaping and slashing. Further out, the tyrannosaur is a crimson killwind surrounded by leaping shadows.

Katya's side is bleeding. One half of her face is streaked with dirt like war paint, and a veil of golden hair has been torn loose from her braid and is now stuck to her cheek with sweat. Her eyes are wild. She has her kopye back. Thrusting me behind her, she spins it in a wheel of blue death, and the hyaena watches, its eyes reflecting the blue sheen. Its jaws drip saliva; the flesh and hair on one side of its head is charred, but that thing's skull is *thick* and strong as stone. Staring into the creature's feral eyes—eyes that hold only hunger—I could retch from fear. We both see its hind legs tense. We're dismounted, I have only a half-chewed stick in my hand, and it's going to pounce! Katya's gaze flicks toward the trees; my heart drums. They're close; can we make it? Katya bolts into a run, dragging me with her by my arm, and I run with her. I glimpse her knife sheathed at her boot again but there's no time to reach for it. No breath to scream, no breath even to *breathe*—just run!

The tall grasses part and there, ahead, are the tangled Catha trees, and between them and us, several hyaenas, snarling. Far to our left, out of reach, I see Daphne slashing at a hyaena whose teeth are buried in her flank, jaws locked. I trill a summons to my raptor, but even as I do, the hyaena behind us tears through the grass and hurls itself into my wife, knocking her aside on her belly. I scream. The hyaena is crouched on her back and I'd leap to *its* back, punching and scratching and biting to get my wife free of it, but another leaps between us and I fall back, screaming at the hyaena. I spin the stick in my hands as if it's a kopye; it's all I have between my body and the hyaena's gaping jaws.

"Katya!" I scream.

The hyaena lunges. I feint to the side and spear the stick right into its eye. Screeching, it knocks me to the ground with a swipe of its paw. Claws rake along my thigh, trailing fire. I roll away from it desperately, my hand finding a loose rock and snatching it up. Then back up to my knees. It's coming at me, and I hurl the rock, connecting solidly with its skull, but its rush doesn't slow.

Then a man leaps in front of me. He seizes a fistful of the hyaena's throat. It barrels him to the ground, but the koschei doesn't let go. As it turns out, being *genomed* and inhabited by "millions" doesn't just give the koschei the ability to rip through rope like it's made of air. It also gives him a feral and unnatural strength and ferocity. He grips the creature's jaws and *rips* them apart. The shrieking, gurgling hyaena spills blood and gore over his face and chest in a red waterfall. Heaving the beast off him, he is on his feet faster than I can believe, and the other hyaenadons are closing. He turns and reaches for the hyaena that's savaging my wife, gets his fist in its mane, pulls its head back; the hyaena turns in one fluid motion and clamps its powerful jaws over the man's side, ripping. The koschei's shriek of pain is terrible.

I stagger to Katya's side and help her up. She's weeping silently and there's blood at her shoulder, but her kopye is ignited and hot as a sun. A hyaena comes at us and she drives the rod into its snout. It falls back with a snarl. Her other hand darts to her boot, unsheathing the knife. Swiftly, she presses the hilt into my palm.

Our eyes meet.

"Alive until sunup," I pant.

She nods and takes rope from her belt, readying a lasso swiftly. I test the weight of the knife in my hand. Let's do this. We're dismounted, but we are *nightwatchers*, battle-skilled women of our people—and wives defending each other. The worn, tough leather of our hearts is braided together. And even if I *am* the weaker strap, Katya is the strongest I've ever known, and she has the strength of our full pack, who love and admire her, braided about her kopye. We will fight. We will survive. We will outlive this night.

Behind us, the koschei stands with a dead hyaena's jaws still clenched over his flesh. He holds his hands spread, fingers ready to grab. There must be eight, nine hyaenas all around him, dark as death. Again, I call for Ihira. Katya and I back away toward the trees, one hyaena still prowling after us, watching the kopye warily, waiting for its chance. I can't see Dmitri but I can hear his trike bellowing. He must have thrown Katya's kopye back to her; I hope he did, and she didn't take it from his corpse—I don't know if he lives.

The hyaenas leap on the koschei, all together, jaws flashing and tearing. He disappears under them. All is snarling confusion. One of the hyaenas is physically *thrown* aside. For an instant I see the koschei again, with a hyaena's jaws latched on his shoulder, teeth punctured deep, blood flowing hot, and another on top of him about to close its jaws over his head, but he presses his fingers together and *stabs* them into that hyaenadon's chest as if his hand is a knife. Then he retracts his hand, clutching some-thing hot, red, and pulsing. The hyaena collapses limply over him. Then the others are on him again, and I can't see anything. But I can hear him shouting now, shouting words in a language I don't know, some language that should never be spoken on Peace.

"Yaga's *teeth*," I whisper. "How is that possible?"

Our own pursuer comes at us, and Katya whirls her lasso, catching its foreleg and wrenching its paw out from under it. The beast comes crashing to the dirt but immediately scrambles up again. Even as it does, Katya lunges in with her kopye, and I with the knife, curved and glinting with starlight. The knife slices open its shoulder and the kopye slams into the creature's neck and it cooks. It backs up, trailing rope, hissing and spitting in fury and anguish. I trill for Ihira a third time, desperate. Then I see her, and my heart is *song*. She flits toward us through the grass. I don't see Daphne. Wait, there—*there* she is, off to the left and limping. Her jaws, and Ihira's, are red.

The hyaenadon turns to face the new threat but when it sees what's coming at it from the prairie it turns and bolts. Not fast enough. My raptor leaps, feathered arms extended, gliding ten meters, her shearing claw flashing. She lands on the hyaena's back, crushing it down, slicing into its snarling hulk in a red spray.

Katya yanks me into the trees, presses my back to one that has low branches, in case we need to climb. Her eyes shine in the ringlight for just a moment, wild as the hyaena's. Breathing hard, I touch her shoulder. She winces but takes my hand in hers, shakes her head. No terrible wound there, she means to tell me, but there's certainly blood enough. I lift her hand to my mouth and kiss her palm, trembling. When I saw her go down under that hyaena, I thought … I feared … I *knew* I was losing her. Losing the only family I have. I blink rapidly because I will not cry, I will *not*.

Katya catches my gaze and nods her head out toward the prairie, her eyes haunted, and I peer around the tree in time to see two hyaenas crouched over a man's legs. Just the legs and hips, no torso attached. The hyaenas bury their snouts in the flesh, then lift their faces red as Yaga's nails. But I can still hear the man's voice, chanting now. Ten meters away, there's movement, a struggle at the edge of the grass. With a shock, I glimpse the top half of the koschei's body, trailing entrails and slime over the ground, his eyes clockwork fire and his fingers buried in the neck of a snarling hyaena. He is trying to choke it. Four others lie dead behind; this one has its teeth in his arm and is trying to drag him into the tall grass to devour. His fingers tighten and the beast squeals. Then two more come out of the grass and take him in their jaws. They drag him into the prairie and I can see only the tossing of the grasses where they've gone, but I can hear his battle chant and the snarling of the beasts.

Deathless, he said.

Farther out, his tyrannosaur is charging across the wild grass with hyaenas clinging to its back and hips, yipping and barking at its flanks. Even as I watch, the tyrannosaur dips its head, lifts another hyaenadon into the sky, and snaps its spine like a twig. Its tail smacks another aside. Its battle coo is resonant and deep and rolls over the prairie like a summer storm. My breath catches at the beauty of that animal—the reaper of death, unbound now and undefeated, taking what lives it pleases in the red night.

* * *

For a moment, Katya and I just hold each other, wild-eyed and panting. Then we stand, shakily, to call our raptors.

Katya ignites her kopye again, and the ends burn such that the air ripples around them. I can hear the hum and crackle of its fire. Just then, Dmitri comes out of the grasses, his jacket torn, a spray of blood across his hat and cheek, one hand gripping a deathclock pistol pointed earthward with smoke rising from its barrel, and in his other hand a scraping tool for his trike's hide. The tool and the hand holding it and the arm up to his elbow are drenched in blood, and he leaves a trail of red drops like Yaga's sweat behind him on the torn soil. Over one shoulder and across his chest, Dmitri has slung a belt with dozens of tiny pouches holding bullets. I recognize it. I last saw that belt coiled on the ground near the fire, beside the gleaming metal of the invader's long saddle-gun.

Old Man rumbles in close behind his whistler, covered with as many scratches and cuts as he has wrinkles. But I guess the trike's leathery hide is too tough for a hyaenadon's jaws. That pride made a mistake tonight, attacking us. Probably the smell of blood brought them, Daphne's blood, the scent of it wafted far over the prairie. Should have expected it—we heard them laughing and whooping earlier. Some nightwatcher I am.

The hyaenas look up from the koschei's legs, debating whether to rush Dmitri, but then Ihira is running at them, and they snarl and crouch. One flees—right into Daphne, who comes out of the grass in a rage, her claw slicing the hyaena open from shoulder to hip. Ihira takes the other. Maybe I haven't been the most alert tonight, but our raptors know *their* work, at least.

Dmitri is pale and shaken but unharmed. He gets his kit and takes a look at my wife's right shoulder, peeling away her jacket and blouse to reveal a sharp cut from her shoulder down across the top of her breast. "Bandage it," he mutters after a moment. "Not deep, but you get dirt in that and it'll be a foul thing."

Katya nods wearily. She closes her torn blouse over her breast and signs to me, *Always wanted a scar.*

It'll look good on you. Like Neveah's.

She smiles weakly. *You been looking at Neveah's breasts a lot?*

Well, she does like to show them off.

Katya laughs—that long, wild laugh of hers, without measure or restraint, a laugh as free as wind and sunlight and wild things growing. And that's when I finally know we're going to be all right, she and I. We'll be all right.

You saved me, Yekaterina, I sign.

We're nightwatchers; we save each other. She leans close and her lips brush my cheek. *Rest. I'll get Daphne and patrol, make sure those things are moving on.*

A quiver of fear at the thought of parting. *We'll both go. Together.*

You rest. Her eyes shine. *The immediate threat has passed. I can handle a little watching. Trust me, Sasha.*

I swallow and nod. *Stay alive until sunup, beautiful wife.*

I intend to.

She walks out over the bloody ground. Daphne comes over, still limping a bit, her claws red and her neck feathers and snout soaked red, too. She has no saddle, but Katya takes hold of her long feathered mane and leaps lightly to her back. My wife lifts her kopye, braided with the colors of all her pack and with my hue too, with what life and strength I have to give her. The ends of her kopye flare with light and hum with violence. She is profiled against the stars and the wild arc of our planet's rings, her golden braid tumbling down her back and some strands loose across her face and blood on her jacket and her face pale in the night. I have never seen her so beautiful. She lifts her kopye in one hand and with the other taps quick signals with her fingers against Daphne's throat, then grips her feathers as the raptor runs haltingly out into the grass.

Dmitri watches her go, breathless as I.

"That's my wife you're looking at, Ticktock." There's no rancor in my voice this time. Just hot pride and gratitude. The fact that we're with each other, she and I, in the midst of this hungry prairie and despite the voracious intent of every invader or predator of earth and sky, seems to me an unquenchable wonder. And worth being grateful for.

"I know it," Dmitri says. He glances back at me, his eyes full of concern. Then he catches sight of the koschei's legs, bloody and half-eaten nearby. "That him?"

"Half of him."

I can no longer hear the koschei chanting. I want to follow Katya, but I am so exhausted I can't move. I find myself sitting with my back to a tree with no idea how I got there. There is frayed rope on the mossy ground. I lift a few strands and look at them. This is the tree we bound the koschei to.

One day needed, he said, *one more.* What did that mean? He was waiting for something. He could have escaped us, maybe killed us—or tried—any time he pleased. But he was waiting.

"We should depart," Dmitri's voice is hoarse from battle. The Ticktock is standing in front of me. I look up at him, my vision a little blurry. "Before the hyaenas come back."

I listen to their distant, whooping cries, then shake my head. "They won't. They're following that tyrannosaur. They've got blood fever; they won't let go. It'll lead them halfway to your mountains by dawn."

He chews the inside of his cheek. "Might be. The blood reek could bring another pride, though."

"Not right away." The prides are jealous of their territory. "Let me rest a bit," I groan. "Sweet Founder, let me rest. Then we'll bury the dead and go."

"Bury *that*?" Dmitri looks at the koschei's legs in horror. "Let your raptors eat it."

I meet his gaze. "You got your justice, Ticktock. You got it red and screaming and plenty thorough. Be satisfied. I'm tired of leaving the dead unburied behind. We don't need his ghost wandering our land anymore than we needed him walking it living." I gaze out over the prairie, and I can see the flash and burn of Katya's kopye in the night, far away now. "And he saved my wife."

***

After that Dmitri leaves me in peace. I lie back and feel every one of my bruises reasserting its existence. Deep scratches in my thigh, too. My lambeohide leggings are sliced and wet and no longer warm. *Eugh.* I wet myself in terror back there at one point. My face heats with shame. I bet my mother never did that. Bet Katya's never done that. I'll have to wash and get my other pair out. Later. When I can stand again. I smell like urine and sweat, but there are other scents in the air here that are worse.

Ihira comes over to guard me, settling beside me, and I rest my cheek on her feathers. She's more comfortable to lean against than a tree. Warmer, too. I just rest against my raptor, looking at those legs severed on the ground over there with chunks torn out of them. Still no chanting in the grass. Guess he's dead and half-eaten, or torn into too many pieces for any Ticktock magic or even one of Grandma Yaga's spells to stitch together again. My hands start to tremble. Rolling to my side, I retch onto the soil, and I keep doing it until I've got nothing left. Turns out bacon doesn't taste as good coming back up.

Ihira chirps her concern. I spit, then wipe my lips with the back of my hand and just breathe; after a moment I reach up to stroke the soft feathers at the base of her neck. I should have been more watchful; watching is what I'm *for.* Was too tired earlier to think, after battling the koschei and battling the dimetrodon and battling the cold grip of despair too. With my thoughts full of everything that might hurtle at us from the stars, I forgot what might hurtle at us from the grass. How could I forget? My mother was not killed by any koschei from faraway suns but by the red rain that is truly deathless, by the relentless blood-hunger of this planet and its creatures. The final enemy is never a Ticktock or a slaver or a koschei; the enemy is our ill-named Peace itself. We should have named the planet Hunger, because there is a hunger at its heart and our people hunger on its soil, striving always to plant and harvest just enough before the red rain falls, or to live off the herds at the risk of falling prey to all the toothsome life that follows, ravenous for flesh. Hunger makes the Ticktocks abandon their children, hunger sends nightwatchers out to check for threats across hundreds of kilometers of wild prairie, hunger drives all peoples to hate and squabble to keep what little they have. Hunger shimmers in Grandma Yaga's eyes when we send her our dead. In the war against hunger, all people must be allies in the dark of night, or the hunger wins.

I glance again at the koschei's legs. Maybe his people haven't learned this yet. Maybe if they are victorious and they take our land, they will learn it too, in the end, at great cost. This koschei fought by my side tonight, saved my wife—whether from sudden and unexpected compassion or from prudence, the awareness that it would require all of us on our feet to beat back the hyaenadons, I don't know—but I know this: the rest of his vat-grown people have not faced the jaws of the screeching hyaenas, and they are still coming, a rain of bullets to pierce and destroy. Panting, I lie back. I hear the tyrannosaur coo in the distant dark, hunting in the grasses, teaching the hyaenadons to fear. With Ihira's feathers warm against my cheek, I gaze up at the night sky. For the first time, I don't see the stars but instead the empty places between them: an endless dark from which unexpected terrors might fall into our world.

14

WE BURY WHAT'S LEFT OF THE KOSCHEI AT DAWN, the legs and a hand and wrist we find in the grass all by itself, torn from an arm that's gone. Too few lines in the palm. Too young, this war-slave from another world. We bury him beneath the Catha trees. Deep, so hyaenadons won't dig him up. I don't know the funeral customs of his people, or even what his people are *called*—only the name of the star system they come from. I wonder what it must be like to be buried in the soil of another world, unbraided forever from your home, your lover, your parents, or your children. We don't have a wrist bracelet of colored beads or a braided feather necklace to lay on his grave, nor many stories to tell of him or songs to sing. But Katya kneels on the dirt, favoring her bandaged shoulder a bit, and signs, *Here is a koschei; he was brave, and he rode a monster with teeth.* Her eyes are dark, but she gets out her drum and makes a song with her fingers for a while, doing her duty to the dead.

Afterward, I kneel beside her and press my palm to the warm dirt while the boughs whistle above me and their pink leaves dance. My voice is soft. "Here is a koschei. He traveled a long way. He is our enemy. But he saved my

Katya from a hyaenadon's jaws, and his battle-beast fought a pride that would have eaten us in the night dark. So he is also our friend." I take a breath. And I sing for the man who is dead:

when you are outcast
when the prairie before you is wide empty as forever
when the hyaenas laugh in the grass
when the frost eats your fingers
and your feet crack and bleed
when you have nothing left

there is still kindness
there is still seeing each other, eye to eye,
there is still holding one another for warmth
there is still sharing your last morsel
there is still kindness
there is still loving
there is still love

He died an exile, far from home, and I have little love for him, but the song is true even so, and who has need of a last kindness more than the lonely dead? Maybe it will be enough to purchase him entry to Grandma Yaga's walking hut, to carry him over the frozen plain. Not even our enemies deserve to wander among the ghosts.

Katya and I stay kneeling awhile. Not in respect but in uncertainty what else to do. And in troubled memory of another body left unburied, far behind, for which this burial cannot fully atone. The wind rises, and the violet grasses of the prairie toss and sigh loudly as the far green sea.

* * *

After a while, I reach for Katya's hand and squeeze it. "A koschei is *not* deathless. He can be killed. Others like him, too. We need to let the other nightwatchers know."

Katya signs, *You think there will be more soon.*

I do. I look out over the prairie. Kilometers and kilometers of mother herd country, quiet here on Peace, though last night this stretch of land was loud with the hyaenas' screeches and the reverberant cooing of the tyrannosaur, louder than any roar, and with the alien war-chant of the koschei. There was arrogance in that chant, arrogance in his heart, arrogance worse than a slaver's, the belief that he had a right not only to our lives but to our prairie and our herds and our corn, that he could scatter us like husks at harvest, if he so pleased. And though he has died, that arrogance has not; it continues, deathless and deadly, in the hearts of all his koschei brothers, somewhere above the sky. I sign to my wife, *These invaders don't fear us.*

Not yet. Her eyes flash. *We'll teach them.*

"Yes, we will, Yekaterina. Yes, we *will*."

We get to our feet and saddle the raptors. I pat Ihira gently on the neck. "Good girl," I whisper to her, "good girl." Then we go to join Dmitri, who is leaning against Old Man's leg, some distance away. The battered old trike has his snout buried in the grass, and we can hear the slow motions of his teeth. Our raptors remain near the Catha trees; Ihira is chewing at one of the hyaenadon dead. Glancing back, I see Daphne limp toward her. My raptor lifts her reddened snout from the animal's soft belly, but she doesn't hiss or snap at Daphne, nor prevent her from approaching her meal, as she usually would. Instead, she takes a half step to the side, and Daphne joins her, and they dip their snouts together into the hyaena's belly. My heart warms.

Dmitri begins belting several pouches to the trike's saddle loops. His wide brim hat is still stained with blood though I can tell he has scrubbed it as best he could. As he did last night, he wears the belt of bullets slung over his shoulder, and I wonder if he's loaded more of them into his gun. I can see that deathclock gleaming and polished at his belt. Mine is at my belt, too; I fetched it from my saddlebags before digging this morning's grave. After last night's terror, I will have *some* weapon at easy reach, alien or no.

The Catha trees are behind us, the prairie ahead. Dmitri lifts a hand in welcome as we get to him. "Yekaterina Nightwatcher," he says, making sure to face her squarely so she can read his lips, "your raptor will heal clean, I hope. Once she does, that stitching of mine will need to come out. You get her to a healer among your people, they'll know what to do. They may never have seen a wound like this and may never have had to dig for bullets, but pulling out stitches … that, anyone with clean hands and steady fingers can manage." He smiles. "Just don't let your Daphne eat the healer's face."

Katya's own smile is warm, and despite her fatigue, her eyes dance with sudden mischief.

"Way I see it, Ellie's had her justice." Dmitri turns and cinches a saddle-belt tight, hesitates. A hoarseness in his voice. "Much as she's gonna get. Thank you both."

"Where you and Old Man headed?" I ask.

"I have a herd straying," he says. "Whistler leaves his herd, that's a bad thing. Set something that big moving and don't watch it, you don't know where it will go, what it might trample, what it might do." He glances at Katya, eyes deep with compassion, but he turns then without speaking and begins checking Old Man's saddle and straps. He sets his foot in the stirrup, but to my surprise, Katya goes to him and touches his arm. One hand on the pommel, ready to mount, he turns, and she kisses his cheek. Dmitri blushes red as fire. Then Katya walks back to me, her braid swaying. Dmitri stares after her a moment, then tips his hat to us and mounts swiftly. Settling in the saddle, he taps Old Man's frill, and the trike lifts his head, mouth full of grass, his horn sweeping upward. A muffled bleat of protest.

"There's still a deathreaper out there somewhere," I call to Dmitri. "Ride with both eyes open. Don't sleep in your saddle by day or by night."

He grins at me. "Whistlers never sleep in the saddle."

He pulls out his watch, snaps it open, and takes a good look, then grunts, closes it, and puts it back. He lifts the bone whistle to his lips. But before he can blow any silent notes on it that might send Old Man rolling over the prairie like a rock rolling downriver to the sea, the sky above us erupts with sound—an eerie wailing, an almost animal scream, some vast leviathan of the clouds in agony. But tipping my head back, I see only the sky pink with dawn and the rings pale and lovely to the north. Then, between one heartbeat and the next, shapes *ripple* into sight in the middle of the air, gleaming metal surfaces, cylindrical, tapering at the upper end. Landers shaped like bullets, just like the koschei said. Falling down at us. I gasp.

Katya's eyes are wide. She runs for Daphne.

It's a moment before *I* can move. I just stare at those descending ships. I can scarce believe what I see. They're in the *air.* They're slowing now, almost floating down at us. There are four of them—*four.* Their metal is white like the hide walls of a domik but pocked everywhere with burns and scrapes delivered during their voyage above the sky. They've had a hard journey. Now smoke billows about them, obscuring them. The wailing drops in tone, becoming low animal groans. The grass flattens in the wind of their descent. The wind blasts my face and my hair; I drop my goggles over my eyes. My hands tremble.

Dmitri, his flesh turned to gold by the tint of my goggles, settles his hat more firmly over his scalp and says simply, "*Shit.*"

"Ihira!" I scream. "Ihira!" I call to her with rapid chirps, and she flashes through the grass toward me, her jaw still bloodied from her meal. When she reaches me, I grasp the pommel in one hand and her neck feathers in the other and vault to her back. Now the landers are down, smoke pouring up toward our sky. Each is a hundred meters tall, a bullet you might fire at a planet instead of a person. The farthest is two kilometers away, out there on the violet prairie; the nearest is two hundred meters off.

One day needed, the koschei had said before he died. *One more.*

I hadn't understood.

"Yaga *eat* his bones!" I cry. "Yekaterina!"

Daphne is limping toward us, Katya in the saddle, her eyes wild with battle. She has her paint kit open in her palm, and she holds onto her raptor with her knees while she applies black paint across her face in quick stripes. You are supposed to wear war paint when you send people to meet Grandma Yaga. Stripes across your face, across your nose and cheeks and brow, one across the eye, one eyelid black, so that you stand half in the day and half in the night, so that when you hear Grandma Yaga's raptor hut screeching toward you out of the ghost prairie, she will see only *half* of you and won't pull you screaming into the cold night with your foes. And so that your enemy will see your face and know that you are a *nightwatcher* and that you are prepared to kill to protect those you love.

I shake my head, *no.*

This is not a time for battle. Not against four of the deathless.

We have to flee.

We have to get to the rendezvous.

We need the rest of the nightwatch!

"Run!" I cry to the Ticktock, knowing his trike is slow. He needs to move *now.* I ride to my wife. "Katya! We have to get out of here!"

There is such fury in her eyes and no intent to listen. For a moment, I believe she might actually ride *at* the ships.

"*Yekaterina!*"

Then she nods tersely, wheels her raptor about.

A shout from Dmitri has me glancing over my shoulder at the landers. My heart pounds. A lone figure, hooded and veiled, crimson cloak billowing in the prairie wind, runs toward us through the grass with inhuman speed. Beyond him, in the middle distance, others emerge from their ships, too, leaping down from doors that have opened in their sides, as if a fall from a height is nothing to them, nothing at all, as if their bones are less brittle than ours, their bodies less breakable. *Koschei.* They're *here.* My blood runs cold.

The nearest koschei unslings two guns from his hips, lifts them. Their barrels are long, and their gleaming metal catches the sun's fire. I send Ihira leaping into a run just as I see the smoke and hear the crack of those pistols, alien clocks telling the time of death. To my left, I see Katya jerk in her saddle, and I cry out. She lifts a hand toward me, eyes round with shock, then topples off her raptor into the grass. I scream and send Ihira toward her. Daphne turns and hisses at the advancing koschei.

Just as I reach my wife, Dmitri pulls up alongside us on Old Man, his face pale. I slide from Ihira's back. Katya tries to stand and her leg collapses beneath her; she falls with a strangled sound; I catch her in my arms. Blood pulses through a hole in her blouse at her left shoulder. More blood running down her leg. She clutches at my arms. She's shaking. She's *shaking.* Daphne limps near, gives a worried chirp.

More gunfire. I see a spray of soil a few meters away.

"She's hurt!" I look to Dmitri. "She's hurt!"

"Get her out of here, nightwatcher." He unslings something from his saddle quickly, tosses a small satchel to me. I catch it. I recognize it by the design on the cover flap; inside are the needle, the spoon, the tools of Ticktock magic, *healing* magic. I stare at that bag an instant, then glance toward the koschei. He's thirty meters away and striding, reloading his guns as he walks. Hate burns hot in my heart, terror courses in my blood.

Dmitri interposes his trike between us and the koschei, and Old Man's bulk blocks out the sight of him and blocks the dawn, too. I stand beside Ihira in his shadow holding my wife and that bag of Ticktock magic.

"Now *get*!" Dmitri cries. "Get her to her people!" He rips the invader's gun from his belt. "I'll make sure these dung-eating hyaenas follow me and not you! Ride, Sasha! Ride!"

Dmitri blows his trike whistle, and Old Man bellows to shake the bones. I lift Katya in my arms, aghast. The Ticktock means to fight for us, die for us maybe. As if we are one people, as if he and we share the same grandmothers, as if he is one of our pack, his life and strength braided to our own. My world quivers, for how has this happened, how can a nightwatcher share such a bond with a Ticktock?

But he is not just a Ticktock.

He is Dmitri.

Hollering, he kicks his triceratops into motion, and in an instant, the great old bull is charging through the grass, galloping right *at* the invaders. Dmitri lifts his gun, steadying it across one wrist, and fires, sending puffs of smoke flying over the grasses. He laughs and whoops like a hyaena. An invader tries to strafe him with gunfire, but Dmitri, magnificent Dmitri, ducks low, and Old Man lifts his horn and bellows, and his bone frill shields his brave rider. Bullets careen off that shield, sending chips of bone spinning in the air. The triceratops does not slow his charge. I can scarce tell what it must be like seeing that mountain of horn and hide bearing down on you with Dmitri laughing on his back and firing that gun, but it must be a fearsome sight.

I have Katya across my saddle now and the Ticktock's satchel over my shoulder. I grasp Ihira's neck feathers and vault to her back, settling in behind my wife. I rip off my scarf and press it to the sucking wound in her shoulder. "Stop bleeding!" I whisper. "Please."

She signs weakly, *Trying.*

"Hold this to your shoulder," I tell her. I feel her fingers brush mine. I give a series of chirps, and my raptor wheels in the grass, with me swaying on her back and Katya retching, vomiting over the raptor's side.

I bend low over my wife, covering her body with mine and making myself less visible. Old Man is a hard target to miss, but give us a hundred meters and my violet-plumaged Ihira will fade into the grass and disappear almost as completely as the invaders' ships do. Dew on the prairie grasses gleams in the morning ringlight. I urge Ihira to wild speed. Daphne can't keep the pace; she limps behind, crying for her rider and her raptor-sister. Katya is silent; she has passed out. There is a bullet hole in my wife's shoulder and one in her leg, and a lot of blood. Panting with fear, I press that scarf hard to her shoulder. I hear Dmitri hollering far behind, and there are gunshots echoing over the grass. I don't know if those are his or the invaders' or both, and I dare not look back.

"Run, Ihira, run!" I cry. At the urgency in my voice, her head drops and her tail lifts for balance and her back goes straight as a kopye, and she *runs*, darting through the grass faster than wind, faster than death, faster than Grandma Yaga's domik, faster than I've ever felt, faster than she ran when I raced Katya to the Catha wood, faster than when we fought the tyrannosaur, *fast.* Daphne's cries fade behind us. The gunshots grow more distant. Soon there is only the wind and the pounding of my heart and the sun rising. The wind ripples through the prairie around us like Grandma Yaga whispering in her sleep, erasing the wake of our passage and the signs of our flight. No line of red ribbons to mark our going. No evidence that we were ever here.

15

I AM RUNNING. All around me, there are screeches and screams.

I am fifteen.

My mother lies dead and half devoured in her domik behind me.

I stumble past others of our settlement. Some are desperately at work raising frames of ceratops hide drenched in Catha sap. Some are running messages. Some stop, see my face, and gasp. The pity that fills their eyes is a horror to me. Somewhere nearby, young women—voices I know, the other nightwatcher trainees—begin to hum, and that is a horror to me too; they are singing for my Mom. Their raptors begin warbling with them, and I turn and run for the dakotaraptor stables. Somewhere to my right, a red larva strikes the ground with a *splat*, a bit of evil hurled at us out of the sky. I can hear the digging of its claws, a woman's scream, the nightwatchers' running footsteps, the hiss and crackle of kopyes as they attack the creature before it can seize anyone. That is how my mother died—throwing herself over my body when a larva shot through our roof at me. It tore into her and sheathed itself inside her flesh, the way a worm slides into soil.

In the stables, I find Ihira, who is no more full-grown than I, both of us lanky young girls. But she can hold my weight. I saddle her through a blur of tears; when she nuzzles my cheek with her soft, soft snout, the sobs burst from me faster. In moments I am on her back, both hands gripping her neck feathers, and urging her out the raptor doors. People leap out of our way. It's getting dark, but we sprint between the domiks and then race away through a field of corn. Red larvae fall to the left, red rain falls to the right, crashing into the corn. But none hits us. We flee, cornstalks whipping my legs and hips.

Out the other side of the cornfield, we leap a fence of kedr wood barely two meters high, built to keep out agonda, not to keep raptors in. Ihira soars over it with an avian cry, and I feel the shock as we land in the dirt on the other side. Before us stretches the prairie, an ocean of purple in the dark. The rings shine in the sky, silver and pure, capturing the sunlight to keep a little of it for us throughout the long autumn night—but keeping none of it for my *Mom*. She will never see these rings again. You can't see the rings in Grandma Yaga's country, or the stars, or the laughter in your daughter's heart, or the tears on her face.

I didn't grab my goggles, and the wind is sharp. I wipe at my eyes, furious at my tears but unable to stop them. I hold to Ihira's mane of neck feathers with one hand as we flit silently over the prairie. I glance back once, but the settlement is so far behind us now, I can't see it. I can't see the low fence or the cornfield or the other nightwatchers with their kopyes seeking to burn and destroy the larvae that have landed among our people. I can't see the stables or the domiks. Just endless waves of violet grass.

Somewhere the lowing of a brachiosaur. And the intermittent, sickening sounds of larvae falling here and there, each the size of my head. I clutch the Founder's book at my belt, my mother's gift, and I tremble as Ihira and I race over the prairie. Aside from my raptor, I am alone. Utterly and forever alone.

* * *

Ihira is running. I cling to her saddle and her neck feathers. All around me the prairie is silent, no sound of Grandma Yaga's raptor hut, nothing but the wind in the grass and the swift, almost silent impacts of my raptor's feet and the shallow breathing of my wife.

I am twenty, and my wife is unconscious in my arms, and I have a panic in my heart. Nightmares are supposed to *stay* in the dream country, where you glimpse them only by the dark of night. But now all my nightmares have lurched into my waking life. First the nightmares of a koschei, and now the darkest dreams I have, the nightmares that don't even need teeth or a knife to wound me: the nightmares of a woman I love dying, and me sitting beside her, sobbing and unable to help. *Mom.*

We're far enough out on the prairie now that I don't hear gunfire behind us nor Old Man's bellowing, nor the screaming of more ships falling from the sky. I bring Ihira to a stop where a dip in the land will help conceal us. I slip Katya to the ground and slide down after her. My raptor's nostrils flare at the blood scent, yet she nudges Katya's hip gently with her snout, worried. Katya makes a tiny sound in her throat that I don't like at all. I have to push Ihira's head away; she trills, fast and high-pitched. "Me too," I whisper. Ihira lifts her head then, her eyes dark and alert. She stands very close, protective.

My wife is pale and still, her eyes closed, her breathing too fast. She has lost too much blood. The scarf I'd pressed to her shoulder is soaked through and my hands are red with it. I rip away the sleeve of my blouse and press it firmly to my Katya's leg, but it does not stop the bleeding. The medicine satchel Dmitri threw me is still over my shoulder; I sling it to the ground at my feet, open it, rummage in it, finding the bone needle and the spoon for scooping bullets. There's other things in there, too, but I don't know what most of them are. My fingers are shaking. Bullet wound in her leg just below the hip, another in her left shoulder. Damn koschei had to try to kill her in *two* places.

I remember the graceful movements of Katya's hands as she signed, *If I die young, I don't want to die with holes in me. I show up like that at Grandma Yaga's domik, she'll take one look and laugh herself silly.*

"Dammit, Katya," I whisper.

I tug her leggings off and hiss through my teeth at the ugliness of that hole in my wife's skin, spewing blood. There's a thing of metal in there somewhere; the koschei *put* that in my wife. Anger and fear chase each other through my veins like wild raptors. I unclip my canteen from Ihira's saddle braids—my raptor gives another worried trill—and I pour some of it out over the bullet hole in Katya's leg, trying to wash it. From my saddlebags, I get some of the wadding that I carry for use during my time of blood, and I get my spare blouse too. I pack the leg wound the best I can with the wadding; I see it redden, but the blood doesn't make it through. I tear away one clean sleeve and bind the wadding tightly in place, because I've only enough hands to work on one wound at a time. Katya's wife braid is soaked with her blood, and with a whisper to her, *I love you*, I unbind it from her thigh. Later, it can be cleaned and oiled.

Now I strip her jacket and blouse and get a look at her shoulders, one sliced by hyaena claws and bandaged, the other punctured by a bullet. I hiss through my teeth. The puncture looks evil. Purple around the edges and just a red hole in my wife's body where no such wound belongs. The bullet went in just above her breast and there is blood all over her. There's thread in the wound, too. As if when the bullet tore through jacket and blouse, it pushed some of it *into* her. I swallow, and swallow again. I lift the needle in my left hand and the spoon in my right. And, bent over her, I hesitate. Several times I try to touch the wound with the needle. Each time, I draw back. I wish I'd watched what Dmitri was doing more closely. He didn't hum or sing as our healers might, but maybe he whispered some spell or used some sign I don't know. I think he washed his hands before and after. What else did he do?

As I look down at Katya, my eyes blur and I see *Annika*, my Mom, red blood flowing over her breast and an obscene rainmaker larva suckling away her life. I blink quickly, and the woman lying in the grass is Katya again. My breath is coming too fast; I fight panic. How can I cut into the body of the woman I love? How can I find what the koschei put there and retrieve it? I am neither a healer of the humming people nor a whistler with Ticktock magic. A terrible certainty seizes me that if I do this, if I dig in her wounds the way Dmitri might, *I will fail.* I will kill her and she will *die*. And then I'll be right back where I started, holding the body of a woman I love while she perishes. And the last night I ever spent by her side will have been a night when we fought. My hands shake so violently that I drop the probing needle. I can't. I *can't.* If I fail she is gone, just *gone*, and I have nothing and no one forever. A scream rises in my throat and I choke it back. I put my head in my hands—my hands that are still shaking.

She's a single strap, a weak strap. You lean on her, she'll break. And then where will you be? That's what Sveta asked my wife.

And the answer is, *Dying in the grass.* That's where she is.

I lie curled and crying beside her. The tears keep coming and I can't stop them. Soon—in a few hours, or a night—I will hold Katya's body, helpless, with these tears hot on my cheek. I will have to *bury* her, to sing at her grave with no one to sing beside me, and I can't, I *can't.* The terror and the dread of it has hold of me like a deathreaper's jaws, shaking me, seeking to break me and crush the life from me. I clutch at the grass stems, holding on to this hungry planet before it can fling me off into the dark. I squeeze my eyes shut against the tears, against the shame and despair of them.

In the dark, I can hear Annika breathing as she crouches beside me.

I can't, Mother. I can't.

Yes, you can.

I keep falling. It's too hard.

Get up, daughter.

Just let me lie in the grass a moment, Mom.

Her hand touches mine. Not cold from Grandma

Yaga's country but warm as my wife's. *You keep falling, do you?*

Yes, I weep.

Her voice is warm and strong and kind. *You know what you have, Sasha?*

No, I cry. *I don't! I really don't.*

Her voice is gentle but not permissive. It is my mother's voice. *You have a bruised hip and burns on your skin, and dirt on your cheek. And you have your mother's stories and the blood of a nightwatcher in your body, and you have a whole lot of hope in your heart. You have hope, Sasha. That's what you have. Hope. It's the best thing that ever was or ever will be. Spun from stories, stronger than medicine, older than this world. Hope is what braids us together. Hope carried our people between planets and hope carries us through the red rain and hope will carry you. So will Ihira. Now get on your feet, daughter, and get those alien bullets dug out of your wife and get her in the saddle and ride. Ride, Sasha.*

Something warm and feathered nudges my cheek, startling me.

My eyes fly open.

My raptor's jaws spill soft breath across my face. As if her breath is warm life, I feel my bond with Ihira beating in my blood—for she is my raptor, my breath and sinew, my warcry and my battle-screech, and I was wrong. I am not alone, because Ihira is here. Katya is too. My bond with my raptor, with my people, with my wife, with my mother—everything she taught reawakens inside me. I flush with anger at my weakness. My mother *hoped* relentlessly; I will have to, also. Because there is nothing that has ever stopped Katya yet, and these bullets sure won't. Not if I help her.

I throw my arms around my raptor's neck and hug her fiercely, startling a chirp from her. "Help me up," I say hoarsely. "Help me up, Ihira. We have to save Katya."

On my feet.

I don't have my kopye, and my wife doesn't have hers—it's strapped to Daphne's saddle, kilometers behind us, but there are *still* lives braided to ours, lending us their strength, and I won't forget it. I brush my fingers gently across the crumpled ruin of the Founder's book at my belt. *Thank you, Mom.*

I've been a selfish fool of a girl, moaning over my own weakness when it's Katya who needs strength right now, every bit of I can provide. Grimly, I make a new strength braid for Katya. To start, I cut a strip from my own jacket. I pluck one of Ihira's gorgeous tail feathers, purple as the early night, startling her, and I pet the back of her head in brief apology. I break off thirty centimeters from the tip of a blade of long grass to stand for Dmitri, who always chews the end of a grass blade like this one. For Dmitri, who my wife kissed. For Dmitri, who is fighting right now so my wife can survive. Our strength—mine, Ihira's, Dmitri's—must be enough to protect her. Three. A firm number, Dmitri would tell me. Torn strip of jacket, tail feather, grass blade: I braid the items carefully around my wife's right arm. It's a braid made of soft and breakable things, but it doesn't need to *last*, it just needs to give her our strength until I can get those bullets out. It may not be enough, but it's all I've got.

I may not be enough, but I'm all Katya's got.

Her breathing sounds shallow to me, and that makes me angry. "No you don't," I tell her. "Don't you *dare*,

Katya. You do *not* get to be weaker than me. Every nightwatcher we know looks up to you—and wants you, too. Now you show us how strong you are, Katya."

Now a braid for me, to steady me and keep my hands from shaking, to remind me I am *not alone* while I work on her wounds. I get the knife from Katya's boot and I cut away a few strands of her hair that have come loose from her riding braid. Those hairs are golden and lovely in my hand. And another blade of grass, for Dmitri who threw me my kopye. Who carried me back to camp safely on Old Man's back. Who rode against the deathless in my stead, so that I might save the woman I love. Another feather from Ihira's tail; she gives me a baleful look and I promise her a soft, plump haia to eat, soon as we get back to a settlement. Next, the slender chain that fastens the Founder's book to my belt, for my mother who gave me that book. For my mother, who put her body between her people and death countless times, and between her daughter and death on her last night. Golden hairs, grass blade, feather, and chain: these, I braid about my own arm. Then I lift a handful of earth to my lips, kiss the soil, and pray, letting the humming vibrate through my whole chest, my whole body.

I am shaking, but I am going to do this nonetheless. I take the canteen and wash my hands with water from it, the Ticktock way. And I take up Dmitri's tools.

"I'm sorry, my love, this might hurt." My voice breaks. She still isn't conscious. That might be for the best.

I get to work.

The day is already hot, and I'm sweating. I prod at the bullet hole with the bone needle, and Katya stirs at last.

She whimpers without opening her mouth, and the sound rips bullet wounds in *my heart.* Because my wife does not whimper. *I* might. But not her. Katya is deep as the sea and strong as mountain rock. Those noises coming from her are not noises I have heard her make before. I bite my lip the way Dmitri did while he worked on her raptor, to hold back any nervous noises of my own, and I dig, as gently as I can, waiting for the needle to strike a metal surface. It must be in there deep.

Blood pulses out over my hand and I try to ignore it, but my hand is slick and I keep losing my hold on the bone needle and damn it I can't find *shit* in this wound. I wish my hands would stop shaking. Damn it. I should have been the one to ride against the koschei back there. Dmitri should be here, healing my wife. I am clumsy. I can't do what he did. But I've got to. I've *got* to. There's no one else.

My throat is scorched. I get my canteen and take a sip and hum a quick prayer to the Founder and then I bend over my wife again and I *work*, because I am a nightwatcher, and nightwatchers protect each other and they don't give up. The needle scrapes against something and I don't know if that's bone or bullet, but I have to try. I get the spoon in her, and she's bleeding more now but I carve at her like I might at a stew that's gone too thick, and I try to ignore her whimpers.

And then I've got it, *I've got it.*

It comes out slick with blood, a bullet of metal with its end a bit smushed where it must have hit bone. I snarl at it and toss it aside in the grass. Then I rifle the Ticktock's bag to see what else is in there. Thread fine as hair—maybe it *is* hair—and a sewing needle. I know what *those* are, at least. I wet the end of the thread with my tongue and I start sewing the wound shut. That part is fast, though my fingers are sticky with blood and her skin is, too. Blood still seeps out even after I've got the wound closed, so I tear off the other sleeve from my spare blouse and bind her shoulder as best I can. I am panting and hot. I get Katya's blouse back on her, but I tuck her bloodied jacket into my saddlebags. I look at her face. She's so pale. She has lost even *more* blood now. I glance up, find Ihira watching me with her head tilted to the side, her eye dark with worry. "You just hold on, girl," I tell her. "When I'm done, you and I need to *ride*."

She chirps.

"You can finally show Yekaterina how fast you are, girl," I tell her. "No lasso this time."

I'm babbling and it hurts, so I stop. I glance past my raptor at the horizon behind us, but I can't see anything over the tall grasses. Can't see if we're being pursued. I wonder if Dmitri is alive or dead, and I shake my head because here I am, Sasha Nightwatcher, wondering over a *Ticktock*, yearning to know if he still breathes. But his strength is braided around my arm and my wife's right now, and I'm glad of it.

Swallowing, I crouch again by Katya and unbind her leg. It's time to look for that other bullet.

And now the koschei's weapons from beyond the stars do me a defeat. I can't find it. The sun is climbing the sky, hot, and I keep looking. She keeps bleeding. Still no bullet. I set the bone needle aside and throw back my head and howl my rage and grief. Panting, I snatch up the sleeve and press it to the wound a moment. I hold it to her firmly, and I can feel the cloth beneath my fingers going damp and warm. With my other hand, I scoop up a bit of dry earth and lift it to my lips, squeezing my eyes shut and praying with all my might to the Founder. All the Founder's music couldn't heal my mother when the red rain ate at her. I had to watch her die.

I lower my head to Katya's breast. My heart wants to weep again, but I won't cry, I won't cry. Feather and chain and grass blade and golden hairs, braided around my arm: I have the strength of those who love me. I won't cry.

Sniffling, I stand and get a fresh cloth from Ihira's saddlebags. I wad it and press it to Katya's wound, then I bind it in place with her scarf. Her scarf is long and I wind it about her body twice and knot it tight. I know how to keep in the blood, at least. If I can't fish that second bullet out of her, I need someone who can. There are healers among the humming people. I need to get her to a settlement, get her to someone who knows better medicine than I. That's her one chance. I need to do *that.*

I get a coatl flare from my saddlebags and light it, and send it on its silent scream into the sky, hoping that koschei with their clockwork eyes can't see it the way the seers, the skyborn, can. I stare after it; the sky is empty but for a few clouds. No coatl glides down toward us. No help.

All right. Fine. See if I have a kind word for a seer ever again. Yekaterina and I are down here hunting invaders and doing our *work,* just the two of us, and even the Ticktock is doing his part, and there hasn't been a seer over this prairie in days. They're supposed to *be* here. They're supposed to see. Seeing is what they *do*. My blood burns.

So I will do this the long way. Whatever it takes.

Bending over her, I slap Katya's cheek lightly, trying to wake her. Her eyes open slightly.

Dizzy, she signs. Then she lifts both hands and jabs her index fingers toward each other. *Ouch.*

"Drink this," I tell her, lifting my canteen to her lips. She gets a gulp or two, then whimpers once and passes out again.

"You keep breathing, wife," I tell her, lifting her in my arms. "And don't you whimper like that." I lift her to the saddle, my vision a blur of wet. "Don't you dare whimper like that at me, wife. Don't you *dare*."

I close up the medicine satchel, tie it to the saddle braids, and mount up with my wife. I gaze across the violet grass toward the rings in the north. The rendezvous point is out there—where the other nightwatchers will be, sooner or later—but it's a good seven hundred kilometers, and the settlements of the humming people are a ways beyond that. The mother herds are somewhere far to my south and east; the koschei are behind me too, who knows where. Seven hundred kilometers until help. That's a long way. "Ihira," I whisper.

Her head curves around on her feathered neck, and she looks at me with eyes wet as a pond.

"We have to get Katya home," I tell her.

Her jaws part, and she chirps. The understanding in her eyes plucks at my heart. She knows.

"You are my brave and beautiful bird." My voice catches in my throat. "Show me how fast you can run." Then I grip her feathers and I chirp the commands, and we come out of the dip in the land. For an instant, glancing back the way we came, I think I see movement out there and I wonder if it's Daphne, following our scent, limping far behind us yet but determined to reach her rider. Then my raptor carries us out across the world on her quick legs, and the grasses flick at my thighs and boots.

I ride with Katya in my arms. Sometimes she sleeps and sometimes she wakes. I tell her where we're going. I try to get her to eat. Sometimes Ihira runs, sometimes I let her walk. The sun rolls across the sky, and then the world goes dark and the rings are a bright glimmer in the sky above us and beyond them are innumerable stars, scattered and twinkling. Nothing in the world can eat kilometers like a dakotaraptor can, and there must be a couple hundred behind us now and still far too many ahead. Once, in the middle of the night, I hear wailing in the sky, but though I gaze into the dark for a long time, I don't see where the bullet is. It's lost somewhere in the air or else on land, in the skin of our world, as surely as that bullet is lost in Yekaterina's leg.

Katya wakes after a while and says she's cold, and I wrap her in a saddle blanket, coarse but thick. I make her drink a little from my canteen. I hope we'll pass a stream soon or find a stand of Catha trees before the sun comes back, because there isn't much water left. We would have refilled at that river with the invader's ship in it, if we hadn't been interrupted by koschei falling out of our sky.

Where's Daphne? Katya signs.

On the wild prairie. She's a raptor. She knows the way home. She'll catch up when she can.

Daphne! she signs, her face full of distress. Her eyes are a little glassy. But just seeing her awake and signing makes my heart beat with hope.

"How do you feel?"

She touches her lips for thirst, and spreads her hands wide. *Like a desert.*

I kiss her eyelids. One, then the other. "Come on, desert girl. You eat a little more, then rest. Ihira and I are going to get you to a healer."

I don't succeed in getting more than a bite or two into her and a sip from the canteen, and then she closes her eyes again. Off to our right, there's a little bit of dawn on the horizon, pink as Catha leaves and faint as coals after midnight. I stroke Katya's hair as she shivers and sleeps, and Ihira warbles as her powerful body moves beneath me. A morning wind sends the prairie grasses slapping against my leg as we rush over the violet plain.

All the while, my mind whispers to me: *You're just a useless girl.*

And my wife's voice, out of the past, not in my ear but in my heart: *I don't believe that, Sasha. I don't.*

You have hope, Sasha, my mother says, *you have hope.*

Yes, Mom.

So I clutch my wife tight and bend lower over my raptor's neck to make less resistance to the wind, and I urge her to run still faster, always faster.

* * *

My raptor and I rush through the dark, and grass blades slap about my boots and her flanks. I don't know how long we've been running. Perhaps we are halfway across the world. Far from home.

I am fifteen.

I bring Ihira to a stand of tall kedr by a dark pool, and I let her rest a moment. Kedr trees are no shelter from the red rain, but I don't care. Let the rain punch a hole in my breast as it did my mother's. There's already a hole there. I have lost everyone I love. Everyone. I am utterly and forever alone.

Ihira's shrill trilling warns me, and I glance to my right in time to see a girl ride up on a raptor even smaller than mine and lighter in hue. A girl my age—I know her. She's one of the others training to be a nightwatcher. Yekaterina. I haven't spoken to her much, but I've admired her, how easily she rides Daphne, how quickly she spins her lasso. Once, our gazes met in the raptor stables while I combed Ihira's feathers and she combed Daphne's, and we both laughed, though I had no idea why. Once, after a hard ride along the edge of the cropland, unsure whether to turn back or go farther and hope to impress the older nightwatchers, I saw the others, Sveta and Neveah, in heated argument, and none of them saw Katya's hands signing. So I spoke and made them look. Tonight, Katya's hair flows golden and loose in the wind, and that hair playing with the wind is the most beautiful thing I have ever seen. She slows her raptor and halts ten meters away. Gently, she nudges her goggles up to the top of her head. Her eyes shine in the ringlight.

"What do you want?" I cry.

She lifts her hands to make sure I can see them in the pale ringlight, and signs, *Red rain in the pool.*

I gasp and peer through the kedr trees at the water. She's right. The water froths, and already several larvae have clawed their way up onto the bank, the claws at the ends of each limb longer than my hand. Their bodies are shapeless, broken by their fall, but that won't matter; once they find animals or people on which to feed, they will mend and remake their bloated, invertebrate bodies easily enough, feeding until they're strong enough to burrow into the ground, their backs hardening like a shell while they hibernate in the soil, to sprout from the earth in the spring and grow like cacti, continuing their vicious life cycle until autumn comes again. Then each rainmaker stalk will explode skyward into a hundred larvae, tiny and weightless enough to be carried on the winds until they grow sufficiently heavy to fall and devour.

With a terrible fascination, I watch the larvae crawl and pulsate among the roots of the kedr trees. Then I dig my heels into Ihira's ribs and chirp to her. We sprint away from the pool and the trees and the horrors, out again through the grass.

After a while, I let Ihira slow. I unstrap my canteen from the saddlebags and drink deeply. A *splat* barely a meter away startles a scream from me. Ihira sprints without any instruction, ten centuries of instinct from her ancestors' life on this planet telling her plainly what to do. My heart pounds; for a moment I can hear the larva following us, clawing and cutting and rolling through the grass, its claws ready to seize and shear and dig into Ihira's body and mine! But nothing on this planet can outrun a raptor, and soon the prairie around us is silent as before.

Almost.

Like a sigh in the grass, the other raptor and her rider appear beside us, still a respectful ten meters away, but pacing us. I sign, *Why are you following me?*

Red rain in the grass.

"I know!" I shout angrily. I urge Ihira to more speed, veering left and dashing wildly over the prairie. I don't know exactly where we are. By now, likely forty or fifty kilometers from the settlement where my mother lies dead. The prairie is empty all around us; the sky is empty, too, except for a few pale stars and that soft silver fire of rings. The grass stirs and ripples. My eyes burn. I yearn now for my goggles and my gear. I bend low over Ihira's neck and hide my face in her feathers, listening. Somewhere, somewhere out here is that walking domik on raptor legs, bearing my mother back toward Grandma Yaga's ghost land. If I can just hear it, if I can only find it, maybe I can catch her. Maybe I can get my mother *back*.

We reach a low ravine and I let Ihira slide down the scree into it with a squawk; it might provide partial shelter from the red rain. We stop at the bottom, a shallow stream wetting Ihira's claws. My raptor is panting, and I stroke her feathers to soothe her.

At a chirp above us, I look up. There she is. Yekaterina walks her raptor along the brink of the ravine, her face lit up by the ringlight.

Go back, I sign to her, feeling fresh tears on the way.

She shakes her head. *Rain still falling. There's peril out here.*

There's peril everywhere. That thing came through our roof.

I know. The look in her eyes tugs at my heart. *I'm not going home until you do, Sasha. No woman should grieve alone.*

"I'm not a woman yet," I cry. "Just a useless girl." Some nightwatcher. I couldn't keep anyone safe. Not even Mom. Not even *Mom.*

I don't believe that, Katya signs.

Go away! I sign furiously. I send Ihira loping swiftly down the ravine, her clawed feet splashing in the shallow water. It isn't safe to sprint here, but I keep her pace quick anyway. After a few moments, there's the sound of sliding scree ahead of us and a squawk. Daphne splashes into the stream a few meters ahead, and Ihira halts, lifting her feathered arms and screeching, nearly dropping me from her back.

Katya's eyes flash in the ringlight. *Will you slow down?!*

"No!" I blink furiously, forbidding tears. I failed Mom. I deserve to be out here. How can I look another woman in the eyes? How can I face her pity?

But it isn't pity in Yekaterina's eyes. *I'm not leaving you, Sasha.* She unhooks a coil of rope from her saddle.

With a chirp, I turn Ihira about and start running her back down the ravine, but abruptly something drops over my shoulders, slides down to my waist, and tightens, trapping my arms to my sides. I am wrenched from the saddle with a cry. I hit the mud hard, on my side. Groaning, I try to get to my knees, but another loop of rope falls over me and tightens. Then I'm on my back. Katya leaps down from her raptor. She stands over me, silhouetted against the rings and the stars, tall and beautiful and impossible to flee. Ihira trills, worried, and her feet splash nearby, but she neither approaches nor attacks; it isn't a hyaena or a medved that has hold of me. Katya pulls me into her arms and I squirm against the ropes, squirm against her. Tears run hot down my cheeks. "Leave," I weep.

I would never, she signs.

And I can't run any further. Not from the red larvae. Not from my mother's corpse. Not from this wild golden girl who chased me across the grasses. She unties me slowly, carefully, and I bend over, my hands in the mud. I dig up handfuls of that wet earth and I hold them to my heart, too exhausted to pray, too tearful not to. I close my eyes. I don't care if anything strikes me from the sky or lands in the ravine and tears its way up the stream toward me. I just can't. I *just can't.*

Katya's strong arms surround me and her hand presses my head to her warm breasts, and I shake, and I clutch at her, and she holds me. Her raptor and mine both nuzzle my hair and my back with their soft snouts. I tremble and hold on, and hold on. Katya has no soothing sounds, no words or song, but her hands are soothing on my hair.

Once during the night, she rises and walks down the stream, lovely as the dawn, snapping her kopye out to its full length. A red larva splashes toward her. Eight times she strikes it or jabs it, sending flame into its body. Each time it rallies and reaches for her again with its claws. Each time, she takes one step back toward me, just one, and thrusts at the creature again. She will not let it at me or the raptors. That shakes me loose of my horror, and with my heart beating fast, I tear my own kopye from its place on Ihira's saddle, and I stride down the stream to join her.

You cannot beat the red larvae back. They don't understand retreat. So we fight it together, cooking that obscene bit of skyfall until it is more charcoal than beast. Even after it stops moving, we keep jabbing at it. Only when my kopye's fire has gone out do I realize I'm screaming. My throat is raw. Katya's eyes shine fiercely. She grips my arm once, then snaps her kopye shut and strides back to our raptors. I follow her, breathing hard. She sits by her Daphne. Curved and graceful and sweaty from battle, Katya combs her disheveled hair with her fingers, then begins binding it in a long braid. I sit with her and help her.

When the braid is done, she gazes into my eyes a while, and I can't look away. She signs, *I'll help you bury her. Your Mom.*

I choke. *Thank you.*

I think of how I sat at first, numb and useless, while Yekaterina struck the larva eight times. I think of how I just *cried* like a child while Mom stopped breathing. My face burns with shame. I blink back the last tears I have.

Katya almost brings more to my eyes when her hand cups my cheek. I turn my face and nuzzle her palm. I kiss her fingers lightly. Then I lift my face to hers and kiss her soft mouth. Inexplicably, though my mother's body lies yet unburied many kilometers behind and a rainmaker larva lies smoking nearby in the creek, in my heart there is suddenly a tiny, hot flicker of hope, like a glimpse of fire far away in the prairie grass. Because even though my tale is a tangle and I can't find the start or the end of it, here is one life still braided to mine, one strong, golden strand that makes sense. I cling to her and twine my legs about hers as if to braid our bodies together, too, and, desperate, I kiss her until I haven't air left to breathe.

16

TELL ME A STORY, SASHA.

I draw in a ragged breath, startled and wild with hope to see my love's hands flickering in sign. Ihira is wheezing, and I slow her to a walk, though time is biting at the back of my neck. We have been riding a long time. Yekaterina's fingers clutch at my jacket. Her face is flushed with fever. She opens her eyes just enough for me to see the glitter of them beneath her lashes.

"A story?" My voice is choked.

She releases my jacket again, signs weakly, closing her eyes: *Need something to entertain Grandma Yaga with.*

"No you don't," I say fiercely.

She can't see my lips with her eyes closed, but she must feel the tension in my body. She signs, *I can see her domik, Sasha, walking toward us over the tall grass. The curve of its claws are cruel, but her face is laughing and kind.*

"Your eyes are shut," I tell her. "You can't see shit."

I touch her cheek with my fingers, and gasp as I feel how hot her skin is. Some infection's got hold of her. I think of the bullet in her leg. I think of the threads I saw in her shoulder wound, and I tremble, thinking there might still be a bit of blouse in there, dirtied and hurting her from the inside. I try to estimate how many hundreds of kilometers remain—and suddenly I wonder if Katya's Ticktock watch is in her jacket, rolled up in my saddlebags. But I wouldn't know how to read it, how to tell distances over the wide prairie the way Dmitri does.

The sound of her breathing tells me she has fallen asleep. Her limpness in my arms reminds me too much of my Mom. Tears burn my eyes and I fight them. Through their blur I see the predawn prairie and the rings like an arc of white overhead, and on the other side of the sky, the fading stars. The prairie is quiet. No hyaena's laugh, no chaka's cry, no scream of a descending ship. As if we two are alone on this planet and our riding through the night has no end and no beginning. I strain my ears, but try as I might, I can't hear the rustle and creak of Grandma Yaga's walking hut. One arm around Yekaterina, with my other hand I pat the barrel of the long gun at my hip, taken from the invader's dead hands. If Grandmother comes at us over the prairie, I will *shoot* her. My wife still breathes. She will go *on* breathing.

I chirp to Ihira and we stop. Talking softly to my raptor to keep her still, I settle Katya gently in the saddle, her cheek against my raptor's neck, and I slide down. There is lather on Ihira's flanks and I feel a pang of guilt, but my fear for Katya overwhelms it. I take a cloth from my gear and dab away the lather. Then I get my raptor bowl and drip water into it, just a few drops. I lift the bowl to Ihira's snout and let her lap it up. She is panting. "Not too much, girl," I whisper, my eyes still blurred. "I'll walk you slow a little while, but then we have to run again. I am so sorry, Ihira. I need you. I need you to save my Katya."

I give her a strip of triceratops jerky; she tosses her head up and swallows it. Then I strap the canteen and bowl to the saddle braids again and get back up, taking Katya gently in my arms. A slow trill to Ihira, and she does not resist me but starts walking slowly through the grass. Blades of it flick against my boots. When I touch Katya's brow, her skin is still full of fire. I reach for the canteen and stir her just enough to force her to drink a little, while we sway on Ihira's back. She chokes but gets some water down, I think. Her eyes flit open and she signs slowly, *Think I'll nap on raptorback, now on. Less work.*

Don't you dare.

A faint smile. *I love you.*

I love you too, my wild golden girl.

She signs weakly, *Don't leave me.*

I would never.

Again that faint smile, and her eyes capture my heart as they shimmer between her lids, before they close.

Then she is asleep again. I scrub at my own eyes with the back of my hand. The fatigue is getting to me, but I tell my Katya a story while she dreams in her fever, because she asked for one and I cannot refuse her now, even if she can't hear it. I tell the story softly while I flex my grip on dear Ihira's neck feathers, tightening and relaxing my fingers, over and over, using the movement and the speaking to keep me alert.

Founder came down in her ship, I tell Katya, my voice hoarse with emotion. Her ship of fire and song, riding the hopes and dreams of the humming people right across the sky through all its stars. Came down hard. Cracks in the metal, air inside the ship gone foul. Lot of our people dead. But some kicked open the door in that ship and came crawling out into the violet grass, their eyes squinting in the light of a new sun. They looked up at that blaze of rings in the sky like the first beautiful thing they had ever seen, and they began weeping, weeping for everything lost and everything found and everything in between. And singing, such singing. There had never been singing like that in the whole universe and there never would be again, Katya, and if you ever get to hear a thing with your natural ears, I hope you hear a thing like *that*, not gunfire or tears or anything else but a song, because you have more music in your heart and your mind than any woman I've ever met and don't you dare let it go silent, don't you *dare*.

I am crying, but I am giving my wife this story and I will continue it. So I drop my goggles over my eyes and urge Ihira to begin her run again, and as I rock in the saddle, I tell my wife:

Founder was carried out by her two daughters, and they set her in the grass, and not even the cancer inside her kept her from standing and singing with her people, though her hair was gone and her eyes were too bright. She just stood and looked at those rings and looked at her people and hummed the first song on this planet. She sang of our exodus from the planets Earth and War, worlds where all lives had come unbraided and undone. She sang of the places where our grandmothers were born, of the slavery and the chains and the eyes of metal and glass that watched you day and night; she sang of the clash of blades and the rattle and roar of guns and the glow after dusk of distant cities ablaze; she sang of the people's ashes falling from the sky onto children's faces. She sang of the screams of slaves starving behind walls of concrete and steel; she sang of the ships that spread their wings like raptors and lifted into the air and above it; she sang of the long night between the stars, of the endless dark where only the distant burning of other suns and the hope you kindled by their fire and carried with you could light the way. She sang of Landing and she sang of sunlight and she sang of hope and she sang of birth.

As she sang, her whitejackets released the herds, triceratops and proud styracosaurs and the hard-snouted pachyrhinosaurs, and even the tiny psittacosaurs that skitter in the grass. From the wombs in the ship they spilled, and ran, and trumpeted to the stars. Founder sang, and the teeming mother herds rolled over the land, and the first nightwatchers protected clutches of eggs. The cancer devoured her body, and still she sang. *Still* she sang, and the herds grew, and settlements sprang up like blossoms on branches. She sang, and the land grew hot and then cold, and the red rain fell. The herds stumbled and broke, brought to their knees; red rain burst screaming from their backs. Thousands died. Our people too, we who live and die by the herds. Founder sang over graves that stretched from horizon to horizon. Then we were few.

Illness made her body weak. Still she sang. The first whistler, who was her lover, tied her with rope to his back in the saddle, and as she shook, pale and dying, he carried her over the prairie on the back of a galloping chasmosaur. From a psittacosaur's femur he'd carved a flute, a whistle; and as the Founder sang, he repeated her melody on that flute—the same song by voice and whistle, one for human ears, one for ceratopsians. Hearing it, the mother herds followed them over the grass, hoping for shelter. The Founder sang by day and she sang by night; she sang when the sun perished from the sky, and she sang when the grass soaked her leggings with morning dew. Under the red rain they rode, dodging death from the sky. Grandma

Yaga came careening over the prairie to rattle along beside them, leaning from the door of her domik and cackling with glee at their daring, at the wild story they were making together! Through the red rain they rode, in search of ravines vast enough to hide a mother herd *in.* And still Founder sang her song, still creating life, pulling coatls out of the sky and brachiosaurs out of the woods to hear her. Under the shrieking sky they rode, singing and whistling, whistling and singing, and the mother herd was thunder behind them, a tumult, a shaking of the earth. Rocks broke at their coming: the great stampede. And still the Founder sang. Sang, vomiting with disease. Sang, shaking with weakness. Sang, even when the rain caught her hand and began chewing. Sang, even when the whistler turned in his saddle with a blade brought from a planet orbiting another sun. Sang, even when he carved her hand from her wrist, tossing the shrieking death aside into the grass. Sang, when he bound her stump in his jacket. Sang as she bled. Sang as she shook. Sang as she stood at night on the edge of the canyon, wind in her hair, calling the herds home, calling them to cover from the rain. Sang as she died.

Even when she lay at his feet, the whistler, with tears on his cheeks, kept the song on his flute of psittacosaur bone, and herd after herd rolled into the wild canyon.

Nothing could stop her song.

Nothing can ever stop our singing, the hum of our heartbeats, the hum of our lives, the hum of our people.

Nothing.

I kiss Yekaterina's hair and whisper to her, though I know she can't hear me, "I will sing for you, Katya. I will hum. I will carry you to safety and shelter, even if Ihira falls. I will carry you if I have to bind you to my back. If I have to *run* through the grass on foot. I will carry you, and I will hum, and our run will make even Grandma Yaga's eyes shine to hear of it. Keep breathing, my wife. Keep breathing, my love. I will sing."

And I do.

Because

when your raptor's flanks are lathered
when you've only two drops in the cup
when your love quivers with illness
when the red rain is falling and there's screaming in the grass
when you've buried your mother with your own hands
when the prairie before you is wide empty as forever
when invaders tear the ground with bullets
when you've run so long you burn
when your feet crack and bleed
when you have nothing left

there is still kindness
there is still seeing each other, eye to eye,
there is still holding one another for warmth
there is still sharing your last morsel
there is still kindness
there is still loving
there is still love

There is still love.

17

THE SUN FLITS THROUGH THE SKY AND WE RIDE ON, pausing only briefly to rest and send up coatl flares, cries for help that go unanswered. I dab Katya's brow, clean her bandages, make her drink water, then we ride on. She is rarely awake now, flushed and hot. Sometimes she signs to me, but the signs rarely make sense. I weep, and then I don't, and then I weep again. I pull Ihira up, wheezing, near a shock of fever grass. I let my raptor rest just long enough for me to start a fire, pluck the pan from my gear, pour in the last of the water and heat it, and force a few swallows of nofever tea into my wife. I hear Veroshka's voice, and Sveta's, in my head: *You're the weak strap, Sasha. If she leans on you, you'll break.*

And I growl at those shadow people in my mind, *Maybe. But I don't see none of you here brewing nofever tea, and I'm the only strap she's got.* I touch the armlet I made her: tailfeather, bit of torn jacket, blade of grass. Braided just below her shoulder. "I've got you, Katya," I whisper.

Then we ride on because the prairie is wide and Katya needs more than nofever tea. As we sprint, Ihira panting beneath me, I am relieved to find beads of sweat on Katya's face and hear her breathing better. Maybe we have a little time yet, just a little, just enough.

Her eyes open for a few moments, and she signs urgently, *Daphne. Daphne.*

I sign, *She's well but long behind us.*

She was shot.

Ticktock helped her. Remember?

The panic fades from her eyes. *Dmitri.*

Yes. Only Ticktock near. If he still lives. Again, I am startled at the worry for him that is in my heart. How did that whistler come to mean so much to me?

Yekaterina presses her fingers to her lips, then to my cheek. Her hand is weak.

My throat tightens. I hold her to me more tightly.

She passes her hand in front of her face, from brow to chin, then presses her palm to my heart. *You're pretty.*

"You're pretty, too." My voice is choked.

Sun in your hair, rings behind your head, just my wife and the wide sky.

"Silly girl. Rest."

A small sound in her throat. *Think I might.*

I sign to her, *You are not riding with Grandmother today.*

A ghost of a smile touches her lips.

The sun climbs the sky. We start to pass stands of Catha trees. To my deep relief, I find the pool that waters them. No whistler dead at this one and no lander hiding in the water. I chuck a pebble across, just to be sure. I make sure Ihira drinks deeply, and soon I mount up again with a full canteen. In the distance, I see a troop of brachiosaurs foraging among the higher branches, sometimes lifting their heads against the open sky and sending their long, fluting calls across the prairie. I stare at them a few moments as we leave the Catha trees behind, thinking of the brachiosaur girl. If my Katya could change like that, she'd be too large and graceful for any bullet to hurt her. And if I, Ticktock-foolish, had put any necklace of feathers about her throat, I'd tear it off now. Though I sway in my saddle from exhaustion, I hum to her again. *Keep breathing, wife. Keep breathing. I'll get you help, I will.*

At midday, we reach the rendezvous point, a tower of white stone with old signs painted on the rock, messages and tales from nightwatchers past. Only one of the others is there yet. As we ride up, I see her standing on a ledge halfway up the rock tower, then descending to meet us, leaping deftly from crag to crag, climbing down a cliff face as though her body has no acquaintance with gravity, then running along a last spur of rock that can't be more than a few centimeters wide and flipping off it into the air, to land in a crouch in the grasses below. Seeing that wild agility, I know it's Sveta, and I tense. Her raptor, Inga, an older beast with a scarred flank from a tussle with a medved, stands in the lee of the rock with her head lifted above the grass, watching us. But Sveta runs toward us on foot.

Sveta Nightwatcher can vanish into the grasses easier than any of us—she wears a long violet coat with buttons of polished ubirajara bone, a violet cowl to which she has braided an assortment of amulets, and a violet hood she can draw over her head to conceal her shock of red hair that otherwise would flash like fire on the prairie, standing out as sharply as Dmitri's ribbons. Right now her hood is down and I can see her clearly. The left side of her scalp is shaved, with red battle sigils tattooed into her skin; they also run down her neck, markings from her mother's people. Her irises are red too—a genetic adaptation of the forest tribes. Belted at her left hip is her kopye, and at her right, her shaska—a long blade forged from the steel of melted chains, gleaming in the sunlight. On the high rock, she must have seen us coming from a long way off, but until we got close enough for her to glimpse Katya through her spyglass, we would have seemed only one of her pack returning to rendezvous. It was very like her to be waiting up there; Sveta is always looking for some high place, to gaze out and find omens in the clouds or along the line where the noon sky and the prairie meet. The way others in the pack tell it, once, as a girl, Sveta rode a brachiosaur over the prairie, not by attempting to saddle it but by scaling its long neck and sitting on its head, as calmly as a woman might sit on a carpet in her domik. She should have been a windrider seer and not a nightwatcher at all; she belongs in the air. Or in the treetops, touching the sky, like her mother's people. Maybe that's why she desires my wife so much—Katya is tall, and I am quite sure Sveta would like to climb *her*. There is a jealous flicker in my heart as she races toward us, yet my relief burns brighter.

Ihira is panting and a mess; I bring her to a halt and snap my wind goggles up. Numb with fatigue, I just barely stay in the saddle, holding Katya. Her fever is coming back. The heat from her body cooks against my chest.

"*Katya!!*" Sveta cries in dismay. Reaching us, she presses two fingers to my wife's throat. Then glances up at me, stricken. "Katya! Oh no, Katya! I *knew* the sky was all wrong. Sasha, what happened?"

Is that accusation in her eyes? I'm honestly too scared and too tired to care. "I've ridden two days and a night," I tell her. "Is Violet here? Have you seen Violetta?" Violet knows a little healing, and they saved Nadya after a medved clawed her, the same bear that clawed up Sveta's raptor, a year back.

Sveta shakes her head, face crumpled with worry. "I haven't seen the others. I got separated. Sasha, you wouldn't believe it, there was a tyrannosaur on the prairie. It came at us a day ago all teeth and fury, scattering us, and it had an *empty saddle* on its back—" She trails off. "You encountered it, too? I see it in your eyes." Her voice crackles with anger. "Is that what happened to Yekaterina? Is it an incursion, Sasha?"

I nod wearily. "An incursion like I've never seen. You said the sky's all wrong, Sveta. It's true. Ships plummet out of it. And I've sent up four coatl flares this day to get help, and several days before, and no seer has swooped down from the clouds. And that makes no sense. Are the coatls sick? Are the seers slain? Are koschei ahead of us as well as behind?"

"Koschei?!"

"No time to talk. I've got to get Katya to a healer. What's the nearest settlement? Tatiana's?"

"Tatiana Hidetanner's, two days' ride."

"I'll make it in one," I say fiercely.

"Sasha—"

I toss her my half-empty canteen; she unlatches one of her full canteens and tosses it back. The water sloshes inside as I catch it. I hold her gaze. "Tell the pack I saw four landers. There could be more. They came down on the prairie, two days' ride south of here. Killed a whistler. There's a ceratops band loose and unwatched. The invaders have deathreapers. And guns that spew bullets like—I've never *seen* anything like it. They rip up the grass. They rip up a body." My throat is tight. "And these men, you can't hurt them unless you rip them to pieces. Wounds just heal up in their flesh. We'll need stealth and speed to take them. And cover of night. And all the bravery in the world. Wouldn't have got Katya away at all if the Ticktock hadn't got in their way."

"Ticktock?" Sveta gasps.

I nod. "Met up with him few nights back. He knew where the invader would be."

"Did you slay him? Did he try to slave you and Katya?"

"No, he ... he saved us." My voice falls as I see the incredulity in Sveta's eyes. I stare at her, realizing what a feverdreamer I must sound like. Sveta's father was born in our domiks, but her mother came from the deep forests on the far side of the Ticktocks' mountains. Enslaved by their raiders, then sold to Sveta's father at a barter. Sveta's father freed her mother the moment the Ticktocks were gone, in contempt for their slaving ways. Sveta was born a year later. She has hated the Ticktocks all her life. So have I. And now I'm defending one to her. The realization near knocks me out of the saddle. *Sasha Nightwatcher defending a Ticktock. Well, shit.* It's like the prairie's tilted on its side and I'm sliding off. Nothing makes sense anymore, not nearly.

"Ticktocks threw him out as a child," I tell her briskly. "Guess they do that. Left him to starve in the grass. He caught a trike and made himself a whistler. Can tell you that tale another time. But tell the others about the deathless. Four landed, maybe others. When Yekaterina is safe, I'll ride back. You'll need our help."

"You're winded, Ihira too. Inga and I can take her," Sveta says. Her raptor is already loping toward us through the grass.

I look right in her eyes and I don't flinch. Despite the roar of pain in my heart, I put this in words I know she can hear. "Let the weak get the wounded home. The pack's strongest braid is needed for riding against what's coming."

"Katya's our strongest."

"I know it."

Sveta squints up at me, troubled. She seems to take everything in: my missing kopye, the lather on Ihira's flank, the bandaging at my wife's shoulder and leg, the sliced leather at my hip where a hyaena's claws grazed me. Then her eyes open like the hide flap over a domik's door and for an instant, I see all kinds of things in her heart, and it shakes me. Instead of contempt, there's—admiration there. Grudging but real. How is that possible, when she can see my kopye is *gone* like a pebble dropped from a cliff? How can that be, after everything I heard her say to my wife in the night, scornful and seductive and wanting me gone?

"You really rode all the way here," Sveta asks, "with her weight in the saddle, like that?"

"And I'll ride farther. Ihira can last. Tell the others, Sveta."

"I will," she breathes. She gives Katya's face a worried glance.

I trill to Ihira and she chirps a protest, then tenses to leap into a run, but Sveta catches my arm. I turn on her with my teeth bared, half raptor in my mood, but she doesn't try to stop me. She just takes something from her jacket, something small, and presses it into my palm. Her eyes gaze up into mine, crimson as blood. "That fool girl," she says softly. "Keep her alive, Sasha. For all of us."

I settle Katya in more firmly against my breast and take hold of Ihira's neck feathers, my eyes never leaving Sveta's. "If you see a domik with raptor legs chasing after us, lasso it for me and keep it here a while." Then, with a series of rapid chirps, I send Ihira sprinting through the grass. We flash past Inga, who calls after us in deep trills, though Ihira is too tired to reply.

Sveta stares after us.

I drop my goggles down and I ride out, wind in my face and the roar of my blood in my ears and the kilometers of naked prairie rushing past, Ihira's mighty heart pounding in her body beneath us, three hundred fifty kilograms of beloved and unstoppable bird, wild as the wind and faithful as the sun. Katya makes slight fever-whimpers as I hold her tight. Sveta wishes it was her life braided most closely with Yekaterina's and not mine; there must be a tempest in her heart right now. Yet at this moment I can't hate her. Nothing matters now but getting Katya to our people's domiks. Weak strap or no, this ride will prove things either way. *I will not fail you, Katya.* I touch my armlet, the braid I've made. I have strength yet to get my wife home.

Then I realize there's something in my hand, and I recall Sveta's unexpected gift. I grip Ihira with my knees, hold Katya tightly to my breast, and open my hand to see what's there. It's a night cord with ubirajara feathers, for bringing healers to you in your dreams. What happens in the dream country is real, as real as Grandma Yaga's domik that you can rarely see with your waking eyes. In dreams, the dead might sing to you. Or you might visit a nightwatcher who rides her raptor far over the prairie, many days from you. Dreaming, perhaps Katya might find the others in their own dreams and give them early warning. I braid the cord gently into her hair. Katya stirs and looks up at me through glazed eyes out of a face frightfully pale. She signs, *It's good that it's me who's shot. You are the faster rider. Only my lasso wins the race.*

Your cleverness wins the race, I tell her. Her signing tears at my heart. I kiss her, and her lips are hot.

I will win *this* race. Terrible things have happened to us on this prairie, but I am a nightwatcher, as much a nightwatcher as any in our pack, and taking the tangle of terrible events and braiding it into a tale of hope is what we do. For Dmitri, raised by Ticktocks and abandoned by Ticktocks, justice was an objective thing. Your clock tells wrong or it tells right. Sometimes, the universe's clock is off the hour and has to be set right. Everything must be counted and accounted for, especially blood spent and spilled. But Katya and I are of the humming people. For us, justice is not a matter of the hours told right but of songs finished, melodies made complete, tales that reach satisfying ends, and no teller's tale ending too soon. My Mom's tale ended too soon. I sure won't let Katya's end here. No matter how hard the story, you don't give up until it's told. When you see another trying to sing and they can't, you help them. If someone has no voice, you help them make a drum and you learn sign. If someone is captive, slaved by raiders, you break their bonds, take the gag from their mouth, and get them out into the free prairie where they can sing again. If red rain falls, you get everyone under shelter where the hum of their heartbeats can continue, however frightened and quick. You never give up, just as the Founder herself never gave up. You sing and you love and you hum with life until your very last breath, and you do what you can so others get to breathe and sing, too, until *all* our tales and *all* our lives are braided together.

My mother, a nightwatcher before me, would never have given up. Nor will I. She shielded me with her own body when the red rain fell fierce and early. I press my hand to my Katya's breast and feel her heartbeat as we ride, beating much too fast. I am a *nightwatcher*; I will not let her song perish in the night.

* * *

Even so, well before dusk Ihira is faltering, and the chirping and the trilling and the raptor songs I sing to her have an edge to them now of anger and despair. *She* must not fail me now. I slow and get her raptor bowl to give her water; Katya doesn't wake. There is *nothing* but prairie ahead, no matter how I peer into the distance, hoping for any line of shadow that might be a cropland fence. It's silent, too, all but the wind. No tyrannosaur coo or hyaena laugh or scream of bullets falling from the sky. I suppose the koschei are behind us, rushing on their way toward our settlements with their guns and their war-beasts and their clockwork eyes and all their hate, but so far we have outpaced them. I glance back and gasp. We *are* being followed. But it's not an invader in the middle distance; it's a dakotaraptor.

I continue on my way but it's a while before we can pick up enough speed, and soon Sveta is close enough to shout. "Sasha, hold up!"

Don't have *time* to hold up.

Nor do I need to. She's already drawing near, her eyes invisible behind the gold sheen of her goggles, her hood back, her hair like flame against one cheek. I bend low over Ihira's neck and blink quickly because I am close to having tears and I do not want them seen. I call out, hoarsely: "You were supposed to warn the others!"

"Left picture-sign on the rock. Nadya and Veroshka will know how to read it."

She's right. Pictographs are simpler by far than the symbols and sigils in the Founder's book that few can read, but they can convey a threat, a warning, or a plea for help well enough. I should have thought of it, too. I'm bone tired.

Sveta brings her Inga alongside us and matches pace. Ihira gets a fresh wind, seeing the other raptor beside her. Competitive girl. But Sveta leans in to grasp Ihira's neck feathers and chirp slowly to her. My raptor slows.

"What are you doing?" I demand.

"You can't do this alone. You'll kill Ihira."

My temper flares. "Ihira would never let my wife die!"

"Ihira will collapse. I'll carry Yekaterina a while. Less weight on your bird. It'll give her time to recover."

I hesitate.

"Come *on,* Sasha. Stop *fighting* me! You're going to get Katya killed, going at it like this. You need my help."

"*Why?*" I round on her, and all the wildfire in my heart, the anguish and fury I've held toward her, toward the others, all of it is in my voice, too hot to hold back. "Because I'm weak? Because I'm unbraided? Because I'll *break*?"

I can't see her eyes, but her voice quivers with frustration. "No, Sasha! Because you're *stubborn*. And too scared to trust others to help. But you need help, whether you trust it or not. *Katya* needs help. We all do; nightwatchers don't run alone."

Hurt, I cry, "I've had to!"

Sveta grabs the pommel of my saddle. "Not anymore," she says fiercely. "We will do this together. As a pack." Her goggles flash in the sunlight. "We will save her together."

My eyes fill with tears at last. I nod quickly, and I walk Ihira to a stop. With my help, Sveta gets Katya into her saddle. Katya is shaking and pale; there are strands of golden hair gone astray, stuck to her cheek with sweat. Sveta has a spare night-cloak and she wraps my wife in it. I lean over and give Katya a kiss on her lips and another on her brow, worry clawing at my heart. "We'll save her," Sveta whispers.

I lift my hand to Sveta's face; when she doesn't stop me, I ease her goggles up. I need to see her *eyes*. They are red and full of distress for Katya. Sveta and some of the other nightwatchers have never trusted me to *be* there, and I've never trusted *them* to be there for me. But Dmitri the Ticktock was there, tossing me my kopye before I lost it, and riding with trike and gun against an onset of deathless warriors in my stead, when I needed him to and didn't know to ask. If *Dmitri* can be there for me, come out of nowhere, unexpected, maybe this flame-haired fighter can, too. At least for a little while. A little while is all I need.

I catch my breath. Maybe—just maybe I *don't* have to do this alone.

"Help me save her, then." My voice is raw.

Sveta grips my arm, squeezes, her eyes full of feeling and bright in the light of the setting sun, and I grip her arm too, in silent gratitude. A wild thought takes me: *We're five now—Ihira, Inga, Sveta, Katya, and me. Another firm number. Have to tell Dmitri.*

Then we are sprinting again, the two of us cutting the grass the way spinosaurs cut the surface of a lake, Sveta in the lead with me close behind. I bend low over Ihira's neck, hiding my tears in her feathers, whispering my thanks to her, too. My beautiful bird, my brave raptor, flitting through the grass more lightly now. She nuzzles Inga's flank once with her snout as we run, and Inga trills happily. We pick up speed and the prairie grasses ripple about us. Katya lies too still in Sveta's arms, her braid tapping against Inga's shoulder as we race Grandma Yaga back toward the settlements of our people. When Sveta glances over her shoulder at me, her goggles are down again, ready for the long ride, but her face is set as fierce as mine.

18

EXHAUSTION WORKS ITS DARK MAGIC ON MY BODY, and the journey that follows is a fever blur of rapid movement beneath the wheeling stars, snatches of sleep stolen in the saddle, water forced down a parched throat. Sveta and I pass Katya back and forth in turns between us, allowing each raptor a rest from the carry. Ihira is more exhausted than I; she wheezes sometimes. We slow frequently to a walk before loping again over the prairie. Once I find myself in the dream country. Dmitri is charging his triceratops through the grass beneath a red sky. Half-turned in his saddle, he faces his pursuers, steadying the gun on his arm and firing bullets behind him. Katya rides beside him on Daphne, but I can see through her body and her raptor's to the prairie behind them. She is here then, dreaming beside me. Dmitri doesn't see us; perhaps there is no Founder's music in the blood of Ticktocks. Yet my heart is glad to see him.

Jolting awake, I find we're swifting through a Catha wood, the trees whistling around us. Ihira is leaping over exposed roots. I clutch her neck feathers, weak with fatigue yet needing to avoid toppling from the saddle. Sveta is ahead of me, with Katya dreaming in her arms;

Sveta has braided a night cord into her own hair, too, but I know she hasn't slept yet. There is light enough to see the boles of the trees. A medved stands beside one, its claws set against the tree to carve its mark in the wood. It watches us pass, its phosphorescent hide gleaming in the tree shadow and its eyes glinting with the dawn.

"So tell me about this Ticktock that saved you," Sveta says as I overtake her, as the sun lights the rings on fire. "That's a strange tale." There's an edge to her voice.

I give her a look, not eager to tell Sveta tales. But it will keep me awake, so I do. I tell her as much as I can remember, though I get some of it jumbled up and have to double back and find my trail through the story again. This isn't one of my mother's tales, polished over the years, and I'm still *living* it and it isn't finished yet. So it's a right mess. Not ready for Yaga's ears. But I tell Sveta about the fight with the deathreaper and the koschei's clockwork eyes and the way his skin healed up even though we spilled his entrails out in the grass. I tell her how he stuffed them back in. She goes pale as I talk. And I tell her about Dmitri and his ribbons and his hat and his love for his old-as-the-world, one-horned trike, and the secret he hid in his glove, and the things we learned from him about the Ticktocks, how they hunger not only with lust for slaves but at the very edge of starvation itself. I tell her about the dimetrodon and how Dmitri threw me my kopye, and I gather what bravery I have, and though I blush, I tell her how I rode back safe to my wife in his saddle. He didn't try to tie me up once.

"Not like any Ticktock I ever heard about," Sveta says, too quietly.

"Dmitri isn't like *any*one I ever heard about," I reply. "He was brave and bold like the whistler who carried the Founder at his back, and I think he *did* have the Founder's own melody in his heart."

And I'm about to tell her about the battle at night, but then I see her face wrinkling with disgust. I imagine she wants to remonstrate with me about this Ticktock, about my consorting with a slaver. I can feel the doubt radiating off her like heat from a night fire. *Sasha, the weak strap, letting Ticktocks near our Katya. Letting her get wounded.* Sveta doesn't even have to say the words aloud for them to squeeze my heart in a fist of steel.

So I'm done telling that tale. Bending low, I trill into Ihira's ear, and we ride ahead a little.

I wonder if these days on the prairie, traveling with my wife and a whistler, have changed me. Maybe they have. But this I know: I am *not* as weak, as unbraided, as Sveta thinks me. I touch my armlet, and the Founder's book mangled at my belt. My eyes sting. *I wish you were here, Mom. You always saw everything so clearly, spoke with so much hope, acted with such grace and strength. I could use some of that hope, some of that strength.*

Now we're riding among stands of kedr wood and I can see evidence of cultivation, stumps and splashes of paint on the trees, markings put there on the bark not by feral medveds but by someone looking to cut themselves a wood cache for the chilly autumn nights before the red rain. We pass beneath wind chimes strung on silver rope between kedr trees, slender pipes decorated with beads and gold ribbon, so that each breath of wind brings the Founder's music to the edge of the cropland and warns away medveds and feral dakotaraptors. It doesn't work on hyaenas, though; that's what *we're* for.

This isn't wild country. This is country the humming people have claimed until rainfall. It's as if the prairie and all its nightmares are far behind us—except in my mind I can hear the scream of those descending landers, and my wife is still shaking with fever. I pluck out my spyglass and take a good look around. We come out of a stand of redolent kedr and there is the yellow of corn in the distance to our right. I point and we make for that, running our raptors fast through the shortgrass. Corn means farmers, and farmers mean the settlement is near.

We come up on the corn quick, and Ihira and Inga carry us rushing through the tall stalks. The green leaves of the corn smack our cheeks and shoulders like leaves at the banya. Our passage startles a flock of microraptors, blue-plumaged, none of them longer than my arm; the farmers encourage packs of these tiny raptors to scamper in the corn so they'll hunt and devour pests.

Katya is pale and her cheeks are hot to the touch. "You keep breathing," I plead. "We're almost there. We've almost made it. Just keep breathing, wife." But of course she can't hear me.

"We got to stop a moment, heat some nofever tea," Sveta tells me. She pushes her goggles up her half-shaved scalp.

"We can't stop. She's dying." I give Sveta my coldest glare. "We need to get her to the healer."

"She needs to not be dead when we get her there." Sveta reaches across and grabs my raptor's neck feathers and chirps to her, like she's my mother and she's training me.

"Let *go.*"

"*Damn* it, Sasha!"

A combat commences between us that is fought without any violence except that in our eyes. But then I yield…and slump. Because there isn't really any violence in her eyes, only anger and concern. And I am too exhausted to argue. And the true telling of it is, she's probably right. So we make a small fire, burning a couple cornstalks for kindling. We heat the tea and stamp the fire out with our boots after. That tea is one of the loveliest things I've ever smelled, yet it takes some doing to get Katya to drink it. I kiss my wife's mouth and then, frustrated, I bite her ear. Her eyes open just a bit, and I tell her sternly, "You drink your tea, dear one," and I hold the tin cup to her lips.

As she drinks, there's a rustling in the maize, loud like a killwind. I glance up in time to see a parasaurolophus walk by ten meters away, its long-crested head and sloping back visible above the corn. It lifts its snout to test the air. Its eyes are black pools. It's coming from where we're going; it glances back and gives a worried bleat. The animal is saddled and there are heavy bags roped to its back, but no rider. And the pale fuzz covering its back is stained dark near the saddle. I feel a chill. There must be a scent of blood too, though too faint for my nostrils to pick up, because Ihira lowers her head and prepares to pounce through the grass at the parasaurolophus. I chirp a quick rebuke to her. She hisses but waits. The massive creature lumbers on, upwind, never knowing we're here.

"We have to go," I whisper.

Sveta makes Katya finish her tea while I pack everything up fast and get in the saddle. She lifts my wife up to me. Even as she turns toward Inga, I ride, flashing through the corn. Sveta can catch up.

She rides as fast as I. I had not expected that.

* * *

There are streams here to water the corn, and they all braid themselves into one wide, slow river. Sveta reaches it just after I do; she calls my name and points upriver, stopping me from plunging into the water on Ihira's back. I look. There's a ferry. It's on the wrong side of the river and I almost dive into the water anyway rather than wait, never mind the risk of dimetrodons or venomous hasks, but already the ferry is poling its way toward us along two guide ropes strung between kedr trees on either shore. The ferrywoman beats a brass gong rhythmically as she crosses the river, and I can hear her voice raised in song. So I wheel Ihira about and ride up the bank toward the ferry with my goggles down and Katya in my arms. Sveta rides beside me; we make the air sing with our speed, and when the ferrywoman in her waterhat and cloak pulls the raft up to the sand and shingle, we're already there. She lifts a hand and calls out happily, "Nightwatchers!" Her hair is gray and her cheeks wrinkled, but her eyes are bright.

"Sasha Nightwatcher," I tell her. "My wife is wounded and sick. Can you get us over there fast?"

The old woman gives Katya a worried look. "Nothing on this river moves fast, but I have a second pole, and if you set your hands to it, we'll see."

"I'll take the pole," Sveta says.

We ride our raptors onto the raft, through I have to encourage Ihira with soft trills and warbles. Inga's an older, steadier bird, and her relative calm helps Ihira, I think. Sveta slides from her saddle, gets her canteen; leaning over the side, she pours a small trickle into the river—a custom of her mother's people, sharing your water with the river so the river won't thirst for your life as you cross it. Katya told me once, with a light of mischief in her eyes, that if her canteen was empty, Sveta would have to use piss. I wrinkle my nose. Sveta's custom seems a waste of water on a dry prairie to me, and if you piss in a river, sooner or later someone's drinking it. That's *if* a water reptile doesn't bite your ass while you're trying. I think Katya just wanted to see the look on my face when she said it. I touch Katya's cheek, checking her fever. "I want to hear you laugh," I whisper.

Sveta puts her canteen back and takes the second pole. I sit in the saddle holding Katya, who is shivering despite the heat on the river. The far bank is a steep slope, and I eye it anxiously. The raptors can take it, I'm sure.

I chafe because the ferry is slow, even with two poles pushing at the water. The river is a hue of green that means *warm*, and a spinosaur breaks the surface far downcurrent from us, the sail on its back catching the sun. I watch it with wide eyes, reminded uncomfortably of the dimetrodon. But the ferrywoman knows her work, and between each sweep of her pole, she beats the brass gong hard with a mallet wrapped in hide—a gong likely rescued at barter from arcology cities on the coast. The ferrywoman sings a crossing song to the beat. The spinosaur does not attack. I feel the gong ringing in my bones like that tyrannosaur's coo, and at its reverberation, Katya opens her eyes at last. They're glassy, and I don't like that at all.

That's not my drum, she signs.

It isn't.

She watches my eyes a moment. *It's loud.*

It is.

That's unkind.

It's necessary.

We're on a river.

We are.

Well. Don't drop me in the water, Sasha. She closes her eyes again.

"I would never," I whisper.

The far bank is getting closer. Sveta is questioning the ferrywoman in between gong beats about how quick we can get to Tatiana's settlement, and I listen. It would take the ferrywoman a day's walk. We'll be there fast.

"Tatiana has a healer," she tells us. "Name is Vasilisa. You need to get her quick."

"I know," I say hoarsely. The bank is almost close enough now to spit at. There's a lot of brush and bracken there, but our raptors will leap over that. I give the ferrywoman a grateful look. "My wife's Yekaterina and this is Sveta. You have my name already; it's Sasha Nightwatcher. If you and your kin ever need help, send for us." Holding Katya to my body with one arm, I reach into my saddlebags and pluck out a pouch of jerky and toss it to the deck.

"You're nightwatchers. You don't have to pay me," the ferrywoman protests.

The raft grates against the bank and I ride off without answering. Sveta drops the pole and mounts Inga; then she tosses a tiny packet to the deck, as well. A meal for a crossing, a song for a return, that's the tradition—unless you're in Grandma Yaga's country, where her meal is *you* but a good tale can substitute for your flesh and marrow. I snap my goggles down over my eyes and send Ihira bounding up the slope, her clawed feet sending up showers of loose grit.

"What did you give her?" I call back to Sveta, the ferry already far behind us. "That packet was too small to hold a meal."

"Sea salt."

"You had *sea salt*?"

"My mother was from the deep forest, Sasha. The food here has no taste, and my mouth knows it."

"But *sea salt*!"

"Not just any sea salt. That packet and a dozen like it are from the grottoes where the keet go to mate." Pride shines in her eyes. "The salt is purple and it can make *any* meal good."

"How did you get it?"

"That merchant last barter."

"The one with the steel ring in her nose?"

"That's the one. Got enough salt to last 'til rainfall after next."

"How?" I am aghast. "What did you trade?"

Mischief in her eyes. "A night she'll still be talking about when she meets Yaga."

I laugh, and Sveta smirks. She sounded so much like Katya, just then. They really are alike: two flirts. Still, it's my arms holding Yekaterina, and it'll be my arms holding her when we get the other bullet out of her and get her fever banished from her body. It'll be my arms holding her when she wakes, I vow it.

We crest a rise and before us stretches a broken land but we can see cornfields ahead and a long line of Catha trees beyond. I bend low over Ihira's neck and bid her *race*. Katya is mumbling in my arms now, and I tell her to hold on, hold on, we're almost there.

* * *

We come out of the corn and find a farmer's domik in flames and two men lying dead. A third crawls at us over the trampled ground, and I cry out, because that is *not* one of the humming people. His crimson robes and hood are stained with dirt and soot, and the clockwork eyes above his veil burn with rage. His leg is half torn from his hip and he's leaving a river of blood behind him.

"An invader," Sveta gasps.

"We ride by," I tell her.

We do, but I glance back. The koschei gets to his feet, shaky at first, then strong, his body rebraiding itself, bone and sinew. I take the deathclock from my belt, with its long barrel and its arcane symbols, writing from another world. I turn Ihira and aim over my arm, quickly slipping loose the catch that Dmitri told us was a lock.

Sveta pulls Inga up, too. Her eyes widen. "Is … that a g—?"

I fire twice. Sveta yelps at the sound, and Inga screeches. One bullet flies past the koschei and punctures the hide wall of the Catha-frame domik behind him. The second takes him in the shoulder, knocking him back. He staggers, then straightens, pressing a hand to his wound. Blood pulses between his fingers, red as ours. Red as the blood of every creature that knows death, no matter how arrogant. He shouts at us in his alien language. That's when I realize that bullet hasn't done any good at all. My hand on the gun trembles.

"We ride by," I say again.

I don't have time for combat. *Katya* doesn't have time.

"But—"

"We *ride by.*"

I chirp to Ihira. The koschei comes at us, running along the edge of the corn more swift than any human being I've ever seen or imagined. But our raptors are faster. We make the wind hum past our ears, and the running man falls behind. My face burns with shame because there are two bodies left unburied behind us, again; yet my fear for Katya drives me on too viciously for any shame to ever hold me back. Beside me on Inga's back, Sveta's face is blanched with horror, but Katya isn't conscious. She doesn't see a thing.

* * *

Riding through that last stand of Catha that shelters Tatiana Hidetanner's settlement, we flit between the trees and splash through a stream that never gets higher than Ihira's shearing claws. The light is going end-of-day red. Then we hear sounds I will never forget. Sounds I will hear in my nightmares until I enter the silence of Grandma Yaga's country at last. Distant screams and flames and gunfire, and something else: an eerie wailing in the sky. For a moment, I can't even breathe. I have heard such wailing before.

"They're here," I tell Sveta. "The koschei are here. That sound—that's the deathless."

Sveta's eyes widen. Her hand drops to the hilt of her shaska, the long blade sheathed in a leather scabbard at her hip. *Her* nightwatcher test was different from ours; the night of her test, her settlement was raided, and slavers recaptured her mother, chaining her to a corythosaur's saddle. When Sveta realized, she leapt onto Inga's back and followed them alone, with just her kopye and her terror for her mother's life. She came back from that night with her mother wounded in the saddle behind her, and steel in her saddlebags: her mother's shackles and chain. She talked a merchant at barter into taking all that chain somewhere it could be melted down and forged anew into something violent and beautiful, an implement all her own, to wield protecting the liberty and lives of the humming people.

"The settlement," she whispers now.

I nod, remembering the koschei's words. *Many bullets. And behind bullets, all Mother's children, come for live your domiks, harvest your corn.*

Sveta reaches into her jacket, retrieves a small, round container, opens it gently. She dips her fingers in, and her fingertips come out black. She begins striping her face with the war paint. With the red sigils on her scalp, and her hair like flame, and that paint on her cheeks and across her nose, she looks fierce and lethal. I tuck Katya into my shoulder, get mine, and do the same. The paint is cool on my cheek. I hum quietly, a melody with a quick tempo, one of the battle prayers. Sveta joins me, and then the raptors warble with us, too. Katya's eyelids flicker but otherwise she makes no sign. Grimly, I run my fingertip along her cheek, leaving a slash of dark paint across her skin.

I expect the wailing in the air to stop as the invaders' bullets land in the corn, but the wailing continues. *Many bullets.* Ahead of us, the Catha trees are thinning. There's a red glow in the air.

"Sveta."

She glances at me, her eyes fearful, still shaken by our encounter with the koschei at the farm, by the sight of him unwounding himself. I have a rush of confidence; I don't know where it's from, except that today *I* am the strong one, the one who has faced our enemy before. Whatever any other nightwatcher might think of me, I am the one who is ready for this.

I hold Sveta's gaze, my voice quiet and clear. "Whatever you see up ahead, *they can be killed.* Remember this. They can be killed. We have to be quick and we have to be brave."

Sveta nods.

I finish Katya's battle paint and I put it away. I wipe my fingers on Ihira's feathers gently. Then I put an arm around my wife, clutch her to me tight. And we ride out through the last whistling trees.

The sight before us is more terrible than I could have dreamed. The red glow is fire. The cornfields stretching before us on the downward slope are in flames; smoke pours into the evening sky. Down by a slow river stand several hundred domiks, sturdy yet collapsible structures of tough ceratopsian hide soaked in Catha resin and stretched over frameworks of Catha poles, but some of these are burning too. I can hear cries of panic carried on the air. High above the settlement are vast metal discs, ships spinning slowly in the air, round and gleaming like steel, like floating pages from the Founder's book, like a day of wrath long delayed yet inevitable. The wailing bullets fall from them; already, twelve or more stand like towers of stone at various points in the corn, or in the river, or even among the burning domiks. Other landers descend on columns of smoke.

I pull Ihira up sharply and gaze down in a fury.

Distantly below, I hear gunfire.

"Sweet Founder," Sveta whispers.

A bullet comes down, its wail dropping to a groan, halfway between us and the settlement. It is larger than those I saw out on the prairie, and after a moment men in red spill from it, not one koschei but many, flitting crimson through the corn, running toward the settlement at a speed that is more like a dinosaur's than a human's. Wildly, I look about for Grandma Yaga's walking hut, for surely she must be here somewhere too, rattling through the smoke, cackling in glee at the harvest of stories she is reaping tonight.

"*Those* are the koschei?" There is a squeak of terror in Sveta's voice.

"Yes." My own voice is curiously detached. I am taking it all in, counting up the invaders and the distances like a Ticktock.

"There must be hundreds of them," Sveta says.

"Five hundred I can see. Probably more."

Ihira lifts her head, and I scratch the soft down behind her eyes to console her. "You did good getting us here, girl," I whisper, then warble to her quietly.

I slip my hand to the gun at my hip. How many bullets are left? Not that they will slow men like these, even if I have the luck to send them flying true. How I long now for my kopye or for Katya's, for its reliability and its savage utility. My gaze strays to Sveta's belt. *There's* a kopye and a blade; Sveta will ride in like a raptor herself, tooth and claw. I'm the one naked but for my rage, unarmed but for my love—and a tiny bit of alien metal, a deathclock I barely know how to read.

Breathe, Sasha, Katya is always telling me. *Just breathe.*

So I do.

I take a long breath, filling my body with oxygen and clarity and hope.

Then I take another. And one more.

And I know what I'm going to do.

"Five or five hundred," I say, "they can still die."

Sveta shakes her head. "There's too many. You can't get Ihira through that. We have to go back, wait in the woods, let the other nightwatchers catch up."

"No." I sat and *waited* once, helpless, with my Mom's head in my lap, waited for Grandma Yaga. I almost did it a second time when I was terrified to dig in my wife's flesh for a bullet, terrified I'd only kill her faster. I almost just wept and waited. Never again.

"Sasha, *think*—"

I turn on her, my eyes flashing in the sunset. "Our people are dying down there. Being shot or enslaved, our homes and our corn burned, weeks and weeks before harvest and rainfall. Vasilisa the healer could be dying down there. There is battle paint on my face and yours, Sveta Nightwatcher. And battle sign tattooed on your skin. We are *not* going to abandon our people!"

We're not going to abandon Katya.

Sveta grabs for Ihira's neck feathers to keep us from sprinting away. "And we *will* fight them, Sasha. With our pack, we can fight them. But we are just two raptors."

"Then two is what we have." I step Ihira away, my eyes and my blood ablaze.

Fingers touch my cheek, so gently. Fingers that are too warm. I look down into my Katya's eyes, green as the sea.

Go, Sasha, she signs weakly. *Get away to safety.*

"No." I shake my head. "No."

I'll slow you down, get you killed. I'm dying, Sasha. I need you to live.

"Katya—"

Sasha. You don't get to decide when I die.

Those words near break my heart. "Neither do you," I protest. "Nobody does. No one knows when their song is finished, until it is." I press Katya to me, press my lips to her cheeks and brow. "I love you," I whisper. Her fingers clutch my arm, but her hands keep shaking. "I will get you help. Don't give up. *Don't.* Don't leave me, Katya."

Her eyes shine with fever and with love. *I would never.*

I clasp her close. Trembling, I tell Sveta, "They've got large stables down there. And look, some of our people are collapsing their domiks, the ones that aren't on fire. We'll ride in, get the healer, get everyone we can, get them on hadrosaurs and ankylosaurs and get them crossing that river. You and I can win them time to flee."

"We'll never even make it to the domiks. Our raptors blend in with prairie, Sasha; they don't blend with corn."

"The koschei have their backs to us. We'll ride in fast. With all that smoke and all the noise of the guns, they'll never know we're there until your shaska is taking them through the throat. We don't need twenty nightwatchers, Sveta. We need speed and bravery and warsong in our hearts."

She looks at me in dismay. "You're wild as a medved, Sasha."

"When I need to be."

Sveta gazes at me evenly. Then, in a very quiet voice, she says, "So that's what she sees in you." Her tone is admiring and sad, but she adds under her breath, "You're both damn fools." She runs a hand over the smooth half of her scalp where battle sigils are written into her skin, delicate but strong. "Guess I am, too."

She reaches down, unclips her kopye, and holds it out to me. "Sasha," she says.

I stare at it, aghast.

"I've got a sword. Take it, sister."

Sister.

For several beats of my heart, all I can do is stare at her as she holds that kopye out for me to take. I have lost mine, yet she is giving me—*me*, kinless, failed, unable even to defend my own wife—she is giving me hers. Around it is braided the strength of our nightwatcher pack, the strength I have been denied. Each strap a different color, each a different life braided with Sveta's own. I gasp, for braided among the leather straps is one that is red and dark as the end of sunset—one for me. There I am, braided with a strip dyed yellow, which is Katya, braided about the kopye to give Sveta *our* strength. Despite the night doubts I overheard, Sveta has braided *me*, trusted me enough to do that, trusted she could rely on my strength to help her survive. My hand trembles. Now she is giving me *her* strength—even as she gave me hers and her raptor's all through the long ride here.

"But you hated me," I whisper.

"Oh, Sasha, no. *No*." Her eyes are wet. "I've sorrowed for you. *Envied* you a time or two. And..." She glances away. "Maybe made the mistake of pitying you, which I regret." She presses the kopye into my hand. "We are your sisters, Sasha."

Tears course down my cheeks. I can't hold them back. Not this time.

I take the kopye, my grip strong on the braided surface. Sveta is giving up some of her fighting ability, making herself more vulnerable, to keep me and Katya safe. That is what sister nightwatchers do—they help each other survive, they keep each other safe. That's what we *do*.

I hear my mother in my memory, the love in her voice: *You know what you have, Sasha?*

Yes. Yes, Mom, I do.

I have hope.

"Thank you," I breathe, my heart so full.

Sveta grips my shoulder briefly, even as she did long ago the morning I first became a nightwatcher, the morning she pressed her leather strap into my hand for the braiding. This time, she is crying with me.

She takes a breath and blinks at the tears. "We're really doing this?"

"We're doing this."

Katya touches my cheek again, where my skin is damp, then signs, *Sasha. My Sasha.*

"Hold on tight," I tell her, pressing her to me. I snap the kopye to its full length and ignite it, and its fire crackles in the air like the fire in my heart and the fire in my blood, a fire nothing in this world is going to dowse ever again. The blue of it burns hot, and the air shimmers around the ends of the rod. There's a ringing of metal as Sveta unsheathes her blade. Ihira makes a wild trilling in her throat like she wants to screech a battle-cry into the sunset but is just waiting for me. Below us on the slope, the blazing corn pours black smoke into the air. The invaders' landed bullets gleam with a sheen of reflected flame. I hear more screams now.

I was wrong to think myself without sisters or kin.

I *have* sisters.

Defiant, I lift my voice. "*I have run my raptor on the prairie,*" I sing.

"*I have seen settlements burn,*" Sveta sings, joining her voice to mine.

"*Watched red rain fall,*" I sing.

"*Heard slavers in the corn.*"

I trill to Ihira. My raptor lifts her head, and her legs tense. Sveta's Inga tenses, too, ready to *run.* Katya's breathing slows; her battle against incursion will be fought in her sleep, against an enemy inside her. Mine and Sveta's will be fought awake by the red flame of sunset. "*Smelled wildfire on the wind!*" I cry. Then both our raptors spring forward, and we are singing as we ride down the sloping land toward the domiks burning by the river.

I have run my raptor on the prairie,
seen settlements burn,
watched red rain fall,
heard slavers in the corn,
smelled wildfire on the wind.

We will put our bodies between our people and peril.
If our people are sick, we will find healers.
If our people are starving, we will find the herds.
If our people are captive, we will cut the ropes from their wrists.
If our people are fleeing, we will guard their passage
through cropland and prairie and wild forest.
If our people are silent, we will sing their tales.
We are nightwatchers.
Together we braid the story,
together we finish the song.

And when Grandma Yaga comes for us at last
we will greet her and say, "Welcome, Grandmother.
We are ready for the last ride."

Now, with my sister at my side and my love in my arms, with my dakotaraptor's brave heart and her three hundred fifty kilograms of feather and muscle to carry me to battle, with my kopye blazing in the air, with my face dark with war paint and a war-song in my blood and my heart beating like Yekaterina's drum, I ride down through the burning corn, into a world on fire, into smoke and ash and screams, to find a healer for my wife.

Ihira and I once took a gallimimus in full stampede; we once leapt from a cliff to capture a swooping coatl; we have slaughtered hyaenas and bested a deathreaper tyrannosaur, befriended a triceratops whistler and set fire to an alien ship, and we have *survived*—and if the koschei with their guns and the millions in their blood think they can keep me from getting my wife to that settlement, *I am Sasha Nightwatcher*, daughter of Annika Nightwatcher, rider of Ihira, with a full pack of screaming dakotaraptor riders somewhere in the kilometers behind me, their lives braided about this kopye and braided about my heart, and these invaders from the stars are *very* mistaken.

THE DAKOTARAPTOR RIDERS
WILL CONTINUE IN:

BOOK TWO | INVASION

WATCH FOR UPDATES AT:

https://stantlitore.itch.io/raptor

GO BEHIND THE SCENES
AND SUPPORT THE AUTHOR AT:

www.patreon.com/stantlitore

A BRAIDING

The tale of a planet is a braiding
of many lives and many names.

Here are some of those lives and names
braided together on Peace.

FIRST, THERE ARE THE PEOPLES

FOREST PEOPLE. A term conflating multiple and distinct peoples living in the wetland forests of kedr, Catha, and bamboo east of the Ticktock mountains. Some are of Gaelic descent from the Bailte Ceobhrán on dying Earth, some Vietnamese or Thai from the Storm Cities on Mars, some Chinese from Ganymede and Io. Many landers fled Sol system over the centuries to find refuge on Peace, and many chose to settle in Peace's vast forests, despite their perilous fauna, because of the partial protection the forest canopy provides from the red rain. Sveta Nightwatcher's mother was one of the forest people.

HUMMING PEOPLE. A thousand years ago, Sasha Nightwatcher's people, of primarily Slavic descent, fled the slave colonies on Mars and crossed the void to live free on the violet prairie west of the mountains on the southern hemisphere of the planet they named Peace. The descendants of those refugees are seasonally nomadic, relying heavily on the mother herds for meat, hide, and bone, and for all the goods that can be made from these items. But they also plant crops in the spring and harvest early before the red rain falls—cutting it as close as they dare. Then the humming people pack up their shelters and their goods and try to get to deep ravines and canyons where the people can shelter until the red rain has passed. They often winter there as well, emerging in the spring to establish new temporary settlements. At harvest time, the humming people trade with caravans from the coastal arcologies at annual barter festivals, obtaining goods such as glass beads, kopyes, and other bits of tech. They have a rudimentary pictographic written language—as well as a few books preserved from the time of Landing, relics which few can read—but they are primarily an oral culture, telling tales and singing songs and drumming in the prairie night. They are largely matriarchal; each settlement is led by a "mother" who represents them in dealings with others and who decides when to plant and when to harvest, and to whom the nearest nightwatcher pack make their report and from whom the nightwatchers request supplies. Family units vary. Women typically form female triads for a year or female couples for a lifetime; men are invited into the domik for a few weeks or for a year to plant seed. In many settlements, men provide the labor for sowing and harvest, for digging wells, for tending clutches of eggs, for constructing domiks, for training beasts of burden; women are more typically craftspeople—tanners, potters, weavers—or nightwatchers. These are not fixed and prescriptive roles, however, and gender is frequently more fluid among the peoples of the prairie. The song in the heart is regarded as more critical to identity than the flesh one is born in, and the humming people recognize that sometimes a person is born two (or more), with several songs braided into a single story inside their body, a story uniquely their own.

ICEWALKERS. A term conflating multiple peoples living on the mountain slopes or among the high snows, relying on pachyrhinosaurs and mammoths for their meat and supplies. These peoples trade among themselves, and occasionally with the humming people. Most are of Central Asian descent; their ancestors were people of the steppes who gazed up into a wide cold sky lit by a white moon instead of the arc of Peace's satellite rings.

KOSCHEI. The interstellar invaders whom Sasha dubs "koschei" and who call themselves the "deathless" are slave soldiers from Sol system. Little is known about them on Peace.

NIGHTWATCHERS. The proud, raptor-mounted warriors who defend cropland and prairie, ensuring the survival of the humming people. Some of the nightwatchers named in these tales are:

NAME	HAIR	STRAP	WEAPONS
Sasha	dark brown	sunset	kopye, deathclock
Yekaterina (Katya)	gold	gold	kopye, lasso
Sveta	red	flame	kopye, shaska
Veroshka	midnight	midnight	kopye, bolas
Neveah	bald	blue	kopye, 13 knives
Violetta (Violet)	violet	violet	kopye, javelins
Nadya	green	green	kopye, bladed gauntlets

SEERS. Seers, windriders, skyborn—the aerial patrols of Peace have many names. Attached loosely to the arcology cities on the coast (and thus of East African descent, by way of the Silver Cylinders orbiting Jupiter, in Sol system) yet born and raised in eyries of their own in the high cliffs above the sea, the skyborn serve as the eyes and ears of humanity on Peace. They form deep and lifelong bonds with the quetzalcoatls, pteranodons, hatzegopteryxes, and other pterosaurs they ride, and while seers form a loose kinship, they live solitary lives, ranging alone over hundreds of kilometers of prairie, mountain, or forest. Some wing between ships on the sea, carrying word of vessels in distress or of the migratory movements of marine life. To aid in their scouting, the eyes of the skyborn have been enhanced to permit infrared and telescopic vision. Seers are offered food and shelter wherever they land; they form the most essential communication network of the planet—as well as search and rescue.

TICKTOCKS. A colloquial term for the Keepers of the Clocks, a numerous population living in subterranean communities that have been tunneled and honeycombed inside of the mountains. The Ticktocks keep a tightly controlled yet thriving trade with the arcologies by the sea, and sometimes young mathematicians and engineers from the arcologies—but only men—are permitted by the Clock Keepers to attend schools in their caverns. The Ticktocks maintain iron and silver mines by slave labor and support a small, privileged scholar caste whose members spend their lives in contemplation and the study of mathematics and metaphysics. They remember Euclid and Einstein and Eukelele Jo of Titan; they are aware that time moves faster in the mountains than on the plain; they own clocks dating back to Landing that tell time on other planets; and they maintain pieces of ancient ordinance on the mountain peaks, cannon that have not been used in centuries. Scholars and craftsmen alike in the Ticktock clans indulge in the mystical; mathematics has become, for them, a mystical experience. Within the boundaries of what can be proven mathematically, they soar on flights of the imagination. The driving question behind Ticktock mysticism and philosophy is, "What is Time?" They are obsessed with numbers and numerology. Their homes are carved with geometric precision; as in Earth's *feng shui*, their living spaces are precisely and mathematically arranged. Prime numbers have spiritual significance, associated with wholeness and stability. Living in close quarters, Ticktocks have a cultural dread of disease, physical infirmity, and starvation, and infanticide is a common practice. Rare among the peoples on Peace, Ticktock communities are patriarchal, with deep and persistent inequities in their social structure; women in the mountains have been deprived of voting rights and bodily autonomy, and, with rare exceptions, are consigned to slave status. Most Ticktock men live stationary lives, not nomadic ones; the center of the household is a clepsydra or ceremonial water clock. The male Ticktock who owns the household keeps the clock and sets its time; the others (children and slaves) live by it. Family units consist of a man and his slaves and children, and occasionally other men whose status is that of long-term "guests," a role that entails specific duties and privileges. Aside from the carefully controlled trade with the arcologies on the distant coast, the Ticktocks are otherwise isolationist, withdrawing entirely into their caverns during the time of the red rain, sealing off balconies and windows. In the spring, bands of young men go raiding and slaving on the prairie. Raiding parties bolster the Ticktocks' meager food stores and are also encouraged as an outlet for thrill seeking and aggression that might otherwise be channeled into internecine conflict between the mountain clans. The raiding entails significant risk, because nightwatcher packs travel faster than slaving parties and often overtake them, slaying the raiders and freeing their captives, before the slavers can return to the Ticktocks' mountain fastnesses.

WHISTLERS. Herdspeople, the whistlers are a breed apart. They are (mostly) women of the humming people who desire a more solitary life or whose hearts are drawn to the mother herds that cross the prairie like living seas of hide and horn. Whistlers live with and tend the herds, using their whistles to guide the ceratopsians away from peril and using coatl flares to summon the attention of windrider seers when peril is found. The whistler's primary tasks include monitoring bands of ceratops that break away from the mother herds, preventing settlements from being trampled, and guiding the herds to safety at rainfall. Whistlers travel in pairs for safety, but it isn't uncommon for them to go days without speaking, living life on the prairie in a slow doze like the herds they tend.

WHITEJACKETS. A term for geneticists and fauna-formers—especially those of centuries past, the legendary assistants of the humming people's Founder, who wore long white coats.

NEXT, THE FLORA AND FAUNA OF THEIR PLANET

AGONDA. The primary indigenous grazing animals of Peace. One of Peace's few successfully diverse examples of non-amphibian life, the agonda most nearly resembles a trilobite in appearance. Collectively, agonda comprise hundreds of species, ranging from tiny grass-chewers, dozens living on a single blade of grass, violet and nearly too small for human eyes to notice; to the woolly agonda, so named for the warm, wool-like substance that grows from their shells during winter; to arboreal moss-browsers and wood-eaters; to the vast shelled grazers that still loom on the horizon in the southern latitudes, remnants of once vast herds that, in more temperate climes, have been entirely displaced by the ceratopsians. Subarctic shelled grazers, living off flora that occupies a niche similar to lichens on Earth, can survive extreme cold, lying dormant for years if needed under inimical conditions. Agonda meat is toxic to terrestrial predators, and their hooked limbs make some of the midsized prairie species perilous to unwary feet.

ANKYLOSAUR. *Ankylosaurus magniventris* is a beast of burden on Peace, not indigenous but imported from Sol system's genetic libraries. Eight meters in length, the ankylosaur is quadrupedal, beaked, and heavily armored with a thick bone shell; its tail ends in a massive club of bone that can be swung with shattering force. Ankylosaurs are typically sheltered in stables some distance from the domiks where their human companions sleep (the reason for the distance being the species' tendency toward obstructive sleep apnea and thunderous snoring). Because ankylosaurs can act as living, breathing, defensive tanks, they are a preferred animal for carrying goods and children on long trips; when the red rain falls and the people have to pack up their domiks and flee from the open plain, they use ankylosaurs—as well as various species of "duck-billed" hadrosaurs—to port their disassembled lodges and possessions. Unlike the hadrosaurs that are raised and owned by the community, ankylosaurs are typically attached to a single farming family, in part because of the deep bonds of emotional attachment they form, imprinting on a particular person. They are also fewer in number, and trading for an ankylosaur hatchling is expensive; it is a rare farm where one can be found.

BRACHIOSAUR. The largest land animal on the prairie, an import from Sol system's genetic libraries (*Brachiosaurus altithorax*, from Earth's Jurassic period). Weighing upwards of forty thousand kilograms and exceeding twenty meters in length, brachiosaurs travel in herds, graze on treetop foliage, and are distinctive for their long, arching necks and their slow, trumpeting calls, which can carry many kilometers over the plain.

CATHA. A rhizomatic, fungal organism that roots itself in proximity to water and sends up hundreds or thousands of pale treelike stalks with long, pink "leaves." Aboveground,

Catha resembles a grove or forest of aspen trees, if the aspen stalks were thicker than usual and grew less straight, often twining with and merging with each other. Catha boughs sigh and whistle in the wind in a way that human listeners find melodic and lovely. Catha stalks are tough, supple, and difficult to break, and are preferred over kedr wood in the construction of the domik, or temporary shelter. Catha "sap" (moisture squeezed from Catha stalks, pressed out by the weight of a lambeosaur's tread) is used to soak the hides that serve as roof and walls for domiks and dinosaur stables, because the sap is toxic to the red rain.

CHAKA. The screeching night hunters. An amphibian species the size of a coyote and capable of both prodigious leaps and short bursts of flight. Carnivorous and found near water on the prairie, chaka are hunted in turn by dimetrodons and hyaenas. Chaka tadpoles provide a food source for various fishlike freshwater amphibians, which are in turn hunted by hasks. The adult chaka has long, grasping fingers, skin that exudes a protective slime, and luminous, froglike eyes. The chaka is a versatile predator and a fecund breeder, a survivor of a once diverse genetic family that until recently included the leaping, house-sized quath and the swarming lyagushka, both of which were hunted to extinction by terrestrial species introduced on Peace for that purpose. Amphibian predators of significant size and ferocity persist, however, in the forests east of the Ticktock mountains … and in the skies above those forests. There may be few sights on Peace as terrifying as one of the chaka's giant and froglike and more silent relatives leaping from the treetops after dark, its eyes like sudden pale moons, its long fingers reaching to grasp, sticky fingerpads snatching prey out of the sky—prey that will be devoured even as gravity reasserts its existence and the forest canopy hurtles up to meet both the dying and the fed.

CORYTHOSAUR. Imported from Sol system's genetic libraries, *Corythosaurus casuarius* is a bipedal "duck-billed" dinosaur, a herbivore nine meters in length and distinctive for a radiant crest above its head. A gentle giant, the corythosaur is used as a working animal by the peoples of the prairie. Because corythosaurs don't startle easily, you can often see dozens of children climbing the netting strapped over their backs (for tying supplies to), or swinging from it.

DAKOTARAPTOR. *Dakotaraptor steini* (from Earth's Late Cretaceous period) is the largest of the dromaesaurids imported to Peace, and the dakotaraptors have been bred over centuries for increased speed, agility, and size. Peace's dakotaraptors now range from three to four hundred kilograms and from five to seven meters in length. The raptor has long feathers on its arms and short feathers elsewhere, and has on its hind foot a long shearing claw that can cut like a scythe to hamstring or disembowel its prey. Dakotaraptors are highly intelligent. They are social animals, rather like terrestrial wolves, but they bond with human riders more closely than horses, achieving an emotional attachment nearer that of donkeys, hounds, and parrots. This is only the case, of course, for raptors raised from hatching and paired early with a human rider; wild raptors out in the wide prairie are often feral and highly dangerous, though extremely few in number (the reason being that their nests are vulnerable to haia, which typically prey on small agonda but find raptor eggs to be a delicacy very worth the stealing). When dakotaraptors who are paired with humans lay, their clutches are carefully guarded.

DEATHREAPER. A genetic import from Earth's Late Cretaceous period, *Thanatotheristes degrootorum* is a small and ferocious, long-snouted, temperate-climate tyrannosaur less than three meters tall. Its Greek name means *reaper of death*. It is a deadly hunter, with powerful jaws and seven-centimeter, knifelike teeth. Deathreapers used by the invaders from Sol system possess a striking coat of red feathers.

DIMETRODON. A mammal-like reptile from Earth's Permian period, the dimetrodon was imported in the hope of controlling the population of venomous eels in Peace's freshwater rivers. Dimetrodons vaguely resemble crocodiles with immense sails on their backs. Their mastiff-like heads feature multiple sets of teeth for pinning, shearing, and chewing meat. Dimetrodons often exceed four meters in length, hunt at dawn and dusk, and are capable of extreme speed and ferocity, relying on a swift attack to drag their prey underwater and pin it there.

FAKL. An eerie sight in Peace's rivers, the softly glowing, ghostlike fakl feed on riverbed molluscs. They are nocturnal, bioluminescent, amphibian hunters, fishlike in appearance because grown fakl lose their limbs. Fakl thrive in rivers where dimetrodons have kept hask populations low. Hasks hunt by night, but dimetrodons hunt at sunrise and sunset, and the fakl, who don't kindle like flame beneath the water until after dusk, have little to fear from the larger spineback carnivores.

GALLIMIMUS. *Gallimimus bullatus* is a large, bipedal, ornithomimid dinosaur, two meters tall at the hip and six meters long from beak to tail. The gallimimus has long arms for grasping prey, and a long neck. They travel in large groups and can bolt at speeds exceeding fifty kilometers per hour. The whitejackets most likely introduced these and other ornithomimids into Peace's ecosystem as one strategy for controlling populations of small animals that would otherwise devastate crops. However, the gallimimus and its relatives have done their appointed task so well that they have largely devastated the prairie ecosystem's biodiversity, driving to extinction most of the non-burrowing relatives of the haia. Also gone is the bobr, a fist-sized amphibian that had evolved opposable thumbs and a complex social structure, and which previously had been responsible for damming rivers and creating wetland areas in a manner analogous to the beavers of Earth. With the bobr gone, the prairie has become increasingly dry. That dryness, combined with the high oxygen content of Peace's atmosphere, has resulted in frequent, devastating wildfires on the prairie. Species of bobr still thrive, however, in the wetland forests east of the mountains.

GLOWS. A distant, burrowing relative of the medved and the haia, the nocturnal glow or "slow dreamer" plants itself firmly beneath the soil after its larval stage and lifts its eyestalks into the prairie night. The creature's eyes are luminous, attracting nocturnal species of agonda near enough for the glow to capture them with its concealed, half-buried claws and feed.

HAIA. Small, tripedal non-amphibians possessing three eyestalks, haia travel in vast flocks and provide a primary food source for the prairie's carnivores. Haia are playful, gregarious, and brilliantly plumaged. Though capable of running, leaping, and gliding over the prairie, haia are incapable of true flight.

HAJAKA. A plant whose red leaves, brewed in tea, provide a sedative and a fever reducer.

HARRA. A tiny herbivore, small enough to hold cupped in two hands and softly pelted. Harra can land on their feet like a cat, and their coo is deeply calming. Harra often serve as pets among the humming people, though they can also provide a food source during the longer winters, when trappers search the frozen ground for sign of harra burrows and dig them out.

HASK. An indigenous, blind, eel-like, legless amphibian seven meters in length and inhabiting freshwater rivers. Highly venomous.

HYAENADON. Settlers introduced *Hyaenadon gigas* (a genetic import from Earth's Miocene period) in an attempt to eradicate the planet's larger amphibian predators, such as the quath, which at the time presented a serious threat to human life. As their intended prey became extinct, hyaenadons took to preying on the ceratopsian herds; they proliferated and grew in size and strength. Contemporary hyaenas on Peace often exceed five hundred kilograms and three meters in length. They travel in large hunting prides and have no natural predators.

KEDR. Cedar, an import from Sol system, genetically modified for height and girth—to produce maximum lumber—yet infrequently harvested by the humming people, as settlers have found the indigenous Catha more useful. However, vast forests of kedr have taken hold on the high-rainfall eastern slopes of the mountains.

KEET. Peace's largest indigenous sea life, the amphibian, whale-like keet travel in vast assemblies, and their clicking speech can be heard across the water for hundreds of kilometers. There are legends of keet growing up to five hundred meters in length, and legends of a Mother Keet living in the deep sea. The people of the arcologies on the coast revere the Mother Keet as a goddess and the originator of all life on Peace. On the ocean at night, mariners can often see keet breaching, leaping from the waves, wet and gleaming in the ringlight as they spin in the air, their tiny, vestigial limbs briefly visible, their axolotl faces expressing a serene and ancient beauty. Keet possess a life span of centuries, and mate only once every five decades, and only in the same grottos by the seashore in which they spawned. They have no natural predators, but Peace's settlers introduced mosasaurs into the ocean with the intent of domesticating those prehistoric hunters and using them to hunt keet. Mosasaurs have since overrun the sea, making sea travel and marine fishing perilous, but while they will attack and destroy ships, the carnivorous reptiles rarely trouble keet because of their size and coordinated defense. Nonetheless, keet numbers may be dwindling over time as the mosasaurs hunt the food on which keet rely.

LAMBEOSAUR. Capable of walking on either two legs or four, *Lambeosaurus lambei* is one of several hadrosaurs or "duck-billed" dinosaurs imported to Peace from Earth's Cretaceous-period genetic libraries. Like the corythosaur, the lambeosaur is used as a beast of burden and a working animal; its hides are frequently tanned for clothing, being softer than triceratops leather. Lambeosaurs are ten meters long and have a hollow crest on the top of their head in the shape of a hatchet. Often, a settlement has a small herd of lambeosaurs, and they can be heard lowing, soft and deep, at dawn and dusk.

MEDVED. An indigenous and quite massive predator. Like its distant relations the harra, the haia, and the olen, the medved is a survivor of a non-amphibian branch of life on Peace. Like its relatives, the medved has eyestalks, but it uses sight less than other senses, and these are normally retracted into the head. The medved otherwise resembles a cave bear and is named after the bears that once inhabited

Eurasian forests on old Earth. Unlike the terrestrial bear, the medved on Peace maintains an entirely carnivorous diet. The medved weighs over a thousand kilograms; has long, silky hair and knifelike incisors; hibernates during rainfall and winter; and is solitary and fiercely territorial, marking trees with its claws to warn off others of its kind. Its coat of hair is inhabited by a microscopic, bioluminescent symbiote that makes the medved glow faintly in the dark. Yet because the medved is diurnal and because it primarily hunts the burrowing agonda, pursuing it with claws curved and adapted for rapid digging, and the haia or the psittacosaur, pursuing its prey by scent through the long grass to seize the weakest and slowest of the flock, the nighttime phosphorescence does not present a disadvantage in hunting. A sleeping bear is among the most beautiful sights on Peace, though it is perhaps unwise to approach too closely or to risk waking one.

MICRORAPTOR. The smallest species of dromaesaurid imported from Sol system's genetic libraries, *Microraptor zhaoianus* is feathered, lighter than one kilogram, has a wingspan of less than a meter, and stands shorter than a woman's knee. Microraptors are lovely, with dark, iridescent plumage and long tail feathers that flash in the sun. Farmers entice flocks of them into cornfields with morsels of meat, in hopes they will stay in the fields and hunt vermin that would otherwise devastate the corn. Microraptors pose little threat to humans—even to children, despite their sharp claws—and when they are seen gliding low above the cornstalks, they are considered lucky.

MOSASAUR. Seventeen meters and five thousand kilograms of muscular, fast marine reptile, *Mosasaurus hoffmannii* is the apex predator of Peace's ocean—and a genetic import from Earth, originally intended to assist settlers in hunting and harvesting assemblies of keet, the amphibian giants of Peace's seas. Mosasaurs have long, powerful tail flukes and are capable of incredible bursts of underwater speed. These leviathans give birth to live young and nurture them to maturity. Mosasaurs have thrived, making shipping and sea travel extremely perilous.

OLEN. Named after the small deer once found in Eurasia and Siberia on Earth, an olen is an antelope-sized, indigenous hexaped with slender, multiply jointed legs, a coat of short feathers rather than fur (vestigial wing nubs can still be glimpsed upon a closer look), a mouth adapted for sifting through grass for the more diminutive agonda species, and two long eyestalks. Prior to the arrival of human colonists on Peace, oleni used their eyes to peer over the prairie for any glimpse of grass moving against the wind that might signal an approaching predator. In recent centuries, oleni have adapted to the introduction of terrestrial species by traveling amidst of Peace's vast ceratopsian herds for greater security, though they can still be seen instinctively lifting their eyestalks above the backs of triceratops and styracosaurs to scan the horizon for danger.

ORRA. A tree-like plant, slender and tall, that produces a delicate and sweetly scented white wood. Orra are not common, but, catching their scent, brachiosaurs will travel many kilometers to feast on their leaves.

PACHYRHINOSAUR. *Pachyrhinosaurus canadensis* and its cold-weather cousin *Pachyrhinosaurus perotorum,* genetic imports from Earth's Late Cretaceous period, are the most successful ceratopsians on Peace, adapted to a wide array of climes. Pachyrhinosaurs can be found among the mother herds on the prairie, and *perotorum* with its smaller size and thicker hide can be found in small bands on the mountain slopes, even among the high snows. Pachyrhinosaurs lay more eggs than most species and the young mature rapidly, attaining a third of their mature size within a single year. The largest are eight meters in length and mass four thousand kilograms. Rather than growing long horns as triceratops and styracosaurs do, pachyrhinosaurs have a thick bony shield over their snout. In rutting season, the collisions of pachyrhinosaur males are like thunderclaps. The sound travels far over the grasses.

PARASAUROLOPHUS. *Parasaurolophus tubicen*, a genetic import from Earth's Late Cretaceous period, is the largest "duck-billed" dinosaur on the prairie, a bipedal herbivore exceeding twelve meters in length. There is a long, slender crest at the back of its skull resembling a curved horn a meter long. Parasaurolophus breed quickly and have proven hardy and robust. While other species are preferred plowbeasts, the parasaurolophus is a favorite saddle lizard for farmers patrolling their fields and for scouts attached to trade caravans, because of its speed, endurance, and height; from the saddle, it's possible to see far over the prairie.

PSITTACOSAUR. A ceratopsian dinosaur imported from the genomes of Earth's Early Cretaceous period, *Psittacosaurus mongoliensis*—as well as several smaller species—are bipedal, hornless, and beaked. The largest species is two meters in length, half a meter tall at the shoulder, and less than twenty kilograms—about double the size of a large turkey. They are quick, intelligent, and gregarious, found both among the larger ceratopsian herds and in families of less than a hundred roaming the prairie alone. They are a favorite prey of hyaenadons, medveds, dakotaraptors, and other large predators, as well as a food source for the humming people; it's a rare domik that doesn't have strips of salted psittacosaur bacon hanging by the door. Psittacosaurs have teeth adapted for cropping the prairie grass but are unable to chew; instead, they swallow small stones, which serve to grind the plant matter inside their belly. Along with the stones, psittacosaurs frequently swallow blednyforma, an indigenous fungus, and they must be examined carefully for signs of this fungus before being butchered for food. Blednyforma has little adverse effect on the psittacosaur but is highly toxic to the human body.

QUETZALCOATL. A long-necked pterosaur originally hailing from Earth's Late Cretaceous period, *Quetzalcoatlus northropi* is a flying lizard of extraordinary size, with a ten-meter wingspan and the musculature needed to bear a human rider aloft. Coatls are among the most popular companions for the seers, the skyborn, the windriders. Coatls bred for life on Peace are adapted for long, soaring flights in the high air. The coatl's six-meter, stiffened neck is incredibly powerful, and at sunset, quetzalcoatls can be seen stalking through the grasses on foot, plucking animals off the prairie, tossing their heads back, and gulping them down as easily as a heron might gulp down a toad on old Earth. The creature has a coat of pycnofiber, a plumage that resembles fur more than it resembles feathers; the pycnofiber grows in stripes of black and white like a zebra's fur, and a coatl feeding at sunset is a striking sight, a towering lord of prairie or sea-cliff who neither desires camouflage, nor needs any.

RED RAIN. Humanity's terror on Peace is rainfall, an annual phenomenon occurring shortly before the onset of winter and typically lasting for a period of sixteen to twenty days. Between four and six days prior to rainfall, the crimson rainmaker cacti dotting the prairie burst, spewing millions of red larvae into the air. The rainmaker larvae drift high, ballooning like spiders, then grow larger and eventually fall to the ground, victims of gravity, where they seize any nearby animal life, digging in with deep claws and devouring flesh and blood for sustenance. Their long claws dig into the body like roots, then into the soil beneath. Once the larva has consumed enough of the body to fuel the next metamorphosis in its life cycle, it burrows deep and lies dormant underground beneath the frost and snow, while the world is cold. After sunthaw, while the world warms, the animal begins growing rainmaker stalks above ground—small at first, ever larger as the next winter approaches. The next generation of larvae gestate inside the stalks, awaiting release into the air. This deadly cycle governs the rhythm of life on Peace. Farmers have to harvest quickly, timing their crops just right; it isn't safe to wait for the full harvest. Then they pack their homes and food and families onto the wide shells of ankylosaurs or strap them to netting draped over the powerful backs of lambeosaurs and corythosaurs, and then they *go*, hurrying to find cover from rainfall, hoping they're on time. Not everyone makes it. They retreat to deep ravines that can be roofed with Catha boughs and hides treated with Catha sap, which is toxic to the red rain. Whistlers guide the ceratops herds to vast canyons as well, some of them natural, some artificial, carved out of the earth by their ancestors during the tumultuous early years when rainfall threatened humanity's extinction on Peace. During the summer months, masked men volunteering as "diggers" ride out on saddled therizinosaurs—herbivorous dinosaurs with meter-long, curved digging claws—to scour the prairie and find all the rainmaker cacti they can, dig them out of the soil, and destroy them. Nightwatcher packs protect bands of diggers from roving hyaenadons, medveds, and Ticktock slaving parties. Diggers find only a fraction of these carnivorous cacti, but it is believed that their efforts lessen the rainfall, which according to legend was cataclysmic during the Founder's time, with red larvae falling thick as hail. The arcologies on the coast and the Ticktock caverns in the mountains shut all their windows, lock all their balconies, and hide inside for the long winter months. Ships are beached and battened down. Only the forest people near the equator proceed through the winter largely as they do any other season, protected from the worst of the rainfall by a forest canopy that is poisonous to the red larvae. The flora and fauna of the planet have adapted to rainfall in different ways. Peace has more burrowing species than most planets, and humans rarely travel anywhere without shovels. Red larvae fall over both land and sea, and marine species have adapted for deep diving. Amphibian species that travel the oceans possess both lungs and gills and are capable of remaining submerged for days. Though red larvae will seize on marine animals, the larvae eventually drown. Nor can sinking larvae withstand deep sea pressures.

SKITTERDEER. See *olen*.

SPINOSAUR. An aquatic freshwater dinosaur, carnivorous and voracious, the spinosaur reaches eighteen meters in length, much larger than a tyrannosaur. It possesses a long, narrow, snapping jaw, a powerful tail that helps it achieve high velocity underwater, and a sail on its back that cuts the water like a shark's fin. Spinosaurs can be found in many deep rivers in Peace's forests and prairies, and were originally imported from Sol system's genetic libraries to hunt and exterminate some of Peace's larger amphibian predators. Like terrestrial cats, spinosaurs find many human melodies unsettling, and people ferrying across rivers on the prairie will use chanting and a gong to keep spinosaurs away from the raft; river ferries in the deep forests use an array of instruments ranging from vuvuzelas to syrinxes.

STYRACOSAUR. A mid-sized ceratopsian found both in small bands by itself and among the mother herds, usually located toward the rear of the herd, cropping the low stubs of grass left after the larger ceratopsians have fed. Six meters in length with a russet hide, the styracosaur grows a single long horn like an impaling spike at the end of its snout, and a fearsome, spike-edged bone shield behind its head. Despite its formidable appearance, the styracosaur is among the most amiable of the horned dinosaurs, placid and gentle toward the human whistlers who tend the herds. That deadly horn comes into play only when the young are threatened. There is a popular story among the whistlers about a young girl whose kin died and who was raised by a band of eighty styracosaurs, unbraided from all other lives but theirs. One night, she wandered away from the herd, enticed by the long, graceful eyestalks of the nocturnal glows, the slow dreamers tossing above the tall grasses in the prairie breeze. While she wandered, a pride of ravenous hyaenas came rushing through the grass, and the styracosaurs closed in a protective circle around the herd's young, with their bone shields and their long horns facing the predators. But the girl was alone, away from the circle. Her scream of terror brought a styracosaur cow charging like a thunderstorm through the grass. The styracosaur planted herself in front of the girl, legs braced like the trunks of Catha trees, horn lowered. The girl hid beneath the dinosaur's body. Brave was the styracosaur's heart, fierce her horn, deadly the sweep of her head. By dawn, hyaenas lay gored and dying in heaps around her feet, and the styracosaur lay dying, too, bleeding from a hundred wounds. The girl put her arms around the dinosaur's head and wept. When the styracosaur breathed her last, the girl took the dinosaur's long horn, and she took the ribs of one of the female hyaenas and made herself a headdress of bone spikes, which she tied into her hair. Then she ran back through the grass to her herd, her eyes shining, naked except for her long hair, the styracosaur horn strapped across her back for a weapon. The herd accepted her as the ghost of the fallen styrac, and to this day the girl defends their young from hyaenadons and feral dakotaraptors, charging through the grass to gore predators with that horn. In some versions of the story, the girl becomes a styracosaur herself while she wields the horn. When the whistlers tell the tale, they conclude it with the hope that they might one day find a stray band of a few dozen styracosaurs crossing the prairie and catch a glimpse of the styracosaur girl. Such a glimpse is considered very lucky, and a few of the oldest whistlers claim to have seen her.

THERIZINOSAUR. In the late summer, masked men ride out on the prairie, saddled on therizinosaurs, to find the carnivorous, red rainmaker cacti of Peace and dig them out of the earth—a dangerous task for which the men's masks and the therizinosaurs' feathers offer only limited protection. *Therizinosaurus cheloniformis* is a distant relative of tyrannosaurs and dakotaraptors but eats no meat. It's an immense dinosaur, weighing three thousand kilograms and reaching ten meters in length, with a long neck, a massive fan of feathers on its tail—its plumage is glossy black in hue—and with the longest claws of any land animal from Earth's genetic libraries. Its digging claws are over half the length of a human body. Therizinosaurs are occasionally used in the plowing and tilling of crop fields in the spring, but they are extremely temperamental and their claws can be perilous, converted in an instant from shovels to scythes, when they are startled or angered.

TRELL. A migratory amphibian species known for gliding over the ocean waves for vast distances, like the albatrosses of Old Earth.

TRICERATOPS. This nine-meter-long, rhinoceros-like dinosaur crosses the prairie in herds of tens or even hundreds of thousands, in a living sea of ivory and muscle and hide. They can drink a river dry. In stampede, they can flatten a forest. Other ceratopsian species travel with them, mingled with the herds. All these species have powerful, bony skulls, though they vary in size and armament. The triceratops has three horns—one long, curving horn above each eye, and a shorter one at the end of its snout. The triceratops is beaked and has a protective bone frill behind its head. Triceratops are highly affectionate and social, yet dangerous when threatened; they can charge like a hippopotamus, shatter a tree on collision, or impale a predator. They provide much of the hide used in the shelters of the humming people, as well as meat. Triceratops bones provide the material for many tools and implements, from needles to knives to shovel blades. Most tools used by the humming people are of wood and bone; very few are metal. Exceptions include the kopye, which is manufactured far away in the arcologies by the sea and is traded for at the harvest barter.

UBIRAJARA. A goose-sized dinosaur with two legs, a long tail, and resplendent plumage, as well as four long, stiff fans of feathers that burst sideways, two from each shoulder. Much like the fan of a peacock's tail, these can be unfolded in a rainbow and riot of color. The ubirajara also has a mane of feathers that lift when the animal is startled. Farmers often keep flocks of ubirajara for their eggs, for delight in their beauty, and because it is believed their presence will bring good luck and a high crop yield.

WANINI. Small, indigenous amphibians that burrow deep in search of subterranean water deposits.

YACCA. One of the tallest "trees" on Peace. Actual tree species are of extraplanetary origin, yet vast treelike organisms, fungal in nature, proliferate in many climates on Peace. These include Catha and yacca. Yacca resemble slender spires, pale green in hue, and can grow several hundred meters in height; they dot the northern prairie near the cropland in groups of seven to ten spires. They are a strange and beautiful sight at sunrise and sunset, gleaming wetly with the sky's flame. A symbiotic, vine-like plant frequently twines around yacca spires, yielding a nut-like fruit called sekaya, considered a delicacy. A certain oil or "sap" is harvested from yacca spires and used to treat leather and braided rope, keeping it soft to the touch while surprisingly tough.

YURRUP. Appearing to the eye like a turnip-shaped root roughly twenty centimeters in diameter, the yurrup is actually fauna, not flora. However, the yurrup extends hundreds of thin silver cilia, up to two meters in length, to sift the surrounding earth for nutrients. No part of the yurrup is visible above the soil; however, soil "drained" by a yurrup eventually appears gray in hue. Yurrup are difficult to locate and harvest but are much sought after, because the oils squeezed from a yurrup have medicinal and narcotic properties.

THEIR HOMES, ENVIRONS, AND TOOLS

ARCOLOGIES. An arcology is a nearly self-sustaining habitat, an enclosed city that provides its own food supply, water conservation and purification, and power (from solar panels and long ranks of wind turbines along the seashore). A few dozen arcologies stand along the coasts on Peace. They are variously designed, some towering a kilometer into the sky with greenhouse gardens and farms on many levels, others forming domed cities. Most of the arcologies on Peace were built by settlers of East African descent during the Uhamiaji, the great migration from Sol to Other Shores. The peoples of the arcologies are variously governed, as each constitutes, in effect, its own environment and civilization. The arcologies trade with each other, and some maintain trade with other peoples on Peace, seeking pelts, carpets, beaded art, and songs and stories from the humming people, iron and other ores from the Ticktocks' mines far to the east, and pharmaceutical ingredients gathered from the flora and fauna of the forests beyond the mountains.

ARENAS, COLOSSEUMS, DINODROMES. In Sol system, dinosaurs were engineered not only for work and for keeping as pets but also for gladiatorial games in the arena, ranging from ceratopsian and raptor races aboard privately chartered dinodromes, both planetary and in orbit, to majestic state affairs proclaiming the glory of the Republic. The first such games were held prior to the settlement of Peace, and the peoples inhabiting the planet retain some cultural memory of them. In the centuries since, Sol system has added games far more elaborate than Sasha Nightwatcher's ancestors could ever have imagined, from the annual Running of the Tyrannosaurs to the Mosasaur Marathons on Mars. The slave gladiators who compete are nanotechnologically enhanced, rendering them capable of superhuman feats. They are also drawn from leading families throughout the planetary cities and space stations of Sol System, serving as ceremonial sacrifices of firstborn to bind wealthy families to the Republic and discourage rebellion. On Peace, some of the arcologies by the sea maintain their own dinodromes; few outside the arcologies ever see them.

BANYA. A specialized domik comprising a steam room and various baths; the rooms are separated by light folding screens. The water is heated by taking rocks from a fire and setting them in the baths. The banya is attended naked but is a frequent fixture in the lives of all the people, not only wives and lovers but families. In the steam room, attendants have the visitants lie down and then beat them with supple, broad-leaved Catha branches, scented with various herbs and spices; both the aroma and the action of the leaves against the back and thighs is intended to drive stress and grief from the body. At sunthaw, when a band of the humming people settle after the winter migration and raise their domiks, the banya is the first raised, so that the people may cleanse themselves of the griefs of rainfall and winter—seasons when Grandma Yaga has come for some of their kin.

DOMIK. A round, temporary shelter or lodge used by the peoples on the prairie, constructed from a frame of supple and surprisingly light Catha wood, with ceratopsian hide stretched over the frame—in appearance, somewhat similar to the Mongol yurt on old Earth or the airlocked kaf on Mars. Thanks to the sturdiness and flexibility of the wood, a domik can be quite large, ranging anywhere from five meters in diameter for a small family consisting of three or four members, to twenty meters for a large familial clan. Under the domik's roof, the ground is carpeted with rugs of ornate and elaborate design, woven from agonda wool. Folding screens might be set up to separate rooms within a large domik. In the roof, stretches of hide can be rolled back to let in sunlight by day or ringlight by night, or to let out smoke from a fire. The domik is a place for councils, for meals, for dancing and song and telling of tales, and for religious observances—but not for lovemaking. There is very little privacy, as you can hear everything happening inside the domik. Lovers and wives more typically walk or ride out into the corn or the grasses, or to a trysting place. While there is very little shame about sexuality among the humming people, lovers tend to prefer an uninterrupted tryst.

FAUNAFORMING. The practice of modifying a planetary ecosystem or climate by means of the deliberate introduction of species bioengineered for specific purposes or to take over specific ecological niches.

KILLWIND. The prairie tornado. During the hot season, supercell thunderstorms have been known to spawn dozens of tornadoes simultaneously, chewing across kilometers of prairie. Although primarily a threat just before harvest, the killwind comes earlier in the year on especially hot days, and nightwatchers and whistlers are vigilant when there is thunder in the sky.

KOPYE. One of several weapons manufactured in the coastal arcologies using ores bartered from the Ticktocks and organic materials bartered from the forest peoples. The kopye is a slender, collapsible rod that can extend to lengths between 1.5 and two meters. It is a weapon designed for versatile and graceful forms of combat. It can be spun like the quarterstaff or Japanese *bo.* Chemicals stored within the rod can be used to ignite small blades of flame at either end similar to a blowtorch, or to spew liquid flame. The kopye also has a built-in taser, firing wires almost too slender for the naked eye to detect but capable of delivering rapid pulses of electricity before being detached. The kopye was developed for martial arts and for combat in the arenas of the arcology cities, but also serves as a frequent trade item, allowing caravans from the arcologies to secure pelts, rugs, salt, spices, ivory, rare pharmaceutical ingredients, and tales and stories from other peoples inhabiting the planet.

LANDING BY THE SEA. The location where the Founder's colony ships first touched the planet. The hulks of these ancient vessels, long since emptied of anything usable, can still be seen on a green cliff above the sea, overgrown with mosses and wild plants in a dozen hues of red and violet.

MILLIONS. A way of referring to nanites. The slave soldiers from Sol system, whom Sasha dubs "koschei," use this term to describe the microscopic biomechanical devices that exist inside their bodies in autonomous ecosystems. These nanites modify the soldiers' bodies at need to heighten their strength, speed, endurance, and agility, and to repair injuries rapidly. The "millions" come at a high metabolic cost; nanite-enhanced soldiers are capable of superhuman feats but require an extravagant caloric intake to replace the expended energy.

OLDTECH. Prairie-talk for technology from the past, from Sol System. Distinct from the technology and engineering seen in the arcology cities along the coast, *oldtech* usually refers to technologies, especially biotech, that were lost or abandoned during the tumultuous early years of the colonists' struggle for survival on Peace.

RINGLIGHT. The softly diffused sunlight reflected from the elaborate ring system surrounding Peace. The rings, more extensive than Saturn's in Sol system, are the remains of multiple moons. Peace still has several extant satellites of such diminutive size that they are barely distinct from stars to the naked eye when gazing up from the planet's surface. Formerly, the planet had several larger moons; however, like Saturn and old Time, Peace ate its children.

AND THEIR GODS AND NIGHT BEINGS

EATER OF CHILDREN. A deity feared by the Ticktocks—Time, who eats his children if left unwatched. Eater of Children is also the name by which the humming people remember the sixth planet from Sol, in the system they migrated from. The name derives from an ancient myth wherein the god Time devoured each of his children at the moment of their birth; the one child to escape became Father, for whom Sol system's fifth planet is named.

FOUNDER. A thousand years ago, Yelena, called the Prophet-Singer by her disciples, led a successful slave revolt on Mars. Yelena gave the slaves a song, a narrative that united all their people across all the slave colonies on that planet, a melody that stirred their hearts, awakened their courage, and inflamed their hopes. After the revolt, Yelena's people seized a small fleet and fled Sol. Many of the ships perished in the dark, yet a few reached their destination system—albeit in terrible shape—and landed on Peace, by the sea. According to legend, they brought with them extensive genetic libraries stolen from Olympus Mons University, and were able to create the first ceratopsian herds, as well as other fauna they hoped would be useful in preserving human life on Peace. They also brought a great supply of seeds, including potatoes, strawberries, kale, tomatoes and many other dry-weather fruits, wheat, and enough varieties of maize to establish a sustainable crop of corn. These settlers were hunted by the large amphibian prowlers that were the apex predators in Peace's ecosystem at the time. At each death, they buried the body, if recovered, and sang Yelena's song over the grave. It was a song Yelena herself had never sung, only hummed—her throat was not able to form the phonemes of human speech, but she signed the words. Over the centuries, the humming people have told many legends of their Yelena, the woman who Found Home and found the song and helped others find themselves. The Founder still lives, the humming people teach their children, because her song does. You hear that song when you hum at play, when you dance and sing nonsense words. You hear it when your body hums with adrenaline or love. You hear it in your last moments, when the world goes silent except for the song beat of your heart, which is the song beat of Yelena's heart, too. We are all braided to her and to each other, braided together in that song. That is what the humming people teach. According to their stories, Yelena died in the first rainfall after Landing, after leading their ancestors and the herds to safety from the red rain. In her memory, the humming people sing many songs. And it is their belief that justice and community consists of the effort to ensure everyone's song is heard, everyone's tale is told in full, and that at each death, the story and song of one's deeds is recited and remembered.

GRANDMA YAGA. An entity or deity appearing in many tale types and rituals of the humming people. The Yaga tales are incredibly syncretic, absorbing or adapting elements from a range of Slavic traditions that featured forms of a *baba yaga*, as well as the ghost ballads of Mars and the 'holy kidnapper' stories developed during the long transit from Sol system to Peace. As oral storytellers compete to tell the best tales, Yaga stories evolve rapidly while maintaining key central elements. Yaga is said to dwell in a walking domik that strides over the prairie on raptor legs. She can braid spells. She can curse or bless children. She has a hunger for human flesh and devours the unworthy, but her primary function is to test the strength, resilience, cunning, and daring of the people who encounter her. You meet her upon your death, and if the kin and community you leave behind can tell a tale of your life that entertains her—if you have lived a life worthy of such a tale—Yaga will grant you passage across the ghost prairie to a forest of rest and delight and song.

KOSCHEI THE DEATHLESS. Personifying hunger and predacity, Koschei the Deathless visits a woman in the night and consumes her ghost, leaving a breathing but emptied body behind, like a husk shucked from corn. Koschei can travel wherever his shadow can, so he is difficult to keep out of a home. And because Koschei has removed his own ghost from his body and hidden it within some other object (or even within nested objects), he is impossible to kill, and he can only be slain once the object in which his life lies concealed has first been located and destroyed. It is Koschei's separation from his ghost that drives his hunger to devour the ghosts of others. Koschei tales, popular among the humming people, draw heavily from Slavic, Romanian, Turkic, and other traditions, merging elements from previously distinct tale types on old Earth involving vampires, specters, and an ancient folkloric figure by the same name.

MOTHER. The leader and goddess of the "deathless" slave soldiers from beyond the sky. Little is known of her on Peace.

MOTHER KEET. The largest amphibian being on Peace, rumored by mariners to be kilometers in length and dwelling in the deep sea. Whether or not such a being exists, the peoples of the arcologies on the coast revere her as the first of all living things, a creature nearly as ancient as the ocean, who birthed all other life. It is said that she swims both in the earthly sea and in the dream country, and those who encounter her in their dreams and hear her music are forever changed.

SCREAMING SHIP. According to legend, a sentient and haunted vessel, the last ship to bring humans to Peace; the ship went mad and threatened the settlements with flame and death. Previously, the Screaming Ship had been able to communicate with women in their minds, but now its screams of pain broke the minds of all who tried—until a woman named Nadya stood in the path of the Screaming Ship with a vast cloak of feathers, one feather contributed by each living human being on Peace; with all of her people present in spirit, she was able to withstand the telepathic assault on her mind and speak with the Screaming Ship. Rather than torch the last settlements of the people, the Ship retreated instead into the ghost prairie. In some later tales, a youth seeking Grandma Yaga encounters the Screaming Ship instead; in others, Yaga herself rides the ship instead of her walking domik with raptor legs; in still others, the Ship sleeps endlessly under the earth—and if the pain and grief of the living above ground grows too great, if the people are not protected, then the screaming in the minds of widows and bereaved mothers and orphaned children will wake the Ship, and she will again rise, screaming and lethal, to murder the world.

Now the names are known,
the tales are told,
the braiding's done.

Until tomorrow night.

Until the next braiding of tales.

ACKNOWLEDGMENTS

TO EACH OF US ARE BRAIDED MANY LIVES, and none of our winter tales are told alone. I will name with gratitude a few of my pack who rode with me. My thanks to Richard Ellis Preston, Jr. and Andrew Hallam, my editors, who are masters of story; to Shoshanah Holl, Isidore Nettleship, Vivian Caethe, Mike Long, Jenna Bird, and O.E. Tearmann, who generously read this manuscript and offered their suggestions; to Stevie Rae for bringing Sasha, Yekaterina, and Ihira to life in her gorgeous art for the book's cover; to Jason Philip and the entire crew of the Dino Punk group, for flooding me with intriguing articles about deathreapers and ubirajara and other species from Earth's past, and who celebrated with me when we first learned that spinosaurs were aquatic; to my Patreon members for funding my work and uplifting my heart; to all the writer colleagues who dropped off unexpected boxes from the farmer's market at my doorstep during the height of the 2020 pandemic, keeping me and my immunocompromised daughter and the rest of my family fed, who helped us plant our garden this spring, who brought their kindness to our door, who reminded me that however long the night, we can get through it together; to my many readers who expressed excitement (or, in some cases, amusement) at the prospect of a new Litore dinosaur novel; to Rex and Vennessa Robertson for unfailing friendship and encouragement; to the staff and volunteers at Dinosaur Ridge in Colorado, who proved to be fine storytellers themselves during the season before the pandemic, when I took my children to see fossils and footprints; to my elementary-school speech therapist, who long ago helped a young boy overcome a speech impediment by reading dinosaur books together and then standing me in front of a tall mirror to practice enunciating *tyrannosaurus, triceratops,* and *diplodocus*; to my children River, Inara, and Círdan, who find dinosaurs as fascinating as I do (or who find them, in Inara's case, edible), and to my wife Jessica for her laughter and her love and her gift for asking just the right questions; and to all of you, my readers, for gathering to hear this story at the fire, after rainfall, while we remember our dead and grieve with our living and wait for it to be safe to emerge beneath the sky again. Since I began writing this novel of catastrophe and hope, 1.6 million of our people (300,000 in my country) have died. It is with my whole heart that I sing,

when your love quivers with illness
when the red rain is falling and there's screaming in the grass
when you've buried your mother with your own hands
when the prairie before you is wide empty as forever
when you've run so long you burn
when your feet crack and bleed
when you have nothing left

there is still kindness
there is still seeing each other, eye to eye,
there is still holding one another for warmth
there is still sharing your last morsel
there is still kindness
there is still loving
there is still love

There is still love. And hope, which braids us together. Let us ride hard through the burning corn.

Be well and safe, my readers, and full of good stories. I look forward to bringing you *Invasion*, the second book in this series. Thank you for joining me for this tale of the dakotaraptor riders.

STANT LITORE
DECEMBER 2020
DURING THE COVID-19 PANDEMIC

About the Author

Stant Litore writes about zombies, aliens, and tyrannosaurs. He does not currently own a starship or a time machine but would rather like to. He lives in Aurora, Colorado with his wife and three children and hides from visitors in the basement library beneath a heap of toy dinosaurs, tattered novels, comic books, incomprehensibly scribbled drafts, and antique tomes. He is working on his next novel, or several. You can read more of his current fiction by looking up *Ansible: A Thousand Faces, The Zombie Bible*, or *Dante's Heart.* However, venturing into these worlds may have unpredictable effects, and Stant offers no assurances that you will emerge from any of these stories unscathed. Best leave all non-essentials behind, take with you only what you need to survive, and venture into the books cautiously and ready to call for backup. Enjoy, and good luck.

www.stantlitore.com

www.ingramcontent.com/pod-product-compliance
Lightning Source LLC
LaVergne TN
LVHW041106080826
845145LV00007B/1704

* 9 7 8 1 7 3 6 2 1 2 7 1 4 *